Sweet Boundless

ROCKY MOUNTAIN LEGACY

Honor's Pledge

Honor's Price

Honor's Quest

Honor's Disguise

Honor's Reward

DIAMOND OF THE ROCKIES

The Rose Legacy

Sweet Boundless

01B

MINNEAPOLIS, MINNESOTA

Sweet Boundless

Cover by Dan Thornberg

Published by Bethany House Publishers
A Ministry of Bethany Fellowship International
11400 Hampshire Avenue South
Bloomington, Minnesota 55438
www.bethanyhouse.com

Printed in the United States of America by
Bethany Press International, Bloomington, Minnesota 55438

Library of Congress Cataloging-in-Publication Data

Heitzmann, Kristen.
Sweet boundless / by Kristen Heitzmann.
p. cm. — (Diamond of the Rockies ; 2)
ISBN 0-7642-2382-8 (pbk.)
1. Woman pioneers—Fiction. 2. Mine accidents—Fiction.
3. Married women—Fiction. 4. Colorado—Fiction. I. Title.
PS3558.E468 S93 2001
813′.54—dc21 2001001302

To Al and Mary Jane Heitzmann
for the gift of my husband

With your whole heart honor your father;
your mother's birthpangs forget not.
Remember, of these parents you were born;
what can you give them for all they gave you?

Sirach 7:27–28
The Apocrypha

One

The rosy kiss of the sun on the newborn day
is God's own touch upon His world.

—Carina

IT WAS MAE'S IDEA. With Berkley Beck, the Carruthers, and all the roughs hung by the neck, why shouldn't the house be hers? Carina stared at the small clapboard house caught between Mae's boardinghouse and Fletcher's Stationery. It was plainer than it had appeared in the illustration—no chimney, no gingerbread trim, no shrubs, and only one window. Hardly the dream house she had thought she'd purchased. Never mind that the deed was a forgery and the sale a fraud.

Carina figured her claim was as good as any, however. And in a city where claim jumping was a sport, no one had jumped that claim, not since its last inhabitants had been choked to death at the end of a rope. Carina cringed, the sight imprinted on her memory. All those men hanging like hams from the rafters of the livery. *Oh, Signore . . .*

She crossed herself, then brought a hand to her throat. How close she'd come to joining them. Thoughts of that night two months ago still raised the flesh on her spine. But now the sun was shining sharply through the dust-clouded air, and the noise of commerce was all around her. No torches, no shadows, no vicious hollers to "get Beck's woman."

If anyone still thought her that, they didn't say it to her face. Tempers were short in Crystal, but so were the memories of heinous deeds, especially their own. No one spoke of that night. Just days after the bodies had been cut down and buried, the men were about their business as though none of it had happened.

If only she could put it away so completely. Carina wrapped herself in her arms. She was not yet thick-skinned enough for that, but she was trying. Crystal demanded it. Only the hardy survived a place like Crystal, Colorado. And even then it took a bit of luck.

Had she not been dubbed Lady Luck? Dubbed by Joe Turner and the host of miners who believed it was by her hand he'd found wealth and glory? Maybe taking a shovel to one piece of ground instead of another was nothing more than luck, but most of life didn't work that way. Every choice had a result. Why else would she be standing on a rutted street before a shabby house and imagining?

She tipped her head back and looked again at the house. With scarcely four feet between its side wall and Mae's kitchen and the long yard behind . . . She considered the possibilities. It could work.

"Pardon me, ma'am."

Carina turned and looked into a broad, pleasant face. Brown eyes, brown hair, square jaw, high forehead. A look of intelligence. "Yes?"

"Could you tell me where to find Mr. Shepard? Mr. Quillan Shepard?"

She stared at the man. Tell him where to find

Quillan Shepard? She was the last one to ask. After all, Quillan was just her husband.

"I have a letter here to meet him at Mae's boardinghouse." He held out the paper.

Carina's heart jumped. Two months had passed since Quillan had left. After the first month, he'd sent money to Mae for Carina's keep but hadn't come himself. Did this man's letter mean Quillan was returning?

"This is Mae's." Carina gestured toward the two-story structure beside the little house. "When were you to meet him?"

"Well, today."

Today!

"He said in the letter I might find a room at Mae's."

"Then you'll be staying." *And Quillan might be, too. . . .*

"If we conclude our business positively." The man removed his hat. "I'm Alex Makepeace, mining engineer." He held out his hand.

Carina took it. "And I'm Mrs. Shepard."

His eyes widened. "Well, now. It seems I'm on the right track. Is your husband home?"

"No."

Alex Makepeace filled his chest with mountain air, then choked. He would learn not to do that in Crystal's streets where the dust was thick. With a hand across his mouth, he cleared his throat. "Then I'll see about a room."

"There's no vacancy. Except . . ." Didn't this make her decision for her? "As a matter of fact, there's one room being relinquished today. You're in luck, Mr. Makepeace."

"Please call me Alex. I hope to be working closely with your husband."

She half smiled. "Then you don't know my husband."

Alex Makepeace surveyed her. "Has he fangs and claws?"

Carina laughed. "No. But if he works closely with anyone, it's news to me."

"Ah."

"Now we'd best see Mae together. The room being vacated is mine."

"Ma'am!"

She smiled. "Don't worry. I'm moving into this fine house next door." Carina waved her arm. "Who could ask for more?"

They shared a laugh; then he sobered. "Truly, Mrs. Shepard, I can't take your room."

"Well, you'd better. It'll be filled before the cot cools." She would never have said something like that four months ago. But that was when she'd learned that it was literally true. In fact, she had stolen her room from Joe Turner, whose deposit was already down. Well, not she; Berkley Beck had stolen it for her.

Carina sighed. Too much had happened in four months' time. She led the way up the front stairs, still hardly weathered, having been so recently replaced after the flood removed the old ones. Mr. Makepeace jumped ahead and held the door. Carina walked in.

Mae was at the desk, doing her books. Nearly a foot of blue dress fabric extended on each side of the chair back. Mae had lost no weight while she recovered from the bullet wounds she had received. But then, while Mae was laid up, Carina had fed her on pasta and bread and good Italian cheese—until the ingredients Quillan had brought her ran out.

Mae looked up, but the rolls of flesh still connected

her chin to her chest. "Well, what is it?"

"Mae, this is Alex Makepeace, Quillan's mining engineer."

He started to protest that nothing was settled yet, but Carina interrupted. "He needs a room, and I told him he could have mine."

Mae widened her violet eyes. "You're taking the house?"

"Why not? I bought and paid for it." Along with any number of people with deeds exactly like hers. But in Crystal, possession was nine-tenths of the law, and everyone else believed it haunted. "I'll be packed and out in an hour." It would take ten minutes, thanks to her husband, who had rid her of all her belongings.

Of course, he had done what he had to, clearing the road of her broken wagon and its contents so that he and others might pass. And he hadn't been her husband then. It had been their first encounter. *Bene.*

The difficult part would be making the house livable. She cringed at the thought of Walter Carruther and his foul brothers who had lived there. If anyone could haunt a house, they could. And she had seen enough of them in life, *grazie.* She didn't need ghosts to remind her. Still, the house was hers.

Mae heaved herself to her feet. "I'll need your name in the book there, a deposit, and the first week's rent. Rent's due at the front end every time." It was her standard proclamation, in case they met with an accident so permanent Mae could not collect.

Carina left them to handle the details and climbed the stairs and entered the canvas-walled cubicle only slightly larger than a horse stall that had been her home these last months. Though she'd been desperately lucky to find it, she wasn't sorry to leave it.

Only through her diligence had she not acquired lice from the thin mattress on the cot. And the small toffee-colored *topo*, whose acquaintance she'd made her first morning there, skittered regularly across the floor and under the door. No cats, Berkley Beck had told her. No cats lived in Crystal to limit the rodent population.

Bene. Fine. She had learned to live with things as they were. She took from under the bed a carpetbag and black leather satchel. The satchel was heavy with Nonna's silver, the books she'd rescued from the mountain, and the letters and photographs she'd brought up with her, mementos of a life so different from now. It also contained the sea green gown she'd worn for her wedding.

Carina thought of the gown. Like the ceremony for which she had worn it, it was not what it had once been. Though she'd carefully brushed the silk and repaired the remaining lace, most of it had been torn off and thrown away. Still, it was maybe not past saving, and her other clothes were few enough, the trunkload she'd brought having landed in the creek far beneath the cliff, along with her wagon.

She gathered up her spare skirt and blouse, undergarments, and nightgown and put them into the carpetbag. A hairbrush and mirror, tooth powder and brush, and the remains of a bar of soap given her by a hawker the day she came to Crystal were the extent of her possessions. It was little enough to make a home with.

From under the thin straw pillow, she took a red leather book and caressed the name within. *Rose Annelise DeMornay*, Quillan's mother. The words inside were precious, bringing to life a woman Carina might have known if life were not so cruel. But God knew best. She placed it gently into the leather satchel. One last look around the room showed nothing else. She took the bags and started down the stairs, straining with the weight of them.

Mr. Makepeace saw her and hurried to her aid. "Let me help you with that." He reached for the bags.

Together they walked next door. Carina halted on the stoop and girded herself before trying the door. It was open, as it had been the last time she'd tried the knob. The floor was still littered with blankets and garbage, and two months of vacancy had not removed the smell. Ghosts did not smell. But the house did.

She looked at the brown stains on the walls and floor and recalled the scarred Carruther spitting tobacco at her feet. Bene. She could rid this place of them. "Just leave the bags there on the stoop," she stated. Carina turned and saw Alex Makepeace's expression. It was almost comical, so like her own first look must have been.

"Mrs. Shepard, you can't . . ."

"If you would be so kind as to help me remove these blankets."

He looked over the floor. "Where would you like them?"

"Out back. Far enough so that the flames won't reach the house."

Again they laughed. He stooped and filled his arms with the rotten-smelling wool. Carina did the same. When everything from the floor was heaped in a bare spot in the center of the yard, Carina doused it with kerosene from Mae's kitchen and lit the pile. She stepped back beside Mr. Makepeace, who stood with a bucket of water to douse anything that strayed too far. The blankets kindled and blazed; then Carina watched the flames die. Alex Makepeace extinguished the ashes with the water and his boot.

"Thank you." She turned again toward Mae's. "The rest I can handle myself."

"Then I suppose I'll gather my baggage from the livery. You're absolutely certain about the room?"

"Absolutely. By the way, the little topo, the mouse, is quite tame."

Alex Makepeace smiled, then stopped walking. "Mrs. Shepard, this has been a most pleasant welcome. Thank you."

"You're welcome. Watch your pockets."

"What do you mean?"

"Although Crystal has recently purged itself of violent men, there are still quite a number with sticky fingers."

He raised his brows. "Then I thank you for the warning." He paused a moment. "Do you know when your husband might . . ."

She shook her head. "I have no idea." Nor did she want to think about it. Two months apart after only one night together and then the horrible things that followed and her near escape. . . . No, she couldn't think about it. Quillan would come when he came. She was obviously not important enough to notify.

Alex Makepeace headed off toward the livery, and Carina went into Mae's kitchen. She filled a bucket with green lye soap and boiling water, then carried it and an armful of cloths back to the little house. It was a single room, with a black cookstove on one wall that vented out the roof. The floor was wood planks, better than her friend Èmie's cabin floor which was pressed dirt.

Carina set down the bucket just inside the open door and surveyed the room. Without the detritus, it was only filth with which she must contend. Bene. The sooner begun, the sooner done. She dipped the first cloth and started on a stain halfway up the wall.

Quillan reined in his blacks, Jack and Jock, and his wheelers, two heavily muscled Clydesdales. The team had pulled his freight wagon, loaded to its limit, to the livery on Central Street. He stopped outside the two huge doors he'd helped Alan Tavish hang on his rebuilt livery after the flood had washed away the first.

Tasting the dust of the road, he jumped down from the box, lifted his hat, and shook back the hair that hung to his shoulders. There was a definite chill in the air, but then, at this altitude, September was chancy. Quillan surveyed the street, choked as always with miners, and hawkers who made money off the miners, and freighters who made money off the hawkers, and thieves who made money off anyone who left his pockets unguarded.

Crystal had become a boomtown. Joe Turner's mine, Elden Jeffries' mine, and Samuel Furber's mine were all producing silver almost to the tune of the Leadville giants. And soon Cain Bradley's mine would do the same. Quillan dropped his chin. Yes, it was Cain's mine, though the title had transferred to Cain's son, D.C., and to him, as equal partners.

He didn't think of it as his, though Quillan supposed he ought to start, since he was hiring on the engineer the eastern investors had sent out. Meeting with him today, in fact. He expelled a slow breath. He hadn't looked forward to this—still didn't. And he had dreaded returning to Crystal.

Two months on the road wasn't long enough to again face the streets where vigilantes had avenged Cain Bradley's death. At least that had been the final excuse.

The town had risen against the roughs who'd terrorized it for so long. Since then he'd heard that Ben Masterson had been elected mayor and the trustees were purged of Berkley Beck's dogs. All positive, but it didn't change the fact that Cain was dead. Quillan was twenty-eight, and in all those years, Cain was the only man he'd have liked to call father.

He turned and whistled to the dog still sitting on the wagon box. The brown-and-white mottled mutt stepped to the side and leaped down to accompany Quillan as he started for the open livery entrance. Alan Tavish was settling with a man whose bags stood around him as he paid the fee for boarding his team. This was one newcomer who hadn't come in on Steven's and McLaughlin's stage.

Alan turned. "Ah, Quillan." And to the other, " 'Tis yer man now."

The newcomer looked up. "Quillan Shepard?"

Quillan advanced into the shade of the entrance. "Just Quillan. Are you Alexander Makepeace?"

"Alex. Yes." They shook hands. "Well, this is fortuitous. I was just coming for my baggage. I've taken a room at Mae's. That is, your wife gave up hers for me."

Quillan released the man's hand. Had he heard right? "My wife? She's leaving Mae's?" Had it taken all of two months for Carina to accept defeat? Was she even now planning her departure? Her escape?

Alex Makepeace shook his head. "I was afraid you wouldn't be pleased. She's moving next door into that shabby little dwelling."

Quillan considered the house Carina had purchased fraudulently through Berkley Beck. What did she mean, moving in there? Did she think to set up housekeeping with him? His heart jumped, then stilled. He knew better than to let those feelings return.

"Have you seen the rooms at Mae's?"

Alex shook his head. "Not yet."

"You might redefine shabby."

"Ah." Alex looked out through the doors of the livery. "Then the sooner we make something of this mine of yours, the better, eh?"

Quillan didn't bother to tell him he was already comfortably set with the income from his freighting and wanted no part of the mine. That was no one's affair but his own. "I'll let you get settled while I make some deliveries. I've a wagon full of freight to unload." It was more accurately sales than deliveries, but Quillan knew exactly where he'd take the things he'd purchased and who would buy them without quibbling one cent on his price. Only Carina thought she could haggle him down. Only Carina could.

Quillan frowned. "Shall we meet back here in two hours?"

Alex Makepeace raised his brows slightly. "Would you like some time with your wife first?"

Quillan's response revealed nothing. "We'll handle our business first, while there's daylight to see the mine."

Alex's mouth formed a downturned arc as he nodded. "All right."

Quillan watched him walk out, arms filled with baggage. He tried not to imagine Alex Makepeace sleeping in Carina's cot, but then, he'd tried hard enough not to imagine her sleeping there. He turned to Alan and gripped the old ostler's shoulder. "How are you, Alan?"

"Well enough. And what's so pressin' ye can't see the lass?"

"Don't start."

"Mary and the saints, man, she's your wife!"

"I know she's my wife. I offered to let her out of it."

"Ye what?"

Quillan lifted his hat and forked his fingers into his hair. "It was misbegotten from the start. Cain would—" He dropped his hand and looked away.

"Cain would what, boyo?"

"It doesn't matter."

"Aye, it matters. Ye've got some twisted idea keepin' ye from what's important."

Quillan closed his eyes with a weary breath. "Leave it, Alan. I've had a long road."

"And it's good to have ye back."

Quillan looked at him, bent and gnarled with rheumatism, his craggy face gentle and honest. Too honest. "I guess I can't avoid her for long."

Alan shook his head. "Ye're daft. Ye've got a bonny lass, one any man would be proud to call his own, and ye talk of avoidin' her. Ye've been too long in the sun, man."

Quillan smiled. "Maybe I have. But just now I have the fruits of my labor to collect. I'll bring you my team when I'm done. You have stabling?"

"For yours? Always."

Quillan patted his shoulder and walked out with the dog on his heels. It would take all of two hours to unload his goods at their various locations. Just now he was glad none were going to Mae, though he did have a dozen eggs for his wife. Why he'd picked them up, he couldn't say. It was certainly no peace offering.

Two

One breath in the presence of God
is worth more than a lifetime away.

—*Carina*

CARINA'S BACK AND SHOULDERS ACHED. Still on her knees, she pressed a palm to her lower spine and arched up. Bene. Here she was scrubbing like a maid, the daughter of Angelo Pasquale DiGratia. She threw the cloth into the grimy pail.

The end of her braid brushed the floor behind her as she knelt and stretched her back. She would soak in the hot springs for hours after this. Èmie wouldn't charge her, and it would feel good to steam away the aches once she finished. She looked around her. The room was almost habitable.

Some of the stains were still faint on the walls. She would ask Joe Turner for paint. He had just built a three-story house and would have paint to spare. He would gladly share enough for this small room. The floorboards were now scrubbed clean, but Carina shuddered to think of sleeping on the same floor Walter Carruther had inhabited. Somehow she must acquire a bed, but with what?

She thought again of her idea. Was it possible? She eyed the wall between her house and Mae's. A door there and a wall connecting the two structures, a door on Mae's side into the kitchen . . . Once, she wouldn't have dreamed of invading Mae's kitchen. Now she thought of it as her own. They could both use it. And if she built onto the back, a room just large enough for tables and chairs . . .

What would Mae say? Would she like the idea, or would it offend her? Carina would do nothing to hurt her. But if Mae agreed, she could borrow from Joe Turner and build. Then what? Where would she get the ingredients and all the other things she'd need? The only freighter she knew was Quillan.

Her stomach flipped. Just the thought that he might come, that she would see him . . . It was crazy, *pazzo*, to think that after two months of silence he would be eager for her. She mustn't hope. God would bring good from their marriage, but she couldn't guess when.

She gathered up the soiled cloths and lifted the pail of slimy water. She emptied it where she'd burned the Carruthers' last effects, then headed for Mae's back door. Was Quillan in town? Was he meeting with Mr. Makepeace even now? And what did that mean? What did Quillan have to do with a mining engineer?

She shook her head. *Signore, you're teaching me patience, but it feels like long suffering.*

She found Mae in the kitchen stirring an enormous kettle of stewed beef on a stove large enough to hold two such kettles with four burners to spare. Carina breathed the aroma. It was so constant now she nearly dreamed it. Stewed beef, stewed beef with potatoes, stewed beef with onions, and on Wednesdays it was bear meat in the pot. Bene. One thing she would never cook Quillan was stewed beef.

She stopped short. What was she thinking? Cook for Quillan? One meal she'd made him. One meal only. And he'd enjoyed it; she knew he had. But it hadn't happened again. Why should she think because he was here to meet a mining engineer that anything would be different for them?

"Well?" Mae looked up.

"I no longer smell Walter Carruther."

Mae laughed her deep, throaty laugh. "I guess that's something."

"It's a lot of something." Carina dropped the cloths in the wash barrel. She would do all the laundry for Mae tomorrow.

"It's not a bad little place, really." Mae jabbed in the fork and tested the tenderness of the meat.

"No, but I don't relish sleeping on the same floor the Carruthers did."

Mae turned. "Land sakes, Carina. You're not thinking of sleeping on the floor."

"What else?" Carina spread her hands.

Mae's plump fist landed on her hip. "You just go on down to Fisher's and tell them you need a bed."

"And pay with what? My good looks?"

"Well, if anyone could . . . but here." She sank the ladle into the stew pot and went to the corner. From the shelf she took a canister, and from the canister a handful of currency.

Carina raised her brows. "Mae! You shouldn't keep money like that in your kitchen. What if someone knew?"

Mae shuffled back with her rolling gait. "If someone wants to steal from me, there's nothing I can do about it. Besides, as long as there's men needing beds and beef in their bellies, there'll be more where this came from." She held up the bills. "Here. Go get what you need."

Carina looked at the money being offered her. So many times Mae had shown her kindness. She held out her palm and received the cash, remembering how Berkley Beck had told her Mae would throw her out if he didn't pay her rent. Lies. And she'd been so *innocente*. "I want to ask you something."

"What?" Mae reached into the second pot and gave the stew a stir.

"Would it hurt your business if I made a restaurant next door?"

"In that little place?"

Carina added a chunk of wood to Mae's fire. "I have an idea, but I don't want to take business from you."

Again Mae's fist found her hip. "Let's hear it."

"I thought we could connect my house to yours with doors into the kitchen and a long hall to the back of my room with space there for tables and chairs and perhaps a fireplace to keep it warm."

"You'd need that for sure with winter coming on." Mae looked at the wall. "A door there? And you'd use my kitchen?"

Carina flushed. "It's a lot to ask."

Mae looked from the wall back to her. "Why?"

"Why?" Carina looked at Mae with confusion.

"Why do you want to do this?"

Carina met Mae's eyes and sank into their violet depths. "What else am I to do? Find another Berkley Beck and sort his files?"

Mae sagged. "Certainly not that. And trust me, any bellies you take off my hands you're welcome to." She replaced the lid on the pot and sat down at the table. "But what about Quillan?"

Carina waved her hand, fingers splayed. "Do you see him around to object?" She raised the handful of bills. "Look at this. I am begging for a bed."

"That's not fair, Carina. If he knew you'd left this house, he'd see you had whatever you needed."

"Oh *sì, un gross'uomo*. The big man who thinks of everything. Did he think of it when he dumped my own bed and feather mattresses in the creek?"

Mae just eyed her. Carina wouldn't push it. Mae thought too much of Quillan to win any argument there.

"How are you going to do it?"

Carina shrugged. "I'll borrow from Joe Turner what I need to build and to buy tables and chairs."

"You'd do better to have someone make tables, and you'd seat more on benches."

Carina sat down across from her. "Does that mean I may do it?"

Mae sighed. "I told you I liked doing for people, and that's true. But it's no skin off my nose if you want to do, too. Besides, I'd like to have you here still. Why would I want this kitchen to myself?"

Carina's spirits leaped. "Do you mean it?"

"One condition."

"Anything." Carina grabbed Mae's hand between hers.

"You have to charge outrageous prices for your fancy fare. Otherwise there'll be no end to the grumbling on my side. At least the men have to think they're getting a square deal at my table."

Carina laughed. "I'll rob them blind."

Mae joined with a belly-rolling chuckle. "Now that's the Crystal spirit."

"Now you have to promise something." Carina brought the back of Mae's hand to her cheek. "Promise you won't tell Quillan."

Mae was quiet a long moment. "Why on earth not?"

"Because he would do it. I want it to be mine."

"What about Joe?"

Carina waved her hand. "I'll pay him back. As soon as I've robbed enough desperate men, I'll pay him every cent, as I'll pay you for my bed."

"You know that's not necessary."

"It is." Carina laid Mae's hand on the table and covered it with hers. "I came here the spoiled daughter of Angelo Pasquale DiGratia, physician and advisor to Count Camillo Benso di Cavour, prime minister to Victor Emmanuel II, king of Sardinia-Piedmont."

She saw Mae's eyes widen and continued. "I never worked for anything, except a few months for Papa's cousin Vincenzo Garibaldi, who was not a nice man. I enjoyed leaving him shorthanded when I came here, but that's another story."

Mae laughed. "Land sakes, Carina."

"The point is, I want to do something myself."

Now Mae squeezed her hand. "I understand. Why do you think I've been here all these years?"

Carina bit her lower lip. "Then it's our secret."

"If that's how you want it."

"Now." Carina stood up. "I'm going to buy a bed." She tucked the cash into an inner layer beneath her skirt. "And then I'm going to soak at Èmie's baths."

"See you don't drown."

Carina laughed. "I won't drown. But it might take days to remove the Carruther grime." If only she could hide in the cave for days. Maybe then she'd be ready to face Quillan.

Quillan held out the diagram, showing the surface diggings where the ground had been stripped first, then the two short tunnels that were begun in the New Boundless. Cain had had it platted before he was killed, but the work had continued in the two months since, so there were discrepancies. It was a start, though, for Alex Makepeace's survey.

They discussed the particulars as Quillan showed him the claim; then they made their way to the heart of the mine. Sam whined softly when Quillan ordered him to stay, then lay down and rested his nose on his paws. The dog had shifted allegiance more easily than he'd expected, and Quillan guessed if anything happened to him, Sam would cotton to the next hand that fed and fondled him.

He led Alex Makepeace inside the candlelit tunnel. This was the first Quillan had seen of the inner workings himself. Walking in was a bitter reminder of his failure. If not for him, Cain would be there showing his Boundless to the engineer who meant to make it a major operation.

"Who's your partner, Quillan?"

"Daniel Cain Bradley. He's Cain Bradley's son."

"I'll meet him?" Alex raised his hat and wiped his forehead with his sleeve.

"He's at seminary."

Alex Makepeace stopped scrubbing with his arm still up. "Seminary?"

"Learning to be a preacher."

Alex replaced his hat. "That's a combination I haven't heard of."

Quillan stared down the short, dark throat of tunnel. "Neither of us is much for working the mine ourselves. I'm a freighter. I have no interest save ownership." And not even that if Cain hadn't needed someone to stand with him when the first Boundless failed.

"I see. Then all the management of the mine . . ."

"Joe Turner lent us a foreman to get it opened up. Your people can choose someone else if they like. I won't interfere."

Alex looked up the wall and down. "Then maybe you'd rather sell out?"

He'd sell out for a dime. But he couldn't. Not with D.C.'s graveside request to look after it for both of them. "No. D.C. and I have an obligation." To the man they'd both loved.

"I see. Well, I think with what you've told me we can work out an equitable solution, profitable for our backers, profitable for you."

"And of course for you." Quillan smiled.

"Of course."

"Have you seen enough?"

Alex did a quick scan. "For now, yes. I'll begin the survey tomorrow if you're ready to proceed. We can get the papers signed if the terms are agreeable."

Quillan nodded. The less he had to do with any of this, the better. "They're agreeable." The investors looked sound on paper, and character was something no amount of references could prove. They shook hands outside the mine, then Quillan stood in the entrance to the New Boundless while Alex headed back to town on a steeldust stallion wearing a gentleman's saddle.

I'm coming up in the world, Mrs. Shepard. In just the way

you expected. He frowned. The Mrs. Shepard in his mind was not his wife but his foster mother. He didn't let his thoughts linger. But then they went to Carina. He couldn't put it off much longer. Whatever his feelings on the matter, she was his wife—as Alan had reminded him. As though he needed reminding.

But there was one thing he had to do first. He replaced the miner's cap in the alcove beside the entrance and took his own hat. Forking his hair back, he put on the broad-brimmed felt hat and mounted Jock. Sam leaped up from his doze, wiggling every part of him. Quillan didn't have to whistle. As soon as he touched his heels to the gelding, Sam followed. From the New Boundless that had been Cain's dream, not his own, Quillan went to the graveyard.

Carina chose the maple Jenny Lind bed over the brass. She had never been one for bright, showy brass, and she liked the lines of the maple headboard. It was the first major purchase she'd made in Crystal, scandalously overpriced, and she did it with borrowed money. She sighed. With any luck that would change.

Luck? No. If it were God's will, her plans would succeed. If not—she shrugged—she could hardly be worse off. She paid for the bed, mattress and blankets, and for a small table and two chairs. So it was wishful thinking, but who was to say he wouldn't come?

She laid the money on the counter for Mr. Fisher. "Send it all to the house next to Mae's. The door is open."

His eyes widened. "The Carruth—" Then he caught himself. "Certainly, Mrs. Shepard. And may I say you look very fine today."

She found that astonishing, as she'd been on her knees scrubbing and sweating, but she smiled. "Thank you, Mr. Fisher."

"If there's anything else you need, Quillan's credit is good here."

She hadn't thought of that. But then it irked her to think it. She would rather be indebted to Mae. Her emotions tumbled about as she passed through the door into the sharp sunshine. When she'd last seen Quillan, she'd felt so confident she could make him love her. How hard could it be?

It was in him to love. She'd learned that the one night they had together. But then he'd left the next morning, fiercely separate, and after the night of the vigilantes, he'd left again. Two months with no word, only his claim that he wanted no part of their marriage. What had she done to make him hate her so?

She reached the entrance to the hot springs. It wasn't a cave so much as a shelf hollowed out of the bedrock with a structure built across the front and several basins inside through which the springs emerged. Steaming water straight from the earth, right beside the icy creek. Èmie had shown her places where the creek ran both hot and cold.

Carina entered the dimness of Èmie's world. Now that her uncle Henri was dead, Èmie worked the hot springs in earnest. She no longer had his thieving to augment what she earned, though the priest Father Antoine, her other uncle, shared what little he could collect with her. It was just that things came so dear in Crystal. Thanks to freighters like her husband.

The thought was unfair. As he said, most of the cost of goods was the difficulty in getting them from the railhead over the treacherous pass and the long miles into the high mountain gulch where Crystal rested. It didn't stop people from coming. In two months the population had swelled by at least a thousand.

Carina saw Èmie approach. In the cave she always looked so stiff and pale. But when their eyes met, Èmie smiled. There was no trace now of the beating her uncle had given on Mr. Beck's orders. No bruises, no swelling, no sign of the pain Èmie had borne because Berkley Beck wanted to punish Carina.

"Well, hi there. Want to soak?" Èmie asked.

"Is it very busy?"

"You'll have to wait for a private basin."

Carina smiled. "That's good news. Good business."

"Oh yes. Everyone new wants to try the springs for themselves. I've put a little by this week."

"How wonderful. What will you splurge on?"

Èmie laughed. "As though I would."

Carina caught her hands. "I'm starting a restaurant. How would you like to work with me?"

"Are you? How?"

Carina shrugged her head to the side. "I haven't worked out all the details. But I'm going to as soon as . . ."

"As soon as what?"

"Quillan leaves." She said it softly.

"Quillan's back? Oh, Carina, I am glad!"

Carina dropped her friend's hands. "I have yet to see him."

"Well, come. I'll shoo someone out." Èmie entered the cave, hung with dim lanterns. "You soak, and I'll scrub that skirt outside in the creek."

"You won't." Carina followed.

"Oh yes, I will. And you'd do the same for me."

Carina watched Èmie's back, straight and unwavering, the thin braid that hung down the middle hardly swaying at all. They reached the first private basin, and Èmie informed the occupant that the time was up. Then they waited until the curtain parted and a man emerged, red-faced and steaming.

Èmie waved Carina in. "I'll bring you soap."

"Thank you."

When Èmie came with the clove-scented soap, she took Carina's skirt out with her. Carina didn't argue again. It was true she would do the same for Èmie if her husband were returned. Of course, Èmie had no husband yet, though Carina suspected a romance with Dr. Simms. Most people thought Èmie plain. Carina thought her beautiful.

She sank into the steaming water with a low groan. She truly needed the healing it would give her sore and aching joints and muscles. If only it could soothe the deeper aching. Would Quillan come to her? Would they speak? What could she say?

There were so many things she wanted him to know. And she thought again of the journal Father Antoine Charboneau had entrusted to her, the diary of Quillan's mother. If she gave him the journal, would he come to know and love that mother as she did? Would he know his parents weren't what he thought them? A savage and a harlot.

Carina closed her eyes and dropped her head back into the water, freeing the hair from its braid. It spread out around her like a rippling black veil, and she threaded her fingers through its mass, then ran her nails over her scalp. She soaped and soaked, ducked under the surface, and let the water work on her.

Èmie returned with her skirt and hung it to dry on the line attached to the wall. "There. Now you can greet your husband, fresh and clean."

"Thank you." Carina had almost succeeded in conquering her inner quakes, but Èmie's words brought them back. God could bring good out of this, now that she was His. She had come to Crystal to spite Flavio, in the back of her mind believing he would come for her, but God had known better. Or she might now be Mrs. Caldrone, forever wondering where Flavio was and with whom.

Was it any different with Quillan? Yes! He might despise her, but she had no doubt of his fidelity. And she loved him. If she didn't, her chest would not be so tight, her thoughts so tumultuous. She must find a way to show him. If she could cook, if she had even one thing she needed to make something wonderful . . . But unless he went to the Italian market in Fairplay, she had none of the *grano*, the tomatoes, the garlic, even the Gorgonzola of which he'd been so leery.

She released a hard breath. What was the use? She could not win him with food. Nor had she impressed him in their marriage bed. Why else would he leave her the next morning with no tender word, no touch at all? She pulled herself up from the water, climbed onto the ledge, and wrung the water from the hair that reached to the back of her legs.

Then she rubbed her skin dry with the towel hanging on the line. So many others had used it before her that it was not much use. But she hung it back and pulled on her clothes. Her skirt, like her hair, was heavy and wet. She went out of the cave without seeing Èmie again. Her friend must be attending someone else in the steamy depths.

Carina walked out to the creek, giving the sun and breeze a chance to dry her hair and skirt. There was a smell of fall and a chill in the air. The light was different, sharper, but not so brilliant. The aspens were splashes of gold among the blackish green pines higher up the mountain. She had a sudden longing to see the mine. The Rose Legacy, where both Quillan's parents had perished.

She had gone up only twice since Quillan left. One of those times she had met Father Charboneau sitting on the burned stones of the old foundation. They both smiled, no longer surprised to find the other in that spot. Together they had visited the grave higher up the mountain, the single stone that bore the names Wolf and Rose.

Yes, she had read the journal and now treasured Rose in her heart. Yes, she understood why Father Charboneau had tried to protect their memory. What would she do with it now? She didn't know. The priest seemed satisfied, but she was restless when she thought of it.

She prayed the time would come when she could share it with Quillan. And she prayed she would know when the time came. But now, when he was grieving for Cain and keeping himself so separate, was not the time. Carina stopped walking and looked around her.

Directly behind the hot springs cave, the creek ran through a small copse of spindly pines. All the rest of the slopes around Crystal were denuded and scarred, studded with stumps and mine workings. Above and below her, along the creek on both sides, were tents and shacks and all the ragged trappings of greedy humanity.

But she no longer judged. They were all doing the best they could. With a sigh, she left the creek and headed back toward the little house she now claimed as her own. It was true she had purchased it from a fraudulent advertisement that had made it all the way to Sonoma, California. But she had purchased it in full. She had a legal right.

She pulled open the door to her house. She would have to get a key made, since Walter Carruther had stolen hers and she had no idea what had happened to it. The bed had been delivered and assembled, the feather mattress an extravagance she granted herself. It had been so long since she'd slept on anything soft. The blankets were folded at the foot. Whomever Mr. Fisher had sent was diligent.

The table stood near the wall to her right, and the two chairs looked ready for use. Again she wondered if Quillan would come. Then she wondered if he'd come already and found her gone. What if she had missed him? The thought threw her into a flurry of concern.

She dashed through the door and rushed across the yard to Mae's back door. It, too, was new, replaced after the vigilantes axed it down in search of her. Carina yanked it open, then stopped and calmed herself. She was Carina Maria DiGratia Shepard. She could walk.

She heard his voice. In Mae's parlor. Mae responded and they laughed. If Quillan was laughing, maybe he had worked out his grief, his anger, his disdain. She stopped outside the door to Mae's rooms. It was open a crack, and she could see him. Heat washed into her belly.

He stood with a day's worth of beard on his chin and his mane of hair tamed with a leather thong at the base of his skull. Did he know how like Wolf he seemed? Or at least her image of Wolf from the descriptions she heard and read. Was it a desire to imitate the father he never knew? Not likely, not with the hatred he felt for him.

Quillan's blue woolen shirt and canvas pants were

clean, the leather brogans almost new. He didn't look like a man just off the road. Had he changed and washed for her? Carina's heart leaped, and she tried unsuccessfully to contain her excitement.

"I told him to think twice before he knocked heads with me." Mae poked her head with a plump finger.

Quillan smiled, and Carina's chest tightened. It amazed her how his smile transformed his face, the hard lines and planes softening, inviting.

"He'd have to know you to fully appreciate the threat."

Mae released her belly laugh. "He caught enough to back off."

Carina touched the door with her fingertips and it swung quietly. Quillan turned, and his smile changed, not in magnitude but character. It became his pirate smile, the rogue smile he kept only for her. He dipped his head slightly, all the while holding her mute with his charcoal-rimmed stormy eyes.

Her throat ached with unspoken words. What could she say? She should have thought before she pushed open the door, but her hand had reached out of its own volition. Betraying her.

"Well, don't just stand there." Mae walked over and swept her in.

She came to a stop before her husband, whose eyes hadn't left her. She felt so small, her five feet four inches hardly significant before his almost six feet that seemed more somehow. Yet she was determined to speak first. "You're back." She was pleased her voice held steady. If he guessed the tumult inside, at least she didn't show it.

"Briefly." He dispensed with the smile and became again the man with the silent purpose she'd met on the road. "I understand you're moving out."

Well. Her business was known before she knew it herself. "It's my house. Why shouldn't I live there?" She should have said "we," but his expression was so hard she couldn't.

"I'll leave you two alone." Mae didn't give them time to argue. In spite of her bulk, she could be quite swift when she wanted to.

Quillan hadn't moved, hadn't shifted his expression. "Have you considered the risks?" There was no deep concern in the question, simply a business tone with a hint of condescension.

"The risks of what?"

"Living alone."

It hurt. She should have expected it, prepared for it. But she hadn't, and it sank deep. She waved a hand, refusing to show her pain. "I am safe here? With canvas walls?"

He glanced briefly out the door Mae had passed through. "Is it habitable?"

"I've made it so."

"I'll have a look."

Carina startled. "That's not necessary." Somehow the thought of him inside those walls . . .

He took up his hat and started for the doorway. Helpless to stop him, she followed. Just outside the door, the brown-and-white dog jumped up and followed, too. They crossed the short distance, circled to the front of the little house, and Quillan pushed open the door. "Do you have a key?"

"No, I—"

"I'll get you one made."

He stepped inside with a hand motion to the dog to stay out. "Where did you get the furniture?"

Her chest heaved with indignation. Who was he to

walk in and ask? What was she to him that it should matter? She waved both arms. "I got it. What does it matter where?"

He turned and eyed her. "Is it on credit?"

"No."

He tucked his tongue between his side teeth, then, "Carina, as long as you insist on this flawed liaison, I'm responsible for you."

Her breath left in a rush. She wanted to kick him, imagined her foot striking his shin, hard! *Signore, it is more than I can stand. This once, just this once, let me kick him!* But she didn't. Instead she drew herself up. "It was *your* decision to marry *me*."

"Don't think I haven't pondered that."

"Bene. Then you might consider what it means."

His eyes narrowed. "I know very well what it means. That's why I offered to let you out."

"You would divorce me?" She splayed her fingers, palm upward, a gesture of fury and exasperation.

"The dissolution of folly is hardly contemptible. What have you to lose?"

She dropped her hand clenched to her side. "I have lost one thing already. Or did you forget our wedding night?"

He turned away and his throat worked as he studied the wall. "Where did you get the furniture?"

She snorted her derision. "Fisher's General Mercantile."

"How did you pay for it?"

"I borrowed from Mae."

"I'll pay that back, and I'll leave you something to use at your discretion."

"Un gross'uomo."

"Carina..." He raised his hand, then dropped it. "Do you have your Sharps?"

She shook her head. The gun had been lost the night the vigilantes struck.

He unbuckled his gun belt and removed it, then refastened it and hung it on the bedpost. "Do you remember how to shoot?"

"Sì." Yes, she remembered, though it would do her little good. She couldn't hit anything at the best of times, and in the stress of the moment...

"This caliber has quite a kick. Use both hands. I'll leave you extra loads."

He would leave her this, leave her that. But he wouldn't stay himself. Bene. Let him go. "When do you leave?"

"In the morning."

"What about Mr. Makepeace?"

He raised his brows slightly. "We've met already."

She wanted to ask about his business with a mining engineer but didn't. "Where will you stay tonight?"

One side of his mouth pulled in an insolent grin. "Here. Since you insist."

Her pulse suddenly rushed in her throat.

"By the way, I brought you a dozen eggs." He put on his hat and walked out the door.

Carina sank down to the bed, her legs no longer steady.

Three

It is the Lord who sees, the Lord who knows.
Search me and fill my thoughts with wisdom and grace.
—*Carina*

UNQUESTIONABLY STUPID. But what else could he do—pitch a tent when he had a wife in a house in a town where everyone knew everything? Quillan ordered Sam to stay. The dog looked mournful, lying back down on the stoop. But for once Quillan didn't want the animal tailing him everywhere he went. He stopped first at the blacksmith's and ordered a key. To his knowledge, Crystal had yet to procure a locksmith.

He eyed the towering Norwegian. "How soon?"

"First thing tomorrow, eh?" Bjorn Svendsen set down his tongs and made himself a note.

"Thanks." Quillan went next to the livery, where he'd left the eggs and his personal luggage with the wagon.

Alan was dozing, but he snapped awake at Quillan's approach. "And what did the man think of your mine?"

"He'll survey it tomorrow. His group will take charge of it. D.C. and I'll collect our share."

"Just like that."

Quillan pulled up a grooming stool and placed it

beside Alan's chair. "More or less."

"And who's to keep them honest?"

Quillan straddled the stool. "Meaning?"

"How will ye know if yer gettin' a fair deal?"

Quillan dropped his chin and kicked a chunk of sawdust. Getting cheated out of profits he hardly considered his own wasn't high on his list of concerns. But he had D.C.'s interests to look to also. "What makes you think that's a problem?"

Alan tapped the side of his head. "I've lived. Gold and silver are beguilin'. They make breakin' the rules acceptable."

Quillan looked out the doors at the street crawling more thickly as dusk approached. "Well, I can't worry about everything."

"But you could stay and oversee it."

Quillan snorted. "I don't know anything about mining."

"That's why you have the engineer. And a manager."

"Then what's my part?"

Alan showed a slow grin. "Your part is to be a presence, a dissuasion."

Quillan rubbed the back of his neck. "I have other things to do."

Alan shrugged. "Might be if you ever stayed, you'd grow roots."

Quillan brushed a spiraling seedpod from his pants leg. "I don't need roots, Alan."

"Ah, boyo. We all need roots."

Well, that was something Quillan would never have. He had no past, no name except the one loaned him by two people he despised, and one given to him by two others he'd never known but whose story had been a torment as long as he could remember. No. He'd live without roots.

"How is she?" Alan spoke low.

"Who?"

"Your bride."

Quillan frowned. "How do you think? Contentious and expensive."

"And bonny."

"Oh, she's beautiful." No denying that.

"Take her to your bed tonight. Get her with child. Settle down and make a home."

Quillan didn't argue, but none of that would happen. He stood up, walked to his wagon, and pulled out the bedroll and the pack that held his immediate necessities. Then he carefully lifted the small crate with eggs packed in sawdust. "Good night, Alan."

"Aye." Alan's smile was misguided.

Quillan hated to deceive him, but even more to disappoint him with the truth. He went out. Up the block he stopped at Fisher's and learned the amount of the bill for Carina's furniture. He'd have provided the things for one sixth what she'd paid, but it was done now. He'd bring that amount to Mae, then request that Carina not shop Fisher's again.

He looked around the town, up the street and down, at all the new and existing businesses. Most had nothing to offer Carina—saloons, gambling dens, houses of ill repute—but there were enough others, including a new bookstore, which might prove costly unless he established some ground rules. And he knew how well Carina took direction. Blowing his breath through his lips, he headed for Mae's.

Carina pulled the long crusty loaves from Mae's oven. She'd used Mae's flour, salt, and yeast, a spoonful of honey fresh from the comb, and olive oil from her own dwindling supply. That and a handful of herbs was all she had left of the treasure Quillan had bought from the Italian market in Fairplay.

It was enough to make the bread he liked drizzled with oil and sprinkled with basil and salt. But she had nothing with which to make the cannelloni or the ravioli, unless—hadn't he said he'd brought eggs? She could dice Mae's beef with a pinch of nutmeg for filling, and with the eggs and flour she'd make the pasta dough and cut the ravioli. Without butter and garlic . . .

Bene. It was the best she could do. Besides, why should she care? What was it to her if Quillan ate well or poorly? But she did care. Especially when he wasn't near to infuriate her. If only she could find a way . . .

She set the steaming loaves on the board. The aroma enticed her nostrils, and she breathed it deeply, thinking of home. She had learned how to adjust to the altitude and make the bread as light and crusty as Mamma's. If she had the right ingredients, she could cook food the men of Crystal would trade their mines for. She smiled at the thought, caressing the end of one loaf. If only she had what she needed.

Sam bounded toward Quillan as he approached Mae's back door. Quillan gave the dog a reassuring stroke, let him lick his hands, then patted him lightly. Why did the animal always act as though his very existence depended on Quillan's affection? Leaving Sam outside the door, Quillan entered Mae's kitchen, only slightly surprised to find Carina there. But then, the stove in her house was good for little more than warmth. A kettle maybe and a skillet to warm something. Certainly not adequate for the kind of use Carina made of a kitchen.

Mae went to the corner shelf and stuffed the bills he'd given her into a canister. He saw Carina frown. Did she think he wouldn't pay her debt? He knew his responsibilities. Mae shuffled to the stove and began slopping beef from one large kettle into a serving pot.

Quillan crossed to the table where Carina stood over two long crusty loaves, the kind she'd served him before. His mouth watered as he held out the small crate. Not much of a gift for a man to bring his bride, but she took it as though each egg were pure gold.

"Thank you." Her eyes met his briefly.

He didn't like the way her gaze made his stomach clench up. "You're welcome." He sat down on the bench at Mae's table.

Near his elbow, Carina set a bowl, and into this she scooped flour. He watched her sprinkle it with salt, then make a well in the center. Her hands made each motion a dance, and he was amazed again by how expressive fingers and palms could be. Her fingers and palms. She lifted one egg from the carton and kissed it.

Irresistibly, his glance went to her lips. Was she playing a game? Enticing him? She cracked the egg and emptied it into the well, never once looking his way. Then she drizzled in oil and water. His brows rose slightly when she plunged her fingers into the bowl and began working the dough by hand.

"Do you always do it that way?" He waved at the bowl.

"How else would I know if the mixture is right?"

He chewed the side of his lower lip where a crack was starting from the long days in the sun and dust. It wasn't hard to believe that her hands told her things. They were more than ordinary hands. He watched them work the dough into a pliant sheen, then divide it into two balls.

She sprinkled the table with flour and rolled one of the balls into a thin sheet. Watching her was like watching a juggler or a musician, someone with a skill beyond that of normal men. She covered the dough with a damp towel and began to mince beef from Mae's pot. Again with her fingers she sprinkled a brown powdery substance, and he whiffed it but couldn't name it.

"What's that?" He jutted his chin toward the substance.

"Nutmeg."

He recalled her tale of misfortune the first time she cooked with nutmeg. She had told it the first time she cooked for him. He warmed inside, but he resisted it. He wasn't here to fall prey to her wiles. He looked away, indifferent to what she did next. But when she began to hum, he looked back.

She had made little mounds of the meat on the first sheet of dough and was laying a second over it all. It looked exactly as though she were tucking them in for the night, and the corner of his mouth twitched with the thought. Once she had it covered, she took a metal circle and pressed it over each mound, cutting them out like biscuits.

Now he knew what she was making, though the name eluded him. It was the little pillows she'd brought to Brother Paine's picnic. He scowled. It wasn't much of a stretch to consider that day the start of it all. If he hadn't wanted to try her fare, he wouldn't have gone back for more.

"Your face is as long as Guiseppe's mule."

He glanced up at her and found the shadow of a

smile. So she thought it amusing. He forked his fingers into his hair. "I'm tired. It's a long road."

"This won't take long."

He wanted to say never mind, he wasn't hungry. But that would be a lie, and the longer he looked at the golden loaves before him, the more he imagined the flavor of it drizzled with oil and basil and salt. She'd taught him that much.

"What do you call those things?"

"Ravioli. It won't be the best without butter or *parmigiano* or garlic."

"You used it all up?"

She spread her hands. "What do you expect in two months?"

He tried not to think of the meals he'd missed. It didn't matter. He could do with a can of something heated over a fire.

She dropped the ravioli into a pot of boiling water. Now that was something he hadn't seen before. He would have guessed she baked them. Crossing to the table, she brushed her hair back from her forehead with her sleeve, then took the knife and began to slice the bread. Steam erupted and filled his nose with the wonderful smell.

His throat worked already. If she wasn't looking, he'd snatch a piece and stuff it into his mouth whole. She laid the slices of bread onto a plate and drizzled the oil over them. He noticed the bottle was nearly empty. The jar that held the pungent basil was all but empty as well.

She placed the plate in the center of the table and turned back to the stove. His fingers itched; his mouth watered. But he controlled the urge. No good letting her see his impatience. Gently she strained the ravioli from the boiling water into a bowl. With a sigh, she poured the rest of the oil and the last of the basil over them. She tossed it lightly with a spoon, then set it on the table.

Mae came in, refilled her pot, and left again, the noise of the men in the other room reason enough for her haste. But Quillan knew he'd have no help from that quarter. She'd find something to occupy her and leave them alone together all evening. Carina sat down, and he reached for a slice of bread.

"We'll bless the food and thank God for it."

His hand hovered over the plate, then returned to his side. If she wanted to pray, let her.

"Grazie, Signore, for this bounty. Bless it to our use. Amen." Her hand made a path from her head to her chest and across each shoulder.

Quillan narrowed his eyes mockingly. "Is it safe now?"

"Sì." She didn't even blink.

He snatched a slice of bread and took a bite. *Heaven.* The most heaven he'd ever know. Carina then spooned ravioli onto his plate. Again the steamy aroma wafted to his nose. She wasn't playing fair. He cut into one and brought it to his mouth. She was right that it wasn't as good as the last time, but he chewed it with relish nonetheless.

"When can you go to Fairplay and get me more?"

"More?" He knew exactly what she meant.

"The market there. I need ingredients." She held a ravioli poised, then plunked it into her mouth.

He swallowed his own bite. "I don't recall that working out so well."

"What do you mean?"

"I ended up in the hole."

She waved a hand, dismissing his point. "You don't know how it's done."

He raised an eyebrow. "How *what's* done?"

"How to buy from an Italian."

He set down his fork and leaned back from the table. "Is that so?"

"Sì. You never pay what he asks."

Quillan took the napkin beside his plate and wiped the side of his mouth where he could feel it slick with oil. He haggled every day in his line of work—on the buying end, not the selling. In Crystal he could ask whatever he wanted and folks would pay.

But it was true that on the occasion she described, he hadn't haggled. It was all so foreign, the things on her list, the man with his broken English. Quillan had taken whatever the man said Carina would want and paid his price. Now he felt like a fool.

"How do you know he didn't ask more than I paid?"

She laughed. "Not even a *truffatore* would ask more than you paid."

"What's a truffatore?"

"A swindler."

Quillan placed a whole ravioli into his mouth. It would save him from responding to that one. He savored the flavor. What would it hurt to keep her supplied? If he had to make a show of this marriage, he might at least eat well. He washed down the bite with a swig of coffee.

"You think you could do better?"

She smiled a perfect smile, soft lips, white teeth. "What do you think?"

He thought the old truffatore would melt into the floor. Quillan crowded his plate and folded his hands on the table. "How would you like to buy for yourself?"

Her breath caught. "Do you mean it?"

Quillan's throat tightened at her earnest expression. He hadn't expected quite such excitement. "If you think you can take the ride."

"Didn't I take it all the way from Denver? Of course I

can take the ride. When do we go?"

He retreated to his bench, angry with himself for suggesting it. If she got tired they'd have to spend the night in Fairplay. But he doubted she'd admit getting tired. "I guess tomorrow."

"Oh, thank you." She grasped his hand a moment, then let it fall and withdrew hers swiftly to her sides.

It was too late, though. She'd touched him, and his heart hammered his chest. He pushed away from the table.

She followed with her eyes, two dark pools wreathed with even darker lashes. "Aren't you going to finish?"

"I have things to do." He stood, leaving the food that had so beguiled him, and walked out Mae's back door. He kicked himself for being vulnerable, for once again letting her lure him with food, and even more than the food, the companionship. For the second time that day, he made for the graveyard.

He hardly noticed the dog following until it lay down beside the mound, as though seeking its old master's comfort as well. Cain's stone still looked new. But then, it took more than two months to weather a stone, even at this altitude. He slumped down beside the grave, feeling the pain of loss as fresh as ever. He looked at the stone.

CAIN JEREMIAH BRADLEY. 1810–1880. He thought of Cain's favorite saying. *"And we know that all things work together for good to them that love God, to them who are called according to his purpose."*

Did they? Did they, Cain? Can you still believe it wherever you are? He shook his head. No, God didn't do good to those who loved Him. He sacrificed them, the same as He had His own Son. Quillan sat by the grave until the stars shone in the clear black canopy, then reluctantly stood.

He'd have to go home sooner or later.

Carina had changed into her gown and brushed her hair a hundred strokes as she always did. She'd scoured her teeth diligently, considering each one a small battlefield. She was determined to take each tooth to the grave without surrendering even one to a dentist. She had a candle lit on a crate beside the bed. She hadn't thought to purchase a lamp, but Quillan had said he'd leave money for such things.

Quillan. Where had he gone? If he intended to sleep here, he'd better come before she put the chair against the door. Once her head felt the softness of a real pillow and her body sank into a feather mattress, she was not moving again.

The door opened behind her, and she spun. Quillan came inside and dropped a bedroll to the floor. "Svendsen will have a key for you tomorrow."

She nodded. Now that he was inside, the walls had shrunk and it was impossible to breathe normally. Would he take her in his arms as he had before, with no words? Would he kiss her, making the love she felt that much harder to bear? She stood frozen beside the bed.

Quillan let the dog inside, and it made a quick circle of the room, then returned to him, tail wagging. Quillan rubbed its head briefly, then stooped and untied the bedroll. He spread it sideways before the door. No one could reach her without stepping on him. The dog circled three times, then lay down at the bedroll's edge.

"You're sleeping there?"

"That's right."

So he wouldn't practice his husbandly prerogative. Was she so undesirable? Her spirit sank, but she raised her chin, looking from him to the dog and back. "Good. Whatever lives down there can eat you first."

He glanced sideways, but she ignored him. Dropping to her knees beside the bed, she crossed herself, then laced her fingers together beneath her chin. "*Il Padre Eterno,* thank you for giving me my house. Please bless Mamma and Papa, my brothers Angelo, Joseph, Vittorio, Lorenzo, and Tony. Bless my sister, Divina." She hardly paused at all over this last. She had forgiven Divina and prayed now for her happiness.

"Bless my uncles, my aunts, godparents, grandparents, and all my family. Please bless Guiseppe and his mules. And bless my stubborn husband. Amen." She didn't look his way, but she knew he'd heard every word. She hoped the order of blessing wasn't lost on him.

She crossed herself and climbed into the bed. She had resisted trying it even for a moment so that her first feel of it would not be diminished. She sank into its softness with a sigh of pure pleasure. If Quillan preferred the floor, fine.

Quillan watched her make the hand motion and climb into the bed. Her form was hidden in the gown that hung loosely to the floor, and she pulled the covers to her chin and blew out the candle, but he knew well enough what he'd find beneath it all. She was every man's dream, beautiful in face and body, sweet and passionate and deadly.

He couldn't afford to lose his heart. He wanted her too much. And he knew how that was—the wanting. His whole being ached. He could take care of the physical need. It was his right. But what of the rest? He settled onto the hard floor. Better to remember that and sleep alone.

Four

Be my banner, O Lord,
champion of my soul.

—Carina

FOG SHROUDED THE WINDOW when Carina opened her eyes. She had slept soundly in spite of Quillan's presence, which had made it hard to succumb. No doubt it was the wonder of feathers and clean, warm bedding that at last won out. She nestled her head for a moment, then raised it. The dog raised his, too, and looked at her with expectant eyes, but the bedroll beside him was empty.

She looked at the door. How had he risen and left without her hearing? She sent her gaze to the window. The fog was dense and swirling. Had he left without her, crept out through the fog and disappeared for months again? No, he wouldn't leave his dog, Cain's dog.

Carina settled back into the comfort of the bed, stretching luxuriously. Then she thought of Quillan seeing her that way and sat up like a shot. She gripped the covers to her chin and searched the room as though he could be hidden somewhere in its bareness. He wasn't there, but he could be at any moment.

She slipped out of the bed, her feet jumping at the cold planks. At Mae's the floor had held a little warmth from the rooms below. Here it was only cold ground beneath the wood. She washed hurriedly with the pitcher and bowl she had borrowed from Mae and set on a crate by the window.

Rubbing her face dry, she looked out. The fog had brightened with the coming dawn but had not cleared. The town looked ghostly pale. Maybe Quillan wouldn't ride out in fog like this. Maybe he would stay with her for the day. She anticipated the thought hopefully. All things were possible. She cleaned her teeth and loosed her braid, then brushed the hair and left it down.

It was her finest feature. Hadn't Flavio . . . Carina stopped, amazed. That was the second time she'd thought of Flavio. Did Quillan's difficult behavior bring to mind the first man she had thought she loved? Would it always be so? Would Quillan wound her in the same way?

She pressed a fist to her breastbone and dropped to her knees. *Grazie, Signore, for this day. I know you are bigger than my troubles. And I am a lot of trouble to you.* However, Carina sensed God's love now in a way she hadn't before. Crystal had made her know Him, made her need Him. And she had surrendered.

She no longer tried to boss and bully God, to chastise Him when things didn't go her way. Her thanks were not empty acknowledgments that He had done as she wanted. He knew better what she needed, and she tried—*tried*—to submit.

I ask only that your will be done. You know the desire of my heart. If it is your desire as well, let my husband love me. She remembered Father Antoine's words. *"You don't have because you don't ask." Bene. I'm asking. I'm asking for his love.*

But you know best. I surrender to your will.

It was the best she could do with such a wayward spirit as hers. She stood and went to the bed. Stooping, she pulled the carpetbag from underneath. From it she took the skirt and blouse she'd worn yesterday and some clean underclothes. When she had time she would put hooks on the walls. But for now, she must hurry. If Quillan came back while she was changing . . .

But he didn't. She pulled on the oversized miner's jacket and went to the door. The dog rose, wagging himself earnestly. She bent and stroked his head. "What's your name? Are you my house dog, my *cane da guardia?* Are you keeping me safe?" The dog's tongue lapped her hand, and she laughed.

"You are a lover, I see. Your master better watch out, or he will lose you to a lady dog, a fine *bella cagna*." She opened the door and the dog leaped out, then frisked on the stoop. She closed the door behind her, and the animal raced off. She was concerned a moment, but he raced back as swiftly, circling her legs.

She wished she felt as carefree as she started across to Mae's. The fog was so thick she could barely see Mae's place. A few spindly shapes wavered in and out like specters. She slowly found Mae's back door and gripped the knob, relieved. Then she realized the dog was still wiggling at her side.

She glanced out where she knew the pump to be. "All right. Come on." She cut across the yard and almost stumbled on the stone basin at its base. She worked the pump handle and brought water into the basin. The dog lapped happily. Carina smiled. If only everything were that easy.

She started back. Suddenly a figure loomed and she cried out. The dog rushed past her legs, leaping and cajoling as Quillan caught her elbow.

"Are you all right?"

"Yes. You startled me." Her heart still raced, but then, Quillan had a way of suddenly appearing without warning.

"Sorry. Down, Sam."

"Is that his name?" Carina let the dog lap her fingers again.

"Second Samuel. Cain named him, not me. The first Samuel died."

"I gave him water." Would he care that she'd seen to his dog?

"Thanks."

"Mae might have something for him. Some scraps . . ."

"I'll take care of it."

Carina clasped her fingers together. "Are you coming in?"

"I ate at the hotel."

She sagged. He had risen and eaten without her. Her spirit shrank. He'd gone to Mrs. Barton, who was, no doubt, all smiles. But what would the woman think to have him there instead of eating what his wife provided? What could his wife provide?

She almost stamped her foot. What did he expect? But then she knew. Nothing. He expected nothing, wanted nothing.

"I'll be leaving soon. This should tide you over." He held out a wad of bills.

She looked from the money to his face, swimming in the fog. "What do you mean? I'm going with you. You said—"

"I can't take you in fog like this. Something's moving in, and it could turn nasty."

"Then you shouldn't be out either. We'll go tomorrow."

"I can't waste a day."

Oh, a day spent with her would be wasted? "How long will you be gone?"

He turned away. "A while."

"A month? Two?"

"There's enough there to last you."

But not to get what she needed. There was no Italian market in Crystal. She shrugged and reached for the bills. "I'll find someone else to take me." She waved her hand. "You can't be expected to, such a gross'uomo, so busy and important. I'll go myself."

"You can't, Carina. The snows'll come any day."

They'd already had several dustings, but what did she care? She waved a hand. "You don't need to worry. Go. Do your business."

He took a step and clutched her arms. "Look at me, Carina. You can't leave Crystal."

She said nothing.

He blew through his teeth. "All right, tell me what you need. I'll go to Fairplay and back."

She raised her chin but said nothing. He'd said she could buy for herself, and she wanted to. She would brave the fog or the snows or anything else to get the precious ingredients she needed.

His hands softened on her arms. "Carina, be reasonable. I can't risk you—"

"Why not? Then you'd be out of this 'flawed liaison.' "

He dropped his hold, his eyes as menacing as the fog, their gray even darker. The dog whined at his side, sensing his master's animosity. "Fine. Be ready to go in an hour." He jammed the wadded bills back into his pocket.

Carina bit her lip to hold back the smile and hid the

satisfaction that burst within her. No good flaunting her victory. He was contrary enough to take it back. "I'll be ready." She hurried into Mae's.

Quillan stalked away. Why should he have thought she'd be reasonable? What possible reason was there to suspect her capable of good sense? He'd worked it all out at the graveside. He'd leave her the money, all his profits from his latest deliveries—except what he needed for his trip down and to procure goods to resell in Leadville.

He'd been freighting to Leadville the last two months, close enough to monitor what was happening in Crystal without being there and lucrative enough to keep him busy. He'd hardly rested, simply changing horses but not giving himself the benefit of even one day free. On the wagon he occupied his mind with literature and poetry he'd read, memorizing it and drilling himself until he had it perfect. Anything to keep his thoughts at bay.

Why had he married Carina, invoked the wrath of Berkley Beck, put Cain at risk, left him unprotected. . . ? Quillan gripped his forehead and rubbed his palm down his face. So Carina wanted to see the freighter's life? He'd show her. He'd let her feel the backbreaking hours on the box, eat the dust, though the fog would keep that down some.

He looked up. The cloud was sitting solidly on the mountain. Every surface and blade of grass was already turning a fuzzy white. A hoarfrost. Snow would follow. It was insane to take her out with the possibility of a storm. He should pack up and go, leave her to her own devices.

But she was just foolish enough to try to make the trip alone. Hadn't she come to Crystal that way? However, that was in June—risky enough, but not the start of an alpine winter. No, he had to satisfy her this once. After this, it would be obvious she couldn't do it again. Even Carina had to see that.

He reached the livery. "Alan!"

"Aye." Alan stood up in one of the stalls. "Ye don't need to bellow. I'm not deaf yet."

"I need my team."

"They've hardly had their rest." Alan let himself out of the stall.

"It's a short trip. Just to Fairplay."

Alan reached his side. "And then where?"

"Back here."

Alan's stump-toothed smile stretched broadly. "Aye. Back by nightfall." Alan gripped his shoulder. "Didn't I say—"

"Carina's riding with me. I'll return her tonight and head out in the morning."

"Ah, boyo." Alan sighed and looked out the doors of the livery. "It smells like snow."

Quillan nodded. "She insists on riding along."

"To be near you."

"To buy at the Italian market."

Alan walked to the doors. "Would you risk . . ."

"You don't say no to Carina Maria DiGratia."

Alan turned, his face troubled. "Don't ye, now."

"I'll get the team myself." He saw his wagon in its usual spot by the back. Alan came and worked beside him. While they hitched the horses, he was aware of Alan's quiet scrutiny. It irked him, but he did his best not to show it. Carina had even spoiled this, the one good friendship he had left. She'd wheedled her way into Alan's heart until he took her side every time.

Quillan led the team out with a silent wave to Alan. He wasn't stupid. He knew weather like this was chancy. But if anyone could take Mosquito Pass in a storm, he could. He had plenty of road experience, and he'd handled the pass in all kinds of weather.

If it proved more than a snow shower, the worst of it would be at the summit. Once they'd started down the other side, it would lighten up again. And a fog like this could as easily lift to clear skies. If it got bad, they'd stay in Fairplay. That would show Carina just how dangerous her impulses were. That would keep her home next time.

But it didn't help at this time. He loaded the wagon with cured wood at twenty-five cents a foot. Scandalous as the price was, he wouldn't be caught without the means of making a fire. Then he loaded a barrel of water, checked his box of hard biscuits and jerked beef, emergency provisions, and a crate of canned vegetables he got directly from Mrs. Barton's larder.

He threw in blankets and an extra tarp, then fastened the main tarp over the bed. The wagon was ready, the horses rested enough for a short, light haul. Now it only remained to fetch Carina. Quillan made a quick check that the rifle was under the box with plenty of loads. It was there, along with Cain's shotgun. Well, that should cover everything.

He released a hard breath. Maybe she'd changed her mind. Wasn't that a woman's prerogative? Maybe he'd get back there and she'd be all aflutter with reasons why she couldn't go. He glanced up at the sky. Couldn't a man wish?

Before returning to the house, he went to find Svendsen. "Is the key ready?"

"Ya, sure." The Norwegian smiled broadly. "I didn't have to make that one."

"Why not?"

"When I saw which house you meant, I remembered. Berkley Beck ordered several for that place. I don't stick my nose out; I don't ask questions, eh? I only made the keys."

"How many more do you have?"

Svendsen held out four on his large calloused palm. "This is the last of them. No one wants them, since the house is haunted, ya?"

Quillan raised a brow, taking the keys. "Haunted?"

"It stood open these two months. How many empty rooms are there in town? Much less a house, ya?"

Quillan considered that. It was probably the best defense Carina had from harassment. Any other key holders would have jumped in before now, but for the superstitious mind of the prospector. As for any actual haunting, Quillan had slept well enough, the only moaning being Sam's rabbit-chasing dreams.

He set a coin on the table and dropped the spare keys into his pocket. "Thanks."

"Ya, sure." The Norwegian went back to his work.

Carina was ready long before Quillan returned. She had run home, filled her carpetbag with a change of clothes, her nightclothes, brush, and toothbrush. What more was there? She added a book, *Silas Marner* by George Eliot. Quillan had taken the gun he'd hung on the bedpost. Why would he leave it if she was going along? It was useful to him. He could shoot the head from a rattlesnake. She knew; she'd seen him do it. He was her protector. So where was he now?

The sun rose somewhere behind the fog, turning it white, and everything she could see through the little window was sugarcoated. The fog moved over the ground, parting and tearing and shrinking into itself, then spreading again. She stood watching, with the carpetbag at her feet. Did she look too eager? He would smirk. But she didn't move.

She searched the fog. A few figures wandered through it, though it was doubtful many would work their mines before the fog lifted. When she finally made out Quillan's form and saw him emerge from the fog onto the stoop, she girded herself. Would he try once again to dissuade her?

He tapped lightly on the door and entered. "Ready?" No smirk, no argument.

Again he surprised her. She thought she could guess his next move, but she never could quite. She took up her bag. "Yes." She pulled the miner's jacket closed at the neck.

"Is that the best coat you have?"

"Yes. The only one." Now he would argue. This would be his excuse.

He reached for her bag, carried it out, and started into the fog. She followed, feeling very like the dog who pranced beside her.

At the corner of Central, he turned and entered Fisher's. He went directly to the shelf on the right wall and pulled down a woolen coat. "This the smallest you have?"

Henry Fisher crossed to him. "Too small for you, Quillan."

"It's for my wife."

Fisher turned and noted her standing inside the door. "You're on the wrong side, then. Here." He crossed to a rack standing near the window, pulled out a brown woolen coat with fur-lined collar, and held it up. "This is what you need for the little woman."

Carina looked from the coat to Quillan and saw him

frown. It cost more than he wanted to pay. She knew. She'd looked at it already.

He nodded sharply. "How much?"

"Two crates of bourbon. The real stuff."

Quillan eyed the coat, jaw cocked, then nodded again slowly. "Deal." He took the coat and headed for her.

Her fingers sank into the fur as she took it from him. It was good of him. Her heart braved a tiny skip. Maybe he cared. Maybe . . .

"Lose the other one. It looks ridiculous."

She slipped the canvas coat off and left it by the wall. Then she slipped into the woolen coat and felt its warmth and the softness of the fur. With unsteady fingers, she fastened the buttons and pulled it snugly around her waist. She couldn't help smiling. How long since she'd donned something new and fine? "Thank you."

Quillan didn't answer. With a firm grip on her elbow, he led her outside. "That's the last time we buy there. From now on, when you need something, write it on a list. I'll get the things when I'm away."

She hurried to match his stride. "You don't like Mr. Fisher?"

"It's just good business. I can get it for less elsewhere. And that goes for the other stores in Crystal."

"I thought it was my discretion."

He turned abruptly. "That was before."

"Before what?"

"Before I thought it through," he ended lamely.

She fit her hands into the pockets of her new coat. "So you don't trust me."

He stopped before his wagon and team, standing ready, and whistled through his teeth. Sam leaped to the bed and climbed to the box. Quillan led her to the off side and swung her up. Sam licked her ear before Quillan ordered him down. She watched Quillan circle back, then felt the wagon sag as he climbed up beside her with the dog between them.

He turned briefly. “It’s just good business.”

Bene. She knew good business. When she had her own, she would shop wherever she wished.

Five

My will is stubborn as leather before the tanner.
Bend it, Lord, to your ways . . . in spite of me.
—Carina

QUILLAN TOOK UP THE REINS. They were damp and frosty from the fog. He pulled the leather gloves from his pocket and worked them on. He realized now that Carina had none, but she could keep her hands in her pockets. Or wrap in the blanket if it was really cold at the summit.

He slapped the reins and whistled to his team. The wagon lurched forward. With a nearly empty bed this portion of the journey would be swift. But not so swift Carina wouldn't know some discomfort. He didn't find that thought as gratifying as he'd expected.

A sidelong glance ascertained her settled against the short back, straight and determined. She was fine. But then, he surmised that even if she weren't, she would pretend to be. "If you get cold, there's a blanket under the tarp."

She nodded.

"You sure you want to do this?"

She turned. "Was the man a Sicilian?"

"What man?"

"At the market."

"How should I know?"

She crooked an eyebrow. "Then I should do this."

He hated her insinuations. His work was not something he wanted scrutinized by a prima donna with an inflated notion of herself and her skills. They rode in silence as they left Crystal with fairly little difficulty. The fog had cleared the road of most traffic. Quillan was confident he could handle whatever came, but others were not so inclined to risk it.

For a long while only the rumble of the bed, the clop of hooves, and the creak of wheels and harness broke the silence. Quillan settled into the rhythm of it, anticipating the long hours of solitude. No, not solitude, not this time. At least it didn't seem that she would chatter.

Another sideways glance showed her gazing through the fog with a slightly pensive expression. Good. She could content herself with her thoughts as he would his. He toyed with several lines from Byron's *Prisoner of Chillon*, then remembered he had promised to lend it to Carina when he'd finished with it. He had never done so.

He'd taken it with him to Leadville, and it was there in his tent even now. Unless the tent had been raided by someone literate enough to appreciate his collection. Oh, well, she had her own books. He'd helped haul them up the mountainside, where he'd put them over with her wagon. What if that chance encounter had never happened?

He returned his thoughts to Byron and left them there, wandering the lines and phrases he'd already committed to memory. It was something he'd trained himself to do since he was young and many of his favorite books had been confiscated. He pictured Mrs. Shepard's face, white with fury whenever she discovered his disobedience. Then the books would be taken, but she couldn't remove them from his mind.

So he'd learned to memorize as he read. Then when the books were found and destroyed, he felt a grim satisfaction rather than the previous devastation. He'd learned the books of the Bible he was ordered to learn, but they never suspected he carried the others in his mind as well.

After a steady two hours, Quillan looked ahead and saw the fog tearing apart as the road climbed. He dared to hope. It could go either way. Sometimes the cloud sat in a gulch and just above it the skies were clear. With any luck it would be that way now. Carina, too, seemed to have noticed the change. She leaned slightly forward, staring ahead.

The road wound upward and the sky brightened. Quillan's chest relaxed when he saw ragged swaths of blue in the sky just ahead. When they reached the section of road that passed Wasson Lake, the sun jumped out and ignited the white needles of the pines and the grasses along the shore.

The lake turned a brilliant blue and Quillan watched it with satisfaction as they passed by, far enough away to catch the reflection of the peaks in its expanse and take in the entire vista. He noted Carina's gaze, riveted. Did she remember his teaching her to shoot on the shores of that lake? Of course she did. It was vivid for him.

"It looks like we'll have clear skies after all." It surprised him that he was the one to break the silence.

"I wasn't worried."

"You don't know enough to be." He didn't say it to

provoke her. It was the simple truth. Until you've experienced the alpine weather, you couldn't imagine its deadliness. Even in early September.

They were climbing toward the summit, and he kept the team at an even pace. Lung fever had claimed many a horse pushed too hard for the altitude. He never expected more of his team than he knew they could manage. Now with a very light load, they could hold this pace and blow once they reached the top. Coming back with a full bed, they'd have to let them rest every quarter mile near the summit.

They continued to climb, the road hitching back and forth as the grade grew steeper and more treacherous. A keen breeze stung his face and the air sparkled suddenly with a snow shower under the blue, sunlit sky.

Beside him, Carina's breath caught, and she released it with an exultant sigh. "It's beautiful. *Com'è bello. Stupendo.*" Her voice was a breathless rush.

Quillan turned. He hadn't heard her language for some time. He liked how it sounded when she wasn't using it to abuse him.

"How can it snow with no clouds in the sky?" She stared upward with wonder.

"At this altitude the moisture freezes without necessarily accumulating into clouds."

"It doesn't look real. I think it's stardust." She pulled her hands from her pockets and raised open palms to the glittering flakes.

Quillan smiled, then rubbed Sam's ear when he wiggled uncertainly. "Don't mind her, Sam. She gets some wild notions."

Carina closed her eyes, ignoring him. Quillan smiled at that, too. Two months ago she would have thrown an insult in return. Now she tried to appear as though she neither heard nor cared. She opened her mouth and held her tongue to the flakes.

He caught his own tongue between his side teeth to keep from laughing. "Don't breathe it in, Carina. It's too sharp to take directly into your lungs that way. You'll risk pneumonia."

She closed her mouth and eyed him. "I want to stop at the top."

"We'll stop. The horses need a blow."

"Blow?"

"Rest. Catch their breath."

They climbed in silence as the sparkling shower thickened without threat. Quillan navigated the road to the highest point, then reined in the horses. Carina jumped down, and he watched her stride to the edge of the road, spread her arms wide, and holler, "Grazie, Signore!"

The air was biting as she hollered, then drew yet more air into her throat to holler again. She believed Quillan that it was unhealthy, but she couldn't contain what she felt. "Grazie, Dio!" This beauty, this stupendous, glorious beauty. How could she not thank God for it?

She dropped her arms and looked down from the summit of the pass. Far below, the river rushed in a narrow, rocky bed. She grasped her hands below her chin and murmured her thanks again. *Gesù* had removed the fear of heights when she surrendered her soul to His keeping and forgave Divina, who had, wittingly or no, given her the fear. God had healed her, and she basked in the scene spread beneath her—something she would not have dared look at four months ago. She felt Quillan at her side.

His touch was cautious on her elbow. "Are you okay?"

She nodded. "Sì."

"I thought you had a problem with heights."

"I did." She stooped and pried a stone loose. Cupping it in her palm, she threw it out over the edge and watched it soar down, down, until it was lost in the landscape.

"You don't seem dizzy to me."

"I'm not." But it was too personal to share why with him. Father Charboneau, yes—but Quillan? He would laugh, scoff, and not believe her. She turned and walked to the black lead horse on the right. The breath from its nostrils turned white in the chilled air. She stroked its muzzle. "Have a good rest, Jack. You've done well."

The horse nuzzled her. Laughing, she walked around to Jock and encouraged him with a pat. "Such strong leaders. You know the road, eh?"

The two Clydesdales behind the blacks towered over her, tremendous specimens of muscle with shaggy hooves. Their eyes were mild on either side of the white streak down their muzzles.

"What is this one called?"

"Socrates."

She touched his shoulder, stroked it with her palm. "And that one is Plato?"

Looking at her over the harness that separated the two pairs, Quillan shook his head. "Nope. Homer."

So he had replaced his first pair of Clydesdales after the flood. Alan Tavish had told her their names, Peter and Ginger. She liked this pair better. "How long do they rest?"

"Awhile."

It was nonspecific, but maybe it would be long

enough to work the pain out of her back. Coming up to Crystal, she'd driven a small wagon with a deep seat to support her while she drove. This freight wagon was a dreadful ride. How did he stand it so long, so many days at a stretch?

Surreptitiously, she rubbed her lower back and walked along the wagon, hoping Quillan didn't see. The beauty had driven away the pain, but now it returned. She tried to focus on the brilliant gold aspens with white trunks that stood out among the tall pine spires.

The snow still flew in sparkling waves. She was cold; her ears ached with it. She climbed up and pulled the shawl from her carpetbag. She tied it over her head as Quillan paced, working the kinks from his legs. She watched him, wondering what he thought, what he did on these drives all alone.

He caught her looking, and for a moment their gaze locked. Then he headed for the wagon. "Don't get down. We'll go on now."

Carina sighed too softly for him to hear as she settled into her space. Sam climbed up beside her. Quillan took the reins and giddapped the horses. Already the ache started in her back again and her seat was no better. Bene. She'd asked to come. She wouldn't whine. The horses would need to blow again—soon, she prayed. To distract herself from the discomfort, she took *Silas Marner* from the bag.

Quillan glanced over. "What's that?"

"George Eliot. *Silas Marner*. Have you read it?"

He shook his head.

"Shall I read it aloud?"

"If you want."

She settled back and opened the book. It was hard to focus with the tiny snowflakes still swirling, but she held the shawl to block most of it and began. Quillan kept his gaze on the road, his expression fixed and a little fierce. The wind picked up, and she had to read loudly to be heard. She paused often to catch her breath and soothe her voice.

During one pause, Quillan brushed the side of his face with his sleeve. "He has an interesting style."

"It's a woman."

"I meant the author."

"I know."

He turned briefly. "Named George?"

Carina shrugged. "What's a name? If I chose to be called Charles, would I be any less what I am?"

He eyed her a moment. "How do you know?"

"I can tell. Certain phrases, certain . . . insights."

"Well, of course, male authors have no insights."

She shrugged. "They're different." She picked up the book and shielded it once again from the sparkling snow dust.

Her voice grew hoarse and her fingers raw from holding the book, but she sensed an intensity in Quillan that kept her reading. It was as though he more than listened; he absorbed her words. If he didn't hear her clearly, he asked her to repeat it. And she did, sometimes twice before he got it exactly.

But the cold was intense and she started to waver. It was a tremendous relief when he stopped once again to let the horses blow. Instead of jumping down, she set the book aside and dug her fingers back into her pockets. They throbbed with cold, sending pain up her forearms.

Quillan came around and reached up for her. Before she could pull her hands free, he'd gripped her waist and swung her down from the box. She fell against him on unsteady legs, and he caught, then released her.

"We'll eat here."

They had come down far enough that the snow shower had ceased and the temperature had risen a little. Would he build a fire and cook something hot? Did he expect her to? He unfastened the tarp and reached into the bed. He retrieved a sack and, from it, pulled biscuits and jerked beef, along with a couple of dried apples. It looked as unappetizing as anything she'd yet eaten in Crystal.

He must have seen her thoughts. "No, it's not a banquet. But it's how we do it on the road."

"Can't we light a fire and—"

"Not if you want to make it back tonight. This is the quick part. It'll be slower with a full load."

Trying not to show the anguish that thought caused her, she took the food he offered. "How much longer to Fairplay?"

"An hour. Unless the wind picks up. We can't keep the pace against a head wind." He stooped and gave the dog the same fare as they.

Carina bit the hard, dry biscuit. It tasted like dust. No flavor at all, only hard, powdery chunks on her tongue. "Is this really food, or do you just pretend?"

That earned his rogue's smile. "I'll give Mrs. Barton your compliments."

"Surely she can do better than this." She waved the biscuit with disdain.

"Not with hardtack. It's made to keep, to withstand the journey."

She forced herself to swallow. "I could caulk my walls with it."

"No doubt." He reached in again and brought out a small water barrel, then retrieved a tin cup. He dipped and handed the cup her way.

She drank greedily, washing the biscuit residue from her mouth and throat, then noticed he was waiting. She handed back the cup and he dipped water for himself. It seemed strangely intimate when he brought the same cup to his lips. His throat worked up and down as he swallowed; the shadow of beard was dark halfway down his neck. To her knowledge, he hadn't shaved since yesterday.

He looked wild and free, and she tried to picture him in the suit he'd worn for their wedding. Seeing him now in the buckskin coat and woolen shirt and jeans, she couldn't envision it. Besides, she'd been dazed and wonderstruck at her wedding.

This was real. This was her husband, this man of the road. What would it feel like to kiss his beard-roughened face? Looking away, she put the jerky into her mouth and gripped it with her teeth. Wiggling it up and down while yanking, she bit through and chewed.

What would Mamma say to such fare? But then, what would Mamma say to any of it? A wash of guilt swept her. She hadn't written in two months. Mamma must be sick with worry. But Carina didn't know how to tell her or Papa that she'd married Quillan Shepard instead of Flavio Caldrone, her distant cousin and childhood love.

Quillan was an outsider. He was not Italian, not highborn, not Catholic, and certainly not one Papa would have chosen. Was he one she would have chosen had circumstance not driven her to it? Yes, her heart cried. But she knew it would never have happened anywhere but Crystal.

She fought the jerky for another bite. She was losing her appetite. She gnawed the bite, then the dried apple.

Then she drank another cup of water. They'd eaten the whole meal standing, but the thought never occurred to her to sit. To be up on her legs, to be off her backside—this was unspeakable relief.

When she finished her drink, she walked briskly back and forth along the wagon while Quillan fed and watered the horses. A raven cawed overhead, swooping upward to the tip of a pine heavy with cones. The sun was slightly past the zenith, and he'd said in an hour they'd be in Fairplay. It was downhill, and even with the wind they would get there. *Just don't think of the trip back*, she told herself.

But then the trip back was the whole point of this. During their trip back they'd be carrying her wonderful supplies, the things she would need to make the food for which Crystal would clamor. How long would it take to build the extra room? She pondered this as they drove, picturing it all and trying to tally wood and proportions and cost. Quillan hadn't asked her to read again. And though she was enjoying the story, she didn't offer. The wind would have sucked her breath away.

"There's Fairplay just ahead." Quillan hollered across the sleeping dog.

She looked up and saw the town. From this side, it sprawled more than Crystal, not being confined to a gulch for its configuration. Beyond that, the similarities were greater than the differences. It was less congested, since all the main traffic wasn't confined to one street. But it was just as loud, just as dirty.

They pulled over on a side street in an obviously less sophisticated part of town. When Quillan helped her down, she tried not to wince. He pointed. "That one, second from the corner. I'm going to care for the horses."

She nodded, then headed for the shop he indicated. The moment she opened the door, tears came to her eyes. Such scents and aromas that met her nose. Such sights as the bottles of olives, the wheels of cheese with black rind and crumbly grain. The sausages. The bread. *Madonna mia,* it was heaven! The shopkeeper stepped out from behind a stack of crates. He was shorter than she by inches . . . and he was Sicilian.

Six

God knows my inmost thoughts,
the desires of my heart.
—Carina

HAVING TRADED OUT THE HORSES and harnessed a new team, Quillan stopped briefly in the general mercantile and picked up a few items that he knew Crystal was severely short of. He could inflate the price over even Fairplay's cost. Then he headed back to the shop where he'd left Carina. She must have had time by now to complete her selections.

He stopped just outside the door and listened to the heated words coming from inside. Actually, he didn't listen to the words because he couldn't understand them. But he saw Carina through the window, following the little man, both of them with arms flailing and exaggerated gestures of disdain and incredulity.

He stood and watched as the man sighed and looked as though he'd just lost his grandmother, then nodded. Carina pointed with another string of words, and the battle began again, Carina scoffing and scolding, the man looking wounded, then angry, then sighing and nodding.

Quillan noticed a sizable pile of goods gathering in the center of the floor, and the storekeeper added another wheel of cheese to this, then with a dramatic swing of his arm seemed to ask what was next. Carina named it, and Quillan pushed the door open just as the man started to rave.

She glanced at him, then returned her attention to her adversary. Quick, sharp words silenced the little man, and Quillan felt sorry for him as Carina smiled and the man huffed an injured huff, then gave in once again, adding the item to his tally. Carina pointed to a long string of papery white garlic hung from the ceiling, then indicated two.

She must have praised it, for the man puffed his chest a little and agreed with her. *"Sì, signora. Stesso buono."*

"Quanto?"

He named his price.

Carina nodded, again showing him her smile. *"Bene."*

The man paused while taking down the strings. *"Bene?"*

"Sì, bene."

The man looked at Quillan, dumbfounded. "At last she no fighta me."

Quillan smiled crookedly. "Take it and run."

The man didn't understand, but he climbed down with that very intention. After laying the garlic on the pile, he added it to his tally and worked the total. He tore off the paper and handed it to Carina.

She looked over the figures, working them in her head, Quillan guessed, then turned to him. "I think this will do."

The man looked from Carina to him with obvious

dismay. "You are witha her?"

Quillan nodded and realized the man must have expected to make up most of what he'd lost to Carina on him. He probably remembered him from the last trip. Quillan looked at the total and whistled. It was high, but not as high as he'd expected for the heap of goods on the floor. Grudgingly he admitted, silently, that he'd been skinned the last time.

He reached into his billfold and counted out the money into the man's hand. Sixty-seven dollars was a lot of money. But it looked as though he wouldn't be making this trip again anytime soon. Carina could feed the whole city with what she had on the floor. It would fill his wagon. It would last her a long while. He thanked the man.

With a pained sigh, the storekeeper threw up his hands. "Eh, what can I do? I'm weak for a *bella faccia*. A pretty face."

Carina smiled and touched his arm, murmuring something.

The man smiled back, waving his finger. *"Oofa, bella signora."*

Quillan half expected him to kiss her hand, he looked so grateful for the chance to be skinned alive by her.

"Addio." She slid her fingers from his arm.

When Carina turned her smile on Quillan, his belly clutched up, and he definitely sympathized with the poor storekeeper.

"Will you load this while I look around?"

"Look around?"

She raised her brows innocently. "You think I'd come here without seeing anything else?"

Quillan frowned. "Didn't you see Fairplay when you came up to Crystal?"

"I spent the night, yes. But I never shopped." She walked out the door, and Quillan watched her disappear down the street.

She had passed one night in Fairplay on her trip to Crystal and, heading from it the next day, hurried on to Crystal, her dream city, where she would make her home and her way. Fairplay had seemed a dirty, ill-bred town until she saw Crystal. Then she had realized what a fool she was.

Carina walked down the street, looking in the windows of any place that was not a saloon or gambling hall. She was aware of the looks sent her way and acknowledged the tipped hats with a smile. She stopped outside a window that held lacy gloves and fans and parasols, colored ribbons and pearl buttons, and even a diamond stickpin.

With her fingers pressed to the glass, she looked until she'd seen it all. One day she would come back to this store and buy the parasol. One day when she had earned enough. The wind whipped her hair. It had a bite to it. And it was bringing clouds.

She sighed and left the window behind. She met Quillan at the wagon, still loading her goods. "I need eggs. Il signore Lanza didn't have any." She spoke over the wind, holding the fur collar tight to her throat.

"That'll be tough."

"Why?"

"They're hard to transport, not always available. If he didn't have them, it's likely no one else does."

"But I have to have them. The pasta requires it."

Quillan paused. "I just brought you some."

"It won't be enough."

Quillan leaned on the wagon. "How much is enough?"

"Dozens." She waved her arm.

His eyes narrowed; then he shook his head. "I can't do anything about that today, Carina. We have to start up. I don't like the feel of this wind." He turned back to the wagon. "Besides you've already cost me enough."

She bit back the retort. Once she had business, she would pay for everything she needed herself. Until then she would have to borrow.

They started up the pass. This time Carina kept the shawl tied over her mouth against the wind and didn't read aloud. She could have read silently, but that seemed unkind to Quillan. She kept her chilled hands deep in the pockets of her coat and was grateful for its warmth. Her canvas jacket would not have been enough.

Quillan reached down and pulled a paper-wrapped parcel from under his feet. "Here."

Carina pulled a hand from its nest and took the package, wonderingly. "What is this?"

He didn't answer, so she tore the paper off a pair of caramel-colored kidskin gloves with a tiny pearl button closure on the side of each. Amazed, she lifted the gloves and held them to her cheeks. They were soft and supple but would be warm as well. Tears stung her eyes as she turned to him.

He scowled. "I could hardly let you freeze. We don't know what we're going into."

"You're kind to me."

He looked away with an expelled breath. "I know my responsibility."

He made it sound like the cross he must bear. She knew he felt that way. But why? The smiles and stares proved she was attractive; she'd always been sought after. Why did he disdain her?

She tugged the gloves onto her hands. They were a good fit and every bit as soft as they'd appeared. Her fingers curled with ease, then stretched out, and she admired the look of her hands in the brown leather. At Quillan's smirk, she brought her hands to her lap. "Thank you."

He said nothing, and they rode in silence. The wind would have made conversation difficult anyway. Nestled against her, Sam whined, whistling softly through his nose it seemed. Carina put an arm around him, and they warmed each other. Quillan drove with grim resolution up the winding pass.

"Why is it so cold?" she called at last.

"At this elevation, September means winter."

She eyed the dark gray sky they climbed toward and remembered the flood that had washed all of Placer and part of Crystal away. Could this sky hold something as dangerous as that? The river was low. There was no chance of flood. But the clouds looked ominous.

Quillan, too, seemed tense, and the dog shivered beside her. Every time they stopped to let the horses blow, Quillan eyed the sky and chafed. She guessed he pushed the horses harder than he normally would, though their load was full. She didn't complain about the biscuit and jerky for supper. She didn't want to stop and make a fire. She wanted to get home.

The horses strained as the grade steepened. The wind beat against them, howling now through the peaks and valleys. Any brief windbreak was a godsend, but it made the next blast that much harder to take. Dusk descended and the wind turned wet. Carina opened her eyes to flakes swirling like dervishes before her face. One moment it was dry; the next, they were engulfed.

Quillan barked something, but she didn't hear what. He reached over and shook her arm, then pointed to the wagon bed, and she heard the word blanket. She turned, worked a corner of the tarp loose, then lost hold of it, and it flapped wildly. She dug for the blanket, pulled it free, and stuffed it under her thigh, then fought the tarp back into place.

Shaking out the blanket, she handed one side over to Quillan, but he shook his head. His concentration was on the team. She pulled the blanket around herself and Sam. The dog licked her cheek, and she could have cried for the simple gesture of reassurance and affection.

She huddled under the blanket, fighting for breath, and prayed. *Signore, per piacere, please help us now. Calm the storm and bring us through.* The snow thickened, a white barrage that dazed her senses and masked the way ahead. Quillan reined in suddenly, and Carina saw the edge of road they'd almost headed off.

He yanked the horses to the right as her heart pounded her chest. This was pazzo! How could they continue? Why didn't he stop? "Can't we stop? Can't we wait?" Her words were swallowed by the storm.

He drove the team on until again he yanked them to a stop. Before she could speak, he jumped down and went to the front. There he grabbed hold of the harness and began leading the team on foot. Carina gripped Sam to her side as the wagon lurched forward. She had to trust that Quillan knew what he was doing.

Soon there was nothing but the white cloud around her—no mountain, no road, no world but the swirling, dizzying white. Sam barked, and it jarred her from her daze, but she couldn't make out even the backs of the horses before her. Quillan was lost somewhere beyond the wall of white.

She trembled with more than cold. Sam barked again, and then again. The wagon stopped moving. The dog jumped to all fours and barked steadily. Quillan appeared at her side, and Carina flung herself into his arms.

He pulled her down from the box, his eyebrows and lashes and whiskers crusted with snow, the hair hanging beneath the broad-brimmed hat, strings of ice. "Get underneath the wagon."

She nodded and climbed under the wooden wagon bed. Sam stood at its side, barking. Carina crouched beneath the blanket while Quillan draped a tarp down from the wagon on either side like a tent. Darkness engulfed her and both the wind and the snow lessened inside her space, though it still howled in from the far side and the back.

Sam came rushing in and circled frantically, then rushed back out. She could see Quillan's legs as he worked his way around the far side of the wagon to the front. She guessed he was doing something with the horses. Could they withstand the blizzard? What if they died?

Then it came to her with a shock that they could all die. She trembled. She had never imagined freezing to death or being buried alive in snow. Now she could imagine it. Sam dove under once again, licked her face, and ran back out, barking. A moment later, Quillan crawled under with two more blankets, and Sam at his heels.

He sat down with his back to the front axle. "Come over here."

She crawled between him and the side of the front wheel.

He pulled a blanket around her. "We'll wait it out."

"Will it stop?" It seemed it might storm forever and there would be no end.

"Sooner or later. No sense driving off a cliff in the meantime."

Carina swallowed the fear in her throat and wanted him to hold her. He didn't. And she wouldn't ask. A gust sent snow swirling underneath the wagon, and she pulled the blanket tight. Soon it would stop. *Per piacere!* But it didn't.

The cold increased. Her ears burned with the howling of the wind and the cold air. Her nose was a point of pain, her fingers in the gloves, icicles. She had ceased to feel her toes. Her teeth chattered, and at last Quillan raised an arm and drew her to his side. She sank into his strength. Dear God, how she needed him. She pressed her face into the hollow of his neck and fought the tears.

He cupped his hand over her head and held her there. "It'll be okay."

She wanted to believe it, wanted to know everything would be okay. But nothing had been. Nothing had gone right since she'd come to Crystal. No, that wasn't true. There had been trouble enough, but God had brought good from it. He was in control now as well. She had to believe that.

She ordered her heart to stop pounding with panic, her breath to come slowly. She closed her eyes against Quillan's neck. He would keep her safe. He always had. Hadn't he brought her out of the darkness of the shaft? Hadn't God used him before to save her from the vigilantes? They would be safe.

The slap was no more than a dim burn on her cheek, the shaking a mere inconvenience. "Blast it, Carina! Wake up!"

She was completely warm, so peaceful. Why would she wake up? And then his mouth was on hers, hard and fierce, and her heart leaped to life. She raised her hands and sank them into his hair, and he kept kissing her until she opened her eyes with a cry. He pulled away, breathing hard and bearing down on her with his eyes.

She dropped her hands and clasped them together at her throat. Why now did he kiss her? Were they dead, or was she dreaming?

"You have to stay awake." His words and face were fierce, as fierce as his kiss.

She shot her gaze to the side. It was dark, but there was the glow of a lantern at the corner of their shelter. It must have been recently lit because there was only a faint smell of it. Beyond the lantern, a white wall surrounded the wheels. It was quiet, so quiet.

Quillan turned her face back to him. "I'm going out now, and you have to stay awake."

How could he go out? There was no out. There was only the wall.

He shook her. "Do you understand me, Carina? You can't sleep."

She swallowed thickly and nodded. He looked another long moment, his eyes charcoal in the glow; then he released her and headed for the side. She watched as he hung on to the undergirding with his hands and kicked his way out from under the wagon. Sam whined at his head.

Carina struggled upright as Quillan forced himself through the wall, hollowing out a space as he went. How long had they huddled there through the storm?

How deep was the snow? Quillan kept working, battling it back, and suddenly she heard the wind again, not howling now, but softer. He must have broken through.

He pushed to his feet and stood. All she could see were his legs as he kept expanding the space. The wagon over her head sagged, and she realized he'd climbed into the bed. She felt him moving around, then the sudden swing as he jumped down. A pile of wood landed at his feet and he crouched at the side of the wagon and began shaping it for a fire. Her spirit jumped at the thought.

When he had the wood blazing, she crawled toward it, the motion painful but necessary. The fire drew her by some primal need. She stretched out her fingers, crying out when they thawed enough to feel the warmth. It was not bliss. It was sharp, unremitting pain.

Quillan crouched at the fireside, eyeing her, then drew her out into the snowy hollow, a circular wall some four feet high. She looked up into a dark, milky sky. Quillan pulled her to her feet, pressed her shoulders to the wagon side, and glared. "Don't you know better than to go to sleep in a blizzard?"

He was so close she couldn't answer. Then his mouth again claimed hers, the whiskered skin rough and scratching, the lips demanding. Didn't he know she would give whatever he asked? He didn't have to take what was his by right. Again her heart beat a sharp staccato. But he pushed away and stalked to the other side of the fire, the flames illuminating his back.

He wanted her. It was in his kiss. There was a need in him for her. That wasn't so much. God had made man to want woman. Quillan was human. But maybe . . . if he wanted her, he could one day love her. *Ah, Signore, that is my prayer.*

Hands clenched at his sides, Quillan fought the desire burning inside him. The fact that Carina was his wife and he had every right under heaven to kiss her did nothing to excuse it in his mind. It was his intention to release her from that bond, not drive it deeper. He forced the heat inside him to subside, closed his eyes, and gained control.

He turned and looked at her across the fire, her hair glowing like a raven's wing, rippling down where it escaped from the shawl. She stood where he'd left her, probably afraid to move, probably wondering what he'd do next. *Nothing. I won't do anything. Anything I do will only make it worse for both of us.* But he didn't voice his thoughts.

He held his gloved hands to the fire. In a small while he'd add another log. He had enough wood to get them through the night, maybe part of another day. But they wouldn't be there that long. As soon as he had light to work with, he'd start clearing a way. They were drifted in, but not all the road would be so deep. He could dig through the drifts.

He released a slow breath. "If you stay by the fire, you can get some rest."

"I thought you said not to sleep." Her voice was small, uncertain, not completely recovered from his actions, he guessed.

"Wrap up warmly and stay close. It's all right to doze. I'll wake you periodically."

"By slapping me?" Her chin rose perceptibly.

Or kissing her? She didn't voice it, but the question was in her eyes.

"A shake should do."

She pulled the blanket around her shoulders and sat down. "Can you get to my book?"

He eyed the box with a foot of snow in it and the leg space filled in. "If I dig."

"You dig, and I'll read." She reached under the wagon and took out the lantern. A gust of wind caught her hair and tossed it as she hung the lantern on the wagon's side.

Well, it would give him something to do. Quillan reached into the wagon bed for the shovel he kept against the side. With it he shoveled the snow down to her carpetbag, then hauled it free and shook it off. Carina took the book from inside, then stuffed the carpetbag under the wagon. She settled down inside the blanket and opened the book.

Quillan took a place near her and the fire. It wasn't warm inside the hollow he'd dug, but some of the edge was off the cold. They would survive the night like that. He hunkered down and listened as she read. Without seeing the words or taking it at a pace he could imprint on his mind, he couldn't get it all by memory. So for once he just listened.

He tried to imagine George Eliot a woman. It could be. It was possible a woman wrote under a man's name. Many authors chose a nom de plume that suited their purpose. But how did Carina guess it? What were the phrases and insights that one woman recognized in another?

As Carina read he watched her, the firelight playing on her face, breaking it into softly defined planes and angles. She was beautiful. Breathtaking, really. He wanted to reach out and touch her hair, to pull it free of the shawl and bury his hands in it. He wanted to taste her again.

Would she resist? Quillan knew she wouldn't. The resistance was his. He closed his eyes and let her voice wash over him. The physical battle with the elements had tired him, and now his muscles let him know. He leaned against the edge of the wheel and eased the strain from his back. He stretched his legs and felt the stiffened joints loosen.

Her voice went on, her English clear but with just a hint of foreignness, more inflection than pronunciation. He liked the sound. It soothed him. The story took a twist, and Carina was in it, coming to him, arms outstretched. He caught her hands and brought them to his chest, sinking into her eyes, so dark, so richly lashed. Her mouth was soft and waiting.

But she shook his arm and kept shaking it. He opened his eyes to her face, just as he'd imagined it. He caught it between his hands. She was his wife. Desire hit him like a kick in the belly, but so did reality. The sky had lightened, and she was waking him. He looked aside to gauge the time, then released her face and pushed himself up.

It was silly to ask if he'd slept. And it didn't matter if she had as well. Day was dawning, and they'd survived. The fire was little more than embers, but there was warmth there still. He reached a hand to it. "I'd kill for coffee."

"I have beans but no grinder."

"No pot either. I wasn't planning on spending the night."

She let go his sleeve. "I'd have let you sleep longer, but you thought it was important to be wakened."

He forked fingers into his hair and groaned. "I didn't intend to sleep myself."

She shrugged. "Your body had other ideas."

That was an understatement, but he didn't elaborate. Instead he let his body know it was time to stand.

The air was still, but with the coming of day the wind would probably return. The sooner they were making progress, the better. He looked around and took stock of their position. Almost to the summit.

This would be the worst of the snow. But more perilous than the drifts would be the slippery slope down. "Can you see to the horses while I make some preparations?"

She nodded. He had covered each pair with a spare canvas tarp that had kept the worst of the snow off them and held their combined warmth together. He watched her tug the tarp from his wheelers; then he started his own work. He dug down to the bottom of the wagon bed, rearranging Carina's goods until he found the square-linked chain and pulled it out.

Carina gave the horses oats from feed bags while he draped the chain within easy reach of his seat and began shoveling the wagon out. He worked up a sweat, clearing the wheels of drifted snow and cutting a path ahead. When he made it around the bend that had formed a windbreak, the road was almost blown clear, leaving only the treacherous ice.

If he led them by hand, he could get the team up the last stretch. Then it was level across the summit for a half mile before starting down. That's where the snow would be even and deep. He returned to the wagon, and Carina met him with a chunk of pungent cheese and a handful of olives. He half grinned. "What, no hardtack?"

With a look that showed what she thought of his hardtack, she broke the ice from the surface of the water barrel and dipped in the cup. Then she held it out to him. He drank gratefully, thirsty from his labor and warmed. The water was icy cold as it went down. *Better go easy*, he told himself. They were a long way from home, and he didn't need to lower his body temperature.

He took a bite of the cheese. It was satisfyingly stiff and grainy, with a sharp bite that was familiar from her cooking with it before. "What do you call it?"

"Parmigiano. Or grano. It's the heart of cheeses. Nothing compares."

Again his mouth pulled sideways. "Not even the blue one?"

"Gorgonzola can only be taken in small amounts."

"I'm not sure I could live on parmigiano either."

She shrugged. "You'll learn."

He popped an olive into his mouth. He'd seen the jars in the store when he'd shopped for her before, but hadn't bought any. He'd never tasted one. He bit down and jarred his teeth.

"Be careful of the pit."

He held his jaw and sent her a dark look. "Now you tell me." He didn't miss the amusement in her eyes.

"Eat around it and discard the pit. They're wonderful." She bit the flesh of one and savored it, then put the rest into her mouth and worked the pit loose.

He watched to see how she would discard the pit. He wasn't surprised when she discreetly removed it with her fingers and threw it into the snow. He made a point of spitting his. All in all, this breakfast had his usual fare squarely beaten. He chewed the cheese with satisfaction and washed it down with another gulp of water, then handed the cup over to her. "Don't drink too much. It's awfully cold."

She sipped. "What now?"

"Now we go."

"Is it clear?" She looked down the road where he'd

dug, lit now by the first pale hues of dawn.

He fit the shovel back into the wagon bed. "Not clear, exactly, but passable. I imagine we'll have to dig in some places, and try not to fly in others."

"Is it safe?"

He leaned on the wagon and gave her a taunting smile. "You didn't come to Crystal for safety, Miss DiGratia."

"No?" She raised a hand and primped her hair. "A fine established city like Crystal? So *affettato*, sophisticated."

He grinned. "Well, we're a long way from town, signora."

He saw her pause at his Italian designation. He'd never used one of her words before.

"Sì," she murmured softly and looked down the road again.

Did he know he'd just called her "wife"? Carina turned to the wagon, reached in, and pressed the black waxy rind closed around the wheel of parmigiano. Oh, it could mean lady or missus, but it also meant wife. If only he meant it that way. She tightened the lid on the jar of olives and made it secure between the cheeses and bags of flour.

Then she reached under the wagon and pulled out her carpetbag. It was still chunky with snow, the temperature insufficient to melt it. She banged it off with one gloved hand and tossed it up to the box. Sam bounded to her, his whole body wiggling. He was eager and ready. Carina turned. "Is there anything else?"

Quillan passed her to inspect the load. "Just let me get this fastened down." He wrangled the tarp into place and made it tight, then whistled for Sam to jump aboard. Carina waited, and he came to her, lifting her in with a strong arm under her hand. He didn't join her in the box. He walked to the front of the team.

Leading by Jock's head, Quillan urged the horses and the wagon creaked forward, the snow squeaking under the wheels, the hooves muffled thumps. Carina lurched side to side as the wheels rolled over the uneven terrain of the shoveled drift. Then the snow abruptly ended and the road was bare.

No, not bare. She noted the milky gleam of ice. How would the horses pull up that? Her gaze followed the grade to the summit. Slowly, the horses advanced the wagon, their hooves clattering sharply on the icy road, their steps uncertain. Halfway up, Quillan stopped to let them blow, and she climbed down.

He glanced from under the broad brim of his hat. "What are you doing? I'm just giving them a minute to blow."

"I know." She held the harness as she passed around the horses to the front. "I can't stand to make their burden harder." She reached up to Jack and stroked his nose with her soft kid glove. "I'll help you lead."

"I don't need help. Get back up where you belong."

She brought her face to Jack's. "I won't make you carry me, *cavallo*. Not on this ice." Jack nuzzled her back. He might be Quillan's horse, answerable to his command alone, but they had an understanding.

Quillan frowned. "Carina, this is hard enough. I don't want to look out for you, too."

"Then don't. I look out for myself." She took hold of the harness on Jack's head. "Are they ready?"

Sam, too, had jumped down and now paced between them, looking eager to help if he could only figure out how. Quillan released a sharp breath of white cloud, then commanded his team. Carina gave Jack's head a tug, but needn't have. He was already responding to Quillan through Jock, his twin. She stepped backward, suddenly aware of her precarious footing. Her boots would not bite into the ice like the horses' hooves.

She turned, holding the harness and took a careful step, then another. As long as she stepped squarely, kept her balance . . . The wagon wheels creaked over the ice, the hooves rang. Another step and more. Step, step, careful. Her breath came in tight gasps. The air was thin and biting cold. The horses labored, and so did she.

At the next blow she would climb back in. But they might not stop before the summit, and she had to keep on. It would be humiliating to stop Quillan now. What was she thinking? Didn't she recall how it had been to walk this before, when Dom gave out and couldn't carry her? Did she want to pass out in front of Quillan and show her weakness?

Nonsense. She would not pass out. She was acclimated. She only had to . . . Her foot slipped, then the other. One hand clung to the harness, one swung wildly as her feet did a dance beneath her. Jack jerked his head, and she lost hold, coming down hard at his hooves. Sam jumped about, barking.

The horse balked sideways. Beside him, Jock shied. Quillan hollered, fighting to hold them steady, but the wheelers had lost hold and the wagon slid backward. Quillan clung, digging with his boot heels and urging the horses to fight. Jock lowered his head and threw his shoulders into the harness. But it wasn't enough.

The wagon slid into the embankment and came to a grinding stop. Shoulders heaving with deep, hard breaths, Quillan dropped his head to Jock's. Then he turned and fiercely gauged her. Carina sat in the road where she'd landed. She already felt chagrined. Did he think his anger would help?

He stomped toward her and jerked her to her feet. "Thank you for your help. Now will you kindly get into the wagon and let me do my job?"

"I'm not hurt, thank you. It's kind of you to care."

He gripped her upper arms. "If you'd cracked your backside, it'd be no more than you deserved. I could have lost my team and wagon."

She swallowed hard. It was true. He had a right to his anger. But her own asserted itself. She hadn't meant to cause trouble, only to help. "And what if I'd been on the wagon, too?" Would he worry about her welfare?

"Then, Carina, we wouldn't be in this fix." He tugged her arm and manhandled her into the box. "Now stay there." Sam climbed up sheepishly beside her.

She felt like a scolded child. Who was he to order her so? She was Carina Maria DiGratia . . . Shepard. Carina folded her arms sullenly across her chest. She'd given him the right, stood in front of him, and the judge, and God, and agreed to obey this man. Bene. She didn't have to like it.

It took him an hour to dig the wagon out and go over it for damage. The physical exertion kept him from wringing her neck; his native control held the words in check. Now he finally had his team and wagon back where they'd been before Carina decided to help.

He growled an oath under his breath, then took Jock's head and started them forward. He should have been to the summit by now. Any more of Carina's interference and they'd spend another night on the mountain. He glanced at her sulking on the box, then turned his attention to the job at hand.

Slowly and carefully he led the horses over the ground they'd covered before the slide, then on up toward the crest. He made himself relax. For the horses' sake he took long, slow breaths and willed the anger from his system. *Just don't think about her.* That was the ticket. *Just don't even think about her.*

Up. Onward. A turn to the right and back to the left. A little more. A little more. The clatter of hooves on ice muffled under the snow as the slope leveled. He kept pulling. The snow was only six inches. They could cut through. "Come on, Jock."

It rose to a foot's depth, but light and powdery enough to manage still. The horses needed to blow, and to be truthful, so did he. Quillan stopped fighting. He let go the harness and dropped his arm to his side. For several minutes he just stood there, waiting for his breathing to slow.

The scene ahead was untouched, unmarred. No stage would pass through in a storm. He looked up at the white woolly blanket above and smelled snow. The wind blasted his face. With his sleeve, he wiped the sweat beneath his hat brim and swallowed the film of residue that had formed inside his mouth from the exertion.

He walked back to the wagon and opened the tarp, levered the water barrel lid, and dipped a cup of icy water. He drank. Then he watered and fed the horses. Not too much. Just enough to bolster them for the next leg. He didn't speak to Carina. Then they started again.

They kept on until the snow reached three feet in depth. He took the shovel and cleared a way, then stowed the shovel and led the horses on. Again he took the shovel and cleared. He was working through four feet of snow now. It had drifted in the windbreaks.

He turned to stow the shovel, but Carina stood at Jock's head. With a word and a tug, she urged the team forward as far as he had dug. Quillan leaned on the shovel and eyed her. She didn't flinch and she didn't speak. He turned and dug, then heard Carina bringing the team behind him.

It was level, and it was snow. She was probably capable of handling such a task without disaster. In that way they made good progress. The snow evened out to two feet in depth and he stopped shoveling. He stowed the shovel and took the harness from her. She walked around and climbed into the wagon without a word.

It tugged him inside. He should thank her. . . . But he looked grimly forward and led the team on toward the first downward slope. He raised his hat and forked his hair back, ascertaining the conditions ahead. It was a steep decline, snow over ice. He had a full load, nowhere near the tonnage of machinery he sometimes hauled but enough to give the horses trouble.

He hadn't yet equipped his wheelers with the sharp steel spikes on their shoes called caulks. But he did have the chain. Quillan nodded to himself. He'd rough-lock the wagon. Removing the chain from where he'd draped it in readiness, he brought it to the rear wheel. He wrapped the wheel with the links square in cross-section, then fastened it to another chain connected to the front axle.

Carefully he led the team forward until the rear wheel locked. He checked the tightness, then climbed up onto the box and took up the reins. He could feel Carina's eyes on him and turned. "Keep an eye on the chain. If the rough-lock breaks, we're in for a wild ride."

She looked down at the chain and back. "How does it work?"

"The chain grips the snow. The wheel won't turn. Makes it hard to pull even downhill." He slapped the reins and the horses started forward. They inched down the hill, the wheelers putting their backs into both pulling and holding the weight of the wagon back. The leaders maneuvered under Quillan's guidance.

At the first leveling Quillan let them blow. He saw Carina's shoulders relax and realized she was as tense as he. He jumped down and checked the chains all along their length. A broken chain could mean disaster. He stopped beside the box and reached up. Gripping Carina's waist, he swung her down. "Can you make us some lunch? I'm going to scout ahead, see how the road looks."

She nodded.

That was settled, but . . . He hooked his hands onto his hips. "Thanks for leading the team while I shoveled."

Her eyes were darkly luminous, sucking him in. "You're welcome."

His steps away were firm and purposeful.

Carina threw up her hands. How was she supposed to make lunch with no stove and no pot and no . . . She turned suddenly and searched the roadside with her eyes. Everything was changed in the snow. But it couldn't be far. It was just past the summit when her mule Dom had taken ill and she had shouldered his load.

She pressed her palms to her temples trying to remember, to recognize the tree she had thought would be a landmark for her to find the things she left there.

Was it that pine by the bend where Quillan was just turning? She took the shovel and followed, then stopped. She would need a fire.

Quickly she dug down to the dirt in the middle of the road, then assembled the wood and got a fire started. The wood Quillan brought had stayed dry under the tarp, and it was well seasoned to light quickly and burn well. She stoked it into a steady blaze that would hold until she got back. Then she went in search of her treasures.

Amazingly, they were there. The iron pot and lid and the dented kettle salvaged from her wagonload of goods that Quillan had sent down the mountain. She dug the lid free from the snow and held it up exuberantly. *Grazie, Signore!*

By the time Quillan returned from scouting, she had sausages sizzling in the iron pot with garlic and onions. Quillan strode up, taking in the scene, arms slack and puffs of white bursting from his parted lips. He was weary, she could tell. Would he be pleased with her efforts?

The iron pot sat directly on the coals and she worked quickly with the stick to turn the sausages and keep them from blackening. It was the best she could do without the proper utensils. All she had found was a leather-sheathed knife under the driver's side of the box. That worked well enough for slicing the onions, but little more.

It wasn't perfect, but since coming to Crystal she'd learned to take what she could get and make the most of it. Now she used the edge of a blanket to grip the pot and remove it from the fire. It hissed and steamed when she set it on the snowy road. Only then did she brave Quillan's eyes.

They held a mixture of wonder and irritation. But he swallowed whatever complaint had been forming and squatted next to the fire, holding his gloved hands to the heat. "I had thought we'd move on."

"You can't keep on as you've been without something nourishing."

He jerked his jaw toward the pot. "Meaning that?"

She nodded. "But I can't find utensils."

"I didn't bring any. All that stuff is stowed in my tent."

And where is your tent? she wanted to ask. *Where do you stay when you're away from me?*

"I thought we'd do with olives and cheese. I didn't know you meant to cook." He looked sharply at the pot melting a puddle in the snow. "Is that the pot. . . ?"

She smiled. "I could only carry it so far. Dom wouldn't walk with iron pots and Dickens banging his sides." She rolled the sausages with the stick to cool the undersides.

Still in his squat, Quillan rested his forearms across his knees. "And it just happened to be waiting here."

"No. I buried it next to that tree." She waved her arm to indicate the one she meant.

"What a coincidence."

She raised her eyes from the pot. "Not coincidence."

"What, then?"

"God."

It was the wrong thing to say. She saw that at once in the lowering of his brows, the tensing of his hands. Heard it in what he said next.

"God. He just had that pot right near where we stopped so that you could dig it up and make this meal."

"Something like that."

Quillan stood. He rubbed his thighs with his fire-warmed gloves. "Are we going to eat or not?"

She stabbed the stick into one of the sausages, releasing an oily red juice and spicy fragrant steam. But not so much steam that it would burn him. The sausages were cooling quickly in the cold air. She held up the stick.

He took it. "What do you call this?"

"*Salsiccia in una sacchetta*. Sausage on a stick."

He almost smiled. He wanted to. But he would lose face. He was not so different from *un uomo Italiano*. She could handle him if he just gave her the chance.

Quillan bit into the sausage on the stick. Steam erupted into his nostrils as he pierced the skin and sank his teeth into the dense ground meat. It burst into his mouth, a strong, spicy flavor, mellowed with garlic and the onions that lay limp and browned in the pot. He closed his eyes and allowed the sensation to fill and overload his tongue. He chewed slowly, deliberately, eking every ounce of flavor before surrendering it to his throat.

Then he opened his eyes and realized Carina had seen it all. She was more dangerous than a rattler in July, as Cain . . . It hit the pit of his stomach like a boot. *As Cain used to say*, he'd almost thought. Used to say. Cain. The pain came, fresh and piercing. He turned away, ate the sausage in a hurry, and stabbed the stick into the pot for another.

She was right. The food would sustain him better for what lay ahead. It would be slow going and he was hungry. Carina had scrounged another stick from somewhere and ate deliberately. He'd hurt her. He'd given her nothing for all her work, not even his thanks.

He yanked off his glove and dipped his hand into the pot. With bare fingers he scooped the onions and brought them to his mouth. Let her think him a fiend. The sooner she realized they had no place together, the sooner she'd leave him in peace.

Not in peace. There could be no peace. Because of him, Cain was dead. And because of Carina. Because of what they'd done, coming together in a sham marriage. And if he wasn't careful, she'd make him forget that. She'd lure him with her talents, her beauty, her vulnerable strength.

He swallowed the onions and reached for more. Another sausage went down in four bites. Then he grabbed snow and washed his hands and face. He tugged on his gloves and turned. Carina had filled the pot with snow and was rubbing it clean as it turned to mush. Her fingers were raw.

"Just stow it in the wagon, Carina. Let's get moving."

She dumped it out and did as he said. Sam lapped at the greasy snow, having already devoured two of the sausages. Quillan whistled, and the animal reluctantly left his feast and jumped to the wagon bed. Quillan kicked the fire out in the snow and ground the last of the coals into the muddy circle.

He unfastened the rough lock for the horses to pull the short distance to the next downward slope; then he climbed into the wagon where Carina waited silently. He took up the reins and urged the horses forward.

Between shoveling and rough-locking, it was dusk before the lights of Crystal came into sight. The blizzard had been negligible as mountain storms go. Soon the road would be snow-packed until May, each storm building onto the base already laid. But for now, the road was mostly clear as they neared the Diamond of the Rockies, which was more a scar and blight than any gem.

Carina was half collapsed against him with her arms around the dog. She must have stayed awake last night while he slept to be so worn-out now. But then, she wasn't used to the rigor of sitting on the box all these hours. And she'd toiled alongside him for some of it.

His conscience weighed as heavily as the hardtack and jerky he'd forced down for supper. She hadn't been hungry. Quillan glanced over, then turned away. He didn't want to be mean, didn't want to hurt her. He just wanted her to see the way it was.

He half carried her into the house over her protests. He didn't want her help to unload, didn't want her working beside him. During his first half dozen trips inside the door with her supplies, she stood in the center of the room and watched. The next she was curled fully clothed on the bed. When the last of it was deposited in the cold back corner, he tugged a blanket over her and went to sleep in his wagon in the livery. By morning he'd be gone.

Seven

A dream worth undertaking must be nurtured.
But I worry. Crystal has not been kind to my dreams.
—Carina

"GOOD MORNING, MR. MAKEPEACE."

"Good morning to you, Mrs. Shepard." Alex Makepeace removed the derby from his head. "Your enterprise is progressing nicely, I see."

Carina smiled her satisfaction at the new walls that connected her home to Mae's and formed a fine long room behind her own. "It's finished except for the fireplace and, of course, the tables and chairs."

"I heard the men worked night and day like gnomes."

Carina laughed. "Joe Turner says they can't wait for their wages in trade. The sooner they finish, the sooner I start cooking."

"Sounds reasonable. Especially as the fare in other places tends toward . . . monotonous."

Carina laughed again. It was easy to laugh with Mr. Makepeace. "Eh, what I make will not be monotonous—I promise you that."

He appraised her cheerfully. "No, I believe you. Any word from your husband?"

She felt her spirits sag but refused to show it. "Communication is difficult up here. He'll come when he comes." He'd left before she woke the morning after their trip to Fairplay. She didn't know to where or how long he'd be gone. For all she knew, he'd never come back.

"Well, I was hoping to discuss some things with him. Regarding the mine."

Carina hesitated only a moment. "Mr. Makepeace . . . which is my husband's mine?"

"Which?" He turned. "You mean you don't know?"

She shook her head. "I didn't know he had one until you came. He keeps his business to himself."

"Well, I . . ." He smiled. "Would you like to see it?"

"I would." Carina unwrapped her arms. "Let me get my coat." She hurried inside. The coat hung on the row of new hooks along the wall by her bed. She tugged it free and shrugged it on, thinking of Quillan. Every time the fur-lined collar touched her neck, she thought of him buying it for her.

She sighed. There was no sense pining. While he was gone she must make the best of it. Anyway, it was less painful than when he was there. She pushed open the door and rejoined Mr. Makepeace, her curiosity piqued. They walked to the livery, passing through the crowd with greetings and smiles. Mr. Makepeace was already known, his amiable nature and expertise winning him a place at any table.

Alan Tavish met them at the door. "Good mornin', lass. Are ye here for a horse?"

"Yes, thank you. I'm going to see Quillan's mine."

He glanced behind her to Alex Makepeace. "Are ye,

now? Touring the New Boundless?"

"Is that what it's called?"

"Aye. 'Twas Cain Bradley's mine. He and Quillan were partners after the old Boundless failed."

"That's not likely with this one," Alex Makepeace said. "Not anytime soon anyway." He went into the stall that held a large steeldust stallion while Alan Tavish saddled Daisy.

Carina greeted the mare with an affectionate stroke down her muzzle. Then she rode with Mr. Makepeace outside the bustle of town to the even more hectic bustle of a working mine. The noise was cacophonous, and as they dismounted, Carina put her hands to her ears.

"Tie this over." Mr. Makepeace handed her a heavy woolen muffler.

She did so, and it muted the din somewhat. The hillside was hollowed out in a bowl shape and Carina remarked on that.

"That was the surface ore first discovered. This much was quarried before I came. Now we're sinking a main shaft inside the shaft house here." He led her to the wooden structure that enclosed the central area of the bowl. "We're following the vein of richest mineral."

She could see the heads of men in the shaft some twenty feet down. The shaft was lined with wooden timbers, but the floor was the raw stone they must remove. Just outside the shaft, a machine puffed and chugged with a hose sinking into the gaping mouth. Suddenly a horrific din erupted from the shaft, and again Carina clamped her ears in spite of the muffler.

"That's a Burleigh drill," Makepeace hollered. "This part's the boiler." He waved to the machine outside the shaft. "Makes the steam that drives the drill at the other end. I can show you better in a side drift."

"Drift?"

"A horizontal tunnel."

He took a candle and led her out of the shaft house and into a tunnel at the far end of the bowl. "This is an exploratory tunnel to ascertain the extent of surface ore." They proceeded into the tunnel and the darkness closed around her even as it had in the shaft of the Rose Legacy. The candle Mr. Makepeace carried was hardly sufficient.

"Why don't you carry a lantern?"

"Fire. A candle overturned extinguishes itself. A lantern can mean disaster. With the amount of timbering underground, an oil spill and flame can take the lives of men more swiftly than anything else."

"Do they burn so fast?"

"Underground the oxygen is limited. In the confined space, a man will suffocate almost instantly in the presence of fire."

Carina shuddered. This was a dark and dangerous world she entered. They walked beside a pair of rails on ties, and she saw a man pushing an ore cart loaded with long steel cylinders. Stripped to the waist, the man plodded past her with a nod.

"He's taking the dulled steels to the blacksmiths outside to be sharpened."

As they continued, Carina felt a thunderous pounding reverberating in her chest. The air was thick and humid with steam and white dust, the heat unbearable. How did men work in it? She peeled off her coat and held it against her. They advanced, and the pounding was now edged with the ringing of steel on stone. Carina felt suffocated, and her ears ached with the thundering din.

"One thing I want to talk to your husband about is

converting the steam boilers to compressed air. Not cheap, but well worth it."

She nodded vehemently. Just ahead a group of men worked the drill that was mounted vertically on a steel column. One man angled it against the wall; the other worked a wrench, turning the steel as it pounded again and again. The men had rags stuffed in their ears. Even so, how could they bear it?

"That's the last hole in this pattern. They'll take it in six feet, then put in the giant powder and pull the entire face. And they'll do it in one tenth the time of the best double jacking team."

"Double jacking?"

"We used to drive the steels by hand. One man held while the other two hammered. Many still do it that way, operations too small to afford the Burleigh."

So her husband's mine was successful. That was good, she supposed, but the work still seemed torturous to Carina. The noise and dust. And the machine itself looked anything but safe.

"Better clear out now. They're gonna set the charge."

"Why don't I see the gold?"

He looked at her a long moment. "Because, Mrs. Shepard, we're not mining gold."

She raised her brows.

"It's silver and lead, mainly. Some small percentage of gold. Just like Leadville. Some operations have gold in white quartz formations, but not in this mine."

They walked out, and she turned her face up to the cold September air, breathing deeply. Her ears felt battered and numb; her head spun. The hammers and files of the blacksmiths rang, and she shook her head. "I wouldn't make a miner."

He smiled. "It seems your husband feels the same

way. He told me he wouldn't interfere, but I did think he'd pay some attention at least."

"Does he need to?"

Makepeace shrugged. "I suppose I can make all the decisions without him. But I've never worked that way before. My backers in the East don't know quite what to make of it either."

Carina waved a hand. "Who does? Quillan goes his own way."

Again she found him appraising her. The questions were in his eyes. Why does your husband leave you? Why doesn't he stay? Why won't he work his own mine? What does he run from? But he didn't voice them. He was a gentleman.

Carina watched while the Burleigh drill was quieted and the men came out of the tunnel. The explosion sent clouds of smoke and fumes into the air. Carina felt the ground shake under her feet and instinctively caught Mr. Makepeace's arm. Mining was a violent business.

He steadied her. "Are you all right, Mrs. Shepard?"

She let go his arm. "Yes. Thank you for showing me." She understood better why Quillan didn't stay and work the mine. If he could make money with his wagon and team in the open air and the quiet of the road, why would he choose this?

"Shall I see you back?"

"No." She took Daisy's rein. "I think I'll ride up the gulch."

"Lovely day for it. I can hardly believe it's snowed twice."

Carina looked up into the startling blue sky, then to the snowcapped peaks and the slopes below. The autumn colors were almost gone, the white-barked aspens bare of leaves among the dark pines. But it was still beautiful, and she knew it would be so even when it was all cloaked in snow.

"Good-bye, Mr. Makepeace."

"I really wish you'd call me Alex."

Carina smiled and pulled herself into the saddle. She had no intention of using that informal address. She'd been through it already with Berkley Beck . . . and Quillan. And look what that had gotten her.

Alex Makepeace watched her go. He considered himself a reasonable man, a solid Presbyterian, raised in Maine, Harvard educated, a man of his times—or maybe ahead of them—especially in his field. He'd excelled in engineering from an early age, showing both aptitude and interest.

This opportunity to develop a mine from start to finish was a feather in his cap. The investors, Harrold and Sterk, along with the several small partners, one of whom was his uncle, were watching his success closely. At this point in his career, the decisions he made would build his name and credentials and, to a great degree, determine his future. One wrong step and a man could undo years of diligence.

And there was his grandmother, who had moved into his father's home and raised him after his mother died. She had told him never to meddle in people's personal affairs, especially those between a man and a woman. Sage advice. She always held that half the world's conflicts would be settled in a day if everyone else stayed out of it.

He watched Mrs. Shepard's slender back, straight yet willowy, as the mare carried her away. Maybe it was a trick of the sunlight, but her hair seemed to shimmer, and she had an otherworldliness that made him pause.

Shaking his head, he turned away. It was purely coincidence that he'd walked into the livery that dawn three weeks ago and seen Quillan Shepard sleeping in his wagon.

A man had a right to his privacy. And pondering that situation was not the way to ingratiate himself; that much Alex knew.

The wind blew lightly in Carina's face as she rode along the creek up the gulch. Though the air had a chill with the sun shining, her night in the blizzard with Quillan seemed an anomaly. Three weeks had passed, and she could almost imagine he hadn't been there at all.

Her restaurant was almost ready, and Joe Turner had added a small icehouse, filled with glacial ice, to the back for storing the perishables. Best of all, a freighter had brought eggs to Crystal, and she'd bought every one with the money in Mae's jar. She owed her friends much. But she didn't doubt she would repay them quickly enough.

A buck elk stepped out of the pines to drink at the creek, and she paused to enjoy the sight. He lapped the running water, then raised his shaggy brown head and shook his antlers. He staidly stepped into the creek and crossed before her. When he had passed, she started up again, the Rose Legacy calling to her.

It didn't really, of course. But the closeness she felt to Rose after reading her diary made it seem so. That it was a site of tragedy failed to dissuade her. She felt close to Quillan's mother in the place where she had birthed her son and died in the arms of one who loved her. While she wished Rose could have lived, Carina was thankful to know her through her words, written in the red leather diary.

It had inspired Carina to start a journal of her own, and with one of the few bills Quillan had left on the crate beside the bed, she had bought a diary. Maybe no one would ever read it, but her thoughts and prayers would be there. And perhaps someday her words would touch someone as Rose's had done.

Carina reached the spot where Placerville had stood before the flood. Only gray weathered husks of buildings and sluice boxes and old placer diggings had remained. Now even those were gone. She didn't miss them. She had once imagined ghosts and shades watching her through the windows and cavities. She was glad the old buildings were gone.

She turned Daisy up the slope and started the climb, the Rose Legacy being located at the highest point up the mountain. It wasn't a placer mine like the rest. It had been tunneled into the mountainside like the Gold Creek mine just below and west of it. The mine itself was hardly substantial, a short tunnel and a shaft, though the shaft had seemed to plunge to the center of the earth when she had been trapped on the ledge some twenty feet into its darkness. If not for Quillan, she would have died there. She pressed her fingers to the crucifix that hung at her throat beneath her coat. God had truly intervened for her salvation.

She reached the mine and dismounted beside the square foundation of burned stones. A sigh filled her as she glanced at the square, wondering again whether Rose had caused or merely accepted the fire's claiming her life. She prayed it was the latter. But God's mercy was supreme.

Leaving Daisy in the small clearing before the tunnel, she headed up the mountain. When she reached the grave, she sat, pulling her knees to her chest. It was here she prayed for her loved ones, and they were many. Mamma and Papa, her sister Divina, Tony and Vittorio and Angelo and Joseph and Lorenzo, her brothers, who had bullied and teased and loved her well. Old Guiseppe and Tìa Marta and Tìa Gelsomina, not a true aunt but her godmother, and so many others.

Sitting beside the grave, Carina ached for them all and was convicted in her heart. She must write them. She must tell them about Quillan. She must tell them that she had married—without Papa's permission, Mamma's blessing. Without a ceremony such as they would have given her.

How different it would have been if she'd married Flavio in Sonoma. There would have been flowers everywhere, dancing and singing and wine flowing. Every relative, every friend, dancing and feasting. And Flavio, dark, beautiful Flavio would not hesitate to know her as his wife. He would not leave her for months at a time, then refuse to sleep in her bed.

Carina caught the bitter thoughts. She must not let them take root inside her. She knew only too well her capacity for bitterness and revenge. *Gesù Cristo, help me.* He had before. He had cleansed her spirit and made her His own. Now she tried, but it was difficult. Her own nature wanted to blame, wanted to hurt back.

She looked at the gravestone beside her. *Rose. Wolf.* Quillan's parents. It was dishonoring to think badly of their son here beside the grave. "I want to love him." She said it aloud, as though they could hear. But more so, she said it for her own ears. The longer he stayed away, the more it frustrated and angered her.

What chance had she if she never saw him? How

could she win his heart? But it was more than that. It was a battle of their wills. He was stubborn. But so was she. He knew she would try, and so he stayed away. If he was near, if he allowed it, she would win. He wanted her. There was between them a belonging, a recognizing, a desire.

It was God's gift, this love she bore for him. Where had it come from? She hadn't sought it, hadn't even known it until they'd wed. But there it was, just as it should be. Only Quillan wouldn't see it, wouldn't allow it. Quillan, the rogue pirate, had taken his due, then refused her his heart.

Again the dark emotions swirled within her like a chilling fog. Carina clasped her hands white-knuckled at her breast. *Help me, Signore. I am so angry.* She shook with it. If Quillan were there now she would kick him—hard. She would throw things; she would holler and call him names. Not one word had he given her after their trip together. He had sneaked out like a thief while she slept. Coward. He would not even stay and fight.

She looked again at the grave. Wolf would not desert Rose. He had stayed with her even to his death. Such was the capacity to love that Quillan carried inside him. Why, why did he refuse it? Was she not beautiful? Not desirable? Was she not willing to make him a home, not able to satisfy him?

Feelings of betrayal rose up, strong and deadly. She had felt it before. She had known Flavio's betrayal and came to Crystal, one thousand miles, to punish him. She knew she couldn't let these feelings take hold. But how could she stop them? Prayer. *Signore, per piacere, give me strength.*

She heard a boot crunch on gravel and spun. Father Antoine Charboneau stood behind her, eyes the same startling blue as the sky. He had grayed these last months, and the lines deepened in his face. But he still had the vigor of a younger man. He smiled, showing yellowed teeth, and she returned it with her own scrupulously white ones.

"I saw your horse and guessed where I'd find you."

Carina waved her arm. "I'm conversing with God. I thought if I meant to discuss my husband, it would be only fair to do it here, where his parents could defend him."

Father Antoine laughed. "Very fair." The one brow lowered. "I trust you've not excoriated him."

"Not yet. But I was working up to it."

"Ah, Carina," he said around a chuckle and came to sit beside her. "It won't do you any good. You'd only have to repent of it."

"I know. But in here . . ." She pressed a fist to her breast. "I'm willing to face the consequences if just once I could kick him."

Father Antoine laced his fingers and dangled his hands between his knees. His face took on a puckish look. "I feel guiltily inclined to see that."

"Maybe between us we could make a deal with God."

The priest rubbed his chin. "What would you propose?"

Carina raised a finger. "One kick, hard to his shin. And for my part any penance you name."

Father Antoine dropped his head back and studied the sky. "And then what? After you maimed your husband, what then?"

"Then I would heal him. Didn't I work beside Papa when I was small, and in the infirmary here after the flood?" She waved her arm over the expanse below them. "The men were thankful for my aid."

"So I heard. Do you really think that would heal your marriage?"

Carina cringed. She hadn't meant to let him know how it was with her and Quillan. But then, he would know. He saw inside her like no one else. She sighed. "No. But it would feel better than this helplessness."

" 'Therefore I take pleasure in infirmities, in reproaches, in necessities, in persecutions, in distresses for Christ's sake: for when I am weak, then am I strong.' "

Carina locked her knees in her arms. "So God would have me meek and helpless?"

"Blessed are the meek."

"But I've tried!" She sprang to her feet. "I've held my tongue. I've obeyed him. I've been willing in every way." She stalked along the grave. "And all he can say is I should leave him, annul the marriage, dissolve our flawed union."

Father Antoine refolded his hands. "And what's kept him from doing it himself?"

She stopped pacing. "How should I know? Responsibility."

"It could be worse."

"Oh sì. He could be a drunk and beat me. Or gamble everything away and leave me starving. He could be base and animalistic. He could be blind and deaf and dumb, malformed and simpleminded. I've thought of it all, consoled myself with such thoughts when I lie alone night after night." She drew a breath, thinking she shouldn't speak so to a priest, nor mention intimate things like sleeping with her husband. But Father Antoine only listened.

She threw up her hands. "What chance do I have if he won't even stay?"

"What do you think keeps him away?" Father Antoine asked softly.

She dropped her hands limply to her sides. "He doesn't trust me."

The priest stood. "Why?"

She shook her head. "I don't know. Because he saw the worst of me."

"No." Father Antoine turned and sent his gaze over the mountainside, down the slope and across the gulch. "He was trained not to trust by all of us who failed him. The mother who gave him away, the woman who raised him, the priest who wouldn't." He turned back to her. "I hoped by reading Rose's diary you would see more of Quillan than he'd show you himself. Not that there was much of him in the words, his being an infant only. But that knowing Rose and even Wolf, you would see Quillan's potential."

She nodded. Hadn't she thought the same? Hadn't it been just so?

He drew a slow breath. "I wrote once to the Shepards. A simple inquiry as to his welfare. The letter I received in return showed me just how wrong I'd been to put Quillan into that woman's hands. Even so, I left him there. With regret, but no more. I shook my head and thought it a shame for the boy. Then I went my way and put him from my thoughts."

He pressed his hands to his face, then slid them down to nestle beneath his chin. "When Quillan came to Crystal a man, I knew he had suffered from my neglect. Oh, he was strong, mind you. Too strong. And solitary. Driven. He'd learned to ignore adversity and make his own way. Did I approach him? Did I tell him I'd known his parents, that his mother had trusted me even so far as to give me her son if I would have him?"

Carina's heart ached for the priest, for Rose, for Quillan.

He shook his head. "My first words with your husband were to marry you."

She took a step toward him. "Do you know that wasn't God's will? How can you say it wasn't ordained to happen exactly as it did?"

His flesh formed a deep line between his brows as he eyed her. He glanced at the gravestone, then at the rocky mound where he'd buried the diary until giving it to her. She watched him puzzle her words. Where had they come from? Did she believe it?

He looked back to the sky. "Could that be why I wasn't driven to interfere? That I heard right, thinking I only wanted my own way?"

"Even if it isn't so, God will bring good from it." Carina spoke ardently.

He smiled. "How often you console me."

She smiled back. "I no longer want to kick him."

The priest laughed. "Then we've both gained something."

She nodded. There was peace inside her and hope. She would reach Quillan. Somehow she would reach him.

Eight

One must be careful of dreams;
they can become more than imagined.
—Carina

QUILLAN REINED IN THE TEAM and brought his wagon to a stop in front of the Matchless Mine, the new investment of the man whose name was linked with luck, Leadville, and silver: Horace A. Tabor. The man's luck was legendary already, and Quillan knew enough to hitch his wagon to a star.

Not only did Tabor seem to know where to be and when, he was a generous and congenial man. Quillan honestly liked him, liked being part of his success. And he was. Without the freighters to carry supplies, the mines would be inoperable, even when the rails of the iron horse came through. And Quillan knew at least three railroads were vying for the privilege.

Freighting as he knew it would not benefit from the advance of the rails. But one thing was already established; the trains would not carry the giant powder needed to blast the shafts and drifts of the hard-rock mines. That's where Quillan's fortune lay. And he and Mr. Tabor had already established a relationship through the Tabors' store. Carrying giant powder to Horace Tabor, Quillan could double what he earned freighting to Crystal. Crystal might be booming, but it was nothing to Leadville.

He jumped down from the box and opened the back hatch of the wagon. Sam pranced around his heels until Quillan ordered him to sit. Then Quillan climbed up and bent close to inspect his load. With extreme care, he peeled open the red paper of a stick of giant powder. All over the normally pasty substance he saw delicate white crystals. The temperature overnight had dropped well below fifty-two degrees, and he wasn't surprised to see that the nitroglycerin in the giant powder stick had separated and frozen.

With extreme care, he laid the stick back with the others in the crate. In its frozen crystalline form, the explosive was as sensitive as the liquid. When Tabor's workers came to take what he handed down, Quillan gingerly lifted the crate and bent close to one miner's upraised hands. "It's frozen."

The rough, scarred miner took it into his arms like a new baby. "At least we don't have to thaw it on a stove."

Quillan nodded. Horace Tabor's Matchless, like most of the big operations, had a heated powder house. His men didn't have to hand-thaw the powder, which couldn't be used frozen because the first tamp would set it off. Other miners weren't so lucky and many had lost flesh, limbs, and lives thawing frozen powder in their ovens or on their stoves. The point at which the crystals liquefied was the least stable of all.

Quillan reached for the next case and handed it carefully to the Cornish miner, who stood ready. He had no intention of blowing his wagon, team, and himself into oblivion. But for now, the pay was unbeatable, and he could work as many hours as he could stand.

The muscles in his back flexed and stretched with the motion and tension. He was thankful for the strain. Crate after crate he handed down until his bed was empty. Then he jumped down himself and started around the wagon to unharness the horses.

"Quillan."

Quillan turned to meet Horace Tabor's mustached face. Quillan's own winter beard couldn't match the man's bulging whiskers. The eyes smiled and probably the mouth, but you'd never know it.

"Mr. Tabor." Quillan held out his hand and they grasped hold like two old friends.

"Thank you for bringing my powder." Tabor always made it personal, his gratitude sincere.

"You're welcome. It's not in the best condition just now."

"Well, it'll thaw. Just let it roost a bit in my storehouse."

"Yes, sir."

Tabor huddled Quillan's shoulder companionably. "Would you like to have lunch with me?"

Quillan raised his brows. This was even beyond the normal courtesy he received. He nodded.

"Good. We'll have it over at the hotel." He motioned Quillan into his buggy.

Quillan ordered Sam to stay, waited until the dog had settled at Jock's hooves, then climbed into Tabor's buggy. As they rode, Quillan eyed the city around them. For a city that had sprung out of nothing, Leadville was truly magic. They passed the gas works, which fueled the gaslights on the main streets and the more affluent homes. It made Crystal seem arcane, and Quillan thought briefly of Carina's small shelter with the wood stove to warm her. Frowning, he looked over at the new reservoir.

Tabor caught his gaze and laughed. "Where else than Leadville will you find a city water system with pipes soldered with silver bullion?"

It was true. Quillan had already heard how the city had used silver, which was more plentiful than any other soft solder. Even the streets were paved with the slag from the mines and shone with hints of silver.

Tabor pointed his crop to the cold, shimmering water. "The reservoir itself was excavated from land with promising color, Quillan. Indications of good mineral now lie beneath that water. Why, there's more money under the waterworks than in it." He laughed again.

"But people can't drink mineral."

"No." Tabor sobered. "More's the pity. So, *voilà,* the waterworks."

As they neared the center of town, Quillan saw a tall pole with wires strung from it. Leadville was serviced by a Western Union Telegraph, running lines over Mosquito Pass, but this was something new.

"There she is." Pointing to the pole, Tabor looked ready to pass out cigars.

"What is it?"

"Telephone. I've organized the Colorado Edison Telephone Company. Much of the city can now converse over those wires without ever leaving their doors."

Quillan stared. He'd seen telephone wires in Denver, but to think of them here in Leadville seemed . . . impossible.

"I tell you, my boy, Leadville is second to none, legendary and almost mythical." He spoke as though it were his private kingdom, and so it nearly was.

Quillan looked around. He wasn't oblivious to the wonder of it, but neither was he inured to the undesirable aspects of the rapid and disorderly manner in which the city grew and flourished. The niceties did little to establish respectability. The place was as much a den of corruption as Crystal and more when you considered the numbers.

But there was a contagion in Leadville, an undaunted spirit—the promise that one hundred dollars could set up a miner to make his fortune. It was true, though the hundred-dollar miner stood little chance against the consolidated interests that were quickly making any real competition impossible. One man, or even a handful of men with hand steels and a wheelbarrow, could hardly compete with an adjacent consolidated interest that could be underground already laying claim to his mineral.

And then there were the tangled claims, counterclaims, and jumped claims, and sometimes only three feet of stone separated men with steels from men with rifles ready to keep one outfit out of territory they considered their own. No wonder the place swarmed with lawyers, many as crooked as Berkley Beck or worse.

But Quillan didn't care about the community aspects. He'd been burned in Crystal by caring. Let the roughs in Leadville have their way. Let the crooked lawyers connive and the saloons and fancy houses rule. He was there only to get rich and get out. And even getting rich was only because he needed something to do.

They stopped at the hotel and Quillan stepped down, suddenly not very hungry at all. "What did you want to see me about, Mr. Tabor?"

Tabor crooked a brow. "See you about? Quillan, I just want to express my gratitude for the job you do. There's little enough appreciation for your work, and I want you to know I'm aware of the danger and hardship you suffer for me and my operation."

Quillan wasn't certain how to take that. If the man was anything but sincere, it would take a keener wit than his to discern it. But why would Tabor feel the need to express such gratitude for his work? Work was the elixir that took away the pain.

At least it kept his mind from brooding on his loss. Maybe it was inordinate for him to grieve Cain so deeply. But he'd had so few people to really love, and he hadn't loved Cain as well as he should have. He'd resisted Cain's efforts to bring him to God. For the old man's sake he should have made a show of it.

But then, Cain would have seen that it wasn't real. And that would have hurt him more than Quillan's honest refusal. At any rate that question was settled. Without Cain, Quillan had no need for God. He could live his life by his own compass and conscience. It was better than most men's, and even some who claimed to revere God.

Quillan nodded to Mr. Tabor, and they went in together to eat.

Joe Turner was the first to seek a table, and though she wouldn't earn a penny from him, Carina was thrilled to see him at the door they had fitted into the hall between Mae's kitchen and her own room. The hall kept people from parading through her private space to the dining room behind.

She smiled broadly and led Joe Turner and his two Cornish mine managers to a table directly before the fireplace, where a cheerful blaze warmed the room against the cold October chill. As they seated themselves in the newly wrought pine chairs, Carina was thankful she hadn't considered benches. Hers was not a feedlot where men could press in and shovel food into their bellies.

The fare for this opening night was a favorite of Papa's, *gnocchi con salsa di fegatini*, potato dumplings with liver sauce. But to start the meal, she had *antipasto di peperoni e pomodori*, pimento and tomato antipasto, which she was forced to make from canned tomatoes, though the pickled pimentos had been a grand find.

By the time she brought this first course to Joe Turner and his companions, men were lined up outside the door. Èmie brought them in until the six tables were full, and still others waited outside for someone to leave. Carina stared out the window of the new door. "Goodness," she muttered under her breath. Where had they all come from?

In the kitchen she threw up her hands. "What will I do? I'll never have enough to feed them all."

Mae snorted. "Raise your prices."

"I'm already charging four dollars a plate. It's indecent." Carina crossed the room and back.

"Make it five and send the rest away when you run out."

Carina squeezed her hands together. "I don't want to disappoint them."

Mae laughed. "They'll be back tomorrow."

"Let them sign a list." Èmie took four plates of antipasto from the board and started back toward the dining room. "That's what I did when the hot springs filled up. Then they'll be assured seating for the next night." Èmie walked straight and unwavering through the door with two plates on each arm.

"I need trays. There's so much I didn't think of." Carina threw up her hands again.

"You'll learn. Fill the need as you see it," Mae said.

"I thought I was ready. How could I overlook so much?"

Mae only laughed and poured a serving pot full of stewed beef. "You'll learn to keep it simple."

No. Not simple, not plain, not monotonous. Even if every night showed some oversight, she would not compromise her vision. The Piedmont House would be a place of refinement, a distinguished restaurant in which she could make her fortune and her name, in true Crystal fashion. Hadn't she ordered the room finished with ornate moldings and painted the walls a rich mulberry?

Her own room might be scarcely more than a shack, but she had made the dining room something special. The food would be no less. It was how it should be. She must learn to do it well; that was all. She hurried into the dining room with three plates of gnocchi for Joe Turner and his men.

Joe Turner leaned back as she set the plate in front of him. "Mrs. Shepard, just look at this place. Every seat filled. I told you, you were lucky. Everything you touch turns to gold."

"No." She smiled. "This isn't gold, just gnocchi con salsa di fegatini."

Joe Turner laughed. "My digestion will prefer it."

As Èmie brought the third steaming plate to the table, Carina gathered up the antipasto plates. "*Buon gusto.* Enjoy your meal." She hurried back to the kitchen, staring at the crowd that waited outside. Bene. Did they think she was magic? How could they fit? How could she feed them all? "Èmie, can you serve alone if I make more gnocchi?"

"Yes. But it's you they want to see. Every table's asking, 'Where's Mrs. Shepard?' "

Carina squeezed her hands. "I didn't know it would be so . . . popular."

"You've never been in business before."

Carina crossed the kitchen and looked out the door window. Just a few short months ago, Crystal wanted to hang her with the roughs. Now men stood with their breath misting in the cold air for a chance to taste her wares. Among them she saw Alex Makepeace and Ben Masterson, the mayor. She caught her breath. "Èmie, the mayor's out there!"

Èmie laughed. "Why not? He eats."

"I can't make him stand in the street!"

"Well, there's nowhere to put him."

"Oh, Signore, why didn't you warn me?" Carina opened her hands to the ceiling, then yanked a large bowl from the shelf. "Quickly, Èmie, serve the rest of the tables. I'll make a fresh batch of gnocchi."

"What about the sauce?"

"This one will be served with butter and oregano." Even as she spoke, she was putting potatoes on to boil. Her supplies would not last long if every night was like this. While the potatoes boiled, she sautéed the butter with minced garlic and oregano and two precious anchovies ground to paste. Already she saw she would have to be creative. But that was how she liked to cook. A little of this, a little of that.

She lost herself in the process, rubbing the boiled potatoes through the sieve into the bowl, then working in the flour, butter, four equally precious eggs, and salt and pepper. When it was smooth, she dampened her hands and shaped the mixture into small balls, then dropped them in to boil until they floated to the top.

Èmie hustled back in. "Joe Turner wants to say goodnight."

Carina wiped her hands. "Good, there will be a table free." He might be insulted by her sentiment if he had heard it, but she couldn't think past the men outside expecting to be served. She hurried down the long hall, wondering how many others might be ready to leave.

Joe Turner stood. "I congratulate you, Mrs. Shepard. That meal was delicious and satisfying. Expect me tomorrow."

"I'll expect you every night until I've repaid my debt."

His eyes softened. "I told you it's not necessary. I owe all I have to you."

She waved her hand, dismissing that. "You come tomorrow for ravioli." She headed for the door and saw them out, then looked in dismay at the line. It stretched almost to Central Street. Without another word, she went into her room and brought out a sheet of stationery paper. Then she stepped outside. "Put your names on the paper. If you don't get served tonight, you'll be first tomorrow."

"Are you serving lunch?"

Carina pressed a hand to her head. "Not until I can think straight." She passed the paper among them, then looked at the next men in line. "I have four chairs if you want to share a table." She thought ruefully of benches.

The first four stood forward eagerly, and she led them in. Another table had cleared, and Èmie showed her the money. "What should I do with it?"

Carina looked about the kitchen. "Here." She dried out the small jar from the pickled pimentos. "Put it in here." Carina hurried back to the dining room. Quickly she shook out the cloth from the empty table and mentally noted two others ready to clear. She took their money, then led another four men inside.

One cheesecloth covering was soiled, and she carefully

wiped it clean. She would need extras of those and twice as many dishes. When Quillan came, she'd . . . No, she couldn't wait for him. She'd have to make her own arrangements. She hurriedly reset the table.

When she opened the door, she met Alex Makepeace's smile. It settled the bees in her stomach. "Hello, Mr. Makepeace. How many are with you?"

"Just me."

She looked behind him. "How many with you, Mr. Masterson?"

"My wife and I."

Carina eyed the perky blond woman beside him, then looked beyond to the miner in a slouch hat and flannel shirt. "I have a table for four if you don't mind sitting together."

Mrs. Masterson glanced at the man behind them, and Carina held her breath. Would she be offended at the thought of sharing her table? With a man from the mines? How would Mamma respond if asked to share a meal with a strange *contradini*?

Mrs. Masterson turned back. "That would be lovely."

Carina felt elated. "Come this way." She led them in and saw that three more tables had cleared. Èmie was quickly resetting them, and Carina could only guess that she'd collected the money as well. With hardly more than a *buon appetito*, Carina hurried to the kitchen and finished the gnocchi.

The pimento salad was gone, so she sliced a salami thinly and arranged it with olives and parsley. These she sent out with Èmie as quickly as they were ready. Then she made up the plates of gnocchi and carried them as swiftly herself. Back and forth she went until she was sure she'd worn an inch off the new floor. When there was nothing left to serve, and even the crusty white bread was exhausted, she told the rest who waited outside that their names would be first tomorrow. Then she closed the door, half staggered back to the kitchen, and collapsed at Mae's table. "Oofa!"

Mae pressed her hands between the rolls that marked her hips. "Bit off more than you could chew."

Carina's stomach rumbled. "I haven't had a bite yet." She'd hardly had time to breathe.

"It's just an expression. Took on more than you could handle."

Èmie came in, beaming, and put a handful of bills into the jar. "That was the last of them."

Carina stared at the jar, wondering if it was half worth it.

Mae set a plate of stewed beef before her and another for Èmie. Carina ate automatically while Mae shook out the jar and counted their earnings. Six tables seated three times at four dollars a plate minus Joe Turner's threesome, who weren't charged but left a five-dollar bill on the table anyway. Two hundred and seventy-six dollars. And she had a page of names to be served tomorrow night.

Carina looked from Mae to Èmie and threw up her hands. "I'm pazza! Completely and totally crazy."

Èmie bit her lower lip and grinned. "You're rich. You've struck gold."

"That's what Joe Turner said. But I can't do this every night." She sighed, dropping her head into her hands. "I have to think."

Èmie's fork clinked on her dish as she ate the beef, but Carina's stomach was too tense to finish hers. There must be a way to make it work without losing her mind. She looked up at Mae, who was stuffing the money back into the jar. "Wait. We divide it three ways."

Mae shook her head. "No, Carina. You and Èmie work out whatever you like, but I've got my own operation."

"It's your stove and wood I'm using."

"Pay for the wood if you like. You'll have to replace your supplies with this as well. You have to think in terms of business, Carina. Pay Èmie a wage, cover your cost, then pocket the rest."

Carina took the jar and shook the money out again. She counted out what Mae had lent her for the eggs and slid it across the table, then added five dollars for wood burned in the stove. "I'll keep fifty to buy more dishes and tablecloths, also trays, and more ingredients. A hundred goes to Joe Turner toward my loan on the building. That left ninety-two dollars. She split it with Èmie.

But Èmie took twenty and pushed back the rest. "We'll need someone to clear and set and wash dishes."

Carina raised her brows. "Hire someone else?"

Èmie nodded. "It's too much for two of us."

And Carina wouldn't do as Mae did, serving the second shift on plates unwashed from the first. "Do you have someone in mind?"

Èmie nodded.

"All right. Bring her here in the morning and we'll see." Carina folded the money into bundles according to their use and put them back into the jar. Then she put the jar on Mae's shelf next to the canister where Mae kept her own earnings. "I will sleep tonight."

Quillan ached when he lay down to sleep with the dog sprawled at the foot of his bedroll. The tension that built up handling frozen giant powder was harder on the muscles than heavy work alone. October was drawing on, and it was time to consider his options. With temperatures over the pass what they were, he didn't relish hauling the giant powder frozen over mile after mile of treacherous road.

And it had been more than a month since he'd gone to Crystal, seen to Carina and his responsibilities there. He rolled to his side. What were his responsibilities there? Pay for her keep, surely. See that she was warm and fed. Beyond that? He'd given her ample opportunity to end the sham. If she refused, he couldn't be held accountable.

He tossed to his other side, yanking the heavy blankets over himself. It was getting cold to sleep in a tent. The Rocky Mountain winter was no place for inadequate shelter. By the end of October a tent would not suffice. But then, he had a house, didn't he? A single room cabin in Crystal he could share with his wife.

Quillan punched the sack of stuffing that passed for a pillow. When had he grown so discontent with his accommodations? When he'd left her lying in the overstuffed bed? He frowned, rubbed his face with one hand, and settled onto his back. He wouldn't move again. He'd will his body to stay still and his thoughts away from Carina and the tangle of their lives.

He stared at the dim canvas above him. Think. John Donne.

Go and catch a falling star,
Get with child a mandrake root,
Tell me where all past years are,
Or who cleft the devil's foot,
Teach me to hear the mermaids singing,
Or to keep off envy's stinging,
And find
What wind
Serves to advance an honest mind.

Quillan tucked his arms behind his head and spoke aloud, " 'If thou be'st born to strange sights, things invisible to see, ride ten thousand days and nights, till age snow white hairs on thee . . .' " He scrunched his brow. Oh yes. " 'Thou, when thou return'st, wilt tell me, all strange wonders that befell thee, and swear no where lives a woman true and fair.' "

He drew a long breath. " 'If thou find'st one let me know; such a pilgrimage were sweet. Yet do not; I would not go, though at next door we might meet. Though she were true when you met her, and last till you write your letter, yet she will be false, ere I come, to two or three.' "

Not a flattering depiction. How much of it did he believe? He'd surely seen the worst of the women in his life from the harlot who bore him to the woman who raised him. And even the woman he'd married. Whatever game she was trying to play—the dutiful wife, the dew-eyed lover—it didn't matter.

She had paid him with interest for sending her wagon off, digging up his past and handing it to the people of Crystal. Then she'd come to him, all trembling and begging for his help. What man could have resisted the need he saw in her? And then their wedding night . . . He groaned. He wasn't licking his wounds. He had no one to blame but himself.

Alfred, Lord Tennyson.

The Eagle

He clasps the crag with crooked hands;
Close to the sun in lonely lands,
Ring'd with the azure world, he stands.
The wrinkled sea beneath him crawls;
He watches from his mountain walls,
And like a thunderbolt he falls.

Quillan closed his eyes. How many times had he done this to forget? How many nights lain awake in too much pain from a beating or too much hunger from going without meals in his stubborn refusal to bend to her will? Leona Shepard. The reverend's wife.

He hated her. If there was a God—and Quillan didn't doubt it—he had surely run out of souls before He formed Leona Shepard. The reverend might have spared the rod but for the lies that poured from her. And Quillan had learned very early that his denials only brought more.

He pictured the resigned face of the man who might have protected him but instead wielded the instrument of punishment. Quillan didn't hate him. The reverend wasn't the source of the pain inflicted on his body, only the tool. Quillan opened his eyes to the dull moon glow that penetrated his canvas roof.

Proverbs chapter nineteen, verse two: "Also, that the soul be without knowledge, it is not good; and he that hasteth with his feet sinneth." Yes, Reverend, you sinned. Believing her, you blundered. Not hearing, not listening, not wanting to know, you missed the truth. All I wanted was a home. A father. A mother.

Quillan slammed the side of his fist into the ground. Sam raised his head, concerned, and Quillan met the dog's eyes, recalling the dog he'd had for so short a time before Leona Shepard had it shot for a chicken killer. He forced the memory away. He was twenty-eight years old. It was all passed. He would never see her or the reverend again. What mattered is what he did now.

Fine. He'd see October out in Leadville, then go back to Crystal, make certain Carina had what she needed, offer once again to release her, then move on. He rolled to his side and pulled the covers over his head.

Nine

Sometimes need wears a face,
and once recognized it cannot be ignored.

—Carina

THE GIRL WHO STOOD BESIDE ÈMIE was bone thin and filthy. Carina recognized the dark Southern Italian coloring and felt automatically disparaging. But that was wrong. How would Gesù see her? The girl had low brows that almost met in the middle and deep-set eyes. She was short, shorter than Carina, and broad across the ribs, even in her malnourished state.

"What's your name?"

"Lucia." She pronounced it with the Italian "ch" sound and confirmed Carina's guess.

"How old are you?"

"Fourteen."

The girl's feet were bare in spite of the mountain chill. Her clothes were rags, unwashed and rotting. Again Carina sought Èmie's eyes. What was the girl's story, and why did Èmie choose her for their help? "In the back, next to the icehouse, there's a washroom. Fill the tub and clean yourself. I'll find you something to wear."

The girl's eyes widened. They were hazel brown with thin lashes and reddened rims. Her skin was blotched but might improve with washing. "Grazie." She hurried around the side of the house, and Carina turned to Èmie. Before she could voice her surprise, Èmie spoke.

"Her father was killed in a fall at the mines. I don't know which one. He left her and two sisters and their mother. Lucia told Uncle Antoine in confession that she would have to work the cribs."

Carina gasped, as startled that Father Antoine would divulge a confession as by the content itself. "How do you know?"

"Uncle Antoine was grim after hearing her confession. He asked if I could think of any way to save the girl from doing something she mustn't. I guessed what that something was. What else is there for her?"

Carina looked around the house where Lucia had disappeared. "There is Piedmont House."

Èmie smiled. "I knew you'd understand."

"Better than you know." She turned. "Come inside." She walked to the crate beside her bed and lifted the red leather diary.

"What's that?"

Carina held it so Èmie could read the name inscribed there.

"Rose Annelise DeMornay?"

"Quillan's mother."

Èmie took the book and examined it. "He gave it to you?"

Carina shook her head. "He's never seen it. Your uncle gave it to me. Rose put it into his keeping when she gave Quillan away to the Shepards. When Quillan and I married, Father Antoine passed it on to me."

Èmie opened it and read an entry at random. Her brow furrowed.

Carina responded with a sigh. "It's not happy, most of it. She, too, had very few choices. That's why I accepted Lucia."

"It's not the only reason."

Carina quirked a brow.

Èmie smiled. "You have a good heart."

Carina released a quick breath. "I've learned a lot since coming here, and God is merciful."

"And patient."

"Grazie, Signore." Carina took the book back and held it fondly a moment.

"What are you going to do with it?"

"I don't know. I thought to give it to Quillan, thought maybe if he read it he would love her as I do. But something holds me back. He's not ready." She laid the book beside her bed again. That was more than she'd meant to say. "I need to find something for Lucia to wear."

She pulled out her only spare skirt and held it up, then shook her head. "She's too wide for this."

"If I had one to spare I'd give it."

"No." Carina shook her head. "We'll buy her a dress." Quillan had asked her not to shop at Fisher's, but he wasn't there to offer an alternative, and besides the money was hers. She took Èmie by the hand and they fought through the traffic to Fisher's General Mercantile.

There was a dressmaker off Pine, but Carina didn't have time to have a dress made up. Lucia needed something now. She walked to the rack of ready-made dresses and chose a blue print with a high collar of stiff, strong material. There must be no question what

Lucia's part was, and she'd ward off any unwanted advances from the start. Piedmont House would maintain the highest propriety.

She bought the dress and also another set of white ceramic dishes and two serving trays. As she walked beside Èmie carrying their goods, she said, "I've been thinking. Your idea of a list is a good one, but it would be better for me to plan if I knew already how many wanted to eat. I think I'll have people sign up in advance for a table. And I'll only seat the room twice in a night. I can't cook for more than that. Not yet anyway."

"Twice twenty-four is enough."

"There might not always be four to a table."

Èmie pulled her shawl close against the chilly breeze. "Why not?"

"Some people might want to dine as a couple, or alone, or three."

"You won't join them up with someone else?"

Carina rolled her eyes. "That was a risk."

"They enjoyed it."

Carina reached the door and quickly stashed the dishes and trays inside. "How do you know?"

"I saw Mrs. Masterson in conversation with the miner all through the meal. Mr. Makepeace and the mayor got downright cozy. It was the same at all the tables."

Carina stopped and turned. "Do you think I should?"

Èmie shrugged, and they made their way around the side to the washroom. Lucia must be thoroughly clean by now, but Carina would make certain she was more than clean. She must be checked for lice, and though she cringed at the thought, she did it herself. Surprisingly the girl's head was free of vermin.

Carina left her the dress and went out. When Lucia came out herself, hair pulled back and face scrubbed, she looked like a new person. Clothes might not make the man, but they did a lot for the woman. Especially in the way she was viewed in a place such as Crystal.

Carina nodded her satisfaction. "What did your father earn in the mine?"

"Three dollars a day." Lucia dropped her eyes as she spoke, as though three dollars was so much.

It was less than Carina charged for one plate. No wonder the miner who sat with the mayor and Mr. Makepeace was the only one of his ilk among the business owners and mine owners, engineers, and managers. Could the discrepancy be so great between those who had in Crystal and those who didn't?

But then, she'd worked for Berkley Beck for room and board and a dollar a week. And his honest earnings had amazed her, even without the forgeries and extortion. Those with education and know-how didn't suffer in Crystal. Not unless they cheated and lost. Like Berkley Beck.

"I'll pay you three dollars a day while you're learning and four starting next week."

Lucia gulped back tears and dropped to her knees. "Oh, grazie. Papa called you Lady Luck, and now I know it."

Joe Turner had started that, claiming she'd made his fortune by putting him out of his room. And his Carina DiGratia Mine, named for her and bringing up the richest ore yet, was halfway to making him a millionaire if the rumors were correct. Though she'd almost been hung by vigilantes not so long ago, it seemed plenty still believed her a legend in the making.

"I'm not Lady Luck. I just need your help. So come

inside and we'll see where to start." Now that Carina was working out of Mae's kitchen for more than her own meals, she set about scrubbing it clean. Mamma had been insistent about that. Cleanliness was godliness. No self-respecting woman would allow her kitchen to be any less.

She didn't judge Mae, or at least she tried not to. It would be difficult—if not impossible—for Mae to get down on her knees and scrub the floor. But that didn't mean the floor needed it less. While Lucia scrubbed, Carina decided her menu. Then she went to the stationery store and bought a pad of paper.

On the first sheet of the pad she wrote the date. Then she divided the page into first seating and second seating. Second seating would begin as soon as each table cleared from the first. Then she numbered down the page one through six with room for four names at each table. She filled in the names of those who hadn't been served the night before, as well as Joe Turner, who had.

There were still two names left over. These she put at the first seating for tomorrow's dinner. She hoped this would bring some order to things. She borrowed a hammer and put in a nail to hang the pad outside the restaurant door. As she did so, Alex Makepeace rounded the corner.

He removed his hat and nodded. "Good morning, Mrs. Shepard."

"Good morning."

"That was a delicious supper you served last night."

"Thank you."

He glanced at the pad hung on the wall. "What would I need to do to have my name on your list every night?"

She raised her brows, surprised. “I don’t know. I haven’t thought past tomorrow.”

“I was thinking of tonight.” He laughed.

Carina spread her hands helplessly. “I have too many names already.”

“Have you considered an expansion?” His brown eyes shone with mirth.

“Expansion! I’ve only just built. Besides, how could I serve more? I can hardly keep up as it is.” She shoved the hair back from her face. “It’s pazzo.”

He laughed. “A very descriptive word. Meaning?”

“Crazy. Insane. Ridiculous. Do you suppose it was curiosity? Will they stop coming once they’ve tried it?”

Makepeace took the pencil that hung with the pad and wrote his name on the next night’s list. “Mrs. Shepard, once they’ve come, they’ll keep coming.”

“But there’s the hotel and all the saloons and—”

“What Crystal wants is the sophistication you’ve brought it.” He flipped up a page, numbered it as she had, and wrote his name again.

“Mr. Makepeace.” She couldn’t help laughing.

“You could make it exclusive. Like a men’s club. Double your prices.”

“Impossible. Who would pay eight dollars for a meal?”

He flipped another page and started numbering. “There are men here making more money than they know what to do with.”

“And others making three dollars a day.”

He glanced sideways as he added his name to a third page. “Which is more than they’d earn in any other unskilled position anywhere in the country. A factory worker in the East makes one dollar a day with hours as long as the hard-rock miner’s. These men are glad for what they get. Why else would they be here?"

"What does my husband earn a day?"

He dropped the sheets and hooked a thumb in his vest. "You'll have to ask Quillan that." He turned back to the pad. "Isn't there another way besides my filling in every page you have? Why don't you keep three of the tables permanently reserved for those of us who intend to come every night. Then keep the others open for sign-ups if you like."

She stared at him. Was he serious? Did he think men would come night after night, pay so much for a meal and the privilege of sitting at her tables? She looked at her pad. She could keep three tables for the first seating at her discretion. Joe Turner would need a place and maybe more than one if he brought his men with him.

"All right. Stop signing every page. I can't help tonight, but starting tomorrow, you may have a place kept for you."

"Madame, you're an angel."

"Oh sì." She waved her hand. "It's your stomach talking. But as you're managing my husband's interests, I suppose I should keep you happy."

"Mrs. Shepard, you know well enough what I have to face every other meal of the day." Again his eyes lit with humor as he saw her silent acknowledgment.

She was a traitor to let him speak so of Mae's efforts and offer no more than understanding. But it was true.

"Now I'm off to the mine. By the way, we've made tremendous headway on the shaft and started a lateral level on a very promising vein."

Carina smiled. "I'm glad to hear it." But she didn't have time to think about it. The mine was Quillan's business, if even he cared. She took down the pad and began renumbering the pages to reserve three tables from each first seating. She would see if they filled and stayed that way.

By evening she had no doubt they would. Joe Turner applauded her idea of keeping his place, and told her he wanted an entire table held for him and the managers and engineers he would have with him. The mayor spoke for a full table every Tuesday and Friday night and promised to fill four seats. His wife had thoroughly enjoyed herself. Mr. Makepeace was only one, but the other seats were quickly spoken for. As he said, too many men in Crystal had money and no one to cook for them.

And now her main concern was how far she could stretch the ingredients she'd bought in Fairplay. How in heaven's name would she get more?

Carina stepped out into the brisk morning air. She felt cleansed and exhilarated after celebrating Mass with Father Charboneau and Èmie and even Dr. Simms. She watched the two of them now, walking with heads together, Èmie's hand lightly on the doctor's arm. It couldn't be argued that he courted her with anything less than the utmost propriety.

It was obvious to every eye that he esteemed and honored her, Èmie, the niece of the demented murderer Henri Charboneau. But then, she was also the niece of the priest. They were two brothers who started out on the same wrong path until God intervened. Carina drew the air deeply into her lungs. One could do so on Sunday, when much of the mining activity was diminished.

She started down toward the livery just behind Alan Tavish. Quickening her step, she caught up with him, then slowed to match his painful amble. "Good morning, Alan Tavish."

"Good mornin' to you, lass."

"I'd like to ride today, if you'll allow me to take Daisy."

He cocked his head. "Quillan didn't tell ye, then."

"Tell me what?"

"The mare's yours, darlin'. Quillan bought her for you."

Carina tried not to look surprised. How would it seem for her not to know? Could Quillan not have told her? Would it have been so much? But then she would have thanked him, and he would have to admit he'd done something thoughtful, something good to her.

"I forgot." It sounded foolish even to her. She should be pleased, grateful. Instead she was confused. Why had Quillan bought the mare? In hopes she'd saddle up and leave him? Probably. She stopped the direction of her thoughts. Instead she hailed Mr. Makepeace coming from the cabin that served the Presbyterians. So he was a God-fearing man.

He turned at her call and smiled. "Mrs. Shepard, you're a balm to the eyes."

"Thank you, Mr. Makepeace. Isn't it a lovely day?"

"It is. I'd thought to see somewhat of the countryside, but I'm not sure where to go." He dropped into step with them.

"Perhaps you'd like to ride with me." She wasn't sure why she'd said it, except that a nagging loneliness was starting to creep in. Mae and Èmie were dear, but having grown up with five brothers and Papa, her uncles and old Guiseppe, she hungered for male companionship as well.

"I'd like that very much. Where would we go?"

"There is Wasson Lake." Again she wasn't sure why she suggested that. It was where she and Quillan had first ridden together. But that had been Quillan's instigation, to teach her how to shoot the gun he'd provided her. She hadn't shot it since the night the vigilantes tried to hang her.

"That sounds bully."

She glanced at Alan Tavish and caught a sour look on the old ostler's face. Did he read more into their adventure than either of them intended? Would others think the same? Carina hesitated only briefly. If Quillan cared two figs, he wouldn't leave her alone in a place like Crystal.

"I'll pack us some lunch. It's two hours to the lake."

Mr. Makepeace tipped his hat with a slight bow. "I'll fetch our mounts." He continued on with Alan Tavish while she veered off for Mae's kitchen. Perhaps she shouldn't be riding off alone with Mr. Makepeace. Perhaps she should ask Èmie and Dr. Simms along. She turned and searched the street behind her, but they were not in sight.

Surely she was making more of this than necessary. It was a friendly overture on both their parts, and Quillan would expect her to entertain his partner. He would do it himself if he were there, which of course he wasn't. She reached the kitchen and went inside. Quickly she assembled bread spread with pesto and sprinkled with parmigiano, a jar of olives, and a small salami. For drink they would have the lake itself, which was so clear she could see to the bottom for a great distance.

It was not connected to Cooper Creek, therefore was uncontaminated by the mining debris and city waste. She remembered her first sight of it as she rode her old mule Dom along the road after Quillan had tossed her wagon. The beauty of the lake with the snowy peak behind had made her breathless, quickened her spirit, and had given her courage to go on.

She was eager to see it again as she met Mr. Makepeace outside with the horses. She looked at the small red mare. So the horse was now hers. *Grazie, Quillan*. He may have meant the gift as a hint, but she would take it as a gift. With a light hand from Mr. Makepeace, she mounted. He had already hung the food sack from his steeldust stallion's saddle. With little interest from anyone, they headed out.

The ride seemed longer than she remembered, and Carina felt more awkward than she had expected. How could it be any worse than the ride she'd shared with Quillan? Especially the ride back, when he was so furious at her insulting his parentage. How was she to know his parentage was worse than she could have imagined?

Not truly, though. Wolf was not a savage, and Rose not a harlot. How would she let him know that? Carina shook her head. From the start her connection to Quillan had been fraught with fury and dismay. Would that ever change?

The lake came into view, and she realized she'd been lost in her thoughts most of the two-hour ride. It was deplorable manners. "I apologize, Mr. Makepeace. I've not been a friendly guide."

He smiled easily. "I've no quarrel with quiet, Mrs. Shepard. That two individuals can share a companionable silence is friendly enough for me."

She searched his face a moment, then directed his attention to the lake. They were not coming toward it from the most dramatic angle, as she had, but it was lovely enough. On the lakeshore, they shared the lunch, which Mr. Makepeace praised profusely.

"It's the mountain air, Mr. Makepeace. It adds God's own seasoning."

"I believe you."

"Now tell me about this vein you're following." It was a safe enough subject, and as she guessed, Alex Makepeace held forth at length while they finished their meal and wandered a short way along the lake. She listened with more interest than she'd expected. He made the operation sound fascinating, and she could hear his pride in the endeavor. She felt herself relax and even questioned him.

"But isn't it dangerous for the men with the thermal instability of the giant powder?"

"Every aspect of mining has its hazards, Mrs. Shepard. Not just the powder. Machinery failure accounts for more accidents than powder explosions."

"What sort of machinery failure?"

"Oh, for instance, the winch that lets the basket down the shaft. If the chain breaks, as all too frequently they do, the basket hurtles down the shaft sometimes sixty feet or more. Men are thrown out or hit bottom with such force . . ." He shook his head. "No, there's nothing safe about the mining trade. But men don't do it for safety or they'd be pushing a plow instead."

"Why do they do it, Mr. Makepeace?"

He formed a solid smile. "There's nothing like it, Mrs. Shepard. You against the very earth with only your wits, strength, and fortitude. You face the danger every day. And when you conquer . . . ah, there's no feeling like it."

There was a sort of fire in his eyes when he spoke, and Carina felt a shadow of the pride he exuded. "Is that how it is for you also, Mr. Makepeace?"

"Now?" He looked surprised. "No, not now. When I went to Cornwall to learn the trade, starting from the bottom up, yes. But that was only the start for me. I went to university and learned engineering. Now I oversee the operation. I'm not involved in the nitty-gritty anymore."

Carina smiled. "You sound disappointed."

He smiled back. "No. But I must admit I miss the fraternity. When your life lies in the hands of your fellow workers, there's a bond with them you won't find outside of it."

"But why is it so dangerous? Aren't there ways to make it safe?"

He hunched his shoulders and dropped them. "There are too many unknowns, and our technology can't cover them all. Hit a pocket of bad air, the canary dies, and all you can do is run. If a fire starts, you better pray you're first to the basket. If a mule backs a cart over you, if a winch chain breaks, if the fuse on the powder explodes before you're clear . . . How could we cover all the contingencies?"

"But what happens to the injured men?"

"Some buy insurance against mining accidents that render a man unable to continue the trade."

She waved a hand. "Such as limbs blown off, blinded eyes, or broken necks."

He turned from the lake to face her. "Mrs. Shepard, life holds no guarantees. Men do what they must and take responsibility for the dangers therein. Even the law says as much. It's called contributory negligence and fellow servant liability. I can't be responsible for every action of every man underground that might contribute to an accident risking the life or health of the others."

Carina considered that. She supposed the men did

share the responsibility for their own safety. "What happens to those who are rendered unable to work?"

"They're let go."

She stopped, one foot on a crisp, grassy clump beside the softly lapping water. "You mean dismissed?"

He looked slightly uncomfortable. "Yes, if they're no longer able to hold the job, they're dismissed."

"But are they able to hold another job?"

Mr. Makepeace rubbed the back of his hand up his cheek. "Not always."

"Then how do they live?"

"Mrs. Shepard, there are cripples and unfortunates in every part of the world. They beg, they borrow, they steal. I don't know how they live. Even the Lord said we'd have the poor with us. The churches care for them."

Carina turned and looked back toward Crystal. "Which churches would that be, Mr. Makepeace?"

He was quiet a long moment, then, "Mrs. Shepard, forgive me for troubling you with concerns not your own."

It was a polite way of telling her to mind her own business and not push him further. Carina recognized that, but she pushed anyway. "And if one day you are injured and unable to work?"

"Then I hope I'll have handled my affairs well enough to see me through."

"I'm sure you will have. But is that possible for a man on three dollars a day?"

He rubbed the heel of one hand against the other and eyed her squarely. "Probably not."

At least he didn't equivocate, and she respected him for that. His arguments had all been sensible and not vindictive. She guessed he was a good foreman, careful in every way he could manage. She wasn't even sure why she had taken the tack she had. What were the miners to her?

Gathering clouds and a renewed chill sent them back to the horses, and the wind made conversation difficult on the ride back. Carina was glad. She had no desire to spar any further, especially with Quillan's man. Did Quillan understand the conditions in his mine? Mr. Makepeace had given her a clearer picture than she'd wanted. How informed was her husband?

Mr. Makepeace left her at her door and, buffeted by the wind, led Daisy back to the livery, behind his steeldust. Carina went inside, wondering what she would do with herself. She had decided not to serve dinners on Sunday. Everyone needed one day free, she'd reasoned. But now her day threatened to stretch unbearably. And she couldn't free her mind from the plight of the hardrock miners.

Ten

I think God allows hardship so that in alleviating it, we might understand His mercy.

—Carina

THE MORNING BROUGHT SNOW, and when Carina stepped out to fill her basin, the air was so cold it hurt to breathe. She pumped the water swiftly and hurried back inside. Before she washed, she stoked the fire in the stove and warmed the water. No sense freezing if she didn't have to.

After washing and dressing, she found Mae in the kitchen frying thick slabs of bacon and pouring hotcakes. Was there ever a morning without bacon and hotcakes? She thought longingly of warm, sugar-crusted *tarrele,* steaming coffee with real cream, sausage and peppers, and hard-boiled eggs. She sighed.

"World on your shoulders again?" Mae didn't turn as she spoke. She flipped a long line of hotcakes, then returned to the front of the line and scooped them onto a platter. "Bring the coffee on behind me, will you?"

Carina lifted the large blue-speckled pot using a cloth around the handle and another at its base. She followed Mae into the dining room, where the men were stacked side by side as tightly as they could fit along the benches. Hungry men, gobbling up whatever they could to sustain them for their day's work.

Some carried pie tins containing the lunches they would eat in the dark of the mines. Others made do with Mae's fare until their ten- or twelve-hour shift was done, then came back for stewed beef. As Carina poured, she looked at the men whose cups she filled.

In the past she'd been disgusted by them, slopping like hogs, not even noticing what they ate or caring that it was the same thing day after day. She poured the next cup and noted the three-fingered grip that held it, the middle two fingers missing at the palm. She glanced at his face, and he smiled his thanks.

She moved on. They were all bundled against the cold, but they'd soon be warm enough with the steam that filled the tunnels. How would it be to go from the snow-filled air to the steam and back to the chill? No wonder so many of them suffered with incessant hacking.

Carina looked up and down the tables. There was not a trustee, store owner, lawyer, or judge among them, though Joe Turner and his managers sat at one end and Alex Makepeace in the center of another table. She emptied the pot and returned to the stove to brew more coffee. Suddenly what Mae did seemed so much more significant than her own dream.

Mae fed the masses wholesome, filling food, food to sustain them over hours of hard, torturous labor. Carina cooked elaborate, palette-pleasing fare for those who could afford more per plate than the men at Mae's table earned each day. She felt . . . wrong.

It must have shown, for when Èmie came in to plan

the day's menu with her, she paused. "Aren't you feeling well?"

"Well enough." Carina suddenly gripped her arm. "Èmie, am I doing right?" She swung her arm toward her elegant dining room, not in sight from the kitchen but clear in her mind. "My restaurant, my fancy food, my fancier clientele. Is it right?"

"Right for what?" Èmie's brow lowered.

"What of all the men who can't afford four dollars a plate? Who don't earn four dollars in a twelve-hour day?"

Èmie caught Carina's hands together between hers. "What is it that's bothering you, Carina? That you've done something special? Created an experience that Crystal appreciates?"

"What Crystal? The glitter that feeds off the poor?"

Èmie smiled. "Is that it, then? You feel guilty for catering to the upper crust?"

Carina threw out her hands. "I don't know what I feel. I've made so much money this last week—and then I think of Lucia. . . ."

"Who is not working the cribs, thanks to you and your fancy food."

"But so many others!"

Èmie brought Carina's hand to her lips and kissed it. "You took me from the baths."

"I know, but . . ."

"There's nothing to say you can't use your money any way you please."

Carina felt the truth of her words. Yes. She could use the money she earned from the wealthy patrons to help those in need. That would be as good as what Mae did. And she could hire another girl. Lord knew they needed the help. She felt the weight lift from her.

"I must talk to Joe Turner about freighters." She left Èmie wondering, no doubt, what freighters had to do with anything.

Joe Turner had risen and was starting for the door when she accosted him. "Mr. Turner, may I have a word with you?"

"Of course, Mrs. Shepard." He waited while his companions politely made their exit.

"I need far more supplies than I anticipated. Could you recommend some freighters who might be amenable to providing what I need?" Even she knew she couldn't again go to Fairplay through the winter. Nor could she consider riding with a freighter who was not her husband. But neither could she wait for her husband.

He frowned in thought. "The freighters I use haul ore. But let me see what I can do."

"Thank you." Carina smiled. Joe Turner would move heaven to help her.

By the time he came for dinner that night he had three freighters willing to make the trip to Fairplay, and one of them to Denver if necessary. Carina suspected Joe Turner had used his influence somehow, but she didn't ask. She was only thankful.

The next morning the first of them took the list she had made up, complete with the most each item should cost. He expected two days to make the trip, barring blizzards. Pleased, she agreed and sent him off. Another thought had occurred to her, but she needed to stock her larder before she could do it. Now it just remained to keep her wealthy clientele pleased enough to keep coming back.

Alex Makepeace listened to the creak and squeal of the winch letting the basket down the shaft. Four men rode together, their heads disappearing below the edge as the machinery lowered them to the depths of the mine. His conversation with Mrs. Shepard made him more aware of things than he'd been in some time.

Perhaps he should have the maintenance team do a thorough inspection. Such things cost time and money, but they saved lives. There was a thin line between profit and loss with the chanciness of silver prospects within the politics and economics of the country. His investors—no, his employers—expected the same margins as the other comparative mines, and many of them cut corners. The easiest corners being those that affected safety.

Setting the timbering farther apart, using fewer braces and planks, which kept the loose rocks from falling on the miners' heads, cheaper grades of lumber more susceptible to rot and mildew—all these were established practices for improving profit. His group expected no less. Alex stepped aside as a new mule was led into the shaft house.

He watched two men tie it securely, binding its legs and blindfolding it so it wouldn't kick itself or the sides of the shaft loose during its descent. They worked the sling under its belly, then hoisted it out over the shaft. The animal dangled there a moment, breathing its last clean air.

Once it was lowered into the mine, the mule would never come out. It would spend several hours still tied up but not blindfolded to accustom it slowly to the new environment. Then it would live the rest of its days in the dark, claustrophobic, muted atmosphere underground. Each day would be a monotony of pulling one-ton ore carts along eighteen-inch rails, feeding and leaving its waste in the tunnels that now comprised its world. Alex didn't envy the poor animal.

Strange, he'd always felt more sympathy for the beasts than the men—maybe because they had no voice in the matter. They were slaves to the human whims that drove them. At least every man down there had chosen the work for himself. And it was a worthy living, if a hard one.

Alex watched the last of the mules disappear and sighed. Everyone played his part, even the beasts, and maybe they minded it less than he imagined. They were certainly docile enough once they adjusted in those first hours. A man coughed beside him, and Alex turned to see what he wanted.

Finney McGough could be anywhere from thirty to sixty, wizened and hacking. He was rocked up, Alex knew, but he didn't mention it. The miners' consumption was a subject avoided on all fronts. Alex had his suspicions of its causes, but he kept them to himself. No sense alarming men over what couldn't be helped. Part of the trade, was all. Part of the trade.

When the freighter returned with a full wagon, Carina was ecstatic. When she saw his bill, much of her ecstasy vanished. Quillan hadn't exaggerated. The freighter's markup was extortionary. She realized now how fair Quillan's price had been even before she talked him down to the deficit amount they'd settled on for that first trip. But she couldn't see any way past paying the bill if she needed to use freighters other than Quillan.

She would just have to get used to higher cost and

smaller profit. She felt better about her plate cost. And with what this freighter had brought her she would implement her new plan. It was two days until Sunday, two days to pass the word and enlist Mae.

Èmie and Lucia she would leave out of it. They needed a day free, and she was determined they should have it. Besides, she couldn't afford to pay them, not when she was charging only fifty cents a plate for any miner and his family. She hurried to Mae's kitchen while the freighter unloaded her goods into the icehouse and larder.

Her pimento jar had been replaced by a crockery canister like Mae's. She stretched up and took it down from the shelf. From it she counted out the money to pay the freighter and shoved it into the deep pocket she'd requested be sewn into the dress she wore.

"Mae," she called into the parlor, but there was no answer. She crossed through to the entry and found Mae at her desk. "Mae, I have an idea."

Mae licked her finger and counted a stack of bills, then entered them into her ledger. "Do I want to know?"

"Of course you do. Because you have to help me. I can't do it alone."

Mae glanced briefly, her violet eyes dark with doubt. She laid down her pencil and folded her fingers into a fleshy mat. "Let's have it."

"Sunday I'm feeding the miners."

"So?"

"I don't mean the mine managers or owners or engineers. I mean the miners. For fifty cents a plate. I wanted to serve them free, but I thought they might not like that. It would seem like charity."

"It is charity. How much are you making on fifty cents a plate?"

"None. But enough the other nights to spare."

Mae shook her head. "You feel guiltier about more things than anyone I know."

"It isn't about guilt. It's about . . . kindness."

Mae heaved herself out of her chair. "And just how do you propose doing this?"

"I'll start serving at noon and serve through dinner. It won't be fancy, but it'll be different—special because it's different. Do you see?"

"I see. Where do I come in?"

"Just tending the pasta and the sauce while I serve."

"And you think the two of us will handle that?"

Carina bit her lower lip. "I admit it won't be easy."

"Impossible, more like. Didn't you learn anything from your opening night? You hang an offer like that out and you'll have a stampede."

"I want to try."

"Why? What's this all about?"

Carina threw out her hands. "Quillan's mine. Mr. Makepeace was telling me all about it. It sounds horrible what the men do, what they risk. I just want . . . I just want to thank them."

Mae was shaking her head before Carina finished. "Guilt again."

"Maybe so. Is it so bad? If it makes you want to help, to do something good? Lucia lost her father. Is it so much to bring a little cheer into their lives?"

"Not so much, I guess. I just hope you know what you're doing."

"Then you'll help me?"

"It'll take a full company."

"It can't. Èmie and Lucia must have the day off. How

else will Dr. Simms ever get the courage to ask Èmie . . ." She realized she'd spoken out of turn.

"I'm not blind, Carina. I've seen the mooning between them two."

Carina squeezed Mae. "I must pay the freighter. I think his name is Peter Marley. Then I'm off to tell Joe Turner my plan."

"Landsakes."

Carina squeezed her again.

"You are the huggingest thing."

Carina kissed both Mae's cheeks, and Mae laughed. "Get out, will you?"

Carina left her still laughing and rode to Joe Turner's Carina DiGratia mine. Mr. Turner balked at her idea. "These men are too rough for your establishment."

"Rough or not, you will tell them, won't you?"

He shook his head. "Yes, I'll pass the word. I only hope it doesn't kill your other business." He clearly enjoyed the elite aspect of her venture, but he did seem genuinely concerned for her as well.

"Don't worry. I know what I'm doing." She left him still shaking his head. She knew it wouldn't hurt business. God had given her the idea, and He would watch over it. She went next to the New Boundless, her own husband's mine. She found Alex outside the mine with a map opened out before him. "That's not a map like any I've seen."

He looked up. "It's topographical."

"Oh."

"That means it maps out the lay of the land. Each of these concentric circles stands for a certain distance upward."

"Oh."

"Never mind. Did you have a purpose here, Mrs. Shepard?" He said the words with a great deal of humor in his brown eyes.

"I did. I want you to tell the men I'm serving miners this Sunday, fifty cents a plate."

"Mrs. Shepard!" He put a hand to his heart. "Fifty cents a plate when the rest of us pay four dollars?"

"It's only fair, Mr. Makepeace, and you know it."

He appraised her in that even way of his. "Well, I'll tell them, but I don't mind saying there are some of us who feel stung."

"If you feel stung, it's your own conscience. When you make three dollars a day, you can come on Sunday, too."

He removed his hat and held it to his chest. "Forgive me for being a clod."

She smiled. "Never a clod, Mr. Makepeace."

"Does that mean you won't have time for a ride on Sunday? I was hoping to see more of the countryside before the winter closes in for good."

"Not this Sunday, Mr. Makepeace. Maybe the next."

"I'll look forward to it." His eyes were warm coffee sweetened with honey. His smile continued the same warmth.

Carina's skirts swished as she passed by him and headed for her mare. That was enough to start with. Word would pass from these two mines to the others. And she had two days to make and dry the pasta. Not to mention starting on her menu for the night. Yes, it was time for more help. She'd see whom else Èmie could find.

Quillan saw the gang of boys huddled too closely to

be minding their manners. Something was inside their circle, but he couldn't make out what. Maybe they were tormenting a stray dog, but it seemed to have more bulk than that. From his distance, he couldn't make out exactly the nature of their activity, but he recognized the mean laughter and the taunting.

He gave Sam a curt command to stay, then strode purposefully closer. The figure inside their circle rose up, and he saw it was a boy, actually nearer a man, a full head taller than the others. The mud on his pants and bulky jacket testified to a roll on the street, and Quillan saw now that one of the others held a stick.

"Come on, dummy, do a trick. Roll over, dummy. Roll over." The taunter struck the boy with his stick, and Quillan hoped for a moment the larger would take the stick and strike back. Then he recognized the expression behind the up-thrown arms. No understanding, just fear and bewilderment.

A surge of rage filled him. What meanness festered inside those kids to mistreat a simpleton as though he were an animal? Quillan reached the group and jerked the stick from the boy's hand. He had no intention of hitting the kid, but the look on his face didn't make that readily apparent.

"Hey." The kid's lip had a natural curl that matched his mean nature. "Give it back."

The others cheered their leader, though Quillan noticed they'd stepped back a pace.

"You want it back?" Quillan balanced the stick in his hands as though testing its weight and measure. "Where do you want it?"

The kid was ready for a fight and not about to lose face. "In my hand, mister, where I had it. Go mind your own business."

Now Quillan did consider striking him, but his own memories held him back. "You like tricks." Quillan heaved the stick end over end into a far field between two cabins. "Go fetch."

The kid's lunge took him square in the belly with a bulky shoulder more developed than Quillan had expected. He tensed just in time and caught the boy in a grip that left his assailant flailing and swearing until he was red-faced with fury. Quillan gripped one dirty wrist and, with a quick twist, jerked the arm up the spine.

The boy bellowed. "You're breakin' my arm!"

"No, I'm not." Quillan spoke with flat deliberation. "Stop your squirming and it won't hurt so much."

The kid aimed a kick for Quillan's shin, but Quillan jerked him back and threw off the boy's balance. "That the best you can do? I saw a girl in pigtails do better than that."

"Let me go!" The boy tried to elbow him with his free arm.

Quillan noted the patched elbow that had torn free countless times and been reattached by someone. "You have a mother?"

That seemed to stump the ruffian. "So?"

"How would she like your behavior just now?"

The boy struggled, realized it only made the arm hurt, and stopped to catch his breath. "She don't care."

Quillan looked around the circle. "You boys feeling proud? Picking on someone like that?" He indicated the large boy still standing there instead of making his escape as any normal person would have.

Several of them shuffled. A few looked sullen, several downright rebellious.

"I'm not going to threaten you. Frankly, you're not worth it."

The boy in his grasp struggled, and Quillan jerked the arm a half inch higher.

"Aah!"

Quillan ignored him. "One day when you're really men, you'll look back on this day in shame. Not because I had the upper hand, but because you were so low to begin with."

Now even the rebellious ones looked uncertain.

"If it were me, I'd follow someone who could prove his own wit, not harass someone lacking. In fact, I'd be hard-pressed to say which of these fellows rates higher on the scale."

A few of them laughed, and the boy he held struggled angrily, but Quillan could tell the fight in him was about spent. He eased his tension on the arm. "I could thrash you, but I'm going to believe you've learned from this encounter. If I see you at it again, I might forget myself."

"You don't scare me." It was false bravado.

"Just so you understand me." Quillan let him go, half expecting a cheap blow once the boy's arm was free.

The kid stepped back, shaking down his jacket and scowling. He turned to his compatriots. "Let's go."

They started off, kicking the dirty snow clumps. Quillan wondered what, if anything, he'd accomplished. He glanced at the victim of their sport. He still stood where they'd left him. Did he even know to get out of the street? And why wasn't someone watching him?

"Go on, now." Quillan waved toward the walk. "Go home."

"He's got no home." Horace Tabor spoke behind him.

Quillan turned.

Tabor joined him. "He does grunt labor for a few of

the mines. Sleeps wherever he can."

"Who's in charge of him?"

"In charge of himself, Quillan."

Quillan frowned.

"I know what you're thinking. But he's not alone. There's more cripples, misfits, and half-wits than can be helped."

Quillan swallowed his argument. If it were any but Horace Tabor he might object, but Tabor was himself a humanitarian. He wasn't speaking without cause. Besides, what business was it of his? Quillan was determined not to care, not to entangle himself in any community's problems. Doing so before had cost him Cain.

He looked over his shoulder at the boys disappearing around the corner of the smithy, then back at the simpleton. Well, he'd spared the poor fellow one hardship. He'd have to spare himself the rest.

"Come on." Tabor cocked his head. "Augusta's expecting me for supper. Join us, won't you? Then we'll go to the opera. I'm showing *Who's Who*. It's a comedy—you'll love it."

Quillan looked once again at the fool still standing there. Then he whistled for Sam and followed Horace Tabor.

Augusta's face was long and plain, her dark hair pulled starkly back with a smattering of small circular curls flattened to her forehead. She was not a handsome woman, but he'd heard she had a head for business and courage to match any man's. Quillan admired her in the same way he admired Mae.

"Quillan, my wife, Augusta. She was the first woman in Lake County, when Oro City was nothing but a handful of tents. The men banded together to build her a cabin, which she promptly made into a store."

Quillan assessed the woman whose hand he took respectfully. He suspected she was at least half behind Horace Tabor's success. She directed him to a place at the table to Tabor's right. He took his seat and watched her carry several covered dishes to the table.

"Nice try with those boys." Tabor settled into his place and arranged his vest. "Not that it'll have any lasting effect." He turned to Augusta, who took her place on his left. "Quillan broke up a gang tormenting JoJo."

"You remind me of Horace." She laid a hand on her husband's arm. "Doesn't he, Hod?"

"He does. Same fire, same grit."

"Less hot air." She almost smiled.

Quillan returned the sentiment with a half smile of his own.

Tabor took the ribbing with his usual good nature, then sobered. "Softhearted like me, too. Heard what you did for the Shultzes."

Quillan felt suddenly uneasy. "Kids were starving. Nothing more than anyone would do."

"That's where you're wrong." Tabor eyed him through his monocle. "You could do better than freighting, Quillan. Though in my own self-interest, I hope you don't."

Thankful for the change of subject, Quillan nodded. "Plenty of freighters in Leadville, Mr. Tabor." And with the cold deepening every night, he was not long for Leadville himself.

"For heaven's sakes, man, call me Hod. Everyone does." He clapped Quillan's shoulder. "And as for that, there's freighters and there's freighters. Take old Chicken Bill." He laughed until he snorted, though Quillan had yet to know which Chicken Bill story he'd be treated to.

Tabor swiped a hand over his mouth. "Old Chicken Bill. Never knew what he'd turn up with. Heard about the chickens?"

"The ones that froze, or the ones whose feathers he found in place of his ore?"

"Aw," Tabor clapped him again. "I suppose you've heard them all."

"Bill isn't actually a freighter."

"Privateer, more like. You know he sold me the Matchless? Salted it first, of course. I knew that from the start." He tossed Sam a chunk of bone.

"Sure you did, Hod," Augusta said.

He puffed his mustache out, offended. "I only made out that I didn't, for the men to have a good laugh. Few enough good laughs around here. A man bamboozling Horace Tabor—now, that's a good one. But I'll be laughing last. That mine's a beaut, Quillan. It'll make my fortune."

"Again." Quillan half smiled.

Tabor guffawed. "Yes, again! Oh, there's no place like Leadville to make your fortune. You stick by me and watch. Better yet, jump in yourself."

"No thanks, I already have a mine."

"You have." Tabor crowded the table. "What mine?"

"The New Boundless. In Crystal."

"Crystal!"

"That's right."

Augusta adjusted her circular spectacles. "Then what are you doing in Leadville, Quillan?"

"Freighting, ma'am."

"Mine's busted, eh?" Tabor looked sympathetic.

"No. Last I heard it was doing well. Producing nearly a thousand dollars a day, eight thousand ounces of silver per ton. Even an occasional pocket of gold leaf."

For the first time that evening Tabor was quiet. "And you're here hauling giant powder to the Matchless?"

Quillan shrugged. "Word is, the Matchless does twice that in a day."

"That it does, my boy. But that's not the point."

Quillan shook his head, knowing what was coming next. "I'm not a miner, never intended to be. My name's on the deed, but it's more of a mishap than anything else."

Tabor looked at his wife. "I told you there was more than meets the eye with Quillan, didn't I?"

"You did."

Horace hunched forward over the table. "What keeps you in Leadville, when you've a perfectly good mine in Crystal, even if you aren't a miner?"

Augusta did smile now. "That's no mystery, Hod. He's looking for a wife."

Quillan started. He did not need the conversation to go that way.

"Is that so? Looking for a Leadville lady to make your own?"

" 'Fraid not."

"Don't tell me; you've got one of those already also."

Quillan felt distinctly uncomfortable. Say no now, and the Tabors would be introducing him to every eligible damsel in Leadville. "Yes, sir, I do."

Again Tabor was silent. Then he exploded with mirth. "By george, she must be one for the history books! Cross-eyed is she? Snake-tongued? Must be ugly as a walleyed pike for you to run off and hide."

Quillan didn't answer. He felt a fierce desire to defend Carina, but that would only bring more questions.

He quirked his mouth slightly and Tabor took it for assent.

Augusta, however, was not put off. "That's tasteless, Hod. Of course his bride is comely. He must have his own reasons for leaving her behind. Maybe he finds Crystal a safer place?"

"Crystal safer? Where they hang men like hams?" Tabor smacked his hands on the table.

"We've done our share of hangings." Augusta gave him a pointed look.

"She has friends in Crystal." Quillan surprised himself by speaking. "She has a house."

Tabor lowered an eyebrow and puzzled him. "You're an enigma, Quillan."

"Just doing my job." Both Tabor and Augusta eyed him, but he offered no more. Carina was no one's business but his, and if she'd just come to her senses, she wouldn't be his any longer.

Sunday went better than Carina had hoped, and partly because Mae knew better than she the reality of such an endeavor. She opened her dining room as well as Carina's and between them they served from noon until six, when not a single noodle was left. Èmie had wanted to help, but Carina refused her.

"Make dinner for your uncle and your doctor. Leave me alone." Carina had laughed, but she almost regretted it by the end of the night when her feet were aching to the shin and her back was one long pain.

She collapsed into a chair beside Mae. Their gaze met, and they burst into laughter. "I don't know if I'm giddy or pazza." Carina pressed the back of her arm to her forehead.

"Both," Mae said, wiping the tears from her eyes. "But landsakes, that was something."

Carina dropped her arm. "I can't do it every week."

"Do you know how many we served?"

Carina shook her head. "I lost count by two o'clock."

"That long?"

Carina nodded, hiking up her skirts and rubbing her lower leg. The pain was kin to the exhaustion, but she felt radiant inside. The simple gratitude and appreciation she'd seen in the men's faces had warmed her, and she glowed with it still. Not even the success of the regular nights compared.

"Oh, Mae, it was *grande*."

"Yes, indeed."

"Once a month. I think I could handle once a month."

Mae groaned.

Eleven

Each day is a new challenge that strengthens me.
I am more alive in Crystal than I have ever been.
But for what am I being honed?
—Carina

ONE WEEK LATER CARINA rode up the gulch on a glorious October Sunday afternoon with Alex Makepeace beside her on his steeldust stallion. The air was keen enough to nip her nose, but it drew no fog from her breath. The sun shone brightly but had lost its sting. Very soon winter would hold sway over the mountains.

Carina looked at the powerful gray steed beside her own small mare. "Where did you get your horse, Mr. Makepeace?"

"New York. Isn't he a beaut?"

"He is. My papa would admire him."

Mr. Makepeace looked pleased. "Where is your papa now?"

Carina sighed. She had tried twice to pen a letter to her family. Both times it had started well until she tried to speak of her marriage. What could she say? She couldn't bring herself to lie about something so important. She could gloss over Crystal's deficiencies and even tell them of her success as a restaurateur. But she couldn't explain her marriage when she didn't understand it herself.

"My papa is in Sonoma, California. Do you know it? Sun-swept hillsides thick with vines, grapes turning plump and ripe, and the harvest . . . Oh, Mr. Makepeace, the harvest." She described the work when all gathered to pick the grapes to make the wine. The sharp knives with which they snicked the branches off and laid them in the crates. The huge vats in which they crushed the grapes by foot, the work itself a dance *and* the music to which they danced! Her heart ached as she spoke with such longing to see and hear and smell the crushing grapes, the foods cooking for the feasting, the rich aroma of the land itself as it surrendered its treasure.

So swept up was she in her memories that she only noticed when she finished how directly Alex Makepeace was watching her. She flushed and turned aside. "I suppose I sound like every homesick woman."

"Mr. Shepard brought you here, away from all that?"

How easy it would be to say yes, to place the blame of her loneliness on Quillan. But she shook her head. "I brought myself."

She saw his brows rise with ill-concealed amazement. No, he would not have surmised that a woman of refinement would come to Crystal City of her own volition. But once again he exercised tact. He would not ask, and she offered no more.

She pointed ahead of them. "Had you come here before the flood, Mr. Makepeace, you would have seen Placerville in this valley."

"Oh?"

"You know Placer was the first camp in this gulch?"

"Yes. But I didn't know exactly where it lay."

She waved her arm over the area as they passed. "All through here were the placer mines with the sluice boxes rotting and the gray buildings filled with ghosts." She smiled at this last comment.

"Was it all placer mining? Shoveling gold from the stream-bed gravel?"

"There were two hard-rock mines. The Gold Creek Mine up the way." She pointed toward the path that led up the steep mountainside. "And . . . my husband's other mine."

"Your husband's? I had the impression he didn't mine, hadn't ever mined."

"He didn't. It was his father's mine."

Mr. Makepeace whistled. "Must have been a piece of work to blast these hills before the Burleigh. He had a crew?"

"He worked it himself. His name was Wolf."

"German descent?"

She shrugged. "I doubt we'll ever know. The Sioux named him Wolf when they found him orphaned. Cries Like a Wolf, they named him."

He looked up the mountain, taking her words in stride. They would not haunt Mr. Makepeace, not conjure feelings of fear and sadness. Wolf was nothing to him but a curiosity.

"Want to show me?"

She shrugged. "There's not much to see. Just a hole and a shaft. The shaft is very deep."

"It can't be that deep, one man working alone through this kind of bedrock."

"It's deep, I assure you. I fell down part of it to a ledge. The rest went forever."

He smiled. "I'm sure it felt that way."

She turned Daisy. "Come, I'll show you."

Approaching the circular landing outside the Rose Legacy Mine, Carina eyed the burnt stone foundation that had been their small cabin. She hoped Mr. Makepeace didn't ask about that. She already felt uncertain bringing a stranger to this place.

They dismounted and Alex Makepeace headed directly for the mine. The drift was short as she'd told him. She followed him inside six paces, then said, "You're near the shaft now."

He lit a match and surveyed his surroundings. She went into the tiny anteroom and brought out a handful of candles, which Quillan had found when he rescued her from the shaft. Mr. Makepeace lit all three and held them together over the shaft, studying the timbered sides, the ledge, and the deep shaft, just as she'd said.

He whistled. "Well, we're both right."

"Oh?" She leaned over just enough to make out the ledge that had saved her falling down forever.

"That ledge is the floor of the shaft, as far as this Wolf blasted on his own. From there, he must have broken through to some subterranean cave or it gave way on its own."

"You're saying there's a cave beneath the shaft?"

"Listen."

She got very still and heard the faint dripping that had sounded so clear when she was in the shaft. She also heard a soft moaning like the wind over the strings of a guitar.

"Water probably means a limestone cave. The wind signals an outside opening somewhere. I don't think it's this shaft. See how still the candle flame is?" Mr.

Makepeace leaned closer to the opening, studying the yawning darkness.

Carina tried to see over his shoulder, but the candle-light was swallowed too soon.

"Wish I had a lantern." He looked up hopefully, but Carina shook her head.

"Well, I do have a rope." He stood up.

"You don't mean to go down there."

He shrugged. "To the ledge at least. I want to see from there."

"Mr. Makepeace . . ."

"Don't worry. I've been down holes two thousand feet deep."

She looked skeptical.

"Oh yes. The shafts in Cornwall are something to see."

"But you don't know what's down there." She swung her hand over the shaft.

"But I'd like to. Mrs. Shepard, a cave like that is just asking to be explored."

"It's not asking me."

He laughed. "Well, it's calling my name with every sigh and moan. Here, hold these." He handed her the three candles bunched together. The wax was dripping freely now, and she tipped them forward to keep from burning her hand.

Alex Makepeace went out to their horses and returned a moment later with the length of rope from his saddle. "Now then, I'll just make it fast . . ." He searched about and located the spikes Quillan had driven into the post to climb down to Carina.

She watched him tie a double hitch to make the rope fast around the spikes. He tugged once, then again harder. Seemingly satisfied, he took the candles and extinguished them with a strong puff. The drift was plunged into darkness that seemed darker than before. Carina strained to make out his movements at the edge of the shaft.

"Well, here goes."

Her eyes adjusted enough to observe him lower himself over the edge. Watching him, Carina felt a flicker of her old fear, but she supposed some reluctance regarding heights was normal. She dropped to her knees beside the shaft, listening to the efforts of his climb. Then she heard him land with a muffled grunt. She waited, and a minute later the snick of a match broke the quiet, and its tiny flame ignited the candlewicks one by one.

From her vantage, it was Mr. Makepeace illuminated, but from his? What did he see? She leaned farther, curious in spite of herself. His rope extended beyond the ledge, into the shaft and the darkness. With one hand gripping the rope, Mr. Makepeace stretched onto his stomach and lowered the candles into the gap.

"Seems to be a subterranean well almost directly beneath, but I can see a surface to the right, and a chamber of some sort. Rather large, I'd guess. Substantial speleothem formation, from what I can make out."

His voice had hollowed when he dropped low, and Carina caught a faint echo of his words. The cave must be sizeable. "Please be careful, Mr. Makepeace. I'm not up to carrying you out."

He laughed. "Don't worry. Think I'll let myself down a ways, see what it feels like inside."

"Maybe you should wait for a lantern. We can come again next week." Carina felt a sudden chill as Mr. Makepeace made a series of knots in the rope.

"What are you doing?"

"Won't have a wall to brace against. Giving myself some footholds."

"Mr. Makepeace . . ." Another shiver climbed her spine. "Please come up now."

"Don't worry, Mrs. Shepard. I'll just be a minute." As he spoke he extinguished the candles again and disappeared.

Carina strained her eyes but could make out nothing but the gaping darkness. *Dio. Signore. Il Padre Eterno.* The words throbbed in her mind, but she didn't break the silence with them. The only sound was the straining below and the scrape of the rope.

"Some slight air movement." Mr. Makepeace's voice sounded unnatural wafting up the shaft. It echoed hugely, and she guessed the space he'd entered must be large indeed. She didn't care. She just wanted him to climb back out. Her back felt tense, and she gripped her hands together.

"Can't reach the floor." His voice sounded hollow and too far away.

"Come back now, Mr. Makepeace." Her own voice sounded foreign thrown down the shaft that way. It seemed to wander off, then echo back uncertainly. It increased her discomfort. Was she reliving her fear from being trapped in the shaft?

"Per piacere," she murmured. And then she heard him climbing back, the grunts of his effort music to her ears. She heard him on the ledge; then once again the rope went taut as he scaled the side of the shaft and pulled himself to the floor where she crouched. In the dimness, she saw him untie the rope and coil it without speaking.

"Are you satisfied, Mr. Makepeace?"

He seemed to only then realize she was there still.

He turned. "Mrs. Shepard, I would very much like to come back with more rope and light."

"Why? What did you see?"

"I couldn't see anything in the darkness. It felt vast, but the senses are easily put off when sight is obliterated. Still, this could be a wonderful geological find." With the rope flung over his shoulder, he took her elbow and led her out. "I'd like to come tomorrow."

The sunlight was blinding, and Carina winced. "But don't you think we should leave it alone? My husband—"

"Isn't here to say one way or the other."

She could hardly explain Quillan's feelings about the Rose Legacy. Was he burdened by the dark presence of painful memories?

"Mrs. Shepard, as a geological engineer, I simply can't ignore a treasure like this. I'll tell no one, if that's your concern. I know your husband is a private man."

Private to the point of secretive. Did anyone really know him? She looked at Alex Makepeace's earnest face.

In his subdued way, he was beseeching her. "I give you my word that no one shall know about this but us two. Come with me tomorrow, and we'll see what's inside that cavern. Think of it, Mrs. Shepard. You could lay eyes on something no human has seen before."

Her throat went dry. "You mean go down the shaft myself?"

"Of course. I'll rig you a harness. You won't have to climb."

"But, Mr. Makepeace—"

He laughed suddenly. "Don't look as though you've seen a ghost. It's only a suggestion. I'll go alone if you prefer."

She saw that he had somehow traversed the point of

whether they would go or not. "I don't know what I prefer."

"Then allow me to show you one of nature's wonders."

Carina was shaking her head, but his smile was so convincing that she nodded instead. It was silly in the sunlight to think of ghosts and forces of darkness, things imagined in the recesses of the mine. Surely Quillan would want to know what lay beneath Wolf's shaft. And a flicker of her own curiosity stirred. "All right, Mr. Makepeace. If you insist. But we must go early so I'll have time to prepare my menu for the night."

"As soon as there's light to ride by. Inside it won't matter how bright the day."

She wished he hadn't reminded her.

Quillan felt the rope dig into his back, but against his chest was Carina's softness. She whimpered as he strained against the rope, hoisting them up with muscles already pushed beyond their strength. The shaft wouldn't end, and his arms throbbed and bunched, cramping and shaking, and all the while Mrs. Shepard was laughing.

"You'll never be anything but a savage like your father." And the laugh. The diabolical laugh.

One hand slipped, the flesh of his palm burning. Carina whimpered again, and suddenly the rope that bound them snapped. He lurched, grasping for her, but she slipped away and fell down the shaft, into the darkness, like a small white bird with raven hair.

"Carina!" His muscles cramped and he fell, the air rushing by bitter cold, freezing him stiff, rendering him mute. The darkness was complete.

"Quillan." Light streamed in, and Quillan opened his eyes to Horace Tabor.

"What are you trying to do? Freeze to death?" Tabor's breath made a cloud when he spoke.

Quillan sat up, teeth chattering. He was stiff and sore with cold and shaking from the dream. He bunched his blankets against his chest and stared at Horace Tabor as he might an apparition from beyond the grave.

"Great scott, man! This isn't weather for a beast to sleep out in." He patted Sam's head when he whined his agreement.

Quillan allowed Tabor to help him stand. The temperature must have plummeted in the night, and he was weak with cold. Stupid. He could have frozen in his tent, with no one the wiser.

"Come on. Augusta can warm your insides with coffee and I'll make a fire to blaze the chill from your bones."

Quillan walked stiffly beside him with Sam at his heels. Why Horace Tabor should have concerned himself with one stupid freighter too stubborn to sleep in the hotel, where some meager warmth would have kept his body temperature at a functioning level, was beyond him.

"Come on, my boy. Not much farther."

Quillan wondered if he'd ever been called "my boy." Alan, of course, had designated him "boyo," and Cain on occasion had called him son. Each time it had sent a liquid warmth through Quillan. This wasn't like that, but it eased something frozen inside. Tabor cared about him. Horace Tabor, silver baron, Leadville king.

Quillan shook his head. His mind was wandering. Soon he'd be muttering like a fool. He looked at Horace

Tabor, who was half supporting him. "Temperature must have dropped."

Tabor spoke around his stump of cigar. "What clued you in?"

Quillan hadn't noticed the cigar. Now the whiff of it reached his brain. One sense functioning. No, three; he could see and hear as well. Now if he could just feel. They reached Tabor's store and Augusta met them at the door.

"Bring him this way."

With Sam at his feet, the Tabors bundled Quillan with blankets and sat him on a bench before the iron potbelly stove. Augusta appeared again with a cup of steaming coffee. "Easy, now. It's hot enough to burn."

Quillan sipped carefully, then held the cup where the steam could thaw his face. It was only October, but sometimes a freeze like this came early. Might mean a long, hard winter. He sipped again, feeling the coffee's heat all the way to his stomach.

Tabor eased down on the bench beside him. "Better now?"

Quillan nodded.

"These mountains do take a man by surprise. But I'd thought you'd been around awhile."

Quillan scowled into his cup. "I knew the season was getting chancy. Just didn't act in time." He drank. "Thanks."

Tabor rested his elbows on his thighs. "Maybe it's time you went home to your house and your wife."

Sound advice, and if anything about his situation had been as normal as Tabor made it seem, he would do just that. Actually, he had to go. He knew it. He couldn't leave Carina through the winter without seeing to her needs at least once more.

The thought brought a pain between his temples, and he closed his eyes, breathing the steam from his cup. The dream was still fresh enough to bring her image clearly to mind. She'd felt so soft and helpless, exactly as she'd felt when he really had climbed the shaft with her tied against him.

His muscles had truly ached after first fighting the floodwaters. But he had drawn her safely out. He hadn't dropped her, hadn't lost her to the darkness. The mocking laugh receded to a vague corner of his mind, but the headache remained. What should he do? What could he do?

"I suppose you're right." He glanced at Horace Tabor.

"There's a time for getting rich and a season for enjoying it. I don't doubt you've amassed enough to see you through the snows."

Quillan shrugged.

Tabor laughed. "What I've paid you alone should make your little lady cozy enough to make it worth staying home." He nudged Quillan in the ribs.

Quillan looked out the store window at the snow falling like fat, lumpy chickens settling down to roost. "Can't head home in this." And it was just as well, because he felt a chill starting inside. His head sounded like rushing water and his throat burned, but not with the coffee. He'd been sick only once that he could recall; then sheer terror had kept him hale ever since.

The symptoms had been similar to what he felt now. But Mrs. Shepard had convinced him that it was no more than he deserved, and as soon as he succumbed he would burn. He'd lain for days with fever and believed every word. If he once gave up the fight, his flesh would burn black just like Wolf's and Rose's, and he'd burn for all eternity.

Quillan started to shiver, even though he'd warmed himself adequately. Under the blankets he began to sweat, though the chill passed up his spine. He felt Augusta's hand on his forehead, thought he saw her nod to Horace before everything got swimmy, and he coughed a raw, chesty cough.

Carina looked out at the snow with mingled disappointment and relief. Mr. Makepeace would not be exploring the cave today. But he did come over a short while later to speak his disappointment.

"Have you any idea how long it will last?" He frowned at the snow surrounding him like curious moths as he stood on her stoop.

"I haven't spent a winter here, Mr. Makepeace. Your guess is as good as mine. One thing I do know, you don't go far from home once it starts." She thought of the blizzard she and Quillan had survived together. It had started as innocently as this one but turned deadly soon enough. Where was Quillan now? Not on the road, surely.

"No, I wouldn't think so." He shook his head heavily. "Know anyone who plays chess?"

Carina smiled at Mr. Makepeace's amiable shift in temper. "I don't know. Alan Tavish plays checkers; perhaps he also plays chess."

He glanced behind her into the small single room. "Will you be all right in there alone?"

She raised a brow. "Would you join me?"

He opened his mouth and paused, uncertain how to take her comment until he saw the amusement in her eyes. "Only if your life depended on it, thereby saving both your virtue and my neck. I rather doubt Mr. Shepard is as lax in his care for you as he is for mine."

Carina almost corrected his misconception but held her tongue. "Oh sì, he is like a watchdog."

He eyed her staidly. "Quite. Well, then, I know when I'm beaten. But at the first thaw we'll take that cave by storm."

On a snowy morning with a warm stove behind her and a day of cooking ahead and Mr. Makepeace's confident smile, she laughed. "Bene. We will take it."

Quillan couldn't stop the dreams. He was a youth again, smarting from a recent caning and wondering what he was supposed to have done this time. He wouldn't refute it. He'd promised himself that long ago. He no longer told his side, no longer countered the lies. He could look for no quarter, and his denials only made it worse, piling the supposed sin of false witness upon whatever accusations already stood to his account.

But he liked to know for what he'd been punished. He'd determined to take up whatever vice it was assumed he practiced. If he was accused and punished for it, then he planned to do it in earnest. That was his pact with the devil, who, regardless of Reverend Shepard's warnings, seemed the lesser of the evils in Quillan's life.

Only this time he hadn't been told. Reverend Shepard had merely taken him aside, rod in hand. With a stern, sorrowing face, he'd used pain to purge the sin. And Quillan was determined to learn what new depravity he could indulge in. But first he had to shake the cough.

It tore his throat down to his chest. He heard voices.

An infection of the bronchi. Fever's too high. *For lo, thine enemies, O Lord, for lo, thine enemies shall perish; all the workers of iniquity shall be scattered.* Quillan felt himself being scattered by the wind. The wind was so cold. Then why did he sweat? He was too close to the sun.

He clasps the crag with crooked hands;
Close to the sun in lonely lands,
Ring'd with the azure world, he stands.
The wrinkled sea beneath him crawls;
He watches from his mountain walls,
And like a thunderbolt he falls.

Quillan felt the plunge. Into a lake of fire. An eternity of flame. *And now also the ax is laid unto the root of the trees: therefore every tree which bringeth not good fruit is hewn down, and cast into the fire.* Quillan felt the heat. He was in the bed between his parents. The flames surrounded and engulfed them. He clung to his mother, but even as he clung, her flesh peeled from the bones, and he looked into the skeletal hollows of her eyes.

He hollered, and a hand came down on his forehead. Something cool and damp, a cloth. It was pressed to his lips and he sucked. *And he made him to suck honey out of the rock, and oil out of the flinty rock.* It was neither honey nor oil, but cool fresh water he sucked. *My doctrine shall drop as the rain, my speech shall distill as the dew, as the small rain upon the tender herd, as the showers upon the grass.*

Quillan trembled with the sheer relief. He felt so weak. Utterly helpless. *For when we were yet without strength, in due time Christ died for the ungodly . . . for the ungodly . . . for the ungodly.* Cain's voice, but Quillan couldn't conjure his face. How could he have forgotten? He groaned.

Again the hand soothed his forehead. *Christ died for*

the ungodly. But Cain died for the ungodly as well. Cain died for him. Quillan forced his eyes open. It was the only way to stop the thoughts. A woman hovered near, large and long of face. Her small oval eyeglasses caught the light. Augusta Tabor.

Now he could put himself inside a place as well. Leadville. He was still in Leadville. Hell receded.

"Feeling stronger, are you?"

He felt weak as a bum lamb.

"Here, let's try some broth." She raised his head and spooned liquid between his lips. He swallowed, but his stomach revolted, and he spewed it back into the cloth she held ready. Then he coughed, and he knew he was coughing out the very tissues of his throat. He dropped back to the bed, shaking with chills.

She wrapped him tighter. "Sleep, then. Just sleep."

And now he remembered. Mrs. Shepard had accused him of visiting the bawdy house. He overheard the reverend's gentle questioning. Was she certain? And her reply: *"What do you expect when he sprang from the loins of a harlot?"* Quillan shook with rage at this particular accusation.

At fourteen, with his body acting foreign and unpredictable, he knew well enough what she was suggesting—the one thing he would never do. The one vice never added to his list. He would never look upon nor touch that sort of woman. His mother's sort of woman. Had she guessed? Did Mrs. Shepard know this was one time she would win? Or did she mean to drive him to that sin, to make him like Wolf. . . .

He thrashed. He couldn't let her win. He thought again of his friend, of his plan to shake the dust of Laramie from his heels, to seek reckless adventure. Quillan would go. All he need do was meet Shane at the bank while he made his withdrawal. Then they'd be off for good.

Off for good. He'd gone off, all right. But not before his friend had left him to take the fall for the robbery, before the judge had warned him off his wild ways with a stern injunction to mend himself or learn the full power of the law. Quillan kept his breath slight to resist the cough clawing its way up his throat. If only he could ward off the memories.

The storm passed as quickly as it came. The next day the sky was clear, though the temperature remained harsh. It warmed substantially by the third day, though when Mr. Makepeace came to her door, Carina still felt a bite in the air. But with the clear skies, she knew he would not be put off again. She bundled into her coat and the caramel kidskin gloves Quillan had given her. She was ready.

Together they rode to the Rose Legacy, Mr. Makepeace well equipped with rope, lantern, a blanket, even a kit of the tools and gadgetry of his trade, she assumed. He lit the lantern at the top of the shaft and gave it to her to hold. "We'll leave that burning up here, though I shouldn't with all this ancient timbering."

"What will we use for light down there?"

He held up two tin-encircled candleholders. "Once we're down we'll light these. We'll have to descend in darkness, though."

Carina looked into the shaft. Alex Makepeace had assured her the rope would hold firm and she would not plunge to the bottom of the well, if it even had a bottom. But the thought of sinking into that blackness . . .

He took the lantern and set it firmly on the floor of

the drift at the mouth of the shaft. "Now, step into this." He held out the harness.

Beneath her fur-trimmed coat, Carina wore the miner's pants and woolen shirt she had bought to disguise herself before the vigilantes rid the town of the roughs. She stuffed one panted leg through the rope harness, then the other.

Mr. Makepeace worked it up around her waist and tugged it tight. "Now take hold of this section, and let yourself over the side. I'll lower you slowly."

"I'm to go first?"

"How else will I let you down?" He smiled indulgently.

She looked at the hole again. "You'll come right behind?"

"Right behind."

"Madonna mia, I must be pazza." Carina stepped to the edge while Mr. Makepeace winched the rope over a thick timber, then braced his legs.

"All right. Down over the edge there."

Carina went to her knees, signed herself with the cross, then swung her legs over the plummeting darkness. She slid down to her belly and felt Mr. Makepeace take up the slack. Then she was clinging to the rope and walking down the timbers. She reached the ledge, balanced there for a minute, then swung down into the space of the cavern below.

Before God's healing, she would have fainted. Even now the plunge into nothingness made her heart rush with fear. The darkness was complete. It seemed she hung there forever, disoriented and confused. Then her feet touched, and she gave a little cry.

"I'm down! I'm on the ground!" Her voice echoed mightily.

Mr. Makepeace's answer sounded weak and far. She felt her rope grow taut as he made it fast up above. She would have to climb out of the harness to go anywhere at all. But she had no intention of taking one step without him. How could she when there was no up or down or left or right?

The cavern was about the same temperature as outside. There was no feel of moving air, but she heard a soft moan and prayed it was the wind, though it had a human quality that sent a shiver through her. A minute later she heard Alex Makepeace begin his climb down. He couldn't come soon enough.

Behind her somewhere water dripped, and to her left the subterranean well continued its plunge into the earth. If she dared, she'd drop a pebble and listen for its plunk. But she didn't dare. There was a watchfulness in the silence, almost a malevolence. What was down there did not want to be disturbed.

She crossed herself and said the Paternoster with silently moving lips. Had she the strength she would climb back up before Mr. Makepeace reached bottom and convinced her otherwise. But already she felt and heard his approach. Even when he was directly above her, she couldn't see him.

He landed beside her. "All fine?"

She nodded, then realized how foolish that was when they could not see each other standing only a foot apart. "Yes." Again her voice was caught up into the cavernous hollows. Something rustled overhead.

She heard the scratch of a lucifer match and the tiny white blaze flared up, then sank to a small yellow glow as Mr. Makepeace held it to the candle wick inside one tin holder. The rustling overhead increased, and something brushed by her with the smell of decay. She cried out, and the air was filled with a flapping wind. She grasped for Mr. Makepeace, and he caught her arm firmly.

"Bats. Don't worry." He held the candle up, watching the cloud swirl up and away. "That'll be the direction of our wind hole, then."

"Take me up now." Carina's voice was urgent.

He turned back to her with the candlelight illuminating his disappointment. "Mrs. Shepard. You won't be put off by a few bats, will you? They're harmless. Here, let me free you from that harness."

Against her better judgment and the racing of her heart, Carina climbed free of the rope. Mr. Makepeace lit the second candle and tucked the metal handle into her hand. The tin cupping around the flame kept it from extinguishing when she swept it from left to right before her, scrutinizing the shadowed depths all about.

Long spikes hung from the ceiling, and matching ones poked up from the floor like the fangs of some earth monster waiting to devour them. Some of the teeth met and formed lumpy pillars that had a sheen in the candlelight. She took a step and found the base of the cave soft and slimy. She looked down.

"Guano, I'm afraid. Bat droppings." Mr. Makepeace looked as though he knew the reaction that news would receive.

"I'm not enjoying this, Mr. Makepeace."

Unfortunately that amused him, and he laughed softly. "Bear with me a bit. You might surprise yourself."

"I have surprised myself. I'm down here, aren't I? Do you think I do this every day?"

"Hardly." He started toward the near wall.

Carina followed closer than his shadow. When he

raised his candle she saw what appeared to be a waterfall frozen in place.

"Flowstone. A common limestone formation. The water seeping down this wall deposits its minerals and over time they solidify into sheets and falls such as this one."

"It's beautiful." Carina surprised herself with that sentiment.

He turned. "Same with the stalactites and stalagmites and all the speleothem you see. Water seepage and mineral deposits forming the spikes and columns. A natural miracle of nature. God's creative force continues."

Carina was reminded of Father Antoine's views of nature. *God is all and in all.* She felt a measure of confidence. "Have you seen many caves?"

"My share." He raised his candle to throw light into the shadows above.

Looking up, Carina was thankful the bats had flown. She would not want them hanging over her head. As it was, the vaulted depths of the cavern were shadowed and mysterious. The moan came again, and she took a step closer to Mr. Makepeace.

"Shall we find that mouth?"

"I don't think so." She shuddered, wishing he hadn't called it a mouth.

"Let's try this way. The bats would have flown toward an exit."

"It could be no more than a hole in the roof."

"And probably is." He started forward.

Carina held her candle like a sword, warding off the darkness. She had no choice but to follow. As they walked, the cave floor rose, or the ceiling lowered. If the breadth of the cave changed she couldn't tell because their small flames lit only their immediate passage.

They were definitely climbing. Carina could feel the incline. The moan came louder this time, and the floor dropped sharply into the shape of a basin. The walls came together and enclosed it, narrowing at the top like a teardrop. Carina realized it wasn't just her candlelight that lit this space, but a dim filtered light from above.

She followed Mr. Makepeace into the center of the basin, their whole attention on the opening that angled up from the ceiling, allowing some small light but offering no view of the outside. Then Carina dropped her gaze and held her candle out toward the walls. Her breath stopped in her chest. The walls were covered with paintings in ochre, brown, reds, and black. She circled slowly and realized Mr. Makepeace had followed her lead.

He let out a slow whistle. "Must be a tribal holy place or something like that."

But Carina had stopped turning, transfixed by one scene near the entrance to the basin. There was a crude likeness of a Conestoga wagon, figures of people with ochre-painted skin and others with red. She no longer had to wonder from what details Father Antoine had saved her. She saw the fate of the infant daughter, the mother, the father clearly depicted on the wall. Off to the side, and recurring in every scene of the mural, was a pale wolf.

Carina brought a hand to her throat. They'd found Wolf's diary.

Carina's throat felt dry and tight as she studied each scene in sequence. It amazed her, the emotion Wolf had portrayed with the simple figures—scenes of cruelty, some of pastoral peace, but many more of violence. No wonder Father Antoine believed Wolf incapable of violence. Anyone who had seen so much and carried the pain of it inside so as to paint these . . . Her breath came out in a mournful sigh.

Mr. Makepeace was instantly solicitous. "Probably ritual pictures. Symbolic, Mrs. Shepard, not real."

She shook her head. As quickly as she could, and sparing some details, Carina told Mr. Makepeace about Wolf. She told him how he had come to Placerville the same night as Rose, Quillan's mother, and how they had made their home beside the mine. How he had tried to want gold, to need it, so he would be like others of his kind.

But she guessed now that this was where Wolf spent many of his hours. Had Rose known? Had she ever seen this place? These scenes of Wolf's life? Without knowing, Carina knew. No one had seen this but the two of them now, and the one who had mixed the paint and told the story.

She realized Mr. Makepeace had hold of her arm, and that she was shaking as she spoke. "No one must know of this." She turned beseeching eyes to Mr. Makepeace. "It's his tomb. His memorial."

He seemed to understand the gravity. "Of course, Mrs. Shepard. We could seal it off. . . ."

"No. Quillan might . . ." She had been about to say Quillan might want to see it, but would he? "It's not my decision. But we mustn't tell anyone this is here."

"I give you my word."

Carina looked into Mr. Makepeace's face and saw there his simple goodness. He was solid and trustworthy. Her heart suddenly ached. What would it be like to love a man such as Alex Makepeace? Already she had spent more time with him, seen more and learned more from him about her own husband's operation, and now . . .

She looked around the chamber once again. What must he think? Would he think Wolf a savage as Wolf's own son did? It was pazzo, this twisting of her thoughts. What did it matter what Alex Makepeace thought? "Maybe we should go back now. My candle's burning low."

"I have plenty of replacements. But I think you're right." He turned for the opening.

That was when Carina heard it. Perhaps it was a trick of the wind through the cave mouth high above, but the sound was like the howl of a wolf on a cold and frosty night, a howl of such longing and loneliness it pierced her heart and brought tears to her eyes. She cried softly as she followed Mr. Makepeace back through the guano-slimed cavern to the ropes.

Twelve

What I have seen haunts me.
My mind dwells on images painted on cavern walls.
And I wonder, if I painted my life, what would it look like?
—Carina

THE LIGHT SNOW BLOWING in his face did little to improve his mood as Quillan left his team with Alan and started for Carina's little house, Sam prancing at his ankles. It was obligatory, he told himself for the hundredth time. He couldn't let her go through the winter without seeing that she had whatever she'd need. One more trip with supplies could hold her until spring. And a winter in Crystal might be enough to convince her to leave once the roads became passable.

He felt amazingly up to anything himself. It was so good to be out of bed without a cough racking his chest. And the fever had done no worse than force him to take a much-needed rest. Still, he'd lain abed for a week and a half, and that was long enough. October was raggedly succumbing to winter as this current flurry proved, and he needed to find a place to spend it.

As Quillan turned the corner at Drake, a surge of

panic flooded his system. A crowd stood outside Carina's house. It took only seconds to realize the crowd was friendly and not some vigilante mob trying to lynch her, but his heart still hammered. He forced a slow white cloud through his lips and looked up at the starlit sky. Why would men be gathered outside her door at this time of the evening?

Then he noticed that her house was connected to Mae's by a short wall with a door in it. Through this door, four of the men waiting were admitted by Èmie Charboneau. What on earth? He stood puzzling as more foursomes were admitted and others exited.

Tired of wondering, he pushed through just as Alex Makepeace came out the door with Ben Masterson and two of the city trustees, Harold Black and Jerrod Hopkins. Makepeace spotted and hailed him. Quillan stepped aside to make room for them.

"Wonderful place your wife has." Ben Masterson placed his hat on his head as the others agreed.

Quillan tried not to look as stupid as he felt. "Yes." He nodded to Makepeace. "I'll see you in the morning for a report. On the mine."

Makepeace nodded back. "All right. Plenty of good news."

Quillan was already puzzling over Carina again and hardly heard him. What was she up to now? When he reached for the door, a couple of the men started to protest. Others hushed them with, "Quiet, you numbskull. That's her husband."

Her husband. *Her*, spoken with familiarity and near reverence. Quillan told Sam to stay, then stepped inside to find a hallway open to Mae's kitchen and long down behind Carina's cabin. As he stood there, Èmie Charboneau came from the kitchen with plates steaming. The aroma struck him dumb. Had Carina known he was coming? Had she cooked for him, to entice him, to trap him?

But Èmie passed with hardly a nod and started down the long hall. He followed her into a dining room set with six tables and a wonderful crackling fire. The aroma of rich spicy food filled the room, and he noted that every chair was filled with Crystal's best. Mine owners, store owners, trustees, and lawyers, even Judge Wallace and his wife.

He didn't see Carina, but she was in all of it, the elegance of the room, the fragrance of the fare, the warm and sophisticated atmosphere. Now he understood. This was what she was doing with the things they'd purchased in Fairplay. She hadn't cooked for him; she'd cooked for all these others.

It stung him. He'd come to think of her meals as a sort of private ceremony. Since the first one they'd enjoyed together at Mae's table, he had considered her efforts his to enjoy. He looked into the room, saw her food being devoured with gusto. Frowning, he let himself out the way he came.

As he passed through the crowd, he heard several guffaws. "Guess he didn't have his name in, boys." "Must not be on the special reservations, either." Laughter.

With a curt command to Sam, he stalked to Alan's livery and found his friend reading beneath the glow of an oil lamp.

Alan looked up. "Back so soon?"

"Since when does my wife operate a public eatery?"

Alan raised his cap and scratched his thinning gray hair. " 'Twas finished around about the start of October. Been all the talk since."

"How did she build it?"

"Ah, Quillan, I wouldn't be knowin' that. The lass hardly comes by now she's so busy."

Quillan nudged Sam out of the way, straddled a stool, and leaned his back against the wall. If Alan saw his scowl, so be it. He hadn't expected it would be easy to see Carina, but he certainly hadn't expected this. Should he wait until she was finished serving her crowd? Or could he walk into Mae's kitchen and find her with a plate ready for him?

After the men's comments, he wasn't so sure. What was this about names and special reservations? Was she in such demand? Again he felt the hot twisting inside. He was jealous, jealous for the others to be getting what should be his, what might be his if he'd been there to receive it. Instead she'd turned elsewhere. He forked his fingers into his hair and released a hard breath.

"Did ye see her, then?"

"No. The whole place is swarming."

"Aye." Alan tapped a pipe on the edge of his chair, then dug out the old tobacco. "There's some have a standing place at her tables."

"Who?"

"The mayor and Joe Turner and your Alex Makepeace."

Quillan frowned. "He eats there every night?"

"Has a place held for him."

What did he care? So Carina had done something with her time and abilities. He should laud her. He believed in work and in people making the most of themselves. Better she do that than sit pining.

Alan struck a match, wincing with the motion, then held the fire to the tobacco in his pipe. He puffed unsuccessfully at the stubborn tobacco, then was forced to strike a second match and try again. The reddened crab-apple knuckles were thicker than before, and Quillan watched the pain bloom in Alan's face as he held the second match steady.

"Have you seen the doctor for pain remedies?"

Alan shrugged. "Laudanum would take the edge and leave me in a stupor."

"Maybe there's something—"

"When I get so that I can't do me job, then I'll worry about the pain."

Quillan reached a hand to his shoulder. "I don't like to see you hurting."

"Aye." Alan covered the hand with his own palm. "Ye've a soft heart for the old men, Quillan. Ye were a good friend to Cain."

Quillan shook his head, lowering his chin. "I can't talk about it, about him." He eyed Cain's dog, trying not to picture the old man's hand in Sam's fur. *"You gotta get you a dawg."*

"He'd want ye to have a laugh for old times. Ye know he would."

The pain was sharp and brutal. It spread through Quillan's chest like a fiery flood erupting into tears. But he wouldn't let them fall. He'd learned too well to stop them, to control the pain, any pain. "Maybe someday." His voice was raw.

"See ye let that someday come. He's dancin' with the saints and angels. What right have ye to begrudge him?"

Quillan closed his eyes. "I don't begrudge him, Alan. I miss him."

"I miss him, too." Alan drew on the pipe, then released its sweet tobacco to the air. "But ye've a life to live, and he'd be the first to tell ye so."

"I'm living it, Alan."

"Ye know what he'd say about your driving the giant powder."

Quillan shrugged. "I'm through with that until the season changes. I won't blow up my team."

"What then? Are ye stayin' on?"

Quillan stood and paced the small space of Alan's room. "I don't know yet. I have options."

Alan puffed his pipe. For once he didn't start on about Carina and having children and making a home. Maybe he knew that wasn't likely with Carina's success. What need had she of children and a husband when she had men standing in the cold outside her door? Men whose names were on her special list.

Again the dragon twisted in his gut. And he was hungry. The whiffs of her marvelous meal had nearly driven him mad with it. But he wasn't about to walk in and beg for a table, not after the laughter he'd already brought on. He'd wait. No, he'd eat elsewhere.

It wasn't as though his wife's place was the only decent eatery in Crystal. Though to look at the men outside you might think it. He shook his head and stood. "I brought you some Irish, Alan. But I can't reach it until I've unloaded the rest. I'll dig it out in the morning."

"I'll not say ye nay." Alan puffed with a grin. Laudanum he might refuse, but never the Irish whiskey.

Quillan went to the hotel and ate Mrs. Barton's sweet-and-sour venison steak. It was sinfully satisfying, and Quillan congratulated himself. Let Carina feed the masses. He knew where to get a meal when he needed one. But once he'd finished, it still remained to go home.

Home? That little house wasn't his home. Why should he even think it? It was Carina's domain. And she was his wife. Therefore everything she had was his by right. Including her restaurant enterprise. How would she feel about that?

He swaggered a little as he walked with Sam staunchly beside him. What if he walked in and ordered them all out? How would that be? Would she take it submissively, posturing this new wifely demurring, or would she fly at him like the wasp she was, stinging with sharp words in two languages? The latter, he guessed.

Anyway, he had no need to order them out. There was no longer a crowd outside the door, and while a smattering exited, he stepped inside. Once again Èmie passed him in the hall, this time with a tray loaded with used dishes on her way back to Mae's kitchen.

He didn't doubt Carina knew by now that he was back. Èmie would have told her. Of course she would. What would Carina have answered? *"Oh sì, un gross'uomo. The big man has decided to come home?"*

He entered the dining room and saw that all the tables had been stripped but one, probably the one Èmie had just cleared. A short, dark-featured girl was sweeping around the tables rather poorly. She glanced up when he entered.

"I'ma sorry, we're finished for the night." Her accent was thick and reminiscent of the Italian market vendor in Fairplay.

Before he could answer, Carina spoke behind him. "That'll be all for tonight, Lucia. See Èmie for your wages."

"Sì, grazie," the girl mumbled, carrying the broom out with her.

He turned to face Carina. Her hair was tied back in a braid, but one strand of hair clung damply to her cheek. He guessed she'd left the washbasin to confront him.

"Are you hungry?"

"I ate." And a good thing, too, or she might have lured him to the kitchen and he'd have followed like a dumb beast. Did he imagine the disappointment that flickered in her eyes?

She walked to the table and tugged the last cloth off. "I'll just take this to Èmie." She was gone before he could object, or tell her she could do whatever she liked, or say anything at all. He kicked himself.

When she returned, she had removed her apron, and he noticed a dress he hadn't seen on her before. By the fit it had been tailored to her tiny waist and delicate stature, and he wondered how she had paid for it. Then he needn't have wondered. Her dining room was filled each night with paying customers if he'd heard the diners correctly. She could buy as many dresses as she liked.

"I came to see what you'd need to get you through the winter."

A small quiver of her lower lip showed that somehow he'd wounded her. What was wounding in that? But then her fire rose and she waved a hand. "I can obtain whatever I need."

Without you. She didn't say it, but the implication was clear. "How?"

"There are other freighters in Crystal."

Quillan probably knew every one of the traitors by name. "I bet you're being gouged."

"I am." She said it as though that pleased her, but he knew it couldn't because he'd seen her haggle, been haggled by her.

"As long as I'm here . . ."

"How long will that be?"

"What I meant is I may as well fix you up before I go." He wasn't sure what he expected, but her angry laugh did more to discomfit him than another response.

"Grazie, signore. You are compassion itself. *Veramente compatimento*. So responsible, so important, eh?" She shoved the wayward strand back from her eyes again.

He cocked his jaw to the side. "Look, Carina, I only came—"

"To fulfill your duty."

"I brought you chickens." His retort sounded infantile. He'd purchased the fowl in Leadville, thinking how pleased she'd be to have her own layers since eggs seemed to mean so much to her.

She put her hands to her hips. "You bring me chickens, but you are more chicken than they. At least they will stay." She was certainly showing her true colors tonight.

"Until something eats them," he fired back. "Or maybe you'll cook them yourself and serve them to the whole town."

"How many did you bring?"

"Six." He slacked his leg in the insolent stance he took when feeling attacked. Six chickens had seemed a treasure.

Now she scoffed. "Six chickens would hardly feed the first seating, not the town. I know. I've fed the town."

That thought irked. "Then I guess you don't need them." His arrow found its mark. Now she would have to relent, admit she wanted the fowl. He knew she did.

"Where are they, these chickens?" It was halfhearted at best.

"Warm in my wagon in Alan's livery."

"Perhaps you'll have time to unload them before you run away again."

"I don't run . . ." This was futile. It would gain them nothing to fight. What had set her off anyway? He gentled his manner. "Carina . . . I don't know what has you all worked up."

"Worked up?" She spread her hands in mock amazement. "Where did you eat?"

"What?"

"Tonight. Where did you eat?"

He shook his head dumbly. "At the hotel."

"Mrs. Barton fed you."

"She cooks at the hotel. I fed myself." He knew the difference after being spoon-fed by Augusta Tabor. He didn't tell Carina that.

"Every day I cook. Every night forty-eight men eat my food. But my own husband, he goes to the hotel."

He felt defensive. "I came here. The place was swarming. What did you expect?"

She shoved a chair into place at the table she'd stripped. "Expect? I expect nothing. I have no husband, only a man who brings me chickens."

His anger flared. "I offered to let you out of this."

She spun. "There. You've said it. No visit could be complete without your generous offer." She clenched her hands, and he guessed it took all her control not to fly at him.

The sight softened him. "It's no good, Carina." And the next words came before he could stop them. "I don't know how to love you."

She seemed to shrink even smaller. Her lip trembled, and her eyes glassed with tears. "You did once."

"That's not what I meant. That's . . . only part."

"It's a start." She took a step toward him.

Desire hit like a charge of giant powder. What was she trying to do? She took another step, and he grabbed her shoulders. "Is that what you want?" He stared into the dark, melting depths of her eyes, then gripped the back of her neck and kissed her hard.

If she resisted he couldn't tell, because he had swept her up into his arms and was bearing down on the small door at the end, which he guessed led to her room. He thrust it open, one intention consuming him. He was not gentle. All his rage and frustration vented, and it left him shaken and ashamed. He rolled aside, his conscience smarting. "I'm sorry."

Carina didn't speak.

He forked his fingers into the hair at the nape of his neck. "I didn't mean to treat you like a . . ."

She sat up, chest heaving with unspent tears. "Like a harlot?"

"Yes!" He hollered it, more angry with himself than he could remember being. He fumbled with his clothes.

"What do you know? What do you know about the heart of a harlot?"

Her arm swung past him and grasped a red leather book from the crate beside the bed. He almost hoped she would hit him with it. Instead, she shoved it into his chest.

"Here. This is the heart and soul of a harlot. Rose Annelise DeMornay. Your mother."

Quillan felt the breath leave him. He lifted and stared at the book, the nameplate proving her words. DeMornay. His mother's name was DeMornay? How did Carina . . . A fresh shame enveloped him. "Have you read it?" His voice was rust on iron.

"Sì."

He gripped the book, white knuckled. "You just don't stop, do you?"

"It was given to me. For our wedding."

"By whom?"

"Someone who cared for her."

He looked again at the finely tooled book, the leather old but quality, the name etched in brass, like the tiny key that hung from a ribbon through the center pages. His mother's diary. A harlot's diary. He ought to fling it from him, burn it. As she'd burned?

Stark anguish knifed through him. He staggered to his feet, grabbed his coat up from the floor. He looked once more at Carina, then left her.

Carina lay back, clasped in her own arms, and cried. More surely than Quillan's face, she knew his back, just as she'd seen it now, the honey brown mane tossed to his shoulders, the straight, stubborn stance. He was gone again, she knew. Maybe this time for good.

What had she expected? To provoke him into loving her, into caring? Her own temper, her own hurt at his going to Mrs. Barton had driven her; his rejection of everything she had to give him. No, not everything.

She touched her lips and gulped her tears, but they came again anyway. A start, she had said. This was no start for them. It was the end. She felt it in her heart. And she had given him Rose's journal. In anger she had given it, not as she'd wanted, to help him know his mother's love. No, she'd given it to strike back, to punish him.

She sank into the pillows. Now even Rose's words were lost to her. She clasped her hands at her throat. *Signore, forgive me.* She closed her eyes and prayed that

God would bring good from this. Then she cried herself to sleep.

Quillan left the chickens with Alan. The old man would see that Carina got them, and she could do as she pleased with the birds. What did he care if she diced them up for other men? He hunched himself against the renewed snow flurries, ignored Sam's whining, and steered his team for Denver.

He could winter there. Work was plentiful, and he had enough put by to live in style if he wanted to. He didn't. He'd take a room in a hotel, loosen a floorboard, and continue to stash his wealth. One day, he might equal Horace Tabor.

He wished it mattered. He put a hand beneath his coat, felt the diary pressed there to his chest. It was locked. He had yet to open one page. Maybe he never would. Maybe he only waited until he could throw it away as she'd thrown him, casting him off like so much unwanted rubbish, giving him to Mrs. Shepard.

Rose Annelise DeMornay. Did he care that he now had a name? At least on his mother's side. Did it change who he was? Did it change anything? He pulled up at the sight of a bogged freighter. The wagon listed heavily where the snow had softened the edge of the road and the wagon had slid down to the axle.

Quillan drove well shy of the edge himself, reined in his team, and dismounted. Without a word, he put a shoulder to the wagon and shoved when the freighter hollered to his team. The ore in the bed weighed tons, and Quillan felt like an ant striving against it. Again the freighter hollered; again Quillan shoved, leveraging himself and straining with every ounce of strength.

The wheel turned, rolled back, turned again. Kept turning. Quillan spun himself about and with both arms to the wagon kept the momentum moving forward until the wheel was free. Once settled on solid ground, the freighter halted his team. "Much obliged, Quillan."

Quillan nodded, mounted his own box, and eased his rig around. It might be miles before he met another wagon, but he'd been there at the right moment for Stanley Benson. It felt good to have strained. It took some of the edge from his temper. Plus, he'd helped someone.

He should pat himself on the back? Of course he'd help a fellow freighter, even a stranger on the road. It was his code. Never pass a need by. He hearkened back to Carina's broken wheel. The first time he'd laid eyes on her he'd seen trouble. Yes, he'd mistaken her for a loose woman, though only because his mind made the assumption that no other sort would find her way alone to a camp like Crystal.

He'd been less than forthcoming with charity. He remembered her hand flying in his face with furious indignation after he put her wagon over the side. If only they'd left it at that. If only he hadn't . . . What? Fallen in love? He could hardly claim that after his last performance. You didn't hurt the people you loved.

Or did you? Hadn't he disappointed Cain time and again by refusing to acknowledge God? Hadn't he caused his death by marrying Carina in order to have his final revenge on Berkley Beck? Quillan slammed his fist into his thigh. He should have let her marry Berkley Beck. She would have had more joy in the union.

Thoughts of Beck and Carina together twisted inside him, and with them his own desire renewed. How could he want her now? What kind of base creature was he to want a woman he only hurt? Not only. He'd saved her life three times, given comfort and solace and safety. He'd been gentle once in his lovemaking. But that was before. Before Cain died.

Quillan groaned. Was this some convoluted grieving or a punishment from God? If that, Carina suffered more. A pang of regret seized him. He didn't want to hurt her. Yet he did, every time they came together. He had to stay away. That was the only answer. He had to keep away from her. For her sake more than his.

Thirteen

I am held in esteem by all except my own husband.
Two months of silence.
Is it all I will ever have from him?
—Carina

THE SNOW SETTLED IN, coming in daily flurries and sometimes more, keeping the cave's secret better than Carina and Mr. Makepeace could have. Several times over the past two months they had discussed their find, Mr. Makepeace focusing on the limestone cavern itself, while Carina's thoughts were always drawn to the painted chamber.

She didn't bring Wolf and Rose's story up with Alex Makepeace. She had told him all he needed to know. If he learned more of the tale from the miners, she couldn't control that, but she guarded Wolf's privacy as fiercely as she had guarded the secrets of Rose's diary. Looking out through the snowy window, her heart sank.

Had she betrayed Rose by putting her diary into Quillan's hands? Hadn't that been her intention from the start, maybe even Father Antoine's as well? Quillan had a right to know his mother. At least through her words. Had he read them in this two months he'd been away? Would he?

Turning from the window, Carina walked to her bed and sat. She took her own diary from the crate beside the bed. While the snow fell outside, she turned its pages, reading there the snippets of prayers and thoughts she'd penned these last months. They seemed artificially bright and cheerful. Had she meant to conjure a hope that was seeping away? Or was she just pretending?

She came to the first blank page and sighed. What did she really feel? She took up her pencil. *My heart is heavy. My spirit drags. Ah, Signore, you are far away. As far as the one to whom I've given my heart.*

She felt so tired. She hadn't slept well, nor had she eaten much lately. How could she with the stress that unsettled her stomach? She kept thinking of how she could have handled it differently. What if she'd simply welcomed him?

But no, her temper had shown itself. Yes, it hurt, his rejection. But did that mean she must hurt back? He was afraid to care, she knew that. And now she'd given him good reason. Oh! She set the journal aside and stood up.

A wave of weakness swirled her head as she stalked to the window. She felt trapped. Thinking she had some mild ailment this morning, she'd turned the cooking over to Èmie and Lucia and the new helpers, Celia and Elizabeth. These last were twins, thirteen years old, whose father had been "rocked up."

Alex Makepeace had brought them to her attention. He'd seemed defensive when she pressed him for an explanation of this condition he called "rocked up" or "dusted." It was a sort of miners' consumption, as best she could tell. But he had known she was looking for additional help, and he knew also to choose those who needed the work.

These girls had come to her clean but wary. Carina guessed kindness was something with which they had little experience. She dropped her forehead to her fingertips and closed her eyes. *Signore, forgive me for complaining.*

A figure passed her window, bundled against the snow. Even so, she recognized Dr. Simms making his way to Mae's kitchen, where he'd linger with Èmie until his duties took him elsewhere. It wouldn't be long now before they married. Carina half smiled. She was happy for Èmie, though she didn't think anyone quite deserved her.

There was nothing but goodness inside Èmie Charboneau. Èmie would never have flown at Quillan like a fighting cock. She would have forgiven his injury and welcomed him gently. Carina sighed, surprised to find a tear slipping from the corner of her eye. Her own nature was too contentious, too proud.

Bene. She'd likely have no opportunity to fail him again. Fail him? The thought rose inside like a fanged snake. Was it she who had failed? She touched the lip he had bruised with his fierce kisses. It had long since healed. But the wound in her heart was unrelenting.

Another tear came. What was wrong with her? Why was she so emotional? Perhaps at last she was starting her time. That would account for the stomach distress as well, though she'd felt no bleeding. When she'd missed the first time, she had thought perhaps he'd injured her. But he had not been brutal, only selfish and cruel. Now she guessed it was the heaviness of spirit that affected her body.

She went and lay down on the bed. She was tired. A day of rest would revive her. Tomorrow she would think of something special to prepare. And she would teach Èmie to make it as well. More than anything she enjoyed their time together in the kitchen. Èmie and Mae. Where would she be without them?

Quillan jumped down from the wagon and left it in the Denver city livery. He strode down the street to his hotel, sneaked the dog past the desk clerk, and climbed the stairs to his room. He considered changing course for the dining room, then realized he wasn't hungry, even for the passable fare the hotel offered. He continued up.

The coals in the brazier had all but died since he'd left them early that morning to do some trading about town. As Quillan added coal and encouraged a small blaze, Sam searched out the corners of the room with his nose, then, satisfied, plunked down before the fire and sighed. Quillan warmed his hands a moment, then took a seat in the chair to the side of the fireplace.

Stretching his legs out before him, he made his muscles relax. Absently he reached for the books he'd recently purchased and stacked on the small round table beside him. Lifting one, he clipped the thick parchment shade of the lamp. Lurching to steady its wobbling, he knocked another book to the floor. Two more slid down behind it. The pile was ungainly.

Quillan lifted the books one by one, some small individual sonnets, others tomes he'd collected about town. He piled them in his lap to organize by size and avoid further disaster with the lamp. Near the bottom, his hand rested on the red leather of his mother's diary.

It sat there with its secrets still locked up.

No, he hadn't thrown it away. Neither had he opened it. He stared at it now with mixed feelings. Did he want to know what its pages held? He'd gotten over the shock of its existence, but not past the churning emotions it conjured. What could his mother say in those pages that he didn't already know? What excuse could she give for her life?

He picked it up and laid it with the other small books. Then he stacked the large ones on the table. Beside these he made a pile of the small books with the diary atop. Hesitantly, he touched the nameplate. *Rose Annelise DeMornay*. His fingers slid to the key.

Determination hardening his jaw, he picked up the diary and worked the dangling key into the lock. Carina had read the book. She knew what it contained. He ought to know as much. He opened to the first page. *This is the journal of Rose Annelise DeMornay written by my own hand this year of 1851.*

His mother wrote in a delicate hand. Her flowery script seemed incongruous with his image of her. He clenched his teeth as he turned the page to the first of her entries. *It is the way of dreams to become nightmares. What seems beautiful is seldom as it seems. Can any who have lived not believe in death? Can any who have loved not know what it is to hate?*

Quillan stared at the words, feeling them seep inside him. *Can any who have lived not believe in death? Can any who have loved not know what it is to hate?* His chest was tight, and he released a slow breath. At least he came by his hating honestly.

He read on. His eyes grew grainy, straining in the dim lamplight, but he read on. Certain phrases he stopped and read over and over.

I find myself at odds with my own heart, longing and at the same time despising myself for that longing.

To rise to higher joy is to risk a deeper sorrow. Do I dare reach for the sun?

A single moment of joy can slake the throat of a dying spirit. An act of kindness, no matter how small, becomes a mercy drop from heaven. Where are these drops? Where is my joy? Each moment is consumed by fear and trembling. My anguish weakens me, body and soul. Where will I turn for peace?

In spite of himself he ached for her, not wanting to understand but finding a terrible kinship of feeling. At first he had thought himself the illegitimate offspring of her illicit affair. Then he read: *I am become most despised. Even the result of my forbidden love could not remain within me to be born alive. Had it done so, it would have looked upon its mother's face in shame.*

Quillan looked up from the book into the fire, scarcely more than glowing coals now. A dead sibling. Would this sibling have felt the shame he felt for her? He watched the dog sleeping contentedly. Quillan almost wished he'd stayed as oblivious. But he hadn't. He'd started this book. Now he meant to finish it.

He returned his eyes to the page. He read on about his mother's plight, her search for shelter and acceptance. Where were those who should have protected her? Shielded her? Loved her? Why was she so alone? And then the story changed, and he read about his father. Wolf.

What strange quirk of fate, to be saved from disgrace by a savage. Yet is he more a savage than those who would have bought me? Who is this man? A stranger, yet when he found me with his eyes, I knew him. His name is Fate. He knew me by my pain, and I him, by his. We are bound together, he and I.

Quillan tensed. As he was bound to Carina? He was half tempted to close the diary, cast it away. He didn't want to know more. He'd been told it all already. He closed his eyes and imagined the flames consuming the hand that had written those words. He forced the image away.

She went on to describe Wolf in ways Quillan had never imagined. His kindness, his knowledge of nature and humankind. His belief in a benevolent power, yet his own struggle to understand himself. Quillan found himself wishing for more. Why hadn't she written everything, every word they spoke, every expression? He could picture them only vaguely.

Wolf is the most beautiful man I have ever seen, his hair next to honey, his skin bronzed by the sun, but his eyes the color of a stormy sky. Of his mother there was no physical description, but he guessed he favored his father. At least by her words they shared characteristics, maybe features as well. Their eyes and hair. He gripped the book's edge, wishing he knew.

He read of his own conception, feeling the stirring of shame until he came to a passage that made him pause and read it twice. *Is there a marriage on earth more blessed by God than the joining of two hearts in simple fidelity? Yet when Father Charboneau came to us a fortnight ago, Wolf insisted our marriage be sanctified by the Christian rite. For my part I accepted his wisdom, and this child is proof of God's blessing.*

They were married? Before his birth?

The child grows large within me. I no longer fear his fate will be that of my other's. This one is strong and eager for the world. He will make his own name.

Quillan forked his fingers into his hair. Make his own name? He'd fought to do that all his life, having been deprived of one he might have carried proudly.

If I die this minute I will not have lived in vain. For I have seen the face of my child and his name is joy. He is perfect in every feature, fearfully and beautifully made. Wolf said we will call him Quillan. He has a lusty cry.

Quillan stared a long while at the words, memorizing, planting them in his brain. He had ceased thinking of Rose as a woman despised and now sensed her love for him. It was there in her words. Why, why hadn't it been there in his life?

The very next entry reminded him why. Wolf. Rose wrote the tale he'd heard in many variations, how his father went berserk at Quillan's birth, howling like a banshee driven to murder. He knew now that Wolf had not committed that murder. It was Henri Charboneau. His brother the priest, Father Charboneau, had made that known, but only now a quarter century after his mother's writing.

She had no reason to doubt the deadly possibility that Wolf was in fact crazed. Why? Why had his father reacted that way to his cries? Quillan shook his head, frustrated by the partial answers. And then he entered the most painful pages yet.

I tried to give my baby to the priest. He alone has shown us unflagging kindness. But he won't take my son. I am in anguish, for the one he names is not one I would choose. What choice have I? Quillan's helpless wailings I am unable to quell, for what baby was ever born who didn't make his needs known? Wolf cannot bear his cries, though I will carry them forever in my heart.

He closed his eyes. This woman whom he'd despised, reviled—this woman he'd called a harlot—had faced a terrible choice. He knew now how painful it had been. She hadn't cast him aside lightly, as he'd been told.

Hadn't spurned him to pursue her filthy ways. She'd surrendered him for his sake . . . at least as she believed.

I must think of Quillan no more or I will surely go mad. Wolf wept when I told him what I'd done, but he did not set out to recapture his son. He knows the truth of it. I can't find it in me to hate him, though my soul wants so badly to blame someone, something. There is only myself.

Of course, she had blamed herself. It seemed her nature to assume the guilt, though it was largely that of others, not Rose, not this mother who had loved him. Quillan dropped his face to his hands. He was tired. He could forgive himself the tears that wet his grainy eyes.

Not many pages remained, and his slow tears continued as he watched his mother fade, her mind turn and lose connection with what was real. *Sometimes I see them playing on the floor, Quillan and Angel together. How beautiful they are. But they don't stay. I feel so cold. I feel cold all the time. The sun can't penetrate the chill. It comes from inside me.*

And then the final entry. *I'm bringing this book to Father Charboneau. Perhaps one day he will give it to my son. I can only hope that Quillan will have compassion on the one who bore him. For there is another inside me whom I cannot bear to see. God have mercy on my soul.*

Quillan sat in silence. His eyes dried as he sat reading the words over. His mother's last hopes were for his compassion and God's mercy. Compassion he'd never given her. And God's mercy? There was no such thing. Or he would never have been led to believe his parents monsters unworthy of anything but disdain.

As he thought of the venom that had been poured into his ear, lies and half truths, his anger kindled. Now he knew the truth. Yes, his mother had sacrificed her virtue, been seduced and deserted. She had even entered

Placerville with intentions to degrade herself further. What choice was left to her?

Did that make her an object of scorn? Rose Annelise DeMornay. Who were her people? Would he ever know? Did he want to? He sank wearily back into the chair. Rose must have come from somewhere before she found her way to Placerville. Her writing exhibited a keen intelligence and delicate nature. He pictured his mother young, frightened, horrified by her plight, slipping away from her home . . . where?

Quillan closed his eyes. The clock in the hall chimed four. He felt depleted in every way, but he knew sleep wouldn't come. If it did, it would be haunted with flames and charred flesh. And now he would care. God help him, he would care.

Hollow with fatigue, Quillan emerged into the early morning chill. For once he had no definite plan for the day, his ability to plan, to think, to act as elusive as sleep had proved. The Denver street was scantily peopled, so he jolted when he heard his name. He turned to meet Horace Tabor.

"Quillan. I hardly expected to find you here." Tabor caught up to him and extended his hand. "Thought for sure you'd be holed up with that comely wife of yours." There was mischief in his pale blue eyes.

Quillan ignored it as he shook Tabor's hand.

"You look almost as bad as when I saw you last. Recurrence of fever?"

Quillan shook his head. "A bad night is all. Hod, you know the area, don't you?"

"I should say so."

Quillan deliberated his next question almost long

enough to resist asking, but not quite. "How would a woman come out, say, to Placerville in '51?"

Tabor reached into his coat and pulled a cigar from a chest pocket. He bit the end and spit it on the street. "A woman, you say?" He fixed the cigar between his teeth and from another pocket took a silver matchbox. He paused before removing a match. "Mostly on a conveyance bringing women of repute to perform in a new locale."

Quillan kicked the boardwalk with his boot toe.

"Why do you ask?" Tabor struck the match and held it to the end of the cigar. His cheeks hollowed when he sucked, and his mustache billowed over his lips as he puffed out the smoke.

Quillan shrugged. "No way to tell, then, where they'd come from?"

"Not likely." Tabor took the cigar from his teeth. "Say, Quillan, what's this all about?"

"A woman named DeMornay."

"DeMornay. The William DeMornays?"

Quillan's heart pounded quickly. "I don't know."

"If so, he hails from St. Louis, but as luck would have it, he's a Denver man now. If he's not a relation, he might know something."

Quillan's fatigue became agitation.

"You want me to introduce you?"

Quillan turned as a carriage rolled past. Did he want an introduction? What were the chances there was any relation between his mother and this man? And if there were, what could he say? I'm the son of your daughter? Niece? Sister? The woman who was scandalized and married a savage in a gold field? Quillan felt too weary for words.

"My boy, are you all right?"

"I'm all right. No, I don't need introducing."

Tabor tugged his gold fob and pulled the watch from his pocket. "I've an appointment shortly, but if you change your mind . . . not that William DeMornay's a close acquaintance, but our paths have crossed."

"Thanks, no."

Tabor eyed him a moment, then smiled. "Tell me the truth now that Augusta's not here to spoil the fun. Is your wife ugly as a one-eyed mule?"

Something wrenched inside him. "My wife is beautiful, Horace."

Shaking his head, Tabor tucked the cigar back between his teeth. "If you don't beat all. Nice seeing you, Quillan. I'm sure we'll meet again."

Quillan half waved, then turned back to the hotel. He was weary enough to sleep through any dreams that might come.

Carina looked at the faces of the miners as they ate the holiday meal she and Èmie and Mae had prepared together. Her stores were too low to do all she might have hoped. Freighters had nearly stopped making any trips through the pass, and she was thankful for the six layers Quillan had brought, or she would have no eggs for the pasta at all.

But this meal wasn't her creation alone. Mae had made the gingerbread, Èmie the corn pudding. Mr. Makepeace and Joe Turner had provided the brandy and earned themselves a place at the tables with the miners, extra tables having been added until there was hardly room to squeeze between them.

But no one complained. There were cuts of wild turkey roasted in chokecherry preserves and long crusty loaves of bread. Carina's lasagna bubbled in heavy iron pans, one after another being spooned out, then layered again and put in to bake.

It was odd to make the lasagna with venison, but no cattle herds were driven to the area once the ways were blocked with snow. And seasoned, the venison served as well as beef, though neither compared to the spicy sausage she would have preferred. Carina walked around the tables, smiling as the men thanked her. "You're welcome, I'm glad you could come."

She recognized faces of men she'd tended after the flood. Some she recognized only from the other meals she'd given them. The sheer numbers had dropped as winter drove many to lower elevations. Crystal was almost tenable with the snowpack stopping the dust, and the crowds cut by half. These men were the diehards, those who bore up under any temperatures and conditions.

She caught Alex Makepeace watching her. From his position against the far wall, he raised a glass of brandy in toast, his easy smile already in place. Beside him, Joe Turner also turned. He motioned her over and she obliged.

"Well, Mr. Makepeace, do you still grudge the men these little dinners?"

"Little dinner? It's a veritable feast. And I've never grudged them. I only envied them."

She laughed, turning to Joe Turner. "You see how well his Harvard education stands him? He's never without a reply."

"May I offer you a brandy?" Mr. Turner held up the bottle and a fresh glass.

She shook her head. "No, grazie. I can barely stay on my feet as it is."

"Then sit." Alex motioned her toward a chair, vacated by a miner near enough to catch his motion and move out.

"No, no."

"You do look a little peaked, Mrs. Shepard." Joe Turner's voice was gentle. "Though not diminished in any way, mind you. Fatigued?"

"To hear you go on, I've one foot in the grave." Carina waved a hand.

Mr. Makepeace nudged her toward the chair. "Sit, Mrs. Shepard. Your operation won't go to pieces if you rest yourself one moment."

"Spoken by one who puts in longer hours than his miners." She dropped elegantly into the chair.

He smiled. "I have the constitution for it."

"Meaning I haven't?"

"Meaning . . ." He bowed slightly at the waist. "That you shouldn't have to."

"But I want to, Mr. Makepeace. These men keep my husband in business, eh?"

In the corner someone took up a violin and began to play. It was a lovely, soulful tune that Carina didn't recognize. The violin was joined by a small guitar played by a lanky man with very few teeth. The scent of gingerbread filled the room as Èmie, Celia, and Elizabeth carried chunks of it out on trays. The men cheered.

From her position, Carina scanned the room. This was the first time she'd sat with a full dining room before her. Now that she was down, she doubted she could rise again very soon—her legs were that tired. So she clapped with the men as the musicians struck up a jig and one bandy-legged Irishman used the narrow tile splash before the fireplace as a dance floor. She glanced up to find Alex Makepeace watching her rather than the dancer.

Her hands paused as their eyes met, his inexplicably kind, and hers, what? She dampened her lips with her tongue and returned her attention to the jig. The smell of the pine and cedar fire, the spicy gingerbread, and the softly falling snow out the window just behind her shoulder made the perfect ambiance to revel in the Christmas spirit. She closed her eyes a moment, letting it seep in. *Grazie, Signore.*

Joe Turner and Alex Makepeace stayed after all the others left, then helped to clear and strip the tables. Carina laughed. "I should offer you a wage."

"Never." Joe Turner put a hand to his chest. "It's little enough for all you do."

"Is it so much, Mr. Turner?" Her voice had a plaintive tone.

He caught her hand between his. "Maybe not so much what you do, but how you do it. You raise the spirits, and that, Mrs. Shepard, is what we men need more than food in our bellies."

"Especially at Christmas." Alex Makepeace dumped the last of the tablecloths in a heap in the corner.

She looked from one to the other, then felt the tears spring to her eyes. At once Mr. Makepeace was beside her. "Shame on us, Joe. We've made her cry."

Carina waved them off. "No, no. It's . . . it's only . . ." She suddenly laughed. "I've no idea at all what it is. Go away and let me cry in peace." She swiped at the tears still coming even while she laughed.

Joe Turner took up his hat. "Happy Christmas, Mrs. Shepard."

"Grazie, Joe Turner." She sniffed. "And you."

He headed for the door, but Alex Makepeace lingered, a look of gentle concern on his face. Carina looked up and waved a hand at him.

"It's nothing."

He didn't answer. Instead he reached inside his vest and took out a small tissue-wrapped parcel. "I have something for you. A holiday trinket."

She stared at the package in his palm, then looked into his face.

His expression was slightly amused. "Don't worry; it won't bite you." With his free hand he flipped her palm upward and dropped the gift inside.

She unwrapped the paper to find an oval porcelain pin painted with grapes and leaves. He had listened well, Alex Makepeace. The grapes' rich tones were all the hues of Papa's vineyard, and she closed it into her palm and pressed it to her breast. "Thank you . . . Alex."

His answer was suspended a moment; then he smiled broadly. "A merry Christmas, Carina."

"Buon Natale."

Alex stepped out into the below-freezing chill of the night. He could have gone through the kitchen to his room at Mae's, but he needed the bracing air to bring him to his senses. A shadow moved, and he spun to find Joe Turner still lingering. Joe wore a quizzical expression, and Alex shrugged.

"Was I so obvious?"

Joe nodded.

Alex swore. "Never in all the years of my Christian baptism have I anticipated loving another man's wife."

"Don't worry. Most of Crystal is more than half in love with Carina DiGratia Shepard."

"Carina DiGratia . . . your shaft?"

"Oh yes." Joe caught him by the arm and started

them toward Mae's front porch. "Of course, I proposed before she was married."

"More proper that way."

"But hardly more profitable."

Alex stopped. "So give me the digs on this Quillan Shepard. Why on earth does he leave her like that? Alone in a place like this to . . . well, to . . ."

"Drive the rest of us a little crazy?"

"Not a little, I'm afraid."

Joe Turner shook his head. "I can't answer that. I only know he's always been strange, though I mean not in a wicked way. He'd go hungry himself to see that someone in need was fed. Did pretty much that after the flood wiped out so many. But he doesn't seem to see his own wife's needs." Joe looked up. "I mean he can't really, or he wouldn't leave her, would he?"

"He doesn't seem dim in other ways."

"Dim? Good heavens, he's brilliant. Have him quote you anything sometime. He carries a library in his head."

"Then maybe it's her?" There was more hope in Alex's voice than he intended.

Joe shook his head. "I don't think so. Whatever the case, I'm afraid we must worship from afar."

Fourteen

The bright side of hardship is that small things give pleasure which might otherwise be overlooked.

—Carina

RIDING JOCK, with Jack and Sam in tow, Quillan had gone first to Laramie, where he'd lived with them last. There he learned that they'd moved on. Some thought Rapid City, so he went there and found that they'd been sent on to Cedar Falls. The old caretaker was certain of that, and Quillan found him sharp enough to believe.

Cedar Falls, Iowa, seemed burgeoning and very forward thinking after the Rocky Mountain mining camps. Crystal called itself a city, but even Leadville was backward compared to the sedate white-fenced streets of Cedar Falls. It took asking twice to find the residence he wanted, located next to a squat stone church with a sizeable steeple.

Quillan dismounted before the solid frame house and led Jock and Jack to the neat trough beside the low gate. Sam, too, lapped at the water when Quillan broke the ice from its surface. The gate worked without a squeak, and he passed through and started up the walk.

At the door, he paused. He'd invested enough time already to want this over quickly, but his stomach had clutched up, and he gave himself a moment, then knocked.

The door opened, and Quillan looked down on Reverend Shepard for the first time in his life. Had he grown, or had his foster father shrunk with age? Maybe both. He'd been eye to eye with him at fourteen when he left. Now there was a difference of inches as their eyes met and held.

Then the reverend spoke. "Quillan. I wasn't sure I'd ever see you again."

"You might have preferred it that way."

The gray brows drew together with a deep *V* between them. He shook his head. "I prayed to see you, to speak with you someday."

Quillan frowned. He wasn't there because of any prayers this old man had muttered. He looked inside, behind the reverend. Though he'd never seen it, the house seemed much the same as the other. This one had a smell of age, of faint decay he didn't remember. "Is she here?"

The shoulders sagged; the head nodded. "Your mother's inside."

"Not my mother."

Reverend Shepard waved a hand. "Have it your way." He turned and motioned Quillan inside.

Quillan told the dog to stay, but the reverend called him in as well. Quillan frowned when the dog slipped in against his order. But it was cold, and he could hardly blame him. The room was small and tidy. Quillan didn't see Mrs. Shepard anywhere at hand. That was good. He needed a few minutes before he faced her, confronted her.

"May I get you some coffee? You're a little past bread and milk."

Quillan nodded. Coffee would be good. But why was it the reverend who offered it instead of her? The old man returned with two cups and they drank in silence. The burden of speech was his, Quillan knew. He was the one who had caused the separation and now ended it.

He stared at the coffee in his cup. The reverend must have a thousand questions, but Quillan's were the ones that mattered. He may as well get to it. "My mother had a diary. It's now in my possession."

The reverend laid a hand on Sam's head as the animal took his place beside the rocking chair. "I knew nothing of that."

Quillan was pleased he hadn't tried to argue mothers again. "She left it with the priest in Placer, who gave it to my wife."

"Your . . ."

Quillan brushed aside his surprise, then swirled the coffee in his cup. "The events in the diary are different from what I was told." He glanced up, fixed the old man with his stare. "Not so different in fact, maybe, as insinuation."

The reverend shook his head. "Quillan . . ."

"Did you know the things she whispered to me? The ugly ways she poisoned me? The twisted words she used to form my nightmares?"

The reverend bit his lower lip. "What are you saying?"

"I thought not." Quillan looked away. "I don't remember you being cruel. Just ignorant."

The reverend's hand shook as he raised it, but the reprimand died on his lips.

Quillan almost stopped, the look on his foster

father's face almost pitiful enough to stop him. But not quite. "You always talked about helping those in need. But did you? Where was your Christian compassion for my mother? My father?"

As the reverend bowed his head, faint wisps of white hair were visible. "I'm only one man, Quillan. I can't reach every soul."

"Did you try?" Quillan hadn't come here to hurt him. Her maybe, but not the reverend. Now he was so tight he couldn't stop.

The veins stood up on the hands that folded and unfolded in the old man's lap. "I spoke the truth to any who would hear it."

"That would cover faith. What about hope and charity?"

"Is that why you're here?" The reverend's eyes were suddenly sharp. "To convict me of my failure?"

Quillan wanted to shout yes, to reach out and sweep the lamp and Bible from the table, to kick holes in the wall and pound his fists into the man before him. He wanted to shake him until his teeth rattled. And then he didn't. What good would it do?

"I don't know what brought me here. To learn why, I guess."

"Why?"

Quillan nodded. "Yes, why."

"Then come with me." The reverend stood. Quillan noted the stoop of his back, the bend of arms no longer limber. Though it wasn't the house he'd lived in, he guessed where they were going. To the room that had been sacrosanctly closed to him all the years of his youth. To the bedroom the reverend shared with his wife.

Reverend Shepard pushed the door open, and

Quillan looked in. The woman on the bed couldn't be Mrs. Shepard. The hair hung in thick white strings; the head rocked and trembled, and when she raised it, there was drool from the side of one sagging lip. But he recognized the eyes.

Their hateful depths even now sent pangs of fear and rage through him. She didn't know him. But something inside her hated him still. She raised a clawlike hand and squawked, a prolonged guttural noise that set his teeth on edge. She was a shrunken husk filled with malevolence.

Then her hand fell and she began to cry, wrenching sobs and whimpers. Quillan felt himself grow limp, the anger that held him stiff seeping away as she curled into a ball and picked at the coverlet with hands more skeleton than flesh. It both horrified and compelled him.

The reverend went to the side of the bed and brought the blanket over her shoulders. "There, now." He stroked her hair.

She slapped at him, but it was more defensive than angry, like a wounded animal that bites the hand which mends its hurt. Quillan staggered to the doorway and pushed through to the hall. Forcing deep breaths in and out of his lungs, he clenched his hands at his sides. He didn't want to pity her. He wanted to blame her, to castigate her. He'd gone there to demand answers, but now . . . He felt the reverend behind him, heard the door softly close.

Quillan cleared his throat. "How long has she been like that?"

"Long."

Quillan closed his eyes, feeling cheated, discouraged.

The reverend urged him forward with a nudge to his shoulder. "I didn't want to believe it, of course. The early signs were . . ." He waved his hand. "Not consistent, unsure. She'd known grief, tragedy. The loss of our children was enough to cause instability even in a woman of faith."

Quillan heard the challenge, knew the reverend was daring him to judge her faith. When he didn't move from his spot, his foster father led the way back down the hall.

"By the time you left, I suspected more. A year or two later there was no denying it."

Quillan followed him back to the front room and walked to the window, there resting his sleeve against the frame. "What is it?"

"Some form of insanity." He caught his chin between thumb and fingers. "They know so little, really."

"Why isn't she locked up?"

The reverend didn't answer.

Quillan turned, and the expression he saw on the man's face cut through the bitterness he'd carried into that room. "I'm sorry."

With a sigh, Reverend Shepard sank into a faded horsehair chair. "I am, too. Sometimes I'm tempted to question God's providence."

Quillan eyed him a long moment. "Do you? Question it?"

"In my weak moments."

Quillan swallowed that. The Reverend Shepard himself doubted God. All those sermons, all those words, and underneath his own doubts, his own questions.

"Tell me about your wife. Is she pretty?"

Quillan looked back out the window at the neat and orderly street, cleared of snow that clumped along the sides like old wax. He pictured Carina's delicate form and features, her hair that rippled like a shining black lake, her skin like custard, smooth and warm. "Yes."

"Good?"

A viselike tightening in his chest. "Yes."

"How long have you been married?"

"Not long." Quillan watched a carriage roll by.

"When you've been married long, you'll know why I don't have her locked away."

Quillan turned from the window, and sat across from his foster father. He stared at the old man's knees. The hand of the clock on the mantel ticked around a quarter face as they sat in silence. He felt cheated. He'd gone to some trouble to find them, to blame them, to accuse. How could he accuse a broken old man and a woman who'd lost her mind?

Quillan threaded his fingers into his hair and leaned his head back against the chair. "I came to confront her, to make her tell me why she'd lied about my parents. I wanted to make her squirm, to hurt her, to pay her back."

Reverend Shepard lit the lamp and replaced the chimney. "And now?"

Quillan dropped his hands to rest on his thighs. "It wouldn't do much good, would it?"

"It never does."

Quillan wanted to ask him why he hadn't defended him, why he'd taken her word, her side every time. Why he'd left him to her if he suspected, even wondered if there were problems. Why he'd valued the souls of strangers over the one he'd taken into his own home. But as with the other, what good would it do?

Reverend Shepard put the match on the glass plate. "I don't know much about your mother. I rarely saw her, or Wolf either. They kept to their place on the mountain, living in sin."

"They were married. By Father Charboneau."

The reverend raised his brows, then nodded. "I'm glad for that."

"Removes some of my stain." Quillan saw it hit home.

"Oh, Quillan. I often thought of you as my own."

"Only I wasn't quite."

He sighed. "Mrs. Shepard didn't want it. She agreed it was our Christian duty to raise you, but she didn't want to adopt. Her grief was too great."

Quillan said nothing.

"I brought her to that godforsaken camp with no sanitation, no medical facilities. Yet when our children died, she never blamed me."

"She laid it to my account." Quillan spoke low. He couldn't tell if the reverend heard or not.

"I've never doubted my call. I've led countless souls to heaven. I've gone where the Lord has sent me and served as faithfully as I could." The reverend stood and walked to the fireplace. He held one hand to the warmth. "I've borne hardship and sorrow and supported others through theirs. I've been a voice in the wilderness, and a light in the darkness. I've fought the good fight."

Quillan didn't doubt it. He'd seen the long hours spent in prayer, heard the sermons, waited for the reverend to come home from the bedside of the sick and dying.

Reverend Shepard touched the oval framed photograph of his wife that stood on the mantel. "All that, I can say with impunity. And still, the two people closest to me I failed."

Quillan heard him through a fog of emotion and thought again of Carina. Shame burned inside. It was inexcusable the way he'd treated her. He could only hope she'd had the sense to leave Crystal, and him, for good. His hands gripped the arms of the chair.

"If one day you have it in your heart to forgive me, will you find some way to let me know?"

Quillan looked up. Reverend Shepard was diminished. He stood by the fire looking old. Quillan recalled him towering in the pulpit, his voice strong and certain. He recalled the hand holding the rod, and the arm swinging it with verve. How defiantly he'd resisted the discipline. And yet they weren't so different after all.

Quillan drew himself up. "I don't blame you." It was God who betrayed them, and those most of all who served Him best.

Carina celebrated the New Year with the rest of the city, crowded onto the frozen street. Torches blazed, bells of every size and sort rang out, and someone had even provided fireworks. Carina watched the sparks shoot high into the sky and explode into green and gold with a bang. She clapped her hands with each explosion, laughing and cheering as loudly as those on either side of her.

To her right stood Alex Makepeace with Mae beside him. To her left, Èmie in the crook of Robert Simms's arm. As the last of the fireworks rained sparks from the sky, Dr. Simms turned Èmie in his arms and kissed her. "New Year greetings, Èmie. Let's make it our best yet."

Watching them, Carina felt a pang and chastised herself for it. Should she wish any less for Èmie? She felt a touch on her arm and turned.

"Happy '81, Carina." Alex Makepeace leaned close and kissed her lightly on the cheek. He did the same for

Mae, but Carina sensed a difference, as though that courtesy was only to cover his gesture toward her. She wasn't nearly as naïve as she had been.

Before she could worry, her hand was being shaken by man after man along the street. "God bless you, ma'am. Greetings, Mrs. Shepard. Best to you and yours, ma'am." She laughed and returned them all. Who was to say that 1881 wouldn't be her best year yet?

Her heart swelled with hope and anticipation. Anything could happen under a winter sky so filled with stars in the city that was the diamond of the Rockies. Indeed, anything could happen. She rested her hand on her waist.

They went inside to the kitchen, where Mae had whipped an eggnog to a frothy richness and sprinkled it with nutmeg. Alex dribbled rum into the bottoms of the cups, and Mae ladled the creamy eggnog atop. Carina laughed when it coated the skin above her lip. "I've winter whiskers like the rest of Crystal."

Alex rubbed his own beard and laughed with her. "You've a way to go to match these."

Dr. Simms lowered his cup. "I saw a bearded woman once at a side show in Detroit. The whiskers hung down to her chest."

"Were they real whiskers?" Èmie looked into his face as though she suspected a jest.

"Had to be. A little midget hung his whole weight on it, dangled there until she thumped him off."

Mae laughed. "Must have been a sight."

"If you go in for such things. I prefer women without." And his smile made Èmie blush.

Alex raised his glass. "Here's to women without. May the new year be bounteous."

Carina raised her cup and tapped it to his. Then she

clanked Mae's and Èmie's and Dr. Simms's as well. "May the new year be blessed." She met Èmie's eyes. "Especially for the two joining their hearts."

Èmie gripped her hand, and they shared a smile. Carina swallowed the rest of her eggnog and silently blessed the man who'd provided the eggs laid by the chickens in the lean-to. *Happy New Year, Quillan, wherever you are.*

Quillan brought the spoon to her lips, the lukewarm soup dribbling in over the tongue Mrs. Shepard extended like an animal. His hand shook, and as much soup went down her chin as her throat. He brought the spoon back to the bowl as her hands jerked wildly. The moan gurgled in her throat, and he looked into her terrified eyes. What brought it this time?

She seemed to see something behind him, as her gaze was fixed over his left shoulder. These last two days she'd grown accustomed to his presence, and he no longer set her off just by walking in. He tried to put another spoonful to her mouth, but she backed away, trembling.

"There's nothing there." He spoke low and softly. "It can't hurt you."

Her wrists curled up and the hands gyrated. He remembered her fingers pinched into his ear, dragging him close to hear what nasty thing she had to say. *"I only took you to save your mother drowning you in the river."* He shook the thought away and again raised the spoon. This time she lapped at it greedily. It spilled over his fingers.

"When you've been married long, you'll know why I don't have her locked away."

Could the reverend love her? Was it possible he held feelings for this . . . creature? The face contorted, almost as though she'd read his thoughts. She pawed his arm, petting him, preening him. Sounds that weren't words came from her soup-stained mouth.

Quillan raised the cloth and wiped her lips clean. "Don't talk now. You need to eat." Quillan looked at her wrists, so thin and misshapen he could snap them with no effort at all. The next spoonful made it into her mouth. Maybe she'd remembered how it was done. Maybe it was just luck. He fed her another and congratulated himself when it, too, went down where it was supposed to. Then both her hands came up and pushed the spoon away. He started to protest, then froze.

"Quil-lan."

His jaw fell slack at her throaty utterance. He'd imagined it. Her sounds were nothing but noise, no sense, no understanding.

She reached up and tugged at her hair, humming. Her gaze drifted to the window at the side of the room. Gathering himself, he urged her back to the soup, and like a baby she opened for him. He'd fed her half the bowl before she tensed again, gripping the neck of her nightgown and shrinking back into the pillows stacked behind her.

Quillan searched the room. It was stale and serene, nothing at all that could alarm her. "Here now, let's finish." He raised a spoonful, but she suddenly gripped the tray and flung it from her, spewing soup over the covers and him. Quillan caught her hands and brought them together. "It's all right. It can't hurt you."

She growled and snarled and tried to bite his hands. There was more strength in her skeleton than he would have imagined, but he held firm. "Calm down."

She started to cry, wringing her hands out of his grasp and pushing him away. Quillan stood. He picked up the bowl and tray and dug the spoon out from under the bedside table. From the washstand he snatched a towel and wiped the coverlet. Then he settled it over her as she curled into a weeping ball. He was learning the pattern. The rage, the fear, then the weeping.

Quillan carried the dish out to the kitchen. He wet a towel and rubbed his shirt and the side of his pants. The reverend would be home soon. Quillan would tell him he was leaving. He leaned on the counter and looked out across the yard surrounded by short white pickets. A cold wind blew, and he thought of Carina.

What if she hadn't left? Would she be warm? Would she be safe? That was where he belonged, not here with an aging pastor and his imbecile wife. Yet he hadn't left. He hadn't intended to stay even one night, and here he'd been there two. Today when his foster father asked him to sit with Mrs. Shepard, he'd balked, then agreed.

He hadn't known the reverend would be absent all these hours, hadn't known he would have to feed and care for her alone. Quillan washed the bowl and spoon and put them in their places. His own soup was still in the pot, but he had no appetite for it. He dried his hands on the towel and walked back to make certain she was sleeping.

The huddled form under the covers was so small, shrunken bones and flesh, a fragile heap of misery. She seemed peaceful now, and he took his place in the chair across from the bed. Reverend Shepard had said he needn't sit there all the time; she was too weak to stand. But Quillan sat anyway.

His feelings were awash with confusion. Why had she told him such lies? Why had she made him believe his mother would have drowned him? Had indeed thrown him away? That his father was a black-hearted, greed-infested animal? That he was doomed to be wicked as they were wicked.

Were they wicked? Was she? Could he even believe that now, when it was the illness that warped and twisted her mind? He dropped his face into his hands. Where did the truth lie? What was truth? Like Pilate before the scourged Savior, he wanted the answer.

Cain might have told him. But Cain was gone. Somehow the thought didn't bring the debilitating guilt it had even a short while ago. Yes, Cain was dead. Yes, in a way he was responsible. But in a world so convoluted and inscrutable, what use was there in blaming himself? The blame lay squarely on God.

He looked at the woman lying in the bed, a woman of faith. He thought of the reverend out somewhere even now, in the cold with some member of his flock. Stoop-shouldered, shrunken, yet tenaciously serving a God who would always have the last laugh. Why?

He rested his head against the wall. Why?

Fifteen

A heart in love is the finest beauty treatment yet devised.
I have never seen Èmie look so beautiful.
—Carina

PACKED INTO THE TINY dirt-floored cabin, while snow sparkled the air outside, Carina watched Father Antoine join his niece and Dr. Robert Simms in marriage. Had she looked at this priest with such hopeful joy when he'd joined her with Quillan? Or had her eyes held only the fear and uncertainty of their circumstances?

Could she have known then what a farce her marriage would become? She pressed her eyes closed against the ache, then opened them again, determined to see Èmie start differently. Hers would be a blessed union. It had no complications. These two married for love.

Carina forced back her tears. Hadn't she also? Perhaps. It seemed so in her memory, but her emotions were so confused. It had been so long now since she'd even seen Quillan, heard his voice in the street. She missed him. Even in his cruelty, at least he showed that he knew she existed.

She put a hand to her belly. But did he know

another one existed? A surge of hope filled her. When he knew, when he saw her belly swollen with life, would he dare suggest their union was anything less than God's will? Though her skirts hid the slight bulging of her abdomen and she had yet to feel more than a flutter inside, she knew this child was their hope.

She bit her lip as Èmie raised her hand and Dr. Simms slid the ring onto her finger. How long before Èmie, too, carried a child in her womb? Would their babies grow up together on the streets of Crystal? Carina smiled at the thought. Was this a son she carried, strong and long of limb like Quillan, or a daughter with dark laughing eyes?

How could she have been so innocent of the early changes in her body? Thinking herself ill with some malady when she missed cycle after cycle? By the third she had guessed. Impossible as it seemed, Quillan had made her with child. *Grazie Dio!* She no longer felt so alone. Even in these circumstances, she couldn't help rejoicing. God had brought good from that terrible night. *Un miracolo.*

Now Dr. Simms kissed his bride, and Carina clapped with the others, joy chasing all other thoughts from her mind. How Èmie deserved to be loved. Now she was free of Uncle Henri and could make a home for this man. Carina thought of her own empty room, but she pushed the sadness aside. This was Èmie's day.

The feast was held in Carina's dining room and consisted mostly of game and corn. She had baked a cake of soured cream and poppy seeds, the last of them in her small jar. The air outside was bitter, freezing the moisture into glittering crystalline wind. Inside, the fire's glow and the joy warmed the room and all those present.

She sensed Alex Makepeace beside her and turned. In what short time he had become one of them. She smiled. "Last year I wondered if Èmie would ever marry. Now this." She waved her arm at the joyful assembly.

"You've done well for her."

"Not me," Carina protested, seeing Èmie's face aglow from across the room. "It is Èmie's own nature."

"And a little help from her friends."

Carina started to argue, but he cut her short.

"Do you think she could have blossomed so, trapped in that hot spring cave day after day?"

It was true. Èmie no longer seemed dull and pale. Her lackluster eyes shone with mirth, and she was accomplished both in the kitchen and business. Carina smiled. Maybe she had helped her friend after all.

"I wish there were more I could do. I owe her so much."

"For what?" Alex raised a cinnamon eyebrow.

"For befriending me when I was alone and afraid in a strange place with no money and hardly the sense of a chicken."

He laughed. "In that case I'm deeply in your debt."

She smiled. "Hardly. You know exactly what you're doing. You didn't come to Crystal expecting anything but what you found."

He was silent a long moment, then, "I never once expected what I found."

Their eyes met, and Carina felt a pang. It was wrong, this closeness they shared. Completely chaste, yet . . . She knew they had crossed a line somewhere. She told herself he was a friend, her husband's partner. Yet the room was brighter for his presence. His smile eased her loneliness. She felt free to discuss anything—anything but her husband and their coming child.

What would Alex think when her belly grew? Would he know she loved her husband? A twisting confusion filled her. She did love her husband. Even in his absence, she longed for his mocking smile as she had first seen it, the strength of his arm as he'd carried her from the shaft, the swiftness of his wit as he'd heard and destroyed the rattlesnake. Most of all she longed for the gentle love they'd shared on their own wedding night. How had it all been destroyed? She dropped her gaze from Alex's and felt, rather than heard, him sigh.

"If this freeze holds, I'd like to return to the cave. There are some tests I want to conduct."

Carina nodded. She, too, wanted to see the cave again. Wolf's pictures had haunted her, but this time she wanted to study them, to learn their story, to know it as she knew Rose's. Somehow she felt it would make her understand Quillan. Reading Rose's diary had increased her love for the man she hardly knew. Seeing Wolf's pictures might do the same.

Carina glanced at the window. "If we start now we'll have enough daylight."

"Dare we sneak away?"

Her heart thumped, his choice of words causing a guilty thrill. Carina looked at Èmie engrossed in the man at her side, enclosed by friends and well-wishers. They might be missed, but not for long. Èmie's joy would eclipse all else. Èmie's joy, which ought to be Carina's as well, for she truly loved her friend. Yet . . . Carina nodded, and they slipped out together.

Did she imagine Alan Tavish's frown as Alex requested their horses? Did the bowed head hang lower, the shoulders stoop with more weight than usual? Carina shook herself. She was doing nothing wrong! She was going to her husband's mine to understand more clearly the forces at work on the man she loved.

Carina shivered. On horseback with her mouth wrapped in a scarf against the crystalline air, Carina was chilled more quickly than she could have imagined. She thought of the blizzard that had stopped Quillan and her. What if another one came? What would Alex do? Would they be safe in the cave? At least it was shelter. But she couldn't spend a night alone with him as she had with her husband. Blizzard or no, tongues would wag.

Yet he couldn't be expected to go alone into the cave. What if something happened? Nor could she go without him unless she told someone else of the cave's existence. She had meant to tell Father Antoine, but he'd been absent from Crystal these last two months. She would tell him, though, now that he was back for Èmie's wedding. He would want to see for himself Wolf's depictions of the story he'd shared with the priest that night on the mountain.

Yes, she would tell Father Antoine, take him there herself if he returned to town long enough. Then she wouldn't have to go alone with Alex Makepeace. But today she rode beside the steeldust stallion, wondering what kept Alex so quiet.

Èmie's wedding feast was the only meal she was preparing today. She'd posted as much on the door of her dining room. Her clientele would have to eat elsewhere, and that left her free to pursue this adventure. Funny how Alex had thought of it himself.

She glanced his way. His gaze was forward, but he sensed her movement, turned, and smiled. "Thank you for coming, Carina. That's the first rule in caving. Don't go alone."

"Thank you for keeping this secret."

"I wouldn't break my word to you." He looked away.

Again she felt a pang, aware that his feelings might be more than her own. She rocked with Daisy's gait and wondered if she should be riding in her condition. As she had yet to mention it to anyone, she had no medical opinion to go by. Papa had not given his opinion on the subject since Mamma never rode horseback if she could help it.

Carina sighed. She had yet to write them. Oh, what a shameful daughter to keep something so important from those she loved. One letter had arrived in answer to her earliest correspondence. With the winter roads, mail service was difficult, though not impossible.

But she had yet to tell them of her marriage, much less this child she bore. If only Quillan would return and see once and for all that she wouldn't desert him as so many others had. That must be behind his fear to get close. He'd been rejected too many times. Now he guarded himself. But she knew he could love if he once let himself.

They climbed to the Rose Legacy and dismounted. Alex had loaded his horse with ropes, balls of string, candles in their tin holders, a box of instruments, even kindling. He, too, was a resourceful and forward-thinking man. He helped her down, and she wondered for a moment if he noticed her extra bulk without the skirts to hide it.

How could he? It was hardly enough to add weight, much less substance. She was overly aware of the baby's presence, but it wouldn't be noticeable for some time to others. They entered the drift and Alex lit the first candle. He handed it to her. She held its dim light for him to see as he fixed the rope to the spikes and double-hitch tied it.

Alex turned. "Ready?" Once again he'd brought a harness for her, and she stepped in more confidently than she had the first time.

"I think so." But as she surrendered the candle and he lowered her down, she heard the moaning, and again, her fear kindled. It was only wind through the mouth of Wolf's memorial. But she imagined worse, far worse.

She descended into darkness and fixed her eyes on the faint glow about Alex above. Soon it was nothing more than her imagination as the dim candle flame was eaten by the hollow depths surrounding her.

Her feet touched ground. Heart rushing, she called, "I'm down." The echoes surrounded her like a flood of voices, breathless and eerie. She trembled. What had she thought, returning here? She could be warm and safe at Èmie's wedding feast. What would they all think when they noticed her gone?

Would Mae organize the cleanup? Would Lucia, Celia, and Elizabeth follow with only Mae's direction? What had she been thinking to sneak off like this? What if something happened? Who would know to look for them here? Trembling, she waited for Alex to join her.

As soon as she heard him near, she struggled out of her harness and reached for the end of his rope. She steadied it as he descended, then stepped back for him to land. He handed her a candle and their fingers brushed. Warm, living flesh.

He lit both their candles. "I don't suppose you came to watch me take rock samples and measurements."

She shook her head, wondering if she dared make her way to the circular cave alone. Overhead the bats stirred. She shuddered.

"I'll walk you through to the chamber, then return, if that's all right?"

"Thank you." She touched his arm, and he pressed her fingers. The contact was brief and inconsequential, but it emboldened her. Holding her candle aloft, she followed him once again toward the moaning sound that indicated the direction of the secondary chamber.

Alex stopped once to mark a channel leading off from the main chamber. He nailed the end of one ball of twine there. "I might see how far that one goes when I come back."

Carina had no desire to see for herself how long the dark tunnel wove. She wondered again what she was even doing there in this dark, cavernous hole. But once she entered the painted chamber, she knew. She was honoring Wolf.

"Well, I guess I'll go back?"

She smiled wanly. "I'll be fine."

Alex glanced once around the chamber. "Not exactly gentle viewing."

"No."

"Are you sure . . ."

She swallowed her uncertainty. "I want to know."

Again he brushed her fingers where she clasped her arm with the opposite hand. His touch brought her strength and comfort.

She almost wished he wouldn't leave, but she strengthened her smile. "I'll be fine."

"If you call and I don't answer, stay where you are. Don't try to find me. I might be down some side tunnel, and it's terribly easy to become disoriented."

"You might get lost?"

"I won't get lost, but you might if you tried to find me."

Carina wondered once again what she was doing beneath the earth and how it would be to stumble about in the dark, lost in an endless maze of tunnels. "I'll stay here or in the main chamber."

"Are you warm enough?"

She realized she was. The temperature in the cave was higher than the outside air. The ground must form a barrier to prevent extreme temperatures in either direction. Though cold, the air had none of the wind's bite. Bundled in layers of warm miner's attire, she should be comfortable enough. "Yes."

"Then I'll leave you." He still looked uncertain, but he went.

Carina brought her gaze to the first mural, which she had identified as the scene of which Father Antoine had spoken. The massacre of Wolf's parents, friends, and baby sister. The picture was brutal in its accuracy. Carina could look at it only a moment. Could Wolf have recalled it so vividly, or did he paint what he thought must have been?

No, she remembered Father Antoine saying the memory was vivid for the man, though he'd been only five years old at the time. His memory must be extraordinary, but then, to see your mother . . . She couldn't look at it any longer.

The next picture showed a boy standing alone in a circle of cone-shaped tents. At each tent stood a man painted red with a feathered headband. At some stood a woman also, and at several, more than one woman. The boy was painted with the same ochre-colored paint as the first massacred victims. Beside him, the pale wolf.

She moved her eyes to the next scene. The boy was on his knees, and it seemed those around him beat him with sticks. The next showed him tied to a post by his wrists while boys on horseback whipped him with ropes. Over both of these, the wolf hovered, almost a cloud, though its shape was discernible.

The next showed the ochre figure as a man standing in the river with a spear. On the end of the spear was a great gray fish. The wolf pranced. The next was a scene of the hunt. A brown stag, bloodied but twice the size of a man, stood in a circle of warriors, and though the ochre man was among them, he carried no spear. Had he not been allowed the glory of the kill?

She looked but saw no wolf in that picture until, studying it closely, she noted the ochre man's head was wolf shaped and pale. Somehow that image chilled her. Was he becoming the wolf they'd named him? The one who howled in tortured dismay when his son was born?

Carina felt a chill across the back of her neck and spun. Her candle sputtered and almost extinguished, but it revealed nothing at all behind her. Just a movement of air. Her throat tightened painfully. Her heart hammered her chest, but she was alone. There was nothing in the chamber.

Signore, give me strength. She turned back to the wall and saw Wolf astride a paint pony, his own head decked with a single feather. At his side, the wolf. They were on the edge of a cliff, and a great vista had been painted around them. The cactus all waved and pointed toward the sun, which was rising or setting on the horizon, and above the saffron sun, an eagle spread its wings. Its shadow reached Wolf on the cliff, the wingtips just touching his forehead.

Carina reached out with one finger and touched the spot where they met. The stone was smooth and dry, probably because of the air hole above. Had Wolf known his pictures would be preserved? But what was their significance? What was the eagle, and why did it touch Wolf now?

The next was a war scene, and the two beyond. In his ochre paint, Wolf did not participate in the bloody acts shown too clearly for Carina to bear. He and the wolf were shown apart, unarmed, heads hanging as though shamed or despairing. Did he choose not to make war, or was he forbidden it? She recalled Father Antoine's words. *"He was the most humane man I've ever met. It wasn't in him to kill."*

Not to war for his people must have cost him greatly in respect and esteem. Or did they refuse him the honor, sensing what Father Antoine had said, a humane spirit that set him apart? She passed the battle scenes and saw now a painting of a maiden. She was naked and broad. Only the wolf stood beside her, no ochre-colored man. Had Wolf believed that only his Indian side could join with a woman of the people?

The next picture showed the maiden on a high platform in the trees. Other platforms were around hers, but each held a skeleton. She had died, then. The ochre man knelt below her platform. The wolf again hovered above like a cloud. If only Carina knew what it all meant.

Now there was a mountain, and on its side, the man and wolf together. The man had his arms upraised and she saw, very small above him, the eagle. One feather drifted down and she wondered if Wolf would catch it in his open hands.

The next scene showed Rose, and Carina's heart leaped. She was painted nearly white, with dark hair and red skirts. The picture seemed more symbolic than real, the two of them standing beside a simple depiction of a cabin with a starlit sky above. The stars formed the shape of the wolf.

The last picture showed the ochre man raising a

newborn child above his head . . . in exultation? Or offering? The wolf beside him had its head thrown back, mouth open to the sky.

Wind came through the opening above her, and Carina staggered back, her legs suddenly spongy. Her candle sputtered and went out. She cried out, then clamped a hand to her mouth. Something moved in the darkness. A bat, perhaps, startled by her cry. Its presence was not a comfort.

With the dim filtered light from the opening above, the darkness was not complete, but close enough that even when straining she could not make out the walls of the chamber or even more than a few inches from her eyes. "Alex." Her voice came as no more than a strangled whisper, and the sound of it scared her more than the silence.

Signore! "Signore!" She shouted it this time. "Gesù Cristo!" She fumbled in her pocket for the matches Alex had given her to carry. Her fingers shook as she struck, then struck once again before it caught. She held it unsteadily to the candlewick and breathed her relief when the light enlarged and once again warmed the chamber.

Her pants were soiled by the guano on the floor, but she sat a moment longer, letting the strength return to her legs. Why had she come? Why did she want to see once again these horrifying images? The wind moaned, and standing swiftly, she felt a wave of dizziness and panicked at the thought of fainting there.

She staggered to the entrance and looked swiftly back over her shoulder. The chamber was still. Candle held high, she made her way back into the main cave. Her candlelight shrank to a mere firefly glow in the immense opening.

Alex was not there. Now she understood his

warning. Without it she would have gone in search of him. She might not have even considered the danger of wandering off, searching one tunnel after another. Neither did she want to stay alone in this echo chamber with the painted one at her back.

She found the side tunnel Alex had marked with the string earlier. With one hand she felt the string pulled tightly along the wall and entered. She held the candle in her left hand, and felt her way along the string with her right. She would not let go of the string for one minute. That way she couldn't make a wrong turn.

It seemed that wouldn't be a problem. After only ten paces the tunnel shrank down until she was stooping, then seemed to disappear altogether. The string, though, kept on, and she dropped to her knees before a small opening above the floor. Here the walls and floor were damp.

Surely Alex hadn't crawled through there! But the string continued through the hole. He must have. Well, that didn't mean she would. But what was the alternative? To turn back to the empty chamber? She shuddered, then looked at the hole again. If Alex Makepeace could fit through, she could.

But not with her candle lit. The very thought of extinguishing it made her tremble. What if she couldn't get it lit again? She closed her eyes and stilled her breath. Maybe she should call to him. But then she remembered how disturbed the bats had been the last time something startled them. She didn't want bats filling this small tunnel with no room even to cringe.

Resolved, she blew out the candle and crouched down to the small space. Flat on her stomach, she pulled herself inside. Immediately she felt trapped and terrified. How long would it last? It was hard to feel the twine and keep pulling herself, so she reached up after every pull to make sure it was there. As though it could go anywhere else.

Soon she was able to crawl on her knees, then once again to stoop. She stopped and relit her candle. In its light, she saw that the floor was rising. The whole tunnel climbed upward. "Alex?" It was a soft inquiry, not enough to disturb anything lurking there. Nor did it bring an answer.

Carina sighed, wondering whether to go on or turn back. But turning back meant crawling again, and she wasn't ready to do that again so soon. She followed the string a few paces upward and came to a very steep rise. The surface was uneven, and she climbed like a goat, using any jut or indentation for a foothold, while clasping her candle and using her one free hand to pull herself up.

She reached, and something gripped her wrist. Screaming, she dropped her candle and nearly fell backward. A flood of bats washed over her, and she fended them off with one hand while the other was held fast by whatever had caught her. Again her heart rushed and beat wildly inside her.

The grip on her wrist tightened, and she realized it was Alex Makepeace who had a hold of her. With one jerk, he pulled her up and held her steady.

"You scared me to death!"

"I'm sorry, Carina." He caught her shoulders.

She could see his face in the dim light of his candle, which he must have set on the floor to catch hold of her. If she hadn't been so intent on the climb, she might have noticed the extra glow from above and his motion to reach for her. As it was, she was thankful not to have lost control of her bodily functions. "Don't you know better than to grab someone in the dark!"

"I didn't want to speak and disturb the bats. I guess it might have been better if I had." He smiled sheepishly.

"Indeed." Carina pressed a hand to her galloping heart.

"Did you think Tommy-knockers had your arm?"

"Tommy-knockers?"

"Ghosts of men buried alive in the mines."

Carina shuddered. "Don't tell me any more."

He looked down the way she'd climbed. "How'd you get through that tunnel?"

"I'm smaller than you, Alex. And I didn't want to be alone."

Alex released her. "Those pictures would be enough to spook a body. I shouldn't have left you. I hope you don't intend to go in there again."

She shook her head. "I've seen it all now. But what is this? What have you found?"

"A crystal cave." Alex stooped and raised the candle. Its light danced all around them on the sharp-pointed facets of the small aperture. It was like being inside a geode. The rounded space glittered with soft hues on the circular ceiling scarcely a foot over their heads and eight feet around.

Carina stared at its beauty, awed. There was no sense of evil here, only wonder. She reached out and touched one crystal as long as her finger and twice as broad. Alex was silent as she walked slowly around the chamber.

"Is this the end of the tunnel?"

He shrugged. "I don't see another way out. Be kind of hard to miss it."

"It's beautiful."

He nodded. "A true wonder of nature."

Carina returned to him. "I'm glad I followed you."

"And I know better than to waste my breath next time."

"I followed the string. I wasn't wandering."

He didn't scold as Quillan might, just took his knife and cut the end of the twine, then nailed it into the wall with a thin spike and small-headed hammer. "There. Now we can find it again."

"Alex . . ." She looked again around the sparkling chamber. "Do you think we should?"

"Should?"

"Find it again."

He narrowed one eye. "Why not?"

"It seems . . . like a secret."

Alex stroked the crystals over his head, then dropped his hand. "We'll leave it for now. Come on." Before starting for the opening, he reached down and picked up a thin rosy-hued crystal shaped like the spire on a church. "Here." He gave it to her, and Carina tucked it into her pocket.

Alex helped her down the steep drop, where she retrieved her candle. The wax was broken, and he replaced it with a fresh one. "There."

She took the holder. "I'm glad it was you holding my wrist and not some Tommy-knocker."

He laughed. "You nearly split my ears with that scream in all that crystal."

"You deserved it."

"You're a hard woman, Carina."

Was she? Was that why Quillan didn't come home? She didn't speak while they climbed out, then wrapped her muffler about her mouth once outside. The cold seemed fiercer on the ride down, and by the time they reached Crystal at dusk, the snow was coming in earnest. Carina fended the flakes from her eyes as she dismounted outside her door.

Alex took the reins of both horses. "Good night, Carina."

"Good night." She watched him lead the animals into the storm. Then she went inside. Mae must have kept the fire stoked, for the room was warm and inviting. Carina lit the lamp and studied the crystal in its light. Had Wolf found the crystal cave? Or had he only immersed himself in the teardrop chamber?

She closed her eyes and pictured his last painting. The pale wolf had been man-sized, howling its grief and fear to the world. Had the ochre man offered his child, whose cries he couldn't bear, to the eagle whose shadow wingtips had brushed his forehead? And who was the eagle to Wolf?

Sixteen

So many questions.

Will I ever know the answers?

—Carina

"WHO IS IT?" Carina turned at the tap on her door.

"Mae."

Carina hurried over and opened the door that connected her hall to Mae's kitchen. She felt a twinge of guilt as Mae swept into the room, breath labored as always. "What is it, Mae? Are you all right?"

"Me? I'm all right. But I could ask you the same."

Carina studied her face, searching out her intent. "I'm fine, Mae."

"Do you mind telling me where you were all day and why you simply disappeared? Or do I have to look any farther than Alexander Makepeace?"

Carina was horrified. "What are you saying?"

Mae raised a plump hand. "I'm not saying I understand Quillan or condone his absence. But he's your husband, Carina, and unless you want the tongues to wag, you'd better consider well before you sneak off with Mr. Makepeace again."

"I didn't sneak off with him."

Mae made it sound dirty. What they had done was above reproach. Yes, they had been alone together, but in no way compromising or . . . But how could Mae know that? How had it looked?

"I know what it is to be lonely, Carina. Why do you think I fill my house up with people who need me, or at least my cooking and cleaning?"

"I'm not lonely. I have you and Èmie." Though now that Èmie was married things would change.

Mae shook her head. "I'm not blind, Carina. And what I've seen, others have seen. Don't you think Quillan's had enough marks against him?"

Confused, Carina pushed the hair back from her cheek. "What do you mean?"

"He's had to fight for every ounce of respect he's won. How will it be if he learns his wife is . . ."

"Is what?" Fire filled her veins.

"Taking up with another man."

Carina's breath came out in a burst. "Is that what you think?" It hurt more than she'd known to have Mae doubt her. And it was so unfair. "What about Quillan? Where is he, and with whom? Do you doubt his faithfulness? Or is it only me you blame? What have I done but wait and be willing?" She threw up her hands and stalked across the room, shaking now with unspent anger toward Mae, toward Quillan, toward herself for the pleasure she did take in Alex Makepeace's company.

"I'm not saying it's so. Just telling you how it looks."

Carina spun. "How it looks? How does it look when my husband won't spend one night with me? When he sleeps on the floor or in his wagon? When he eats at the hotel instead of my table? When he leaves for months with no word, no thought for me, no—" She burst into angry tears.

Mae's hand was warm on the side of her head. "There, there. I'm sorry I upset you."

"I don't know what else to do. I've tried to understand. I thought by knowing Rose, by knowing Wolf . . ."

"What are you talking about?"

Carina raised her tear-streaked face to Mae's. "I had Rose's diary. Father Charboneau gave it to me. I felt her love for Quillan and loved him better for it. And now the cave . . ."

"Carina, you're not making sense."

"Alex Makepeace and I found a cave under the Rose Legacy."

Mae stepped back. "The Rose Legacy. Wolf's mine?"

Carina nodded.

"You went back there? After falling in the shaft?" Mae said.

"I've been back dozens of times. I . . . I visit the grave."

Mae paled. "Landsakes, Carina."

Carina sniffed, swiping at the tears beneath her nose. "Mr. Makepeace and I went down the shaft to the cave. There's another chamber that's painted. It's Wolf's story."

Mae sank to the bed. "Are you telling me Wolf went down into the cave and painted the walls?"

Carina nodded. "That's what he must have been doing when Rose thought he was searching for gold hour after hour. He was painting his life. It's all there. Some of it horrifying, some just sad. Some I don't understand, but . . . but that's where I was with Alex Makepeace."

Carina realized she'd broken her own injunction for secrecy, but she had to. She couldn't bear for Mae to think badly of her. She reached into her pocket and brought out the crystal. "There is also a crystal cave, no bigger than this room, with crystals like this growing from the walls and ceiling. It's beautiful."

Mae fingered the crystal Carina laid in her palm, then held it up to the light. She sighed. "I'm sorry I doubted you. It's just you're so young, and it's hard to be alone."

Carina sensed Mae's own loneliness as she had when they first met. One year of happiness with her husband was all Mae had known. But, Carina thought bitterly, it was more than she had with Quillan. "Mr. Makepeace is my husband's partner . . . and my friend."

Mae nodded slowly. "Unfortunately, folks judge by appearances."

Carina dropped her hands to her sides. "Then I am judged already. What kind of woman cannot keep her husband home?" She walked to the window. "Half a year ago Crystal would have had me hung. Beck's woman, they called me. What do I care now what they think they see?"

Mae stood, holding the crystal out to Carina.

Carina shook her head. "Keep it." When Mae went silently through the door, Carina stood a long while at the window, looking out into the night.

The moment he heard the explosion, Alex knew something was wrong. Years of unconsciously gauging a blast gave him the ability to register any differences and mark them in his mind. Even before he heard shouts of "fire!" and "cave-in!" he had jolted into action, running toward the main shaft where already men were lowering the winch in a desperate effort to have it in place for the fleeing men below.

Cave-ins were bad, often deadly, but nothing was so bad as fire. It sucked the oxygen faster than a man could run, and they would drop like canaries, crumpled and suffocated within yards of freedom. Alex's heart hammered as he hollered orders, directing the men in procedures he'd practiced in his sleep whenever the nightmare possibilities tormented his rest.

There was so little they could do, and so little time to do it. Now it seemed each moment hung on a thread, and he worked and hollered as though he'd stepped outside himself and watched from a distance, safe from the agonizing knowledge of his own futility. Billows of smoke and dust rose from the shaft as the first winch platform of men was raised. Two of those who surfaced were bloody, but they were dragged free and flung where they lay, and the winch dropped the platform again, careening down as fast as the chain would spin.

"Watch the heat!" Alex shouted, and the winchman poured water over the chain to cool its burning links. He didn't want another accident to compound the first. "Now oil it!" A quick dose was all they had time for before they were raising the platform again with more men.

Alex helped his foreman, James Mires, to his feet. "How bad is it?"

The man doubled over and coughed. "Bad. A dozen men at least behind the wall."

Behind the wall meant anywhere beyond the cave-in, even in the rubble itself. Alex gripped his arm and steadied him. "The fire?"

"Think we stopped it." Mires choked again, banging his chest as though he could expel the bad air that way.

The next platform of men confirmed that the fire was out, and Alex had a modicum of hope. Once the dust settled they'd deal with the cave-in, but the immediate danger of fire had lessened. When all the men had been retrieved from the shaft, James Mires saw to their injuries and counted heads. Thirteen men were unaccounted for, and now it was Alex Makepeace's turn to take charge.

Using the maps of the operation he'd drawn and the men's information, he located the collapse on paper. If the explosion had been caused by a pocket of toxic air, there would be only bodies to retrieve. But if it was powder error or any other such cause, the missing men could still be living. Time was critical.

Hours passed as they worked on the best route to the men; then shifts were taken to first fortify the surrounding tunnel, then begin the process of clearing the rubble. The first men retrieved were beyond help. Alex looked at their crushed bodies and hung his head. It wasn't the first carnage he'd viewed, nor would it be the last. Yet it didn't make it easy to imagine their moments of fear and pain.

He stooped to help carry one of the dead to the platform. There would be families to notify, widows to comfort. He didn't want to think of the orphans. But these men knew what they were facing, what dangers were inherent to the job. They knew when they signed on. But Alex kept thinking of Carina, and what she would say when she heard of today's disaster.

In shifts, they worked through the night. Alex staggered with fatigue, but his expertise was needed at every step. Each time they reached a point of decision, it was his call. Build up first and lose valuable time, or break through and risk a tumble. His call, his responsibility.

Alex sank to a pile of timbers and swabbed his face with a kerchief. He was black with soot and sweat and dust. His eyes felt scratched and burned. Already they'd removed too much rubble to raise any hopes for the men inside. This whole length of tunnel was likely collapsed. But he was determined not one body would lie unretrieved. No Tommy-knockers in this mine. Alex looked roofward and prayed silently. If even one man could be saved . . .

The winch squealed, and Alex turned slowly to see who was coming down now. His spirit sank as Carina appeared in the dark shaft. This was not something she should look upon. He stood slowly, knowing as he did how futile it would be to ask her to leave. And truthfully, he didn't want to.

She stepped from the platform and carried a candle lantern toward him. He waited. She stopped before him, and he saw that she'd been told enough already. "How much farther?"

He shook his head. "Three hundred yards of tunnel. How much is collapsed, I don't know."

She looked at the bodies, covered but not yet raised to the surface. "May I have the names of all those dead?"

Alex swiped a drop of sweat from his ear. Carina was bundled against the cold outside, but down here with the pressure and anxiety of the situation, it felt like an inferno. He took a pad from his pocket and from memory began listing the men whose bodies had already been removed.

He handed her the page. "Four still missing."

"What contingency is made for these families?"

"None."

She released a sharp breath.

"This is part of the job, Carina. Part of the risk. Yes, I hate it. But they know. . . ."

"Do the women know? The children?"

"They know, Carina. They accept it. Doesn't make it any easier, but they know." His fatigue made him sharp. When Carina reached a hand to his arm, he gripped her fingers. "I'm sorry." And he was. As bad as he felt, he could see she was taking it even harder. Why?

She spoke evenly. "Each of these families and any others yet to be found will receive a severance large enough to see them through the winter. Take it out of my husband's share."

Alex shook his head. "That's not the precedent, Carina. It will cause trouble with the other mines."

"I don't care about the other mines. This is my mine, my men. You will do this, Alex." Her eyes were dark coals, their intensity unmistakable. His heart jumped with an emotion foreign to him, but recognizable enough.

He gripped her fingers still on his arm. "Carina . . ."

She turned away. "How did it happen?"

"I don't know yet. I'll have to study the scene. Right now my first priority is clearing it out. Finding the men."

"Could they be alive?"

He hesitated, then, "They could." If she heard his doubt, he couldn't help it. Yes, it was possible, but what were the chances?

"What can I do?"

"Pray." He lifted her fingers from his arm, pressed them briefly, then started back down the tunnel.

Carina rode the platform up the shaft. The nightmare scene below was reminiscent of the dark night of hangings and bodies lying covered like furrows in the road. How much life would Crystal claim? *Signore* . . . She stepped from the platform and handed the candle lantern back to the winchman.

Word had reached her early about the accident, but she hadn't been able to leave the restaurant until the last of her diners had gone home. How strange and pointless it had seemed to be serving plate after plate of elegant fare when somewhere below ground men were gasping their last under tons of crumbled stone and timbers.

But what could she do? Alex had looked terrible, bone weary and discouraged, but he at least had a purpose and the means by which to work. She knew the burden he felt, even though he spoke the company line. Precedent. What did she care for precedent?

There were widows and children now. She would see that they had what they needed through the winter until the roads were passable enough for them to leave. She didn't care whom she offended in order to do it. If Quillan were here . . . oh, how she wished Quillan were here. He had been so good after the flood.

She knew from what she'd seen and heard how he helped people, providing what they needed at his own expense. Surely he would agree with her now. He couldn't know how conditions were in his mine. He wouldn't refuse these families in their need. She put a hand to her belly. "Your papa would do the right thing."

But Quillan wasn't here. So she must do it for him. She clasped the list of names Alex had written up for her. Tomorrow she would find these families and tell them not to worry. Their grief was terrible enough. They would not starve as well.

"I'd like you to come with me this morning, Quillan." Reverend Shepard cinched the soft tie that held his wife into the chair beside the window.

"No thanks."

"Not to hear my sermon—I've said enough to you over the years. Just to be present, to allow God—"

"I said no." Quillan looked at his foster father. "I'll sit with her."

"Martha Reisner from the ladies' aid sits with her the last Sunday of the month." Reverend Shepard fixed Quillan with a look too reminiscent of his stern pulpit manner. "She'll be here any minute now. There's no need for you to stay."

"Then I'll find something else."

The reverend dropped a heavy hand on his shoulder. "As a favor to an old man."

Quillan's heart twisted. He didn't want to care for this old man. Cain, maybe. He'd suffered Preacher Paine for Cain's sake. Alan, even. But this man, this reverend . . . His hands clenched at his sides. Then he released them. "All right." He could always recite poetry in his head.

As they headed for the door, a broad woman came through the gate. Quillan cocked a brow. "Martha Reisner?"

The reverend nodded. "And leave your uncharitable thoughts."

Quillan wondered how he'd known. But then Martha Reisner could hardly engender much else. She was squeezed so tightly into the dress that it was a wonder she could take a breath at all. He caught his foster father's eye and let it go.

They walked next door to the church. The wind buffeted the minister, and once Quillan caught his arm to steady him. How old was the man anyway? Quillan had thought him old when he was a boy, but he supposed most kids thought the same about their parents. He couldn't help noticing the stares as he walked inside with the reverend.

"Just take a seat anywhere." Reverend Shepard smoothed the wind damage on his hair and suit.

"How 'bout the steps?" Quillan waved out the door toward the wooden steps that formed his escape.

"This pew should do." The reverend nudged him to the side, and Quillan plunked down on the hard wooden bench. He wanted more than anything to get up and run, but he'd conquered that urge early on. This was one more test of his fortitude, and he would rise to the challenge.

The hymns were no problem. Quillan liked music, and if folks wanted to sing about God and his heavenly promises, let them. Then the reverend took the pulpit. Quillan noticed the quiver in one hand, and the man's eyes brushed his once. He opened the Bible and threaded the ribbon into place.

" 'And he said to them all, if any man will come after me, let him deny himself, and take up his cross daily, and follow me. For whosoever will save his life shall lose it: but whosoever will lose his life for my sake, the same shall save it.' " Reverend Shepard looked now at Quillan, and Quillan felt the force of his gaze.

What did he want him to do, jump up and cry out his need for a savior? Isn't that what Cain had wanted?

"Take up his cross daily." The reverend searched the crowd. "What is it to take up one's cross, but to accept the sufferings the good Lord sees fit to visit upon you?"

Quillan frowned. Well, at least they saw eye to eye on the source of the suffering. But accept it? He'd rather fight.

"Why, you ask, would a good and loving God allow

pain in the lives of His people? What place has suffering in victory?" And now he boomed, "'And he said unto me, my grace is sufficient for thee: for my strength is made perfect in weakness.' Beware your strength, for it takes you from God. It is in your burdens, in your failings, in your pain, that His power is made perfect."

Once again Quillan locked eyes with his foster father. He should rejoice over the torment he'd suffered, suffered at the hands of the reverend and his wife? So God could be powerful? Quillan wanted to laugh.

"'For whosoever will save his life shall lose it.' Do you love your life more than you love your Lord? You will lose it! Anything that comes before the Lord is forfeit. 'If any man come to me, and hate not his father, and mother, and wife, and children, and brethren, and sisters, yea, and his own life also, he cannot be my disciple.'"

Cain had told Quillan God wasn't condoning hate, only drawing a line beyond which no one could raise someone or something before God. So vast should be the difference in reverence that it was like love and hate. For Quillan, the two had seemed hopelessly entwined.

"'But whosoever will lose his life for my sake, the same shall save it.'" The reverend rested his gaze gently now. "Must you die for the Lord to know His salvation? No. You must only die to yourself. How? By taking up the cross daily. What is the cross in your life? Take it up. Bear it bravely as Simon bore the cross of our Lord."

Quillan fought the scowl. What was his cross? Ignominious birth. Loveless childhood. Rejection. Shame. Fear. Not fear! Yes. Fear to risk his heart, fear to love. That was why he hurt Carina. Not because he'd failed Cain. But because she might fail him.

"Take up your weakness, your pain, your failing. Be

weak that God might be strong. 'For when we were yet without strength, in due time Christ died for the ungodly.'" The reverend seemed to shrink, though his eyes remained firm. "He has accomplished your salvation. But He has not yet perfected your circumstances. Do not be confused in the two."

Reverend Shepard stepped down from the pulpit, and Quillan saw the quivering in one leg. Almost stumbling, the minister took his seat as another hymn filled the church. Quillan drew a slow breath. In the old man's weakness, did he see God's power? He'd ignored the fiery sermons easily enough, but it was in the gentle moments, when the reverend was at a loss, that Quillan had been most perilously close to seeing God.

He shook his head. He hadn't intended to listen, certainly not to ponder the words of this man. Maybe they weren't just the reverend's words. Maybe they were God's. But he and God were not on speaking terms. Quillan wet his lips and swallowed the dryness from his throat. Cain had believed he refused to surrender. Maybe he feared to.

What was he doing there? He should go. To Carina? Something inside him lurched at the thought. Something rebellious and altogether untamed. Why did his heart have to jump that way at just the thought of her? What if he went back to Crystal and found her gone?

But he couldn't stay away forever. For better or worse he owed her something. If only her freedom. That thought hurt. Seeing the conciliatory care the reverend gave his wife these last weeks had shown Quillan a sort of love he didn't understand. A giving with no return, an accepting with no sense.

Quillan shrank from the thought of so exposing himself. To be so vulnerable . . . *And he said unto me, my grace is sufficient for thee: for my strength is made perfect in weakness.* Quillan sat straight and stiff, showing nothing of his thoughts. What if he returned to Carina. Asked her to love him. After their last encounter! Not a chance.

But what if . . . He thought of his mother's diary, the despair he'd read in those pages. But she'd found Wolf. And whatever his father's story, he, too, had found joy with Rose. An image of them charred and entangled filled his mind, but Quillan fought it back.

If only he could purge it forever! But maybe that was his cross. Maybe the pain was what he needed to embrace. The loss. The sorrow he felt for two ill-fated lovers too damaged to survive. Quillan closed his eyes and lowered his jaw. Let them think him in prayer. He swallowed the lump in his throat. Maybe he was.

Seventeen

My heart aches for the lives that were lost in my husband's venture.
What more can I do but bring succor to the wives
who no longer have a man to call their own?
—Carina

CARINA WALKED FROM SHACK TO SHACK. Seven of the men were unmarried, but six had wives, and five of those had at least one child. Carina entered the sixth house when the thin blond woman opened the door.

The woman stared as though Carina weren't real. "I heard you were coming, but I didn't believe it. Why would you do this?"

"You are Mary Billings?"

"Yes. My man was killed last night. But what's that to you?"

Carina reached into her velvet purse for the last packet of bills. "I'm very sorry for your loss. My husband would want you to have this. Mr. Makepeace has authorized it." She held out the bills. "To see you through the winter, until the roads are passable."

Dazed, Mrs. Billings took the money. Then, her legs collapsing, she landed on a crate beside the door that held a saddle and some blankets. "I always knew it would end like this. When I married him I knew." She began to sob.

Carina ached for her. "I'm so sorry, Mrs. Billings."

The woman raised her eyes doubtfully. "Why? Why are you sorry? You don't even know me."

"You came last Sunday to my restaurant."

"You know that? There were so many all through the day."

Carina stopped before her, took Mary Billings' hands between hers. "I didn't know your name. Or your husband's. Not before Mr. Makepeace gave me the list. But I remember your face." She was ashamed that she couldn't recall Mr. Billings' features. But the men were so many.

Her throat tightened painfully. "I know the money cannot replace what you have lost."

The woman gripped the bills to her chest and cried again. "Nothing can, nothing will. But at least... at least I won't starve."

"If you need anything..."

"When I walked into that fine dining room of yours and saw you all petite and sparkling... I despised you. I thought you made us look bad. Your fine cooking making what I put on the plate every night seem like dirt." She swiped her sleeve across her face. "But now this."

Carina lowered her face. "It's little enough."

"It's more than anyone else would do."

Carina stood up. "Please accept my deep regrets."

Mary Billings also stood. "If you'll accept my apology."

Carina embraced her. "No apology is needed."

Carina then left, her own eyes tired from sharing the tears of these women. Mary Billings had been the only one to speak her resentment, but they had all been wary. Had they, like Mary, resented her efforts toward their husbands? It didn't matter. What mattered was that now they would have what they needed to live.

Carina tried to imagine Mary's grief, knowing that each day her husband left for the mine might be the last she would see him. And then to receive the word that yes, her husband was killed in the mine, and to be all alone. Carina drew herself up, staunchly defending in her own mind this small kindness.

No, she hadn't known their names, perhaps had never spoken to them personally. But she felt these deaths. And she wished there was more, much more she could do.

Alex Makepeace looked at the dozen men assembled before him, their scowls and fierce disapproval no more than he'd expected. He'd lost thirteen men to the mine, yet these men were not here to protest the loss of life. One burly thug with a cauliflower ear shouted, "It's not done, Makepeace. You'll have our men jumping ship, expecting favors, demanding what we can't give."

Alex held himself straight. "It wasn't my decision."

"Since when does a bleeding-heart woman run your mine?"

"Since her husband owns it."

"Partially!"

"Partially," he conceded. He could have thwarted Carina, could have denied her the funds, the names, the access to the families. If his personal involvement had not gone beyond the bounds, he might have.

"Our investors won't stand for it. You've set a precedent we won't allow."

"It's only once." Alex knew the argument was feeble. He'd told Carina from the start how her actions would be perceived. No eastern investors would stand for a mine taking responsibility for the accidental deaths of workers. No mine could afford to insure against the mistakes and misjudgments of its workers. He knew it! He had no quarrel with their thinking. So why was he standing there, defending Carina's actions toward the families of those killed in his cave-in?

"Once is all it takes! They'll be clamoring for restitution all over the district! Take it back, man, or there'll be trouble."

"I can't take it back. Those families and widows need some way to survive until winter breaks. Then they'll be gone."

The man bristled. "And what of the powder blast at the Iron Horse? Three men dead."

Alex swallowed the tightness in his throat. "That's their business."

"Their men are shouting for fair treatment."

Alex understood the fear behind their objections. It would be chaos if the mine owners took responsibility for every mishap. It would be ruin. The miners accepted employment knowing the risk. They were paid to take the risk. "The accident at the New Boundless was the worst to date. Minor errors will not be treated with severance. No severance will be offered again." He slumped with the weakness of his argument, but he determined he would stand against Carina if she ever suggested as much again.

"Our own men say they'll go directly to her."

Alex turned to the voice. James Mires, his foreman. Alex saw the concern there, knew its depth. Yes, their own miners would be the hardest of all to deal with, wanting for their families what the others had already received.

A short redheaded engineer called out, "I had one man who was crippled last month by a falling Burleigh come today demanding compensation for his family."

"You hear that?" The first man raised a fist. "We'll have every rocked-up hacker demanding justice!"

Alex sagged. It was true. He would be reprimanded by the investors, maybe replaced. He rubbed his face with stubborn resolve. "What's done is done. It won't be repeated." It was the best he could do. He couldn't ask Carina to take back what she'd given, couldn't demand it back from the women and children who could starve before they made it out of Crystal. It wasn't his responsibility, but Carina had made it so.

He heard the grumbling, knew these foremen and engineers were not satisfied. They had the same responsibilities as he. Their jobs, their reputations were at stake. They'd be required to handle the situation so the investors didn't lose revenue. And he'd just made their lives very difficult. They were caught between his generosity and their quotas. So was he.

In his mind he cursed Carina. Then he cursed himself. He should never have listened, never have allowed, even for a minute . . . Had he thought with his head instead of his heart he would have squelched her plan, no matter the hurt he saw in the depths of her eyes. His responsibility was to his employers, not his employer's wife!

"It's on your shoulders, then." The burly man raised a finger. "If the New Boundless takes on one of Charity

Jane's men, you'll be dealing with me."

"I won't take on any of your men." Which meant he'd be running short through the entire winter, having lost thirteen workers. He saw the dismay on James Mires's face. But what else could he do? The other mines would lose men the minute they thought they could find a better deal at the Boundless. He'd rocked the boat, and the ripples were spreading.

"You've not heard the last of this. Trouble will come of it." Grumbling, the crowd dispersed. They'd accomplished nothing. Alex could only hope that, like the snows, this would melt away come spring when the families left Crystal and the memory of a misguided generosity was forgotten. It was a faint hope, and when he met Mires's eye, he knew it would be a long time until spring.

Carina sensed a change in Alex Makepeace when he came in for dinner that night. Was he angry with her? Had she overstepped his consideration for her? Had he lost face because of her? He hadn't looked happy when he turned over the funds, even though they came from the monies Quillan would have counted profit.

Now he looked miserable. She wanted to ask him, to make him tell her what weighed on him so heavily. Maybe it was losing the men. Maybe it had nothing to do with her. Either way she couldn't ask. Mae's suspicions had warned her not to display a relationship beyond the accepted courtesy.

But it ate at her while she worked, cooking the hare with wild onions, tomato paste, and the last of the anchovies, and continued as she served the laden plates to the tables. Alex had seemed discouraged and almost hostile. Had she once again alienated someone who mattered to her? First Flavio, then Quillan, now Alex. No, it wasn't the same with Alex. It couldn't be. She had loved Flavio, loved Quillan still. What she felt for Alex Makepeace was . . . what? *Oh!* She slapped the towel on the stove.

Mae glanced her way. "What's flustering you?"

"Am I trouble, Mae? Do I . . . do I give people trouble?" Even as she said it, she recalled the bullets thumping into Mae's body, bullets meant for Carina Maria DiGratia. "Oh!" She threw up her hands and stalked across the kitchen and back. "I don't mean to cause trouble. But somehow I end up in it."

"What trouble are you in now?"

"What trouble? My husband won't stay home. You think I've taken up with another man, and he—" Carina gripped her hands together and faltered under Mae's gaze. "He looks like the devil walked over his grave."

"I thought maybe you were coming around to that."

Carina rushed to her, caught her hands together. "So you saw it, too? Do you know what it is? Why is he so angry? So miserable?"

"I couldn't say."

"But you guess."

"Whatever I guess I keep to myself."

"Mae!" Carina gave Mae's hands a shake. "Now is not the time to mind your business. Tell me!"

"You've stirred the kettle." Mae sighed. "I know you meant well. But you don't understand how things work in a mining community. You've put Mr. Makepeace between a hammer and an anvil."

"How?"

"Setting precedent with those miners' families."

Carina stared a moment. "Thirteen men were killed. In my husband's mine."

"It's not his mine. And even if it were free and clear his alone, it would still be a dangerous precedent. You can't go taking responsibility for accidents that no one else can or will pay for. The other mine operators are up in arms, and Mr. Makepeace is their target. That's all."

"Well, he can tell them it was my doing."

Mae snorted. "That'll go a long way in saving him face."

Carina threw up her hands. "Has the world gone mad? Is everyone pazzo? What are the women and children to do if their men are dead?"

Mae was silent.

"What!" Carina demanded.

"It wasn't your place, Carina. Not as your husband's spokesman or in any capacity in the mine. Especially not through Alex Makepeace. Now he's as culpable as you."

Carina swallowed her indignation. So that was it. Her innocence had once again caused trouble. But why was it so wrong to help people in need? Quillan would have done the same. But he would have done it quietly. Not as an ultimatum to Alex Makepeace that set a precedent to the other mine owners.

She sank to the chair. "Will I ever get it right?"

"I don't know about that." Mae smiled. "You act with your heart, Carina. Maybe that's how it should be."

Carina forked her fingers into her hair. "If Quillan were here, he would have handled it better."

"But he's not."

Carina met Mae's eyes. That was the first time Mae hadn't defended Quillan outright or excused his absence as a matter of course. It was almost a criticism, and it so took her by surprise Carina couldn't answer. No, he was not there, and she had acted as she thought best. What more could she do?

Carina stood and checked the stewing hares in the oven. If she had put Alex in a bad place, the best thing now would be to let him handle it. If it strained their relationship, well, that too should rest awhile. Grabbing a pair of hot pads, she pulled the pan of stewed hare from the oven.

Celia came in with a tray and Carina loaded it with steaming plates, then did the same with Elizabeth's tray. Carina would stay in the kitchen until Alex had gone home. No sense making him more miserable with her presence. She fought a deep loneliness that was becoming chronic. Resting a hand on her abdomen, she wondered why thoughts of the child inside didn't comfort her now.

Quillan watched Leona Shepard stare out the window as though something vitally important might appear at any moment. The startled intensity of her gaze had twice made him look to see if something truly had frightened her, but there had been nothing but the neighboring houses and perhaps a passing carriage.

The white cords of her hair were fuzzy with inattention, and her skin was like softly veined wild rose petals. Maybe she'd been lovely once. She could have been now, but for the distorting of the features, the sagging mouth, the bloodshot, terrified eyes. And her lack of flesh that lent the overall skeletal appearance.

He felt uneasy scrutinizing her so, but he had to reconcile this creature once and for all with the image he carried of her in his mind. He wanted that much at least to come from this time. He'd intended to leave after the service Sunday morning, but snow had kept him from starting out. Even if he could have traveled, it wasn't fair to Jock and Jack and Sam. Now it was Tuesday, and the reverend was out and about his charitable duties.

Once again Quillan waited in the room of the woman who had made his youth a torment. Understanding her illness had removed some of the sting, but he was uncertain what more was left to do. If the weather cleared today, he would go. Or tomorrow or the next day. He had already determined it was time.

The reason he had come no longer existed. He couldn't confront her with his mother's journal and demand an accounting of the lies Mrs. Shepard had told. He couldn't even lay the blame to her account. All he could do was put it behind him. He knew the truth now.

His mother had loved him. Enough to put him into hands she thought would be safer, stronger than her own. Safe from Wolf and their entangled pain. He no longer saw Wolf as a monster. Knowing, as Rose hadn't, that Henri Charboneau had been the killer, even that taint was removed from his parentage. Yet what did it change?

Mrs. Shepard gripped the shawl around her shoulders and made a pitiful mewling.

Quillan leaned forward and held her shoulder. "It's all right." But it wasn't right. Nothing was right, not for Leona Shepard, not for the reverend, not for Quillan. And, he thought, certainly not for Carina. Why had he embroiled her in his life?

Because he loved her. He didn't know how to show it, but her incessant presence in his thoughts confirmed it. From the time he dumped her wagon and she'd waved her hand furiously in his face, spitting fire, she'd captured more of his thoughts than anyone before.

Every time he'd passed her in the street, when he had looked at her with smug, taunting indifference, she'd made a new impression on his mind, the sunlight shimmering in her hair as on a crow's wing, her willowy waist, her hands so expressive. When he'd seen her broken and in pain and drawn her up from the mine shaft of the Rose Legacy, feelings had stirred in him too powerful to address.

When he'd told her he'd marry her to keep Berkley Beck from the privilege and first entertained the idea of taking her into his arms as his wife, those feelings had proved as potent as he feared. When he'd seen her on her knees and spoken cruel words to break the terrifying closeness they'd shared, he'd known the feelings could destroy the defenses he'd built over years of rejection. When she'd stood teary eyed after Cain's death and promised to wait for him, he'd almost given in.

What if he had? Would they be snuggled up warmly in that little house of hers, sharing a meal of some fantastic creation that only her hands could prepare? There would be no hallway to Mae's. No hordes of men seated at tables enjoying her rich and savory fare.

He dropped his face in regret. Mrs. Shepard looked away from the window. One clawed hand gripped his, and her mouth worked, the tendons straining in her throat.

He must have startled her, disturbed her with his own regret. "It's all right," he said again, voicing the lie.

She looked at him. "Quil-lan." This time it was unmistakable.

He leaned forward, searching her face. What was she saying? What did she want from him? "Yes. Yes, it's Quillan."

"Quillan." Tears started and streamed from her eyes.

His hand shook as he held her shoulder, searching himself for some response. What did he feel? Did he care that she knew him, that the knowing brought her pain? Slowly, hating himself for weakness, he folded her into his arms. Her fingers dug into the tendons across his shoulders as she sobbed.

"It's all right." And now he meant it.

She softened in his arms like a bird growing limp. Babbling, she petted his arm, playing with his name. "Quil-lan, Quillan, Quillan."

He said nothing, only let her stroke him until she pushed back, catching his face between her palms. Her mouth hanging, she studied him, her eyes almost cognizant. Then, as though a shutter closed, she looked away to the window and grew rigid, picking at the shawl.

Quillan let go of her and stood. Whatever had passed between them, it was over. He left her staring and wandered out into the front room of the house. Should he tell the reverend what had transpired, that she'd recognized him and spoken his name? Did she have lucid moments with her husband? Would he regret that he had missed it?

Quillan sighed. He'd done all he could there, made whatever peace he could with his past. Now it was time to consider his future. He looked out at the sky breaking up into ragged strips of cloud. He could leave today. He went into the room he'd slept in these last days and gathered his things.

Carefully, he lifted his mother's journal. DeMornay. Where were her people? His family? Denver? Should he try? He swallowed the swelling in his throat. Maybe someday. Now he would go to Crystal. If Carina was still there . . . His stomach clutched. He felt an urgency for her. Something was changed, as though a vacuum inside had opened up and only Carina could fill it. *Let her be there!*

He heard the door before he'd finished tying his pack around his meager belongings. The reverend was home, and they could say their good-byes. Quillan shouldered the pack and went out to take leave of his foster father.

The reverend seemed to know what Quillan meant to say. Maybe the pack on his shoulder, maybe the look in his eyes. Reverend Shepard shrugged out of his coat and hung it on his hook, then turned with a sigh. "You're going, then?"

Quillan nodded.

"And did you find what you were seeking?"

"Not what I came for." Quillan glanced toward the bedroom where Mrs. Shepard sat picking her shawl and jumping at shadows. Not the satisfaction of confronting and attacking. "But maybe what I needed."

The reverend nodded, raised a hand to Quillan's shoulder. "God bless you, son."

Quillan looked into the gray-brown glassy eyes. He could tell the reverend he wasn't his son. They'd never seen fit to make him so. But in a sense he was. He carried inside him the lessons the reverend had impressed upon him over years of tutelage, and they hadn't all been learned at the end of a rod.

Quillan pressed the old man's hand. He glanced again at the room where Mrs. Shepard sat. "She knew me. She spoke my name."

Slowly the reverend smiled, just a faint crinkling of the eyes, a slight upturn to the mouth. He nodded, and Quillan saw the reverend's eyes grow bright with tears.

He pressed the old man's hand again and turned away. Shouldering the pack, he opened the door. "Good-bye, Reverend."

His foster father raised a quivering hand in farewell.

Eighteen

For my impulsive nature I make no excuse.
God did not create us all tortoises to contemplate each step.
Yet if I have acted wrongly, I pray the Lord will forgive.
It was my heart which dictated the deed.

—Carina

CARINA KNEW THE MEN WERE TROUBLE when Èmie first showed them to a table. They could only have gotten their names on the list since the trouble with the mines had alienated some of her former customers these last two weeks. There had been no lack of others to take their places, but these four had the look of the roughs who had previously terrorized the town. She knew. She'd seen enough of the roughs in her dealings with Berkley Beck.

Though washed and dressed appropriately, they were unmistakably different from her usual clientele. Did everyone else notice? She could be mistaken, but Alex Makepeace seemed to have been disturbed by their appearance. Did he know them or guess something of their manner? Had he tried to catch her eye?

They had hardly spoken since she'd demanded he

follow her orders. She knew things had grown difficult for him. The relations between his operation and others were strained. Even Joe Turner. And all because of her impulsive act. She sighed. It was better to let things settle on their own, but she missed their chats. She missed his smile. It was not so easy these days, nor so genuine.

Carina passed Èmie in the hall. It was Èmie's first night back to work since her wedding, and they'd hardly had a moment to talk. She was aching to share in Èmie's happiness, just to hear her talk of her husband and the expansion of their cabin and the plank floors he was putting down. But she was busy, so busy. She should be thankful. Such success! Yet the uneasy feeling wouldn't leave her. *What is it, Signore?*

She had little time to ponder it, though, between carrying trays and serving up plates. Celia was up to her elbows in dish suds, and Elizabeth looked like a rabbit hopping back and forth between tables and kitchen with the used dishes. Lucia carried pots of coffee and bowls of sugar. There was no cream.

Carina carried four bowls of steaming minestrone for the men who had concerned her and were now seated in the center of the room. They eyed her darkly as she approached, and again her senses sharpened. Where was the courtesy to which she was accustomed? Did they mean to provoke her?

"You smell somethin'?" One squint-eyed man sprawled in his chair, his arm dangling down the back.

The man across from him made a show of sniffing the air. "Smells like dago."

Carina's breath hitched, and she stopped, tray suspended. She had heard the word before, but not in Crystal, at least not in her presence.

"Sure does." The lumpy man crowded the table.

"You suppose they got dagos in Crystal?"

The first man snorted. "Got dagos everywhere. Like rats. They move in and breed."

Her breath came out hard. They hadn't looked at her, but she knew every word was directed her way. Then the speaker did look at her, and she saw a calculated cruelty she recognized all too well. Her heart hammered furiously. It was not only for herself that she seethed, but for Lucia, who stood frozen some few steps away, and for all the Italian people. Such ugliness had no place in her restaurant.

One step brought Carina beside the squinty man. "Get out."

"What's that?" His head lolled to the side insolently.

"I said, get out."

He curled a lip at his companions. "You hear that? She's mindin' my business."

With every ounce of restraint, she resisted dumping the soup on his head. "Get out of my restaurant."

"You telling me what to do? Need to learn your place . . . . dago woman." In his tone, in his face, was a taunt, a direct challenge.

Carina started to shake. The ugliness of it appalled her, but she held her ground, burning them with her eyes, never flinching. She felt motion and saw that Joe Turner and Alex Makepeace had come to stand behind her. Whatever their frustrations with her, they were her friends. A quick glance to the sides showed Ben Masterson and Horace Fisher also standing. As she watched, every man in the room rose to his feet.

Her chest swelled, and she returned her fiery gaze to the miscreant. "Get out."

The man did a quick peruse, then sneered. "Dago princess has them all by the—"

A flick of her wrist and the minestrone bowls slid from her tray, scalding down the side of his face, into his lap, and crashing to the floor. He jumped up with a yell and lunged.

Ben Masterson caught him around the chest. "Got no more than you deserved, mister. Clear out and don't come back."

Carina felt a hand grip her arm. It was Alex holding her steady. Did he think she would fly at the man like a cat? Or did he show her with that simple gesture that he was there for her?

"You'll pay for this!" The burned man swiped his hand down his face.

The other three scrambled up as Masterson released their friend. Together they stormed out, kicking table legs and shoving chairs as they went. Carina stood shaking. She shouldn't have burned him. Èmie would never have burned him. She turned to Alex Makepeace. "Do you know who he is?"

"I have my guess."

"He works for one of the mines?"

"A number of consolidateds."

So Alex had tried to catch her eye, to warn her to tread carefully. "Why was he here?"

The men had returned to their seats. Alex led Carina to the hall. "He was here to stir things up, to bring public opinion against you. He didn't know how your diners feel about you. He miscalculated."

"Why would he want to turn people against me?"

Alex said nothing.

"It's because of the families, isn't it? Because I brought aid to the families."

"It's not as simple as it seems," he said.

"I know I've caused you trouble. I never meant to."

She looked into his face, hoping he understood.

His brown eyes softened, and he smiled. "I know that."

"What happens now?"

Alex shook his head. "I don't know."

"I shouldn't have burned him."

He rubbed the side of his neck. "It's like the mayor said—he had it coming."

She didn't argue, but her heart convicted her. She'd returned evil for evil. Would she never learn? *Dio, have patience with me.* Èmie came into the hall carrying the broken bowls on the tray. Carina looked at the wreckage. What a waste, for one moment of revenge. Had she changed their minds? Made them respect her? Had she brought any resolution to an already tense situation?

Alex rubbed his beard. "Forget it, Carina."

Like everything else she was supposed to put out of her mind. "Thank you for standing with me."

He touched her hand briefly. "I'd have been outnumbered if I hadn't."

She smiled, thinking of the men standing up in support. How had she won their hearts so soon after Crystal would have hung her? It warmed her, but she knew too well how capricious the sentiments could be.

Alex lay awake with more than the hard, narrow cot and lumpy pillow to blame. His thoughts whirled. He knew all too well how ugly things could get when factions started warring. The miners demanding their dues; the owners refusing demands that would ruin them or, at the least, alienate their investors.

The men here running the operations were the ones in the worst spot, obligated to those who'd put up monies back east, pressed to turn greater and greater profits or see the operation scrapped, and then where would the miners be? Not dead. Images of the crushed and mangled bodies they'd pulled from the collapsed drift filled his mind.

None had survived. It was a toxic gas pocket that had exploded. Those not crushed by the debris . . . Alex shook his head. But they all knew the risks they took when they descended the shaft. Carina's sympathy had been for the women and children. Maybe if he hadn't been raw himself from watching one corpse after another being brought out, he would have refused.

But he doubted it. He wouldn't refuse Carina anything. He'd kept secret the cave that could yield untold treasures. And he'd stood with her tonight against the thugs. Next time it could be himself he was defending. Other miners were demanding aid for their families. No injury seemed too small now that the door was opened. They were using the deaths at the New Boundless as fuel for their fire. And the owners were adamant against them.

Those men tonight had been a warning. Not just to Carina, but to him as well. James Mires was running scared, and God only knew what correspondence he was sending back to Harrold and Sterk. Alex would likely be removed by spring. And all because he couldn't say no to another man's wife.

Was that it? Was God punishing him for wanting what wasn't his? Coveting another man's wife? *I've not done anything wrong. Not once touched her unchastely. Not spoken one word of my feelings.* Yet he'd let her color his judgment. Perhaps cost him his job, his career.

He rolled to his back and stared at the ceiling. He was a moral man. He followed God's tenets. If this was a chastisement for impure thoughts and desires, so be it. *Well, Grandmother, I've landed in it now. What would you say about this one?* But he knew what she'd say. He should have kept out of it altogether. He drew a slow breath and sighed. What sleep he found tonight would not be peaceful.

At the crash, Carina jolted up, wondering if the small shattering sound had been in her dream or was real. If it were real, it must have come from the dining room, for her own room was still and dark. She groped for a candle and lit it. Threading her finger into the tin loop of the holder, she slipped out of bed and made for the door to the hall.

What could have slipped in the night? She pictured the three painted china plates she had stood on the mantel of the fireplace for their ornamentation alone. She jumped when another crash came from the darkened room, then hurried down the hall to the doorway.

Her candle illuminated the mantel, and she saw at once the missing plates and the fragments on the hearth and tile. How had they fallen? A chill ran up her spine. Had the ghosts of the Carruthers . . . No, she stopped that thought before it scared her further. How, then? The one remaining plate seemed steady enough in the groove Joe Turner's men had cut there. She stooped and picked up the central part of one fallen plate with its beautiful floral design shattered. What had . . .

She heard a whoosh, and burning pain shot through her back at the blow. Carina screamed even as the second blow took her knees from behind. She fell. The candle sputtered and went out, and in the darkness she thrashed, screaming, as blow after blow sent fire through her body. Instinctively she curled but was kicked about until she had no control.

Something struck the side of her head. It seemed there were gunshots, but maybe the blows had broken open her skull. Her ears throbbed, and she vomited blood. There were shouts, but she didn't hear them clearly, then a gust of cold. Blood filled her throat again and she retched. Then she felt the hot fluid run down her legs.

"No . . ." she moaned once.

Arms grasped her. "Carina."

She knew him. Alex Makepeace. With another moan, she sank against his chest.

Voices. Darkness. A sweet smell. The taste of blood, and an ache inside worse than the dull throbbing of her body.

"How bad is it?" Mae's voice.

Gruffly, Dr. Felden: "She lost the baby."

Mae's voice, startled. "The baby?"

Carina tried to argue. *No, the baby's fine.*

"It appears her husband stayed long enough for that." A clink of instruments.

But he doesn't know. When he learns about the baby, he'll stay; he'll love me.

Mae spoke thickly. "Will she have another?"

"I'm not a fortune-teller." Water splashing and sloshing.

"Will she live?"

"It depends on the internal bleeding. Now that I know there was a baby, I don't believe it's as extensive as I first thought."

Mae, softly: "I'll sit with her now."

The door closed with a click. Carina wanted to call him back, to tell him he was wrong. She wanted to feel the baby inside her, to know that what she hoped for could still be. *Dio! Signore! Per piacere, Signore. My baby. My baby.*

In the fading light of dusk, Quillan rubbed his grainy eyes and slipped through the doors of the livery. He'd pushed his team hard to make Crystal before nightfall, and he had slept little for more nights than he could recall. He'd been driven by his need, the need for his wife, the need to see her, speak with her, tell her the things he'd learned, promise her . . . what? That he'd be the husband she wanted him to be? Could he?

He sure meant to try. The full wagon of things from the Italian market was just one proof of that. Quillan rubbed a hand over his face and searched the dim horse-smelling enclosure. He'd pushed himself hard. He was cold, saddle weary, and dragging almost as badly as his horses and his dog. But he was home.

Maybe. If she'd have him. Crystal could be home. Anywhere with Carina could be home. "Alan?" At least the old ostler would be pleased with his decision. He could honestly tell him this time he planned to stay.

Alan Tavish came forward with a lantern, but his expression was not what Quillan expected. "Ah, boyo. Sit there." He pointed to a barrel beside the stall.

Quillan sat, too weary to argue, and blew on his wind-chapped hands. It was better he catch his breath before he went to Carina anyway. He ought to wash and change as well. He needed a shave or at least a trim of his winter beard.

"I'll give ye the way of it before ye hear it elsewhere."

Looking into Alan's face, Quillan felt his stomach tighten. "She's gone?"

"Nay. But she's in a bad way." Alan gripped his shoulder. "Quillan, your wife was attacked last night."

Quillan jumped up from the barrel, his heart thumping inside. "What?"

"Beaten."

Quillan gripped the post, wanting to find the lie in Alan's eyes, but seeing only a deep, pitying sorrow. "Who?"

Alan shook his head. "No one saw for sure. 'Twas dark."

Quillan spun. He'd thought that himself last night as he made it into Fairplay, how it was a dark and moonless night. If only he'd pressed on without stopping! One night! One night too late. He ran for the livery door, slammed it open with his palms, and pushed through.

The frozen ground crunched beneath his boots, and the air tasted of smoke and slag. He ran to the small house connected to Mae's, then stopped, feet frozen to the crusty snow beneath his boots. Smoke trailed from the small pipe that vented her stove, and a warm, soft light filled the window, though a curtain blocked his view of the room.

He jammed his fingers into the hair that had grown wild. His beard, too, was shaggy and unkempt. He looked like the animal he'd been the last time he'd seen her, the last time he'd touched her with anger and frustration. He thought he'd changed. But had he? Even if he had, would she care?

Where was he last night when she was beaten? Had he been there to protect her? He remembered how shaken and horrified she'd been by Èmie's beating. It was so inhuman to violate the natural barrier that protected a woman. What beast . . . He swallowed the rage.

Forcing his feet forward, he climbed the steps to the small stoop outside her door. Before he could decide whether to knock or walk in, the door opened and the light that poured out onto the street was mostly blocked by Mae. Her expression was as militant as her stance, but it changed to surprise mingled with disappointment.

"Well?"

She had a right to ask. Quillan had hardly deported himself in a complimentary manner since Cain's death. He'd been so wrapped up in his own pain, his own loss. No wonder Mae questioned his intentions. He questioned them himself, but now was not the time. He had to see Carina. His voice was ragged. "How badly is she hurt?"

Mae pursed her lips, eyeing him. "Badly enough to lose your child."

Quillan's chest caved in with the breath rushing out. His child? Carina had been with child? He stared past Mae into the room, the realization of her words seeping deeper and deeper. How? From their last encounter? It must be, but . . . now she'd lost the baby. It was worse, far worse than he'd feared. What had the loss of her children done to his mother? To Mrs. Shepard? Would Carina ever be the same?

Why hadn't he been there? He straightened. "Will she see me?"

"Not much of you. Doc has her dosed up, and she hasn't wakened." But Mae moved aside and let him enter. "I'll be next door."

Quillan stooped beside the bed that held his wife. Gently, he stretched out his fingers and touched the satiny thickness of her hair. Dried blood crusted the cut on her ear, and a bluish swelling distorted one temple.

Her face was pale and still. No blows had hit her face. He could almost imagine she slept naturally, only her breath smelled of laudanum.

Standing, he slipped an arm under her shoulders and another beneath her knees, then lifted her as he slid in to sit on the bed, cradling her against him as he had when he'd pulled her from the mine shaft. He held her to his chest, overwhelmed with anger, grief, and condemnation. "God, oh, God. God!" His whole body tensed as he spoke through clenched teeth.

He raised his face to the ceiling. Somewhere up there, God watched. Cain, too, maybe. The old man had told him God wanted him; God had plans for him. Quillan hadn't heard, hadn't wanted to. Is this what it took to drive him to his knees?

He curled Carina into the fold of himself, as though he could shield her now from what she'd already suffered. "God forgive me." He held her close with one arm and stroked her hair. When she wakened would she despise him? He despised himself.

He would give her one more chance to be free of him. *No!* The thought hammered inside him like a blow, a chastisement. He looked upward. "What? What do you want from me?"

But he knew. Everything. God wanted everything. Quillan buried his lips in Carina's hair, rocking slowly forward and back. God was unrelenting in His pursuit. It was futile to resist. The fight wasn't in him anymore.

He felt a presence as real as Carina in his arms. *Lord.* He knew Him. He'd known Him when he was small in the darkness of the shed after the pain. He'd known Him beside his dog's grave. He'd known without recognizing. He knew Him now. *Lord.*

Tears he didn't recall shedding dried on his face, and

he held Carina, rocking, rocking her. They were alone, but not alone. She knew and trusted God. He'd known Him, too, before he was able to voice it. He'd known but rebelled. The prodigal son who'd thought he knew better how to handle his Father's affairs.

God . . . He pressed his lips to Carina's hair and closed his eyes, praying that the damage he'd done her wasn't irrevocable. *Let me make it right. No. Lord, you make it right.* He held Carina close, knowing the grief he'd caused her. Then he thought of the baby. She'd been carrying his child, and he hadn't known. He pressed her head to his chest. "Forgive me." He rocked. "Forgive me."

Carina felt the arms rocking her. *Papa.* She'd crawled into his lap, and he rocked her, soothing the terrible dream. *Now, now, tesora mia. Don't be afraid. Papa's here. Papa's here.*

She hurt. Her back, her side, her legs, and deep inside her belly. She moaned. *Papa, it hurts.* But she wasn't a little girl. She was a woman, and she'd lost her child. A wave of pain more piercing than her bodily wounds seized her.

No. Not my baby. The baby was her hope of winning Quillan's love. That hope was gone now. But what did she care? He didn't want her. He didn't want her! Her eyes were heavy, her mouth thick and dry. If only the clouds would leave her head. She tried to push the dream away, but still the arms rocked. It wasn't real. The pain was real.

She forced her eyes to open, saw a cotton flannel shirt, felt it against her cheek, heard the beat of a heart faintly in her ear, felt a beard against her forehead. A hand stroked her hair, and she felt safe and cherished.

She swallowed, pressed her eyes closed, then murmured, "Alex."

The rocking stopped. The hand felt heavy on her head. For a long time she stayed still; then she felt herself lifted, laid down, and covered with the warm coverlet. A breath of cold came over her, then ceased with the click of the door. She curled into a ball and slept.

Quillan walked out into the cold, as chilled inside as out. *Alex.* Makepeace? He reeled as he walked stiffly through the darkness. It could be. Makepeace had a table at her restaurant every night. He lived next door. In her room. Which she'd vacated. For him.

Quillan's boots crunched on the snow. His breath was a white cloud in the lanterns hung along the street, the light pouring out of the windows in golden pools. The music from tinny pianos spilled out as well, but he wasn't enticed. His thoughts spiraled down. Had he lost her? Would God exact even that for his disobedience?

He went to the livery and found Alan drawing slowly on his pipe and talking to Sam, who sat at his feet looking worried. He was suddenly aware of how alone Alan must be. Every night spent in a tiny room at the back of the horse stalls, his only company the animals men left in his care, and those men like himself who sometimes sat for a chat and asked after him.

Quillan felt his own loneliness growing like a void inside, sucking away his very breath. And it was his own fault. He pulled a stool up to Alan's rocker, clenched and opened his hands, then dropped them in his lap. He met Alan's craggy gaze. "Is Carina in love with Alex Makepeace?"

Alan raised hoary brows. "Why, boyo?"

Quillan sat in silence. *Because she spoke his name when I held her.*

"Ye saw her, then?"

"I saw her. She was sleeping. Laudanum. For the pain, I guess."

"Aye, and the healin'. Sleep is what she needs, and to know you're home."

Quillan hung his head. "I'm not sure of that, Alan. She has reason to hate me." Did Alan know about the baby? He couldn't bring himself to say it aloud. His child was killed because he failed to protect his wife. Failed in the most basic, the most sacred of his duties. *God!*

"Then ye'd best be about your courtin'."

"Courting? My wife?" It was far too late for that. Maybe God meant to free her after all. Then he remembered the inner chastisement. *No!* It had been almost a blow. He couldn't think that way. But how? Court his wife? Win her love?

Alan drew on his pipe until the coals in the bowl flashed red. "Aye, courtin', Quillan. 'Tis time ye learned the art."

Quillan scowled. Did Alan need to rub his nose in it? No, he hadn't courted her well. He'd done everything he could to drive her away. Why hadn't she gone? A thought chilled him. Because of Alex Makepeace? The jealous dragon twisted his gut. He'd let it hurt her before, then drive him away. But not this time. God help him, not this time.

Quillan stood and stalked to his wagon, reaching under the box where he kept most of his personal belongings. Fingering through the stacks of books, he found the one he sought. He'd sworn he'd never open a Bible again, not since he'd left the Shepards' house fourteen years ago. Not since the enforced readings that had imprisoned Scriptures in his unwilling mind.

But now he dug out Cain's Bible. He'd protested when D.C. gave it to him, knowing it was a wasted gift and the boy would cherish it far more. Now he blessed D.C.'s decision. *"Daddy would want you to have it. You never know, Quillan. You might want it someday."*

Quillan recalled the book in Cain's age-spotted hands. He held it now, not sure why he'd searched it out. Then he opened to a section he'd never read. It hadn't been part of his expected study. In fact, Leona Shepard had spoken of it once as a dirty book that had no right in the Holy Scriptures at all.

The Song of Solomon. Quillan looked at the page. He'd never read it, didn't know why it came to him so strongly now. But he took the book and sat on a barrel in a corner of the livery. He smelled the fodder and the animal scent, felt the breath and heat of the horses and mules. *Let him kiss me with the kisses of his mouth: for thy love is better than wine.*

I am come into my garden, my sister, my spouse . . . I have eaten my honeycomb with my honey; I have drunk my wine with my milk: eat, O friends, drink, yea drink abundantly, O beloved.

Quillan's breath arrested. These words showed him more than any poetry about the depth of love. A love he'd never sensed before, never embraced even that first time he'd taken Carina into his bed. This was a holy love, a godly love, and he prayed he'd have the chance to show her.

I sleep, but my heart waketh: it is the voice of my beloved that knocketh, saying, Open to me, my sister, my love, my dove, my undefiled. Quillan closed his eyes, picturing his wife as he'd seen her under the spring on the mountain-side. His heart surged painfully. *Open to me, Carina.* And he heard another voice inside him. *Open to me, my son. My son.*

Nineteen

What hateful seed germinates in the heart of men
to find release through their tongues
and fill the air with venom?

—Carina

"HOW BAD IS IT, PAPA?"

"Not so bad, tesora."

"It feels bad, Papa. It hurts."

"Life hurts. You have to be strong. My little tigre."

"It's too hard. Papa? Papa?"

But he was gone, and only the pain remained. If she could open her eyes, would the pain leave her? Carina tried, but sleep would not release her. It was better. In sleep there was forgetfulness. Oblivion. Yes . . . oblivion.

At the first hint of dawn, Quillan sat up in the livery, where he'd lain unsleeping near the potbellied stove that gave the animals some relief from the cold and turned Alan's room into an oven. It didn't seem enough to keep the chill from Alan's joints as he lay huddled under the blanket, breathing in staggered gasps. At least the old man had found sleep.

Quillan's mind had whirled between condemnation and determination. Yes, he blamed himself, as Carina must also. But that wouldn't change what happened. Nothing would change that. Not even God. But God could bring good of it. And the words he'd read in Solomon's book had been both a balm and a promise.

Quillan no longer felt the presence of the Lord. He could almost convince himself he'd imagined it, conjured it out of his need, his dismay, his horror over what had happened to Carina. But the words he'd read stuck in his mind, and he felt such an urging it compelled him. Cain's voice in his mind again. *"If you knew God, you'd understand those urgings."*

Maybe he didn't understand, but he knew what he had to do. God might be the source of the good, but Quillan would have to make it happen. The source needed an instrument. He could almost hear Cain cackle. *"What tickles me is how the Lord chooses His instruments. Not the high and mighty, who think they deserve it, but the lowly, the motley, the old cripples like me."*

Quillan wasn't sure where he belonged in that list. Motley maybe. But he'd do his best anyway. He had watched Cain operate. Prayer and unflagging zeal. Like the Reverend Shepard's.

The reverend served God in his church, but not just there. He served in his life. Available to anyone in need. Most of all in his care for his wife. Each spoonful he placed between her lips, each soothing word that eased her fears, each gentle touch served God.

Quillan had felt it himself when he did the same. He just hadn't understood. While he thought he was making peace with Leona Shepard, was he making peace with God? Could he do so now with Carina?

He pushed the covers off and stood up from his bedroll on the floor. Alan didn't stir. Only a dim light brightened the window, but Quillan made his way into the lean-to and washed. He took his razor and cleared the beard from his face and neck; even the mustache he removed. Then he combed and tied his hair back with a leather thong.

Carina might not care, but he'd present himself suitably. He studied the reflection a moment. How like his father was he? Stormy eyes, his mother's diary had said. His were shot with blood and darkened with fatigue and worry. He looked more than his twenty-eight years. He felt more.

How must Carina feel? Bruised, beaten, and deserted. He had yet to know the extent of it. That was his first priority. He slipped out the back and went to Dr. Felden's home. He banged on the door, knowing as he did that he was waking the man.

The doctor came to the door with exactly the expression Quillan expected. "Well, what is it?" he barked, then, "Quillan! You couldn't wait for the sun? No, I suppose not. Come in, then."

Quillan followed the doctor inside.

"I suppose you want to know about your wife. You've seen her?"

Quillan nodded. "How was she injured?"

"Beaten with a stick, a stout one." The doctor slid a chair his way.

Quillan didn't take it. "How badly?"

Dr. Felden shoved a log into the stove and put a pot of water on to heat. "Contusions. Swelling. I'm concerned about her kidneys. Took a blow high to the right side." The doctor turned. "She lost the baby, you know."

Yes, he knew. Now. When it was too late. "How far was she?"

The doctor frowned. "As far as your last visit, I'd say."

Quillan looked away. She'd conceived the child in that angry union. And now the child was lost. "Is there damage?" *Besides the damage to heart and soul. Would she have another child? Would she even want to try?*

"Too early to tell." The doctor raised the lid and checked the water in the coffeepot. "You want some . . ."

But Quillan had already reached the door and stepped into the brisk morning. The sky had lightened and cast a pinkish hue on the snow-covered slopes. The air was still, winter quieting Crystal as nothing else could. He found Mae in her kitchen, heaping slices of smoked venison onto a platter.

She turned when he pushed the back door open and entered. "Don't let the draft get my hotcakes or they won't fluff up."

He looked at the scorched and stiff hotcakes, the blackened venison. But he wasn't there to judge her cooking. He closed the door and approached her. "How is she, Mae?"

"Still sleeping."

He glanced toward the door that connected Mae's kitchen to Carina's hall. Behind that door his wife lay beaten and in pain because he'd failed to keep her safe. What had she ever asked of him? That he stay home. That he eat her food. That he love her.

Mae flipped the row of hotcakes and set the plate near to remove them one by one. Her silence was heavy. He knew what she thought.

"Tell me what happened, Mae."

Mae poured the pitcher of batter onto the hot griddle in circular mounds. "You know Carina. Every time she turns around, she's landed in it again."

Quillan's throat tightened. Yes, he knew that. She'd caused him trouble from the first time they met. He'd saved her life three times. How could he have thought she'd be safe without him? He hadn't thought. He'd reacted. And run.

"She meant well. But she doesn't understand the industry."

His thoughts caught up to Mae. "What do you mean? What industry?"

"Mining."

Quillan was farther out than he realized. "What does Carina have to do with mining?"

"You own a mine, don't you? Landsakes, Quillan! Don't you understand anything?"

Quillan raised his foot to the bench and leaned on his knee. "Start at the beginning, Mae. I knew she had this restaurant." He waved behind him toward Carina's dining room.

"And a fine success she is, too. She's done you proud."

"But the mine?"

"Oh, she and Alex Makepeace have had a time of it."

Quillan's stomach clutched.

"Carina thought she was doing good, seeing to the families. All those men dead and all."

"What men dead?"

Mae turned from the stove and swiped the steam from her brow with the flesh of her forearm. "Sit down, Quillan. Have you eaten? Coffee?"

He shook his head twice.

"Well, no wonder you're so thick."

He didn't want to eat. He wanted answers. But when

she shoved the plate in front of him, he obeyed, hardly tasting a bite. As he ate, Mae told him about the disaster at his mine and the trouble that followed. His jaw clenched when she described Carina and Alex Makepeace collaborating. But he saw Carina in all of it.

"She went personally? To the families?"

Mae sighed. "Couldn't have been plainer than that. Those who approved applauded her. Those who didn't . . ."

Quillan laid down the fork and sat stiffly. "Who didn't, Mae?"

She shrugged. "The four men in her restaurant were just hirelings. You know how it is. And don't bother looking. They're long gone, whisked away before anyone could tie them to one operation or another. Likely all of them together."

"Why?"

"You're as innocent as Carina, aren't you? She set up expectations no one else could meet."

Mae was right. He was ignorant. He hadn't learned the first thing about his mine or mining in general, hadn't wanted to. He'd left it all in Alex Makepeace's competent hands. Left Carina there, too. It was only natural that what they'd done together would bond them someway. The twisting inside him was almost a physical pain.

Of course Makepeace would crumble under Carina's insistence. Even against his better judgment. Could either have guessed the repercussions of their solicitude? Quillan pictured the four men insulting his wife, the deft twist of her wrist that sent the scalding soup down the man's face, that simple twist that had brought the men back to injure her. They might have killed her. What if he had returned to a grave? The food was lead inside him. He pushed the plate away.

Mae took the plate and set it aside. "So now you know all I do. No one saw a face. When Mr. Makepeace started shooting, the assailants ran."

"Alex Makepeace started shooting?"

"Are you listening to me, Quillan? He fired the shots that sent the men away." Quillan frowned. Makepeace had gotten there in time to save his wife. Had he held her? Soothed her? Is that why Carina thought it was Alex she snuggled into when Quillan held her? But then, why would she think it was he? Had *he* been there? Had *he* sent the thugs running?

Mae hunkered down on the bench across from him. She crossed her arms and leaned forward. "Truth is, you've come back none too soon, Quillan. I've always thought highly of you, starting as you did with too many disadvantages. But I'll say this now, and then it's on your own head. If you're not intending to stay, don't go in there at all. Just walk away, and let her heal from you and the baby together."

Quillan met Mae's eyes, saw in their violet flash that she meant every word of it. "Just tell me one thing, Mae. Does she love Alex Makepeace?"

Mae pursed her lips and studied the door that separated them from Carina. "I think she could, given the chance." Mae turned her gaze back to him. "But before God, Quillan, she's your wife. And if you let her go, you're more the fool than I ever thought you."

"I won't let her go, Mae."

"Then good luck to you." Mae shoved up from the table. "I wouldn't want to be in your shoes."

Quillan half smiled. "Thanks for the confidence."

Mae rested a hand on her hip. "Putting the two of you in a ring, my money would be on Carina."

"Not this time, Mae. Lay your bet on the underdog."

She laughed. "This I've gotta see."

Quillan went outside to the woodpile behind Carina's dining room. Her ax was sharp, and he bet any number of men kept it that way for her. Or maybe it was only Alex Makepeace. Quillan frowned. He had to stop thinking that way. He'd all but abandoned his wife. Why shouldn't someone else step in to help?

He sank the ax into the log, raised it, and swung with such force the ax cleaved the log and bit deeply into the chopping block. He yanked it free and picked up one of the halves that had flown free with his blow. When he had splintered enough wood, he gathered it into his arms and turned for Carina's door. The latch was broken, pried out of the wood, and Quillan guessed this was how the intruders had entered.

He opened the door and went inside, carrying the wood down the hall and through the door into Carina's room. It was warm but not overly. Quietly he set the wood beside the stove and added a stick or two to the coals. Carina stirred, and he turned, but she only slipped back into sleep.

He wished he'd asked the doctor how long it would be before she wakened. Quillan looked around the room, noting the things Carina had added. A cut-glass lamp, a new pitcher and bowl, and books, of course, on a shelf along one wall. He'd known that bookstore would entice her.

He glanced at the crate beside the bed. What was she reading currently? The one that lay there was plain. Carefully, he lifted it and searched the spine for a title. No title. He opened the cover and realized it was a journal. Carina's?

He looked at her face, flushed slightly with sleep . . .

or was it pain? He flipped to the center of the book, just to know if the words were hers. *Dio, you are faithful. I know my prayer will be answered. But how long must I wait, loving a man who doesn't love me in return?* Doesn't love her? Is that what she thought? He closed the book, ashamed to have pried even that much.

And then it occurred to him that she might not be speaking of him at all. What made him think he was the one she loved? Hadn't she loved Flavio before him? Couldn't her affections have shifted to yet another? He was tempted to open the book again and find out.

Firmly, he set the diary beside his wife. He would not pry into her private writings, even though reading his mother's had given him a love and appreciation for her he could have gotten no other way. But that book was given him to read. By Carina. He owed her so much.

He bent and touched his wife's hair. She sighed, but her eyes didn't open. He leaned close. *Look at me, Carina. Know that I'm here.* But he didn't speak it aloud. If she did look, she might not like what she saw.

Carina woke to Mae's hand on her forehead. It felt cool and soft, and when she tried to open her eyes, they opened easily, no fuzzy heaviness holding them shut. Her mouth, though, was dry as down. She tried to swallow.

Mae must have anticipated her need. She held a cup of water to her lips. Carina drank. Slowly she became aware of the pain, feeling the bruised areas with even the smallest motions. It was bearable pain though, and she struggled to sit up.

"Easy now. You've been medicated for two days." Mae stuffed pillows behind her back.

Carina sank into them stiffly. Two days of dreams and pain. But she felt sure now she would heal. Of course she would heal. Papa had come to heal her. No, that was the dream as well. It wasn't Papa who held her. Papa never wore a beard. She knew that much.

The bed sagged as Mae sat beside her. Carina looked into her face and froze. What was wrong? Mae took her hand and held it in silence. Carina's heart rushed. She wanted to send her away. Whatever it was Mae had to say, Carina didn't want it spoken. Not now, when she finally felt that the nightmare might end.

"Carina . . ."

"Don't. Whatever it is . . ."

Mae turned away, but not before Carina saw a tear trickle from her eye. Blood pounded in her ears. There was something she should know, but she couldn't make herself recall. Something in the dream, then, had been real, as real as the blows that bruised her now. She closed her eyes, shutting Mae out.

But her voice came through anyway. "Why didn't you tell me you were expecting?"

Carina wet her lips painfully and opened her eyes. Was she?

"I don't know what good it would have done." Mae waved a hand. "But I just would have liked to have known before . . . before you lost it. Carina, I'm so sorry."

Lost it! She'd been with child and lost it? The thought slammed inside her head, smashing her defenses. Oh, the pain. Quillan's child, gone. Her baby. Her baby gone. Tears stung her eyes as Mae wrapped her in a thick, fleshy embrace. She was warm and soft, so different from that other embrace, that rocking embrace. Or was that a dream?

What did it matter? Her baby was dead, and she was alone. So terribly alone.

"I'm so sorry, Carina. So sorry."

Carina let Mae hold her. Their tears mingled. But all she could think was, why? God had brought good from their marriage, even from the shambles they'd made of it. Then He'd taken the good away. Carina sobbed. "Why? Why?"

"I don't know, darlin'. I don't know."

"I thought . . . I thought with the baby he might . . . I thought he might love me."

"He loves you, Carina."

She shook her head so sharply it sent pain to her temple. "No." Suddenly her sorrow was eclipsed by a choking rage. Her hands formed fists and she pushed Mae away. "And if he were here I would kick him!"

Mae opened her mouth to speak, but Carina had no interest in her defense of Quillan Shepard. She buried her face in the pillows. "Go away. Please go away. I want to be alone."

The bed creaked and swayed as Mae stood. Carina ought to thank her for her care, her sympathy. But she didn't want her sympathy—she wanted to scream! When the door clicked shut, she flung herself to her side, grabbed up her diary and pencil, and flipped page after page to the first blank sheet.

Teeth clenched, she held the pencil aloft, then wrote:

What grief in the severing of mother and child. Bone of my bone and flesh of my flesh. The joining of two lives to make one. The wrenching of one from its resting place. My body is empty. My heart a stone. But in my blood, fire rages. Fire against the men who did this to me. Fire against God. And most of all, fire against Quillan. I wish it could consume him.

Quillan carried the rocker over the precarious ground, careful not to lose his footing and slip. He'd paid an outrageous price for this particular chair because it was similar to the one Carina had lost on the road, the one he'd dumped over the cliff on her wagon. Arms straining, he made it to her stoop and set the chair down. Sam scrambled up and circled him impatiently.

Quillan nudged him aside with his knee. "Don't get your hopes up." He used one of the extra keys he'd acquired from the blacksmith and unlocked Carina's door. He glanced inside, saw Carina lying still on the bed, her eyes closed.

He lifted the rocker and carried it inside. There was room for it in the front corner, and he set it there softly so as not to awaken his wife. Sam, however, had other ideas. He frisked about the bed, then put both paws up and licked Carina's hand.

"Sam," Quillan called softly.

But Carina startled, rolled, and sat up. Sam licked her face, but she didn't look at the dog. Her hair was a tousled mass of dark, shining ripples. The bruise on her temple showed blue against her olive skin as she caught her hair back with one delicate hand. But it was her eyes Quillan couldn't avoid. In their dark, stormy depths, he saw something raw and furious . . . and wounded. Their gaze flicked to the chair, then back to him.

She raised her chin. "I don't want it."

He stood for a full breath, unsure of how to answer. She had a right to her anger, a right to blame him, to strike out. God knew he blamed himself. But that wasn't the way. Quillan slacked a hip and met her gaze.

"Auction it off. You'll get a good price."

Sam slipped down from the bed and pattered over to stand, tail wagging, before him. Quillan motioned him away with one hand. "Lie down." The dog reluctantly obeyed, and Quillan was glad for the distraction when Carina's gaze followed the dog as he circled, then lay in front of the door. When she turned back, he saw she was shaking with pain, weakness, or just plain fury.

He took a step toward the bed. "Carina . . ."

"Do you think I want your gifts? Eggs and chickens. A rocking chair. Do you think they matter?"

He had hoped they did. That's why he'd brought a wagonload of supplies from the Italian market. And paid an exorbitant price for the rocker.

"So." She waved a hand. "You've brought your token. Now you can leave."

He saw that the movement of her arm hurt her. "I'm not leaving."

"Beh!" She made a motion with her hand to her mouth that he hadn't seen before, but its message was clear. She didn't believe and she didn't care. She sank into the pillows and glared.

Quillan straightened. "I'm not leaving Crystal, Carina. I'll be at the livery if you need me."

"Un gross'uomo." She spoke it darkly.

The big man. No, he was not the big man, but he was trying. She must see that he was trying.

Carina glared at Quillan standing there with a hint of his pirate's smile. If it didn't hurt so much to move, she would throw something. But she didn't have to. He went out the door with his dog at his heels. Again he showed her his back. She sat and seethed.

He thought he could bring her a chair and change

everything? Was it her mamma's chair that he'd shattered on the road? It was similar. Of course. He had probably searched every store in town for it. Maybe even carried it from someplace farther.

Auction it off? She would give it away! To Mae. No, Mae wouldn't fit between the curved arms. To Èmie, then. Yes. It would be a wedding gift. To one whose marriage was not a sham.

Carina sank into the pillows. She reached for her journal and pen. *We'll see how long the gross'uomo stays. Will it be even one day? He thinks to win me with things. Does he know the only thing that mattered is gone?* She pressed a hand to her belly, flat and empty, and cried.

Twenty

I know I am wrong to harbor such thoughts,
but I cannot stop them.
They rise up like a well inside me
and I am drowning.
—*Carina*

CARINA HAD SCARCELY KNOCKED when Èmie pulled open her door. "Carina! You shouldn't be up. Robert says healing takes longer if you force it."

"I have a present for your wedding."

"What?" Èmie caught her arm. "You should be in bed. Look at you, pale and—oh, Carina." Èmie closed her into her arms and Carina sagged against her.

Èmie was right. She shouldn't have gotten up. She felt weak and the pain was much worse than she first thought. Not just the bruising, but deep within her, as though her insides were bruised as well. Perhaps they were. But she pulled back and waved at the rocking chair Joe Turner had hauled for her in his carryall. He jumped down and lifted it to the ground.

Èmie caught her hands together. "Oh. It's beautiful."

"You'll have to fight Robert for it."

Èmie was shaking her head, eyes still pinned to the rocker. "Oh, Carina, I've never had anything so fine."

"Eh, you have a home to make." She fought off a wave of dizziness. The corset she'd donned to fit into her dress was pressing so tightly over her bruised and swollen flesh, she thought she might faint. But she couldn't stand to have the chair in her room one minute longer. Not when it reminded her so of Mamma. And worse, when she thought how she might have rocked her own baby in it.

Joe Turner carried the rocker to the door. "Where do you want it, Mrs. Simms?"

Èmie stepped back. "Right in the middle of the floor. I want it to be the first thing anyone sees. Oh, Carina, it's too much. Wait till Father Antoine sees it! Oh, we'll all have a sit."

Carina forced a smile. "Try it now." And when Èmie went inside to sit in the rocker, Carina gripped the doorframe and held herself erect.

Joe Turner didn't miss it. "Mrs. Shepard." He took her elbow and supported her. "Come, now. Listen to Èmie. Don't force it."

She nodded. The last thing she wanted was a fainting scene. She had acted on impulse, anger motivating her up from the bed and through the washing and dressing and finding Joe Turner. Now she leaned on his arm and let him turn her toward the carryall.

"Thank you, Joe. I'll take her now." Quillan stood, jaw set, eyes stern, as he took Carina's other arm.

Where had he come from? What was he doing, standing there like an avenging spirit, hair loose to his shoulders, stance stubborn and protective? Carina seethed, but she couldn't refuse him with Èmie and Joe

Turner looking on. She felt his strength, his muscles hardened from years of strong labor.

Joe Turner released her. "Use my buggy."

No! She didn't want to ride next to Quillan. How she wished she could shake him off and stalk away!

"That won't be necessary." With a single swift motion, he picked her up like a baby.

Carina bit her lip against the pain and fury. He would carry her in his arms for all to see? The humiliation! But her body was rebellious. It sank with relief into his chest. He didn't speak as he carried her. Did he know she'd given Èmie his rocker? It had already been inside, but he might have seen. A sharp satisfaction filled her.

She closed her eyes. It was wrong to feel such vengeful spite. She knew in her spirit what was right, but she couldn't do it. Her loss was too great, and Quillan . . . With her face burrowed into his neck, she felt a vague stirring. Something from before, the rocking . . . No, those arms had been tender, not hard, and the chin bearded.

It must have been Alex. Where was he? She hadn't seen him once since . . . since he held her, broken and bleeding. Carina fought tears of fury and frustration. Who was Quillan to walk in now and demand his place? What did he care? She was his responsibility? Oh!

"Don't stiffen up. Relax." It was the impersonal, imperial tone he'd used when teaching her to shoot. The big man!

"Relax!" She struggled in his arms. "When you're humiliating me for all Crystal to see?"

"Would you rather collapse in the street? Dr. Felden's appalled that you're out of bed."

"I'm perfectly able to walk."

Quillan turned his face to hers, and Carina felt the intensity of his closeness. She wanted to look away, but as always, he held her bound by some magnetism she couldn't fight. His face softened, and for a horrible moment, she thought he would kiss her.

Then he started walking again. "He's concerned for your kidneys. The blows there may have caused damage you don't realize. He's ordered bed rest."

"Bed rest!" Carina fought the feelings of helplessness. "And who will run my restaurant? You?"

There it was, his rogue's smile. Oh! She hit his chest with her fist. He kept walking, not even deigning to answer. He was impossible! *"Omacio."*

"I may be a cad, Carina, but you're stuck with me."

Fire burned up inside her. "Why don't you offer now to end this flawed union?"

"Because it's no longer an option."

"What!"

He stopped at her door, leaned slightly to turn the knob, then pushed it with his foot. He carried her to the bed and eased her down. Every part of her hurt. The softness of the bed only accented it. Closing her eyes, she bit her lip against whimpering. When she opened them, she caught an expression on Quillan's face of such tender concern it stopped the breath in her chest.

Then he straightened. "It seems I'll need to move in here, to see that you obey the doctor's orders."

She opened her mouth to retort, but a sharp dagger of pain seized her back, and when it had passed he was gone. She lay back, gasping. Maybe Quillan was right. Maybe there was more damage than she'd realized. She closed her eyes, suddenly exhausted. Had he even noticed the chair was gone?

Alex Makepeace supervised the removal of the last of the debris from the collapsed tunnel. The next months would be spent building it back up again, and this time there would be no spreading of timber distances, no seconds in lumber. He never wanted to face a disaster like that again.

Of course, there was a good chance he wouldn't be there long enough to worry about it. Especially after this morning's actions. He'd polled every man he knew and learned who was behind the troublemakers who had attacked Carina. Though the attackers seemed to have evaporated, those behind them had not. He'd taken what he learned to the authorities. And there were prominent names among them.

He had no delusions that anything would be done, but his very actions had branded him. He was no longer a company man. Though his loyalties lay with the owners, engineers, and managers of the mines, he'd acted against them. And he'd be blackballed for it—deservedly so. He'd stirred the can of worms Carina had opened. But after finding her, holding her . . .

He clenched and unclenched his hands. He had taken her into his arms and held her as he'd ached to for so long. She was injured and unconscious, but he'd held her, heart hammering with rage at the attackers and equally with joy at the warmth of her in his arms. God have mercy on him. He'd kept away ever since.

Mae had apprised him of Carina's condition the next morning when he'd asked. But he didn't dare see her himself. He'd all but slept in the mine since then, spending all his energy and effort in work. Anything to keep his thoughts and emotions from such dangerous territory.

Carina was another man's wife. And though he'd not seen him for himself, Joe Turner had told him Quillan Shepard was back. Turner had thought it prudent he know. Alex slammed his fist on the table of charts.

Quillan gathered his things from Alan's small room. Though Carina would likely scratch and spit, it was time he took up residence with her. He would not have her turning to Joe Turner or Alex Makepeace every time she needed aid. And Dr. Felden had scared him with his reaction this morning. If her health were that precarious, Quillan would see that nothing thwarted the healing. Not even Carina herself.

Alan was haggling with a customer when Quillan carried his things past, but the old man didn't miss the import of his load. Quillan nodded, and Alan sent a wink after him. In Alan's mind all Quillan needed to do was take Carina to bed and all would be well in the Shepard house.

Quillan knew better. It would be the floor for him. Not only because Dr. Felden had warned him against practicing his rights too soon, but because he would not so much as kiss his wife until he knew she wanted it. And if the fate of his rocker were any indication, she would not want it soon. Presents were obviously not the way into Carina's good graces.

What, then? He glanced heavenward. If he had gone to her meek and trembling, would she have forgiven him? If he'd let her pile his head with coals, would she now welcome him with open arms? He doubted it. Then how?

Love her. The thought was clear and direct. But what did it mean? He didn't know how to order his life now.

He'd hardly had any days in which he hadn't known exactly what he needed to do and done it. He could be on his wagon, even on these winter roads, hauling, driving his team and himself. He could be buying, selling, and bartering. And then he thought of Carina's words.

Would he run her restaurant? Somehow he suspected that was the last thing she'd want, but hadn't he brought a wagonload of supplies from Fairplay? He knew her doors hadn't opened since her injury. Two young girls had come daily to ask whether they were needed. He didn't know who they were, but he'd recalled seeing them working. The other one, too, the one Èmie called Lucia, who didn't speak good English. They all wanted to know what would happen now.

Quillan looked at the building as he approached. Carina had made something of herself, something of the shabby house she'd fought for and won. Maybe he could preserve what she had until she was on her feet again. He let himself into Carina's house, laid his bundle on the floor, and looked at her lying in the bed.

She slept soundly, no doubt worn out from overexerting herself earlier. Her eyes were damp, and he felt a guilty pang. He rubbed his face. How easy it would be to convince himself she was better off without him. But he knew now the covenant they'd made before God was forever.

Just as the Reverend Shepard's was with his wife. For better or worse, sickness or health, until death. Quillan leaned close to Carina, wanting to stroke her hair, to kiss the tears from her cheek. But he straightened and went out the side door, down the hall to Mae's. She was upstairs changing a bed and looked up, surprised, when he crowded into the room.

"Mae, tell me what I need to know about Carina's restaurant."

"What do you mean?" She folded the edge of the sheet and tucked it under the lumpy mattress.

"Can it run without her? Does anyone else know what to do?"

Mae plunked a fist onto her hip. "What are you thinking, Quillan?"

He slacked his hip and leaned into the doorjamb. "I'm worried, Mae."

The other hand joined her opposite hip. "Well, it's about time."

He dropped his chin, accepting her rebuke. "I don't want her thinking she has to get up and work before she can. But I brought a wagonload of the things she likes to use. Ingredients and such."

"You're going to make the ravioli?"

He looked up to see the teasing smirk on her face. "I wasn't thinking that. But if any of the rest of you know how . . ."

Mae swished past him, grabbed up the blanket, and spread it over the bed. "Emie's learned a far sight. Lucia's handy with the simpler dishes. The twins mostly clear and wash. If we took on another to wait the tables . . . yes, it could be done. But does Carina want it?"

Quillan tucked the near corner of the blanket. "I don't know."

Mae grunted as she tucked her edge of the blanket under the foot of the mattress. "I'll gather the girls and see what can be done. I suppose Carina could direct things from bed."

"I don't want her to."

"Then you don't know Carina."

Quillan considered that. He knew her better than

Mae suspected. And, yes, it would be a battle to keep Carina still. But what could she do from bed? He released his breath. He couldn't figure it all out at once. "Do what you can, Mae. Let me know what you need."

Mae laughed. "My guess is you're a little stir-crazy yourself."

"I'm used to keeping busy."

"Get unused to it." Mae fixed him with a frank stare. "If you're expecting Carina to sit still, you might learn to do the same."

It was such an obvious thought, it caught him short. And he didn't like it. Yes, he'd decided to stay in Crystal, but he hadn't thought to be sitting on his hands. Walking over, he'd thought he could take charge of Carina's operation while still attending to his own affairs. There was plenty of work for a freighter in town, ore to the smelters, hauling irons and powder and other supplies to the mines. Work, he knew. Work, he needed—not for the money as much as . . . as what?

"Think about it." Mae swished past and started down the stairs.

The day seemed to stretch already. Could he make himself be idle? He'd sat with Mrs. Shepard, hadn't he? That was idle enough. Except when she had her fits and required a strong arm to contain and soothe her. Or when she needed to be fed or washed or helped onto the chamber pot. No, it had been work, not idleness. *Idleness is the devil's tool.* Or was it?

He headed down the stairs in a daze. What if he sat with Carina, just sat? She'd think he'd lost his mind. He would lose his mind. Or would he? He took the hall back to her room, stood over the bed, and watched her sleeping. At least she could sleep. He walked over and unrolled his bedding. Then he untied his pack and took out the three books and meager foodstuffs it held. Lastly he took out his mother's diary.

He held it a moment, his eyes stroking the nameplate. *Rose Annelise DeMornay*. One piece had been put into place. But what about Wolf? Why did he think of that now? Because in Crystal, Wolf was never far from his thoughts?

He laid the diary beside Carina's journal on the crate by her bed. It was more hers than his. Without Carina he wouldn't know his mother's devotion. Nor would he know his father's innocence of the crime ascribed to him for too many years. Without her prying, none of that may have come to light. But there was still so much he didn't understand.

Quillan perused the single room of Carina's house. The stove was stoked warmly enough. Everything was neat and in its place. That wasn't hard since there was very little to keep tidy. Quillan felt an ache begin. He could have done so much more. He knew, or at least he guessed, the fine living Carina had known before coming to Crystal. Hadn't she told him in no uncertain terms the power and prestige her papa wielded?

Now look at her. The only thing of value was the bed, and he had begrudged her that because she'd paid too much. He hadn't known, hadn't been able to open his heart and see her need. Now he wished it hadn't been opened for him. It hurt to care so much, to want so much.

God. Again the presence was with him. He'd felt nothing since the night he returned. He knew better than to expect feelings of God's presence. But it was there with him now. He looked at Carina, wishing he could wipe out everything that had happened and start fresh.

To everything there is a season, and a time to every purpose under the heaven. A time to be born and a time to die; to plant, to pluck, to kill, to heal; a time to break down and a time to build up. A time to weep and a time to laugh; a time to mourn and a time to dance.

Maybe it had all needed to happen as it did. Could he have loved her and hated his mother and Leona Shepard at once? Would it not have been a war inside him? Hadn't it been already, every time he got close to Carina? *A time to break down and a time to build up.* He had needed to be broken down. Now he wondered what could build them up.

Quillan sat down in one of the chairs at the small table against the wall. He would have sat in the rocker if it had been there still. He certainly hoped Èmie Charboneau Simms was enjoying it. With his elbow on the table, Quillan rested his forehead on his fingertips. He raised his eyes just enough to see Carina's face, flushed in sleep.

There is a garden in her face. Looking at her now, the whole poem ran through his mind, its truth sinking deeply. No matter how much he wanted her, until her lips called cherry ripe, he was outside the garden looking in. And the wall was high and thick.

Carina woke. The lamp beside her bed was lit, and she saw beneath it, glowing warmly, the red leather of Rose's diary. Lifting herself slowly, stiffly, she reached her fingers to stroke it. How. . . ?

And then she saw him through the side of her eye. In the golden lamplight, Quillan's hair was more honey-toned than brown. His face looked weary, and his eyes, fixed on her, vulnerable. There was no look of the pirate tonight. Her heart stirred, but she knew better than to give in to it.

She reached for the diary and brought it to her breast, then sank back into the pillows piled high behind her. Where Mae had gathered such a supply, she didn't know. But she was grateful. Carina raised her eyes to Quillan, saw his gaze drop to the diary. She clutched it protectively. "You read it?"

" 'It is a fact that the human heart differs from all other species. While its function to the body is that same of all animals, its participation with the human soul is both rhapsodic and fatal.' "

Hearing Rose's words from Quillan's mouth gave Carina a pang she couldn't hide. And he spoke it from memory. He had committed his mother's words to memory. Again her heart stirred. "Then you know she's not what you thought her."

He nodded slowly.

"And Wolf?"

The crease in his brow deepened. "I don't know."

Carina expelled her breath and looked out to the night where Quillan had parted the curtain. If there were stars she couldn't tell with the lamp glow so close to her face. She replaced the diary on the crate. She had given him Rose. Did she dare give him Wolf as well?

A nasty voice inside said he didn't deserve it. Why should she give him anything? But unlike earlier, the quickened anger ebbed. Maybe she was too weak to sustain it. Maybe the look in his eyes had dissolved it.

"You know the shaft where you found me? Where I'd fallen?"

He frowned. "In the Rose Legacy?"

She nodded. "Under the shaft, there's a cave. A large limestone cave. But beyond that there's a chamber. If you want to know Wolf, he's there."

Quillan's expression was inscrutable. After a long moment, he said, "How do you know?"

"I found it with Alex Makepeace."

Quillan visibly stiffened. She waited for him to strike out, to accuse her of some new violation of his privacy. Perhaps even infidelity. She saw his throat work and the tension in his jaw. All the softness in his eyes was gone. He was Wolf, warding off all comers with the power of his presence alone.

Then he closed his eyes and dropped his chin. "He can take me there?"

"Ask him." She turned to her side, already regretting what she'd done. What would Quillan see? That his papa truly was the savage he thought him? That he was the pale wolf always off to the side, alone? That he was more like Quillan than he wanted to believe? She sensed motion and looked up over her shoulder.

Beside the bed, Quillan extinguished the light. For a moment he rested his hand on her head. "Sleep now." Then he left.

Quillan stepped out into the night. He walked the short way to Mae's and asked for Alex Makepeace.

"He's not here, Quillan." Mae looked up from the ledger she was balancing. "Try the mine."

The mine. The source of all Carina's trouble. If he'd been there to oversee it as Alan had suggested, she wouldn't have been involved at all. Hadn't Makepeace known enough to keep her out of affairs that didn't concern her?

"This late?"

"He has an office there. Hardly sleeps here since . . . well, that's your best bet."

Since what? Since Carina was hurt? Or since Quillan came home?

He went to the livery and took Jock without disturbing Alan. He rode through the darkness until a lighted window showed where Mr. Makepeace's office must be. He pulled up outside the small log building. With the moonglow on the snow, he could make out the sizeable workings all around him. The New Boundless. He dismounted, tethered Jock, and rapped on the door. It opened, and Quillan tried to read Alex Makepeace's face. Surprise, surely, or was it discomfort?

"Quillan. Come in." He was motioned inside.

Quillan refrained. "I won't stay. I . . . Carina mentioned a cave."

Makepeace's head jerked sideways. "She told you? I guess she would."

Quillan narrowed his eyes, fighting back the jealous surge. What other secrets did she share with Alex Makepeace?

Makepeace turned from the door and walked to his desk. "Come in before all the heat escapes."

Quillan stepped in, wondering why he felt as though he were treading on another man's territory. This was his mine, his property, his wife. He closed the door behind him. Alex Makepeace gestured toward a chair and took the one behind his desk for himself. Quillan sat and waited for Makepeace to speak.

When he did, it was with a soft, throaty tone. "How is she?"

"Not well. Yet."

Makepeace nodded. "Carina—that is, your wife and I—did find a cave. But she wanted it kept secret. I've honored that."

As you honored her marriage to another man?

"It's in your mine. Your other mine. The Rose Legacy." Makepeace glanced up.

"She told me that. She said there's a chamber." Quillan saw the change in Makepeace's face.

"Oh. The painted one, I suppose."

"Painted?"

Makepeace stood and walked around the desk. He rubbed his fingers down the side of his beard. "It's probably best you see it for yourself. I can meet you at first light, weather permitting." He paused again, long enough for Quillan to feel uncomfortable. "She . . . wanted you to see it?"

A flicker of fury licked up like a flame. Who was Makepeace to protect Carina's wishes? Did he dare suggest he cared more for Carina's well-being than Quillan did? Quillan said, "First light, in front of the livery."

Alex Makepeace nodded slowly. "All right."

Quillan stood. He wanted to demand an accounting of the time this man had spent with Carina, to force him to confess his feelings for her. They were there. He could see it, though Makepeace tried hard to keep them hidden. Quillan didn't extend his hand. He put the hat on his head and went outside.

Alex stared as the door closed behind Quillan Shepard. His feelings were a hornet's nest inside, but his head told him to be grateful. If the man hadn't come back now, what might he have done? Lured Carina into a wrongful relationship? Lured her with kindness, compassion for her loveless state, the tenderness she longed for?

Quillan was an enigma. But Alex sensed that was about to change. What would he make of the paintings his father had left on the walls of that chamber? Alex shook his head slightly. His own father was as conventional and stolid as the state of Maine. Alex had never once wondered how the man felt on anything. Whatever the moral position, whatever the just cause, Victor Makepeace held to it. What would he think of his son's conscience?

Alex sighed. He wouldn't have to find out now. Quillan Shepard loved his wife. It was in the fierceness of his eyes, the tension of his jaw. And Quillan Shepard was not a man Alex cared to thwart. Not when rectitude lay with Quillan. God had intervened.

Twenty-one

Hope is a lighthouse on a rocky shore
luring me in through treacherous waters,
promising safety.
—Carina

THE ROOM WAS EMPTY when Carina woke from a deeply restful sleep. Had Quillan somehow charmed her with his soft injunction and the touch of his hand on her head? She'd dreamt again of the soothing arms, the rocking of that strong and gentle embrace. It had to have been real for it to remain so firmly in her mind. Who had held her? Alex Makepeace?

She knew he was the one to gather her up when the attackers fled. And first she had been so sure it was his arms, his beard on her forehead, his chest that rocked her. But he hadn't come even once since then to see her. Because Quillan came home? Of course. Alex wouldn't come if Quillan were there.

Yet it didn't feel right. Something didn't fit in that picture. She hadn't actually seen who held her, only sensed a tenderness, a love that she could only ascribe to Alex Makepeace. He'd never admitted such, but she knew it. Why now did the thought leave her feeling bleak?

Because she wished it was Quillan who had held her? His arms that had brought her such comfort in the darkest point of her sorrow? His mourning joining hers? Looking about the silent room, she felt his absence even as she felt the emptiness of her womb.

Was he gone? Would she learn today or tomorrow that he had slipped away, left again for someplace he found more tenable than her home? Carina looked at the empty space where the rocking chair had stood so briefly. She wished now she'd kept it. She would have crawled aboard and rocked, recalling the strong chest, the embracing arms. Whose? Did Mae know? Could she ask?

As though summoned by the thought, Mae tapped the door and came in. "Ah, you're awake. Sleep well?"

"Like a baby." Then a pang of sorrow swept her. Where did her baby sleep? In heaven? With the angels? With Rose's lost child?

Mae bent and stoked the coals in her stove, then added wood that lay in piles of kindling along the wall. Someone had been busy. Quillan?

"Mae." Carina pushed herself up farther in spite of the dull ache in her back. She wanted to ask but was afraid of the answer.

"If it's the restaurant you're worried about, don't. Between Èmie, Lucia, me, and the twins, we're opening the doors tonight."

Carina stared. "But, Mae . . ."

"We all like to feel indispensable. But the truth is, we're mostly not."

Carina shook her head. "What have you found to serve?" They'd been scrambling to put together anything remotely like the meals she'd started with.

"Oh, I'm not sure. Èmie's figured out the menu. Some of the recipes you've shown her before."

"But that would take ingredients we don't have. And . . . you can do it without me?"

"I'm not laying claim to anything. It's Quillan's doing."

"Quillan!" Carina bolted up and winced.

"He brought a wagonload of things that look and smell like what you're used to."

Carina sank back with a huff. So. More gifts to bribe her. At least he had the good sense not to tell her.

"And he's got us all doing our parts. He's hard to ignore."

Bene. Let him try to run her business for just one night. He'd see. He'd . . . but what if he did it? Oh! The man was impossible! She folded her arms across her chest.

"Now, there's a look."

Carina didn't care how petulant her face was. She was not about to let Quillan take charge of her or her restaurant.

"You may as well face it, Carina. Quillan's here to stay."

"Hah. Where is he now?"

"On his way to the Rose Legacy with Mr. Makepeace."

Carina's eyes darted to the window. To the cave? With Alex? She bit her lip. *Signore, did I do right?* What if it was more than he could stand? It had hurt her to see the scenes. How would it be if it were her own papa? She pressed a hand to her breast. *Be with him, Signore. Make him strong . . . and wise . . . and compassionate. Help him understand.*

Tears stung her eyes as she prayed. Oh, Dio, she loved him. Furious as she was, she loved him!

Quillan reined in outside the Rose Legacy and dismounted as Alex Makepeace did the same. The air was crisp with the smell of snow. The foundation was hidden under snow already. But the mouth of the Rose Legacy yawned before him. As Quillan stood, a single snowflake touched his cheek and melted like a tear.

He looked up to the sky. It was partly clear, but tiny flakes darted about like fireflies. A snow shower, probably. Not a blizzard. He turned to Alex Makepeace. "We'll tether the horses inside."

Makepeace nodded. When the animals were secure, he took the thick coil of rope and attached it to the top of the shaft, using the spikes Quillan had driven into the timber to rescue Carina. Quillan remembered the exultation he'd felt when he realized she was alive. Had God directed him into that shaft? Did He direct him now?

"There's a subterranean well directly beneath. The rope falls just to the right of it. When you land, watch your footing."

Quillan nodded.

"Here." Makepeace gave him a tin candle holder and three candles.

Quillan stashed them in the deep pockets of his buckskin coat. Then he took the rope and let himself down over the side of the shaft. He remembered how fatigued his muscles had been after fighting the flood, every movement a strain. Now his arms were strong.

He remembered the dream. Carrying Carina, climbing the shaft that wouldn't end, his arms throbbing, cramping and shaking, and all the while Mrs. Shepard laughing. *"You'll never be anything but a savage like your father."* And the laugh. The diabolical laugh.

Her laugh had lost its power to horrify him. He knew now the illness from which it sprang. So why did he feel such a sense of foreboding letting himself down the rope into the darkness of his father's mine? No, not his mine—this cave, this natural orifice Wolf had opened up.

Down, down, Quillan descended hand over hand until his feet struck bottom. He landed, signaled with the rope, and stared into total darkness. A chill settled in his spine. This was hell, this total void, this deprava-tion of senses, as terrifying a hell, as everlasting flames. He felt the rope jump as Alex Makepeace started down it.

Quillan stepped away carefully to the right. He dug into his pocket, found the candle holder, and jammed a candle into the socket. Holding both the candle and the matchbox in his left hand, he struck a match and lit the wick. The relief from that little glow was enormous.

Makepeace dropped beside him and lit his own can-dle while Quillan raised his light and circled slowly. Alex Makepeace held his up as well, motioning toward the ceiling. He spoke softly. "Bats. If we're careful we won't disturb them." He lowered the candle. "Floor's slippery as well."

Quillan nodded. He had never been deep inside the earth before. Not even into the New Boundless more than the span of the short drift that Cain had driven. He felt the immensity of the stone around him like a giant tomb. He studied the size and shape of the spikes on floor and ceiling, some connecting like pillars.

"Amazing, isn't it?" Alex Makepeace's voice held both awe and appreciation.

"It is."

"The chamber's this way." Alex swung his arm and started across the cavern floor. "First time we came down, the bats showed us which direction to go."

We. Makepeace and Carina in this dark place together. Quillan tightened his jaw. A low moan started and wailed over them. Stopped dead and clutching his candle firmly, Quillan shuddered.

"It's the wind through an orifice in the painted chamber."

But it wasn't. Quillan's feet felt frozen to the floor. It was a sound that had haunted his dreams from his earliest years. He knew it, but how? He forced one foot to lift and then the next, thankful for the dimness that kept his terror from being apparent to Alex Makepeace.

"Mrs. Shepard wasn't wild about it either."

Quillan stared ahead as they walked. Carina had gone this way, seen what he would see, felt what he felt now.

"Probably nerves. I shouldn't have left her alone there. She wanted to study the pictures, so I went exploring." Makepeace tried to seem casual, but to Quillan he sounded overly familiar with his wife. *He* shouldn't have left her alone? He shouldn't have been there at all.

"How many times did you come?"

"Twice." Alex ducked between two spikes that nearly met and continued on. "Found the chamber the first time when the bats made their exit. Mrs. Shepard did not enjoy the bats."

Quillan heard the humor in his voice and seethed. What right had this man to be alone with Carina in a treacherous place? Was she frightened? Had he soothed her? Quillan remembered her reaction to the rattlesnake. Had she clung to Makepeace when the bats startled her?

The cavern narrowed and lowered into a passage. Quillan followed, hoping Alex Makepeace wasn't leading him down some dark tunnel where he'd lose him and have Carina for himself. Where were these thoughts coming from? Some animal fear conjured by the darkness, the sense of being swallowed alive?

Makepeace stopped in front of him. "It's just ahead here. Quillan . . ." He glanced back over his shoulder. "Well, I'll let you see for yourself." He stepped aside.

Quillan felt a terrible reluctance. His heart thundered so, he was sure Makepeace could hear it. In spite of everything in him wanting to run, Quillan stepped forward into the chamber. It was small and circular. And the walls were a mural. Wolf?

"I'll . . . be out . . ." Makepeace waved toward the main chamber.

Quillan hardly heard him. The moan had started again, but this time it was shrill, the howl of a wolf. His whole being shook. No wonder people thought they heard howling on the mountain at night. Slowly he raised his candle and studied the pictures on the wall. They followed one after the other from the right of the opening to the left.

"If you want to know Wolf, he's there." Quillan pictured Carina standing there in his place, seeing what he saw. He neared the wall, studied the first picture, the horror of the massacre. He saw the child Wolf crouched behind the bush watching the atrocities to his family. Quillan forced himself on to the next image and slowly made his way around the room. Each scene took fresh courage to

look, to learn. This was his father!

There was emotion in each scene, though the pictures were simple. Each one spoke its own story, but one thing was constant through them all. Why was Wolf so alone?

The symbolism of the pale wolf was not lost on him. It was as though the man and wolf were bound together, somehow vying like two selves in one. Quillan came to the picture of Rose. There was no clear definition of features, but he saw her willowy form, her dark hair. He wanted more, wanted to see her clearly. To purge the nightmare images Leona Shepard had given him.

Breath thick in his chest, he viewed the last picture. Wolf with a newborn child raised over his head. Quillan's heart hammered. He'd seen it before. But that was impossible. It was déjà vu. A trick of the imagination. But the longer he looked, the more he knew it. How?

He'd been only a baby when the Shepards took him from Placerville. He knew they'd never gone back, surely had never gone into this cave. No one knew of it except Wolf, and now Carina and Alex Makepeace. It didn't make sense. But this picture was in Quillan's memory as surely as the books he'd committed there . . . with very little effort.

He knew his memory was superior to most. He'd been amazed as a boy that everyone couldn't recall as he could. But this . . . He stared at the wall. Was it possible? Had Wolf brought him into the cave? Had his eyes truly taken in this scene of father-son surrender? And how did he know that was what the picture meant?

Quillan's chest heaved as he strove to keep his eyes on the picture. He sank to his knees. He felt himself torn, even as his father must have been, knowing the animal was inside him, the pale wolf that howled its protest when the man gave his son to God. That howled every time the baby cried. That couldn't stop the howling born of torment and torture and fear.

The howling became shrill, a cold wind filling the chamber, and Quillan's candle flickered out. He knew a moment of sheer terror of the dark. *Jesus.* He spoke it aloud. "Jesus." He didn't relight his candle, but the darkness lessened. In the faint glow from somewhere above him, he saw the picture of Wolf and his son.

Wolf had made the choice. In the end they were separate, the wolf outside the man. Quillan knew this. It was the man who had joined with Rose, and the man who had died with her. And the man had surrendered to God. He wasn't the savage Mrs. Shepard had made him, and Quillan wasn't damned before he started.

Quillan closed his eyes, breath coming hard and swift. *Lord God, I give you my soul.* Wholeheartedly now, and not because grief had brought him to his knees, Quillan surrendered himself. Drenched in sweat, Quillan straightened on his knees, his breath easing. Slowly he reached into his pocket, found the matches, and relit the candle. The chamber sprang to life, a monument to his father.

Quillan laughed. He threw back his head and laughed. Stretching his arms wide and upward, he filled the chamber with his laughter. Then he stood, circled the walls once again with his eyes, and walked out of the chamber. He followed the corridor to the main cavern. Alex Makepeace stood just inside. He must have heard the laughter. It must have rung echoing into the cavern.

Quillan met his puzzled gaze. "We'd better go. Before the snow gets serious." He led the way across the cavern to the rope and handed Alex Makepeace the end. "Go ahead. I'll follow you."

Without speaking, Alex Makepeace extinguished his light and climbed. Quillan stood alone in the dim of his single candle swallowed by the space of the cavern, feeling the stillness of the air. As he reached for the rope he heard a sound, a soft wail that had no power to terrify anymore. He stood, letting it wash over him until it faded into silence, then clutched the rope and climbed.

Carina sighed. Èmie had twice come in to ask about a recipe and each time assured her that they were managing just fine, but it chafed to leave the kitchen entirely to her friend. Especially when she could smell the sausage and parmigiano Quillan had brought. It irked her to wonder so intensely what else the pantry held. But the weakness resulting from yesterday's exertion kept her in bed.

She thought again about Quillan at the Rose Legacy. With the day wearing on and snow fluttering past the window, she couldn't help but worry. Even more than the outer circumstances, she worried about the impact of what Quillan would see. *Dio, soften his heart. Let him see past the horror to the soul of his father.*

She closed her eyes and pictured the cave mural. Oh, the images would be hard to forget. But she prayed Quillan would be able to do so if it was too much for him to bear. Would he come to her? Or would he run away again? It was the chance she took when she told him of the cave. But she didn't regret it.

If he left her now, she would go home. She didn't care that, being married to Quillan, she could never marry another and carry a child inside her. No, she didn't care. It hurt too much to lose them. She dozed, willing the pain to subside, the bruising outside and in. God was good, and He would bring good from it all. She clung to that.

She thought she smelled the snow, felt the cold breath of winter on her cheek. Her eyes fluttered open to find Quillan standing over her. She looked into his face, chapped with cold, yet warmer than she'd seen it before. There was no haunting, as she'd feared. Intensity, yes, but no despair. And his eyes were not closed to her with his rascal's indifference. They were searching, vulnerable, real.

She eased up onto her elbows. "You saw the cave? The paintings?"

"I saw it."

Oh yes, the images were in his mind even as they were in hers. They had moved him, changed him. "Your papa had a lonely life."

He nodded.

"You don't have to." Now it was her voice that softened to a mere breath.

He worked his thumb across his index finger, and she could see that his hands were red with chap or rope burns. "I haven't done so well."

A smile touched her lips. "Yes, you have."

He stood silent a long moment, then stooped down beside the bed and took her hand from the coverlet. His were cold and rough as they cupped hers between them. "I'm sorry, Carina. For leaving you and . . ." His throat worked painfully. "For the baby."

She felt the pain wash over her. Tears sprang to her eyes. "It was . . ." She raised one shoulder. "God's will." She had to believe that, even though it hurt.

Something fierce filled his eyes, and she thought he

would argue, but then he looked down at her fingers nestled inside his. "Can you forgive me?" His voice was soft as dust, yet firm, reaching inside her, demanding response.

Carina's heart quickened. Did she forgive him? Knowing what she knew of Wolf's pain, of Rose's deep sorrow, how could she not forgive their son, for whom each had grieved in their own way? Wolf in his cave; Rose in her journal and her failing mind. Quillan himself had suffered through no fault of his own. She saw it now in the strain around his eyes, the tension in his jaw. Forgive? She had learned to forgive. She answered softly, "Yes. I forgive you."

It was as though years peeled from his flesh. She couldn't say how, only that his face changed without changing. His fingers tightened around hers. "I'll stay here with you. Quit freighting. Whatever it takes."

She drew an unsteady breath. "I want to go home." As soon as the words were out she knew he'd mistaken them. He'd offered to release her too many times, and now she saw the hurt and disappointment as he guessed she would leave him after all. Her heart broke for him, thinking once again he was abandoned. "Will you take me home?"

He visibly relaxed. "To Sonoma?"

"I miss Mamma and Papa and—"

"Five brothers, one sister, aunts and uncles and old Guiseppe and all his mules." His mouth quirked crookedly as she raised surprised brows. "I'll take you. But there's one thing I need to do first."

"What is it?"

"There are DeMornays in Denver. I'd like to know if they're any relation."

"Rose's family?" Carina squeezed the hand that held hers. "Oh yes!"

"I don't know."

"But we have to ask! Of course we do!"

"They may not . . ." He raised a hand and dropped it.

"Even if they don't acknowledge you, you'll know." She reached her hand to his beard-roughened cheek.

He tipped it into her palm and rested it there, his eyes holding her captive as always. Wolf's wonderful stormy eyes.

She smiled. "You need a shave."

His lips formed the pirate grin. "This is nothing. You're lucky you didn't see what I wore into town."

Carina's breath stilled. "You had a beard?"

"No mountain man could have done better. Or worse, depending on your tastes."

Carina caught his face between her hands. "Then it was you."

"Depends what you're accusing me of."

"I knew it. Here." She pressed one hand over her heart. She could see he didn't understand, but then, he didn't have to know everything, eh?

He went down on one knee and caught her hand to his chest. She trembled at his intensity. He had never looked at her with such yearning, such firm decision.

He raised her chin with the side of one finger. "The face of my love is a flower, fair with nectar sweet that harbors there bidding me hover, light and fleet and longing for that honeyed sweet. . . ."

His words jellied her, words she'd never read or heard. "Who are you quoting?"

"My heart." His gaze deepened.

"They're your words, Quillan?"

"They're yours if you want them. And more where

they came from. You drive me to poetry, Carina."

"You? The hard, solitary man of the road?"

"Not anymore." His grip tightened on her fingers.

Her heart soared with hope. *Oh, Lord, you are good. Your grace has accomplished my plea!* She searched his charcoal-rimmed eyes and tightened her fingers in his. She could feel his strength and something more, something beyond Quillan, beyond them both. Something else bound their hands together; it was God's own.

Acknowledgments

My profound thanks to God for grace in all things.

My unfailing thanks to my family and friends.

My humble thanks to you, my readers.